PRAISE FOR PER

"*Perception Check* is a real treat for fans of fantasy and TTRPGs alike. The characterization and world-building is exceptional, and I was hooked from start to finish. I can't wait for the next book!"

— KATHERINE SHAW, AUTHOR OF *GLORIA*

"Right from the beginning, I was invested in the main character, Violet. Her adventures took me on an emotional rollercoaster of my own. When I finished, I needed a moment to return to reality, because my mind very much wanted to stay in the universe Astrid Knight created."

— A.R.K. HORTON, AUTHOR OF *STRUGGLING WITH THE CURRENT*

"*Perception Check* is a thrilling and resounding fantasy for the modern age. An epic balance of comedy, emotional magnitude, magic, and adventure."

— BLAKE R. WOLFE, AUTHOR OF *THE CRYSTAL EYE*

"Reading this book is like rolling a nat 20 for enjoyment. Filled with unforgettable characters, in-depth world building, and heaps of inclusion, *Perception Check* is impossible to put down"

— JAYME BEAN, AUTHOR OF *UNTOUCHED*

The Mages of Velmyra Saga: Book One

PERCEPTION
CHECK

Astrid Knight

ALSO BY ASTRID KNIGHT

Anthology Stories

In the Wake of the Kraken (Tales From the Year Between: Volume 3)

Welcome to Simmins, Detective Spencer

The Mages of Velmyra Saga

Perception Check

The Obsidian Archive

The Wayward and The Wanderer

For Grandpa Van, who encouraged me to never stop making magic.

A NOTE ON THE TEXT

Perception Check deals with themes regarding mental illness (specifically depression, anxiety, post-traumatic stress disorder, and suicidality) as well as mentions of childhood sexual assault, alcohol abuse, and animal violence.

If you or someone you know is struggling with suicidal thoughts, please reach out to the National Suicide Prevention Hotline at (800) 273-8255.

what if I told you trauma was a stalker
　　follows me room to room
　　visits
　　me at work, leaves
　　dead animals on my day planner
　　texts me knives, licks
　　my memory before I have a chance to get it right
　　I am on all fours digging into the carpet
　　learning how to make wool imprints in my kneecaps
　　this is how I learned to dance
　　with half of my body on fire
　　there is not enough whiskey in the world
　　to make any of this bearable

　　　　　— MARY LAMBERT, "THE GOOD NEWS IS
　　　　　YOU WON THE LOTTERY, THE BAD NEWS
　　　　　　IS THE LOTTERY IS POST-TRAUMATIC
　　　　　　　　　　STRESS DISORDER"

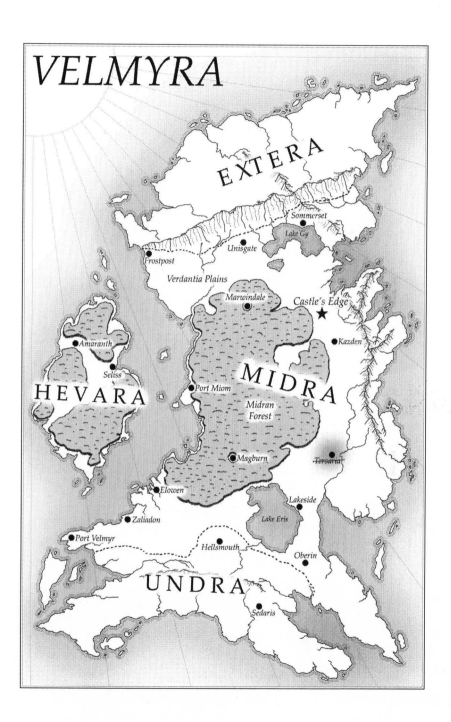

PART I

"There are two levels of perception: what is surface, and what is just underneath. For those things not immediately noticeable, you can run a perception check to see what might be undetectable at first glance."
-*Mages of Velmyra* Players Handbook, Page 23

CHAPTER 1

I see the demon sitting on the bus before it sees me.

I don't notice it at first. I'll admit: I'm distracted. Usually on my bus ride back from the main campus, I read one of the *Mages* modules that I'm obsessing over currently, but it's so noisy today. Too many bodies crammed together, all being too loud. A group of frat guys are holding the railing in front of me, laughing about how wasted they're going to get tonight once their last class is over. Pretty typical for a Friday, but the sound is grating to me. So, I've tightened my headphones around my ears, blasting music that I've been listening to over and over for the past decade and hoping I can drown the world out. But the mishmashed chatter permeates even the heaviest bass lines.

I just have to get through today. This stupid, stupid day.

God, they're just so *loud*. I close my eyes, fumbling in my coat pocket. My heart skips when I grapple at nothing but lint. Fuck. I thought I had it with me. I always have it with me. If I lost it, I swear to fucking *god*—

My fingers finally find something, and I ease back into my seat as they glide over the ridges of a tiny piece of plastic at the bottom of my pocket; a twenty-sided die. I could take it out and look at it, but I don't want to draw attention to it. I close my

3

eyes instead and visualize the translucent red resin and the bright white numbers, digging the blunted edges into the flesh of my thumb. I do the only useful thing I ever got out of therapy, something I should be able to do myself without having to pay a hundred and fifty bucks for someone to tell me how.

I breathe in.

Breathe out.

The bus jerks to a halt. I instinctively look up to the LED display at the head of the bus to see what stop we're at, panicking because I haven't been paying attention to the route.

That's when I see it.

Everything in my body runs cold.

It's exactly how I remember it, and I blink a few times to make sure I'm not seeing things. In the first few months after the attack, I saw them everywhere, but if I would blink enough, they would eventually go away. Just flashbacks, my therapists told me. Like sun-spots in your eyes, they would fade as time went on. And they did for a little while. But then they'd come back, and fade away, over and over.

But this one doesn't disappear. And I stare at it long enough that it turns its bug-eyed gaze on me.

It crouches between a couple of elderly people in the handicap seating. They are none the wiser to the demon that sits beside them. In fact, no one on the bus seems to pay it any mind, all absorbed in their phones or staring out windows or boisterously laughing about the party they're going to that night. Even those who look directly at it don't seem to see it. I rub my eyes this time. Maybe it's just being stubborn. But it's still there when I drop my hands. The bulging black eyes that take up half its face reflect the cold winter light coming in from the windows. Its mouth is fixed into a perpetual grin as its too-big teeth jut unevenly out of its face, and its skeletal frame is covered with tight, oily, reptilian skin with a row of spikes lining its spine. It cocks its head at me like a curious puppy, but it's nowhere near cute. It's bone chilling. We hold our gaze for a breathless moment. Until, unceremoniously, it jumps from the bus seat and skitters away out the open bus door.

It takes me a second to unfreeze, leaping out the door after it. The bus driver curses as he nearly closes the door on me, but I can't bring myself to care. I sling my backpack across my shoulders as I rush onto the sidewalk. Biting February air hits me in the face, and it tastes like it's going to snow. I've ended up at the downtown GVSU campus, thankfully right where I needed to go. Glancing through the crowds of students on the sidewalk, I look for the creature. It's no bigger than me, or at least they weren't that much bigger than me a decade ago...

I push through a group of girls who are idling next to the building, blood pounding in my ears. I don't *want* to see it. The mere thought of them usually makes me feel sick. The fact that it's disappeared is a good thing, right? I'm not curled up in a ball on the ground screaming. So why am I running after it? Like I want to catch it.

I see what looks like a scrawny black foot slip behind the building next to the walkway to the Blue Bridge. I power after it, rounding the corner—

It's gone. There's nothing but a few straggling students laughing and taking selfies by the water. There's no indication that they just saw a monster run past them.

I close my eyes and sigh.

Something heavy falls on my shoulder, and I jump. I'm usually on my guard, but after having just seen one of those things again, all my systems are on red alert. I whip around, anticipating those bug eyes reflecting back my terrified face.

Relief washes over me. It's Eddie.

He laughs at me, but it's good-natured. "Dude, you taking up jogging or something?" His smile falters as he sees the tension start to leave my body. "Sorry, I didn't mean to scare you."

"It's fine," I sigh, glancing back down the walkway next to the river.

"You trying to catch up with someone?" Eddie asks.

5

I look back down the path, but it's in vain. The creature is gone. Goddamnit, it's not gone. It wasn't even here.

"I thought so," I say, breath still shaky. "Guess not."

There's a wrinkle between his eyebrows that suggests concern, but his demeanor doesn't crack. "Come on," he says, "let's get food."

Reluctantly, I go with him. We walk across the Blue Bridge, winter wind blowing through our hair. The familiar feeling of being watched doesn't leave me as we cross and leave the water behind us.

We settle on Big O's Pizza, our weekly go-to mostly due to the fact that it shares a name with a decent anime from the 90s. It's a hole in the wall, or as "hole in the wall" as downtown Grand Rapids gets. It has all the makings of a regular hangout spot— it's near both of our jobs, not far from our apartment, and it hasn't given us food poisoning. Well, not in the past few years. As long as you stick to the pizza, it's pretty safe. The floors certainly haven't been cleaned since 1989, made all the more apparent by how the soles of my tennis shoes stick to the cement floor as I anxiously bounce my foot after we sit down at our usual spot by the window.

Even though the restaurant is below street view, I can still see pairs of feet pass by the window. I flinch every time I think I see a pair of spindly black ones. I force myself to look away, focusing on the laminate red and white checkered tablecloth.

I'm being absurd. I'm recovered. I'm functional. I shouldn't be getting flashbacks or hallucinations any more. The fact that it stuck around so long just doesn't sit right with me. I mean, maybe it's because of what day it is, but come *on*. I acknowledged it, even had a little cry about it this morning before I headed out for class. I was doing all right most of the day. I was managing, which is pretty fucking stellar given my track record. So why did I see one of them?

"I think I'm going to throw a wyvern at them."

I glance back up at Eddie. He doesn't go to Grand Valley like I do, though with his bleach-stained Nirvana shirt and decade-old burgundy zip hoodie, he sure looks like a college stoner. And the scrawled notes and hardcover books spread out in front of him on the table definitely make it look like he's cramming for a final. It's not anything academic, though. Upside down from my perspective, I see a detailed drawing of a dragon-like creature in his open book, a string of lightning streaking from its mouth. I don't know if I've read that particular *Mages* module or not. Some of them have started to run together for me, especially with how many I've borrowed from Eddie over the past year.

"You think they can handle wyverns?" I ask him, picking at the tablecloth. "They're only level eight, and they almost got wrecked by dire wolves a few sessions back."

Eddie waves a hand, not even looking up at me as he scribbles something else into his notes. "That was all shit rolls," he says. "They're capable. If Kaeden wants to use their priest spells for actual healing, anyway."

"They could die."

"If they get close, I have a deus ex machina," Eddie sighs, setting his pencil down and scratching at his scalp, his dirty blond shoulder-length hair going askew before he smooths it back down and tucks the strands in his face behind his ears. He bounces excitedly in his seat as he quickly picks up the pencil and jots another note down. "Oh fuck, I got a few deus ex machinas I could use, actually. Lore shit, baby!" he exclaims.

I grin as I watch him. It doesn't take much to get Eddie's enthusiasm up. He's the human equivalent of a golden retriever, especially when it comes to nerd stuff. But Game-Mastering for *Mages of Velmyra* is where he thrives. He's always been interested in a compelling story. *Mages* is the perfect excuse to create stories and hangout with friends at the same time. Every Friday night, his excitement is palpable—inevitably humming as he makes his morning toast, grinning ear to ear as he sets up his battle maps on the kitchen table before I head out to class. To put it in RPG terms, GMing is his favored terrain.

And I don't blame him. I'm obsessed with the game, too. Though, my reasons are a little—well, sadder, I guess.

The pizza arrives—half pepperoni for him, half ham and mushroom for me—and Eddie pushes his game materials aside before devouring a slice nearly in one breath. I take my time usually, but today, I'm just not hungry. Not after seeing the creature on the bus. I shift in my seat. Every once in a while, I get these almost out-of-body experiences where I'm suddenly aware that I take up space. I'm a tangible object that people can observe and make judgments about. This place isn't the fanciest by a longshot, but poking at my pizza and wearing my "Han Shot First" sweatshirt and ratty grey beanie, I feel too much. Too unworthy. Like I can't quite justify the space I'm occupying. I reach into my hoodie pocket and grab hold of the twenty-sided die that I've transferred over from my coat, rolling it between my fingers and hoping that the self-conscious feeling will dissipate.

"You know," Eddie says between messy bites. "Tonight's session would be the perfect time to introduce you as a player. We got a couple hours. Plenty of time to make a character sheet. I'm thinking you'd make a good crusader for the Outer Realm. Cold damage to all your weapon attacks, and you can teleport at level fifteen. Crusaders are dope as shit."

I snort. "That seems a little overpowered."

"Matt plays a multiclassed thief-warrior-priest. Trust me. You'd be nowhere near min-maxed being a straight-up crusader."

I chuckle a little, jabbing my cold slice of pizza with a fork. "I'm okay. But thanks for offering."

Swiping a napkin over his mouth, Eddie says, "You are literally the only person on the planet who loves *Mages* but doesn't want to play it. Makes no sense to me."

It doesn't make a ton of sense to me, either. Eddie has been playing *Mages* and other tabletop roleplaying games since we were in high school, but it never really caught my attention until last year, when I—

Well, I spent a little time in the hospital. And there was nothing much to do there except art therapy and reading the very limited selection of books available in their piddly collection. Midway through, I called Eddie and asked him to bring me some books to read. Mixed in with the stack of fantasy and sci-fi books was the *Mages of Velmyra* game master's guide. Honestly, I was about to read *Fellowship of the Ring* for the third time before I was going to sit and read a rulebook for a game I knew nothing about.

That was, until I caught a glimpse of the artwork for the Crystalline Mage arc.

That was all I needed to get hooked. Once I got home from the hospital, I ordered new source books to pore through. Player and game master guides, expansions, online resources. Everything I could find. It's my bedtime reading material now. I find podcasts and streams and shows, sometimes so obscure that they don't even have a single Tweet written about them. If they mention the Crystalline Mage arc at all, I find it, and I consume it.

Sure, I'll listen to strangers on the internet record themselves playing. I'll buy all the books and memorize all the rules. I even bought a set of dice at the comic shop Eddie works at. But I've never played, and if I have any say in it at all, I never will. It can be a spectator sport of sorts, but unless you don't have anyone to play with, most people interested will end up playing it at some point. With everything I've been through in the past ten years, maybe I could use some escapism, a chance to be someone else and live another life for three or four hours every week. But something always holds me back. As if I'll dip one toe in the water and immediately drown.

"One of these days, maybe," I tell him, which is the same thing I've been saying for a year.

I lift the limp piece of pizza and take another half-hearted bite. While I meekly chew, Eddie says, "Hey, you're doing okay, right?"

Swallowing, I look up at him. Eddie is a guy who wears his heart on his sleeve. When he's concerned, I know it. And he's definitely concerned. His brow furrows as he rips little bits of his napkin into squares and drops them on his empty plate.

It's common practice for your high school friends to fade into barely-acknowledged social media followers. But with Eddie, there was a tougher glue that held us together. When he started going to my high school in freshman year, I was still getting over the attack. Therapy was every Wednesday—sometimes Fridays too, if my parents thought I needed it—and meetings with the principal were frequent. I wasn't in the business of doing school work, and when teachers told me to do something other than stare at my desk, I had the tendency of lashing out. The other kids kept me at arm's length. I was more of a museum specimen than anything.

That is, until Eddie took an interest in me. He ended up in nearly every one of my classes and he had zero interest in making friends with our wildly social classmates. The only person that he insisted on having lunch, doing lab experiments, and waiting for the bus with was me, the silent girl who resembled a CPR dummy more than a person. I've been transparent with him when it comes to spiraling back into a bad place, and he doesn't rest until he makes it right.

And that was how I ended up in the hospital last year in the first place.

"I'm good."

"You've just been kind of off today. Quiet."

I shrug a shoulder. "I'm quiet a lot of days."

"I know," he says, quieter, more somber than he was just a few minutes ago. "I just thought with it being the tenth anniversary and all—"

"It's honestly not been bad," I lie. "I'm good. Everything's good."

Eddie nods, his worried expression relaxing just a hair. "Okay. Just—if you're not fine, tell me. Okay?"

Here's the thing: ever since that night ten years ago, I haven't been fine. There are some days when my best friend being kidnapped by demons isn't the first thing I think of when I wake up. There are days where I think I can have normal adult conversations with people, and that they aren't ignorantly thinking I'm some traumatized child who's one chipped nail away from sticking a pencil in her jugular and calling it a day. But no matter how deeply I bury it all with source books and shitty podcasts, it's all still there just under the surface.

He wants me to tell him when I'm not fine, but he doesn't realize that if I were to do that, I would never stop. It would come out in an endless pained stream of noise that no one would be able to suffer.

I look him in the eye and manage to smile. "I promise," I say. "I'm fine."

For a moment, even I believe it.

Anyone could look it up on Wikipedia. I've done it before, when I'm feeling particularly low. All the facts are there, at least the ones that the police know.

February 11th, ten years ago: two thirteen-year-old girls—best friends since elementary school—snuck out late at night to meet some of the boys in their class at a nearby public park. When they arrived, none of the boys were there. Upset that they walked miles in the cold for nothing, the girls decided to head back. Before they could leave the park, though, they were ambushed. One of the girls—Violet Spence—was found the next morning by a jogger, unconscious on the sidewalk, face mangled. She was taken to the hospital, her face stitched up and her broken nose set back into place. It would take a few more months for her to get her teeth fixed properly, but she was alive.

The other girl—May Beaufort—was gone. There was no body, and no trace. She had just disappeared.

The thing that people find strange—the thing that all the true crime weirdos latch onto and theorize about like the whole thing is a story and not something that actually happened to us—is what I told the police. The thing that got me ridiculed in school, the thing that's kept me in therapy twice a week for ten years. I told them what I saw.

May wasn't taken by people. She was taken by monsters.

Dozens of those nasty black demons—at least, 'demons' is the only word I have for those things—descended upon us in the park that night and dragged her away screaming into the void of night. Like a darkened doorway had opened up behind her and swallowed her whole. I can see it all perfectly, a detailed brand seared into my memory.

No one believed me, of course. Every therapist I've ever had has told me that my mind couldn't handle the stress of what was happening to me, so my mind created demons where there were none. It was people who did this to me and May, not other-worldly monsters. It took me a long time to admit, but they were probably right. That doesn't make the flashes of those creatures go away. It doesn't make going through my day-to-day life feel any less like walking on broken glass in silk slippers.

The internet doesn't know about the night terrors, the Xanax prescriptions, the hospitalizations, or the very public panic attacks. They certainly don't know that I'm obsessed with a certain tabletop roleplaying game. Or that the reason I'm obsessed with said game is because I think I found May in the game as a character.

CHAPTER 2

"God, I fucking hate wyverns."

From my perch on a stool at the kitchen countertop, I see Eddie's friend Samantha—the party's nature diviner—flop back into her chair at our chipped old dining table with a heavy sigh. She runs her hands through her green hair, which has been fried after years of bleaching and box dyes. The rest of the group looks just as worn down. The battle took over two hours, after all, and they ran out of Doritos pretty shortly after the fight started. Everyone is exhausted, as if they had actually just fought a dragon. Kaeden—the priest that Eddie moaned about back at the pizza shop—makes an unenthusiastic effort to get everyone's characters healed, while Matt the Min-Maxer inspects the body of the deceased wyvern. He rolls a three on his inspection check and doesn't find much of import. Angela's armorer-warrior is already harvesting wyvern scales to use for future projects, but everything is half-hearted.

They barely made it. I'm entirely certain Eddie nerfed the wyvern's hit points midway through the battle because it was going so poorly, but he doesn't seem to really mind. He's grinning like an idiot, rubbing his hands together behind his cardboard game master's screen. "Hey, you guys killed it! Not bad for a bunch of level eight dipshits, huh?" he says, forcing as much encouragement into it as he can muster.

The group grumbles back in response as they all erase and scribble on their character sheets, white printer paper now a mess of black pencil smudges after keeping track of their own health points and Residuum allotments. I take the opportunity to look back down at my own notes and textbooks, but they're not for anything nearly as exciting as taking down a lightning-spitting wyvern. Psychology 403 involves a lot less magic and a lot more stats and double-blind studies. I've been pretending to do work for the past couple of hours, but I've gotten nowhere. All my focus has been on the battle.

"Jackson, do you want to do anything post-battle?"

I've been paying more attention than some of the players, actually. At the sound of his name, Jackson looks up from his phone, pushing his horn-rimmed glasses back up to sit on the bridge of his nose. "Sorry?" he asks, shutting his phone off hastily.

"Anything you want to do before y'all move on?" Eddie asks, more patient than I would be.

"Oh," Jackson says, staring at the gridded battle map in front of him and the miniature figures of players and a massive draconic beast tipped over on its side. It almost seems foreign to him, like it's the first time he's seen it all night.

I keep myself from rolling my eyes. Jackson does this every session—distracts himself with his phone or folding a stray piece of paper into one of the two shapes of origami he knows or taking his pen apart and putting it back together over and over. He's a quiet guy in general, but it's like he has to be brought back from whatever world he's living in to actually participate in the game. I've made some not-so-subtle remarks about it to Eddie before, and he's defensive as hell about it—probably because he's been in love with the moody and aloof Jackson King since tenth grade. "He's just got focus issues. I'm fine with it as long as it doesn't hinder the game." Whatever. Not my game, I guess.

"Uh, well. What's not already covered?" Jackson muses to himself, thumb on his chin as he thinks.

I hold back a snort. *You'd know if you'd been paying attention.* I'm being pretty snotty, I know, but at least I keep my thoughts to myself. Jackson and I never had a lot of interaction in high school. We had friends who were friends, but those circles never really intersected. He and Eddie didn't even start hanging out until recently when he joined the Friday night game. Even with the lack of familiarity, he always seemed to look at me with some kind of disgust, like I was perpetually walking around with shit on my shoe. And I never have figured out why. Part of me wonders if maybe I accidentally said his dead name once or twice when he first came out as trans, but he's always been pretty forgiving with other people who have slipped up. I don't think it's that.

Another part of me has always thought it had something to do with May. They knew each other back in middle school, occasionally hung out at some parties. I'd say they were okay friends, but nowhere near as close as she and I were. When she went missing, though, he got mean. And call me a bitch, but if he's got something against me for what happened to her, I don't feel all that bad for making shitty comments about him to myself.

"Actually, Jackson," Eddie says, steepling his fingers under his chin. "Could you make me a perception check?"

Oh shit.

Something is about to go down. And given the little grin on Eddie's face that he's trying desperately to suppress, it's something good.

Wide-eyed, Jackson nods. He picks up his twenty-sided die and rolls it hastily onto the game mat. He looks up toward his forehead, doing some mental math before saying, "Nineteen."

Coyly, Eddie raises his eyebrows. "Nineteen," he repeats, lacing the word with as much mystery as he can muster. Throwing his shoulders back subtly, he looks Jackson directly in the eye, which causes Jackson to stiffen. "It's strange. Everyone else has a handle on the wyvern and healing and recuperating, so you don't pay much attention to all that. You look past, out into the snowy landscape of the mountain pass that you've just fought in." Eddie has been cultivating his GM voice for years. He's watched endless streams and podcasts of other people's games, surgically taking their best qualities and grafting them into his own performances. It always astounded me that he never did theatre in high school, because the man knows drama. As he describes the eerie scene, his facial expressions mirror the ones at the table—curiosity, doubt, and just a slight hint of fear. "For a moment, it all just looks like snow, as far as the eye can see. And then you look harder."

He pauses for dramatic effect, his eyes looking past Jackson to the front door of the apartment. His furrowed brows gradually unknit in convincing surprise. "There's something approaching the group. Something that puts a chill in you that isn't from the wind."

That same chill runs through me.

Shit.

I know what this is.

"Uh, I yell at everyone," Jackson stutters. He glances around between the other players nervously before clearing his throat. "Hey," he says, a bit more gravel to his voice than his normal tone. That's his best attempt at getting in character, I suppose. "Everyone. I think there's something coming."

"I immediately nock an arrow in my bow and aim where he's looking," Matt says, a little too quickly. He's probably been sitting on that since Jackson was asked to roll. The others all mutter out that they're readying weapons, prepping spells, all looking in the direction of the oncoming intruder.

The corner of Eddie's mouth twitches as he holds back another smile. I've read this part in the module so many goddamn times that I can practically see the words on the page as he recites it, occasionally looking down at his own copy of the book. "As it draws closer, it looks almost as if part of the icy mountainside has ripped itself away from the rock and come to life. You see angles of clear, glimmering fractals moving through the gentle falling snow around you, almost like a golem of crystalized ice. As it draws closer, though, it's astounding. Because this isn't a golem. It's a person—a woman. Everything about her is colorless—her skin, her hair, her eyes. All white. As if someone siphoned the color out of her image." For dramatic flair, Eddie runs his hands up and down his arms as he says, "Her arms are covered in a layer of moving crystal, undulating and shifting as she moves, as if it's another layer of skin. And a flowing dress trails behind her, so long and so white that you don't know where it stops and the snow begins."

"I yell, 'By order of Queen Veridian, halt!'" Angela chimes in, holding her hands out as if she's actually holding a spear out in front of her.

Shaking his head, Eddie says, "She doesn't stop, at least not at first. When you say that, you think you see a smirk on her face, as if it's absurd that you even suggested it. Gradually, though, she stops, leaving a wide distance between all of you."

Jackson exhales, rubbing his hands on his jeans. "Do we know who this is?"

Eddie looks around at all the other players, a playful arch to his eyebrow. "Everybody, make folklore checks."

They roll. There's a pause as everyone consults their stats, but they soon call out numbers. Matt's is the worst—there's no real success when you roll a one, no matter how great your intelligence stats are. But the rest all get above a ten—Kaeden gets a twenty-five, so they may as well know the exact day and time this mystery woman was born. Eddie leans back in his seat, though, crossing his arms over his chest. "It's not a difficult check. Because most of you have seen iconography of her or those before her in Old God's shrines. Her name is whispered with fear and reverence in every shadow of every city you've been through. You know that this is the Crystalline Mage."

The group lets out a smattering of curse words. I don't blame them. If I didn't know this exact scene by heart and that it's not supposed to be a fight—or at least not a winnable one—I would probably be panicking too. In the game, the four Mages are the equivalent of demigods. Infernal, Earthen, Heavenly, and Crystalline. It's said they were mortals once. But when the Old Gods abandoned the world to make new ones, they granted a select few people to take on a fraction of their power in order to protect their creation. What really happened, though, was what happens whenever you give anyone a shred of power: they abused it. They lost control. The Mages aren't peacekeepers in the game. They're forces of raw destruction and chaos.

Even though I've totally abandoned all pretense that I'm studying, I don't react to the Mage's appearance. I wait. Because it's what comes next that I'm really interested in.

Eddie directs his gaze back at Jackson, who has taken off his glasses and started rubbing his face in a show of nerves. As soon as Eddie's eyes fall on him, his dark brown eyes go even wider. "With that perception check, I will say that you notice something else. Or someone else."

My stomach winds itself into a knot.

"Standing behind this viper of a woman is a girl."

Everything inside me has halted—no heartbeat, no breath. I wait for him to continue.

"She's a foil of the Mage—dark black hair and bright blue robes. Her brown eyes dart back and forth between you all, warily sizing you up. She stands waiting behind the Mage, silent, hands behind her back almost as if she's an attendant of some kind."

Samantha frowns. "How old is she?"

Wavering his hand side to side, non-committal, Eddie answers, "Eh, maybe twelve or thirteen. Young, but not that young."

More muttering between the players, and Eddie revels in the confusion. "I will say," he interrupts, "that out of all the stories you've heard about the Crystalline Mage, you never heard anything about a girl being with her or her having a child of any kind."

"Is there anything special about the girl that I can see?" Matt asks.

"Roll it."

Another clattering of dice, a shuffle of a character sheet. Matt gets a shit eating grin on his face as he looks at Eddie in defiance. "Natural twenty."

There's a round of ooo-ing and ahhh-ing and congratulating, as there usually is for the granddaddy of rolls. "Dude, those dice are giving *me* whiplash, holy shit," Kaeden comments.

Matt doesn't respond, simply staring down the GM. And Eddie matches the energy, giving him a slow, regarding nod.

And he finally says it. The sentence I've practically tattooed onto my grey matter.

"The only special thing you can really see on this girl is that her right earlobe is split in two."

It never ceases to make me shudder. That earlobe. Everything else matches up too, of course. Black hair, brown eyes, a look of inherent distrust. It's the earlobe, though, that I could never ignore.

I was with her the day she ripped it. We were ten. She was so goddamn happy because she had snuck into her mom's jewelry box and worn a pair of dangling, teardrop earrings to school that day. Always the exaggerator, she said they were diamonds. Thinking back on it, they were more like the fake crystal you could buy at Macy's. She showed them off all day anyway, living for the jealous looks from the other girls in class. It all came to a painful end at recess, though. She jumped off one of the swings and landed on her back instead of her feet, and before she could catch her breath, one of the boys that was playing catch nearby wasn't watching where he was stepping.

The earring ripped right through her lobe like it was tissue paper.

Up until the attack, that was the most blood I had ever seen come out of someone. I was the one who cried as we waited for May's parents to come pick her up in the principal's office. I was sobbing like a toddler while May held a wad of gauze up to her ear and kept a hand on my back, insisting she was fine.

She never did get it fixed. It was always split in two, right up until...

I have to look back down at my textbook now, otherwise it'll start replaying in my head again. I focus on the words "cognitive behavioral therapy," running them over in my brain until they don't look like real words anymore. It isn't until Eddie ends the session on a cliffhanger that I rip my eyes away from the page. I realize the die is in my hand again, hidden in my pocket from the others.

At the command of the GM, the room falls into an orderly chaos. Everyone packs up their dice and tucks away their minia-tures, all while chattering about how the night's session went down. One by one, they trickle out of our apartment. Eddie and Samantha are left talking after most everyone else leaves, but she starts inching her way slowly toward the door. I try moving her with my mind closer and closer to the exit with all the determi-nation of a kid who thinks they have telekinesis. Once it's just Eddie, I won't have to feel "on" anymore. I just get to be me for the first time in hours. It's the social equivalent of taking your bra off after getting home from work.

As Samantha leaves, though, I glance over to the one remaining straggler. Jackson King leans against the couch, messenger bag thrown across his body, a tan hunter-style coat buttoned up with a red knit scarf peeking out of the neckline. He stares at the floor, eyes wide and unfocused. It isn't until the door closes that he blinks, and his eyes meet mine.

Out of instinct, I look back down at my notes, pretending that we didn't make eye contact. We both know, though.

Jackson stays behind and talks to Eddie for a few more minutes about his thief's backstory and motivation that he's been tweaking. It's odd that he actually sounds invested in the game when his attention in game doesn't seem to match up. Eventually, he's out the door. I don't look at him as he goes, but the icy prickle that creeps along my neck as the door latches closed makes me think he was certainly looking at me before he departed.

The air in the apartment shifts after that, and I let out a breath. The social bra is on the floor.

"Told you they weren't going to die," Eddie says, grabbing an open bag of chips off the table and crunching on one in satisfied glee.

"You are a fearsome yet benevolent god," I say, shutting my books and stacking up my loose notes.

"Indeed. All shall look upon me and weep."

"Not because you're a god. Trust me."

"Hilarious," he deadpans, throwing a broken piece of chip at me that I deftly bat away. "If you ever do end up playing, I'm not gonna go easy on you."

My mouth goes dry as he says that, and I'm quiet as he starts to clear off the table, putting away leftover snacks and rolling up his gaming mat. "You didn't tell me you were doing the Crystalline Mage module," I finally say after a moment of getting my mouth working again.

"Well, I'm not straight up doing the whole module. Little bit of homebrew thrown in. I just thought it would be good to introduce her for some drama."

"I'll say," I mumble. Eddie doesn't know about my obsession with the Crystalline Mage arc. He knows I like the game and like listening to other people play, but not why. It's my one secret, one that I don't have to reveal to any therapists or parents or friends. It's something I keep with me like you might keep a lock of hair in a locket around your throat. A keepsake. May and I never had any Best Friends Forever bracelets or secret notebooks. This module is all I have to remind me of her. Just a paragraph in a game manual. I've thought about telling him, of course. But when you're nothing but transparent with someone, it's nice to have even a tiny thing that's not for them or anyone else.

He waggles his eyebrows at me as he passes by, throwing the chip bag back into the cabinet above the sink. "Still plenty of room for your crusader…"

"If I change my mind, you'll be the first to know." I scoop up my books and notes into my arm. "I'm turning in for the night."

"You sure?" he says. "We could play a round of Smash Bros. After the WoW session I had this afternoon, I feel like winning something."

I ignore the subtle insult toward my gaming skills. "I don't know. I'm just wiped," I lie.

He pauses then, looking me up and down with that same look of concern from earlier. I think I should tell him about the creature I saw on the bus earlier. It's too odd, and it's clearly shaken me to the point where he knows something is up. But how do you even start a conversation like that? How do you tell someone that you've started to see monsters again after a decade of everyone telling you they're fake?

"Rain check, I promise," I tell him, forcing another smile.

"All right," he says, conceding. I start to walk out of the kitchen, but he soon exclaims, "Oh, hold on!" Dashing back over to the table, he crouches down to his backpack that sits on the floor, rifling through it until he pulls out a flat, laminate hardcover book. He walks back over and extends it to me. "Just picked this up at Vault yesterday. They re-released the original game master's guide in a special edition. Thought you might want to take a look. A lot of stuff that hasn't been seen since the first edition."

I take the book from him, looking it over. It's got the same dramatic, detailed artwork that all the other books have—this one is a sprawling portrait of a cloaked figure wreathed in flames, hovering in the air with arms extended outward in a show of force, while a group of generic adventurers looks up at him in terror. I give him another forced smile. "I'll give it a read. Won't keep it too long. I'm sure you haven't looked over it all yet."

"Eh, least I could do," he shrugs. "I'd lend you my left kidney if you needed it."

I wrinkle my nose at him. "Ugh, you're such a gentleman after you play *Mages*. It's gross."

"I can't help being impossibly charming and endlessly kind, Violet," Eddie says through a cheeky grin. "It's just who I am."

I snort, finally turning away and walking down the hall to my room. "Whatever," I call back to him as I walk off. "If you call me 'm'lady,' I'm kicking you in the dick. Fair warning."

"Noted," he shouts back.

Despite what I told him, I'm not the least bit tired. I crack open the book he lent to me, skimming through the pages for the next few hours. I'm always generally looking for the word "Crystalline," because I'm always wondering if that means the girl with the split ear will be there, too. It's mostly been in vain, of course. The only mention of the girl is in the Crystalline Mage module, and really the only thing said about her is what Eddie gave to the others earlier. I've listened to other podcasts that branch off and do their own thing with her, but nothing official from the game publisher has been written except for that brief mention. Doesn't mean I don't still look.

Of course, I don't actually think it's May. A split earlobe means nothing. A lot of people have those. Still. When I first found that bit about her in the book, it was as if I met up with her for the first time since she disappeared. A visit from an old, long-lost friend...

So of course, I keep looking.

It's about two in the morning when my eyes really start to get heavy. I run a hand over my face before stretching my arms above my head, feeling every hour I've been curled up in the same position pulling at my muscles and joints. I flip over the next page in the book, just to see how much more of the section I have left to—

The breath gets sucked out of me. Illustrated on the glossy page is a highly rendered and detailed picture of a familiar creature. It's hunched and skeletal, with a spine full of jutting black spikes. Its eyes bug out of its head along with rows of overlapping razor-edged teeth.

It's one of them.

My heart hammers against my rib cage, and I instinctively reach out and shut the book completely.

Breathe in.

Breathe out.

I force my breathing into something normal and sustainable. Through my exhausted fog, I try to form rational thoughts. It's just a drawing. It can't hurt you. It's just ink on paper. You're fine. You're okay. Stop freaking out, you stupid piece of—

I look back at the book. Innocuous now that it's closed.

First, on the bus. Now here? I close my eyes. It's been ten years today. Ten years, and I'm losing it over a picture.

I'm too exhausted to berate myself. I crawl into bed, shutting off my lamp and forcing myself to try and sleep. I lie awake for another hour, though, staring at my desk and the outline of the module sitting amongst the unread library and psychology books. It's only after I get up and throw the guide underneath my bed that I can get any sleep at all.

CHAPTER 3

I wake up at noon the next day—only an hour before my work shift. I hurriedly throw my hair up in a bun, smear my day-old makeup around my face enough that I don't look like a depressed clown, and head off to work. I check my phone on my walk. Dad called and texted. Just checking in to see how I'm holding up. I text him back hastily saying I'm good, just to let him know I didn't down a bottle of pills over the anniversary or anything.

My therapist Amy also sent me a text—she does that sometimes, especially if she hasn't heard from me in a bit. She knows when the anniversary is, so she's probably making sure of the same thing Dad is. I let her know I'm still alive too. She responds saying that's great news and to schedule my next appointment if I need it. It's been a few months since our last session. Right now, I think I'd rather eat glass than sit in a freezing room and talk about all my stupid-ass feelings for a hundred and fifty bucks an hour, so I don't send a reply

I work at one of the trendy coffee joints downtown, which people find strange since I absolutely *hate* coffee. I hate everything about it—the taste, the smell, the look, and the everything else. But it pays something close to a livable wage, and they are flexible enough with my schedule that I can keep going to school. Besides, I'm used to a base level of misery during an average day. Coffee and customer service isn't going to add much more to that.

My shift is hazy as I navigate the monotonous tasks of cleaning out espresso machines, washing dishes, and taking out garbage. The exhaustion leaves me bleary-eyed, but I can handle it. This isn't the first time that I've stayed up far later than I should have and then had to work the next day. I doubt it will be the last. By the time my five-hour shift comes to an end, I can see a few flakes of snow falling outside the windowed wall of the shop. The thought of curling up on the couch, wrapping myself in five blankets, and blissfully losing consciousness while hoping I don't have to trek through a foot of snow tomorrow is all that's keeping me on my feet.

I'm hanging my apron up and shouting my hurried good-byes to the rest of my coworkers when I see Jackson King at the end of the counter.

In typical fashion, he isn't paying attention. Actually, he's the way I remember him from high school for the most part—eyes down and nose buried in a book. The end of the counter is where you wait for your drink, and with how bundled up he is, he doesn't look like he's about to sit down anytime soon. I don't know a lot of people who just casually get in a bit of reading before getting their coffee. Usually they're checking their phone, but I guess Jackson would be the one I'd point to if asked. Whenever we had class together back in high school, he regularly got called out for reading when he should have been taking notes or working on subjects that obviously weren't English. It was practically the only thing he was interested in. I even caught him retreating to the library to spend his lunch hour there instead of eating in the cafeteria with everyone else. Some things never change, I suppose.

As I'm dwelling on all that, though, his eyes briefly break

away from his book and lock on mine. And I don't look away fast enough that I can pretend I didn't see him.

Goddammit. Does that mean I have to make small talk?

I take a few awkward steps forward, closing the gap between the two of us but maintaining distance still. "Hey."

"Hey," he says with a nod, leaning away from me on instinct.

"Uh, never seen you in here before," I offer up, awkwardly. "Do you come here often?"

He raises an eyebrow at me, probably thinking the same thing I am—"come here often?" What kind of 90s sitcom is this supposed to be? But he moves on from it, saying "I had a job interview nearby. Thought I would get myself something afterward."

"Cool." Oh my god. *Kill me.* Straight up, someone please just murder me. I should have just bolted out the door when I had the chance.

"Yeah, super cool," he says, dry as cardboard, looking back down at his book.

I could use this opportunity to leave. He seems about as interested in this conversation as I do. "So, the fight last night was pretty intense." *Fucking*—why am I still opening my big trap?

"Yep," he says, not looking up at me and turning a page.

"And the whole Crystalline Mage reveal was pretty neat."

"Definitely neat."

"Interested to see how that's going to—"

"Violet, do you do this to everyone who's just waiting to get a coffee?" He closes his book, pushing his glasses back up and glaring at me with what I can only describe as contempt.

"S-sorry," I stammer. "I was just—I thought since you and I were seeing more of each other now, we could—I don't know—"

"Become best friends?" Jackson asks.

"No, of course—just, at least not—you know."

"I don't know, actually."

I don't even hold back my eye roll this time. "You don't have to be an asshole about it. I'm just trying to be an adult."

Dianne, one of the baristas still working, calls out Jackson's name, and he stuffs his paperback into his messenger bag hastily before grabbing his to-go cup. He mutters a thanks to her before turning back to me. "Listen," he says, "the 'adult' way to handle it is to exist in each other's spaces and keep it at that. We don't have to make small talk. We don't have to do anything. You don't bother me, I won't bother you. Pretty simple concept."

"I wasn't *bothering* you."

He scoffs and opens his mouth to say something but stops as a buzz comes from his pocket. Digging out his phone with his free hand, he glances at the screen and sighs. "Whatever," Jackson mumbles as he shoves it back into his pocket. "If you want me to appease your anxiety or whatever, I'm not interested. I don't owe you an explanation. Have a good one." Without any fanfare, he turns on his heel and walks toward the front entrance.

That's not good enough for me, actually. I do think I'm owed an explanation.

I grab my coat off the coat hook by the counter and bolt off after him, calling his name as he walks out the door. Piercing winter air hits me in the face as I hold the door open and step outside. "Jackson, hold on. Just—"

I stop. Because he's not there.

The whole city is gone.

I sway on my feet for a moment, disoriented. The city buildings have disappeared. The people, the cars, the pavement beneath my feet. They've vanished. In their place is paradise.

All around me, the sloping hills of a grassy valley curve up toward the sky, enveloping me like a lush green hand cupping me in its grasp. The hills are dotted with specks of color. Wildflowers in bloom. And the whole plain is lit by warm, buttery sunlight. Sunlight. It's been months since the sun was truly out. The breeze rolls by, and it's still bitterly cold, raising the flesh on my arms into goosebumps. But it looks so bright. So alive.

I'm not in Grand Rapids anymore. I have no idea where I am.

I hear a rustling, and instinctively, I whip around. Stupidly, I wonder if Jackson has followed me into whatever hallucination I've found myself in. But it isn't him skittering around in the tall grass.

It's the demon.

We have our stare down, just as we did on the bus—eyes locked, daring the other to make a move.

As it was the last time, it goes first. It clicks its mouth and runs off, soft grass and flowers swaying after it. It's then that it dawns on me. Maybe I'm completely off base, but I think it *wants* me to follow. It's a white rabbit, and I'm Alice.

I've never really been much of an Alice, though.

As it trounces away, I stumble backward. It should be difficult to walk backward through the thick patches of grass and foliage, but it's not at all. Nothing impedes me as I turn and stagger in the opposite direction, the vastness of the valley in front of me overwhelming. I stop for a moment, but the rustling behind me reminds me that it's still there. I pick up speed, running through the thick grass like it's air—

And then I'm back.

I stop before I trip over the curb. Everything is back—the buildings, the people. I look behind me, noticing I've moved. I'm half a block away from the coffee shop. The snow has stopped but the chill still runs through the air, electric against my bare skin. The sun is hidden away behind clouds again, and around me is only concrete. Not a patch of green in sight.

The demon is gone again. Down the rabbit hole.

I straighten myself out, throwing my coat on and hoping that no one saw me stumble around like I just saw a ghost. Grand Rapids isn't New York City—people *do* care if you wander around like a crazy person. I can feel some of the stares burrowing into the back of my head as the bystanders walk past me. I put my head down as I turn around and make my way down the block, my mind racing.

I can officially say that this isn't normal. When I would have my flashbacks, they would be brief glimpses of images, not full-fledged hallucinations. It would just be flashes of the attack, of those creatures' faces. This is new.

Both those demons—maybe they were the same one, I don't know—wanted me to follow them. Where, though?

I think back to the picture I saw in the *Mages* book last night, and I sprint down the street toward Vault. I have no idea why this is happening. But if there's one person who knows anything about what you can find in a *Mages* book, it's Eddie.

Vault is only a handful of blocks away from the coffee shop, nestled between a line of delis and upscale hotels. Eddie has built his resume since graduating high school on working in hole-in-the-wall comic shops, but Vault is the first nice shop he's managed to get into. "Nice" meaning the ceiling isn't caving in and the employees mop the floor more than once a year. There are nights he laments about missing his old jobs, back in the shops that had "character" and that weren't part of the gentrification that has plagued the city. But whenever he gets his paycheck, he shuts up about it. None of the shops with "character" can offer him full time at fifteen bucks an hour.

I'm glad I don't have to walk into a dilapidated mess in the state I'm in. A stable environment is what I need right now, when I can't tell if what I've seen is real or not. As I walk in, I run my fingers over stacks of comics, blind boxes, and packs of Japanese candies, just so I'm sure that what I'm experiencing is physically here. That *I'm* physically here.

Eddie's coworker—god, I'm so bad with names—is working

at the register, and she eyes me as I walk up. They don't have name tags here, either. Fuck. "Uh, hey," I say awkwardly. "Eddie's working today, right?"

She raises a perfectly drawn-on eyebrow and casually adjusts her septum ring. "Yeah, he's in the back."

I wait. She stares at me.

"Could you..." I say. "Could you go get him?"

She rolls her thickly lined eyes and walks off behind the stacks.

I breathe in. Breathe out. How am I going to talk to him about this? If I tell him I'm seeing things...

I'm not, though, right? I actually saw this place. It was real.

Right?

"Vi, what's up?" I nearly jump at Eddie's voice as he comes around the corner. He looks concerned already, and I don't blame him. I glance in the mirror behind the register, and I'm a mess—coat rumpled and uneven, my dark brown hair a wind-blown disaster, my face paler than usual. I try to smooth my hair down a little bit and straighten myself out, trying to shake off any Doc Brown vibes I've acquired on the way over.

I open my mouth, but Septum Ring comes back behind the register, pretending to be interested in some new issue of *Squirrel Girl* but clearly listening. I grab hold of Eddie's forearm and drag him further into the stacks. Soon we're hidden back in the games section of the store, a wall of *Ticket to Ride* and *Settlers of Catan* blocking us from the rest of the store. Eddie looks at me with a furrowed brow as I glance around nervously. "Are you okay?" he asks, a lot less jovial than he was a minute ago.

I nod, but I'm still breathing pretty hard. "I'm fine. I just— that book you gave me last night? The *Mages* source book. That just came out recently, yeah?"

He glances around to the rest of the shop before crossing his arms. "Well, kind of. It was the original source book when they first published the game, but it's been out of print for like five years. That was a re-release."

"Did they add anything new? Any new monsters?" I'm trying so hard not to sound frantic, like his answers are the key to defusing some bomb, but I don't think I'm doing a stellar job of it. My face is still flush from the cold, and it's hard enough to catch your breath after being in February air anyway, much less when you're trying not to have a panic attack.

"A few of them are new, yeah. What is going on?" Eddie asks. "Did something happen? I don't—"

"No, nothing happened," I say a little too quickly. "I'm fine. I just read the book last night, and—one of the drawings looked like..."

"Like what?"

My chest tightens. Ugh, he's really going to make me say it. "Uh, I don't know. I didn't get the name. The little black things with the huge teeth and the—the eyes—"

"Hellions?"

"Sure, sure. They, um, they looked like—like—" God, it's so hard to breathe in here. The edges of my eyes sting as I suck in another big breath, but it comes out broken and uneven.

That's when it dawns on him. "Oh shit," Eddie says like a sigh. "Fuck, Vi. I totally didn't even realize."

"It's fine," I say, waving my hands dismissively. "That's— whatever. It's whatever. But they looked just like them, Eddie. Like, *just* like them."

He's back to looking confused. "Okay..."

"Like—god, it was uncanny."

"What are you getting at?"

What *am* I getting at?

Because they aren't *real*. They've never been real. Like I've been told a thousand times by a thousand therapists: they're nothing but fabrications. A way for my brain to process trauma. If I'm saying they're real, that just proves to everyone that I'm as crazy as they all thought. So of course I'm not saying they're real, right?

Why am I even here then?

I must be too quiet because Eddie puts his hands on my shoulders and looks me in the eye. "Okay, hey. Why don't I tell Brian I have to take off and then we can go somewhere and get food. Or we can order takeout and marathon Doctor Who. Whatever you want to do, all right?"

Closing my eyes and shaking my head, I say, "No, no. Don't do that. I don't know—I don't know why I came here. I don't want to worry you. I just—"

"Violet, it's fine."

I bite my lip. Because I want to scream at him that it's *not* fine. Nothing is fine, and every time I've told him I was fine before has been a disgusting lie. I shake my head again. "I'm sorry," I say, my voice breaking as I pull away from him, striding back out of the stacks back into the main store. "I'm not going to bother you anymore. I'll see you at home."

My feet feel like they're moving by themselves as I take off, boots squeaking across the tile floor. "Violet, hold on!" Eddie calls out after me, but I don't listen, barreling toward the door. I have enough foresight to pull my jacket around me since I see it's snowing out again.

I open the door and step out, and it takes me a moment to blink back the tears enough to see that I'm back.

It's not the same valley I was in before. This time, it's a hilltop looking down on another plain full of rolling, luxuriant grass and trees. The green is so vibrant that it almost hurts to look at. Off in the distance is a massive rock formation that stands against the blue sky like a stalwart guardian. The sun beats down on me—why does it still feel like the dead of winter, then? I shiver, but I can't tell if it's from the frigid air or the fact that what I'm looking at is just so goddamn beautiful.

I glance around. There's no demon this time. I'm alone here.

Until I feel a hand clasp around my wrist.

Instinctively, I pull my arm back, ready to fight with all my pathetic might against whatever has a hold of me. A jolt of adrenaline rushes through me at the thought of looking down to see the demon and a pack of his friends all grinning up at me, ready to finish the job they started ten years ago.

But the thing that has hold of me is human. It's Eddie.

And he's not looking at me. He looks past me.

"Holy shit," he says, a mere exhale of breath as he stares out in awe.

I gape at him. "Do you see it?" I ask.

It takes him a moment, but he slowly nods, not taking his eyes off the horizon. "Yes."

I follow his gaze back out to the expansive plains surrounding us, the breath still knocked out of me, but for an entirely different reason now. Tears that I had so desperately been holding in roll down my cheek, the bitter wind chilling it instantly as it streaks down my face. There's so much rushing through my mind that I can't process. I opt instead to just stare at the massive red rock formation and take in the strange foreign beauty of something I can't possibly understand yet.

It only takes a blink before everything snaps back in place. The hilltop is there one moment, gone the next. We're back in front of Vault again.

Before I can say anything, Eddie speaks. His expression looks bewildered, but beneath the utter confusion, a grin of unbridled joy breaks through. "Vi," he says. "I think we were in Velmyra."

CHAPTER 4

I fill Eddie in on everything as we wander around looking for somewhere to eat. About seeing the demon on the bus, the drawing in the book, May's doppelganger in the module, the valley I saw stepping out of the coffee shop. Once I've sufficiently spilled my guts, we end up at a sushi place. On any normal evening, we wouldn't have gone to Soho's since we've joked that it's been shut down for health code violations more than once. The nice thing about that, though, is we know it'll be empty. And it is, save for the apathetic waitstaff who don't look up from their phones aside from bringing us our orders. We're left to nibble on our spicy tuna rolls and stare blankly at the bland wall art, reeling from the shock of what we just saw.

I've opened my mouth to speak several times already, but glancing at Eddie's pallid expression, I've stopped myself. Neither of us can figure out the right thing to say. And if I open a can of worms, I at least want to make sure it's the right can.

"How did you know it was Velmyra?" I ask.

"Hm?" Eddie hums quizzically, mouth full of rice.

"You said it was Velmyra, the place we saw," I explain. "How did you know? It was just a big open plain."

He swallows and exhales, putting a chopstick up to his forehead and closing his eyes. "It wasn't just some grassland," he says. "It was the Verdantia Plains near Frostpost. I saw the outline of Fort Myr in the distance. And I recognized Rogue's Rock from the guidebook drawings."

I look at him, impressed. "You got all that from a glance?"

Eddie shrugs with one shoulder, looking a little stunned himself. "I'm a GM. The illustrations in the guide help me visualize. I guess I just remembered them well."

"And you're sure, right?" I ask. "You weren't just…"

"What, seeing things?"

"Well, I don't know, man," I say. "What's that French term that means two people are crazy together? It was a Fall Out Boy album."

"*Folie à deux*," he says. "Not their best work."

"Eddie," I say.

He scrubs at his face. "I'm sorry, I'm sorry," he says between his fingers. "I just don't know what to do with this information, you know. Velmyra is *real*." He laughs a little as he says it, stunned. "And it was way more vibrant, way more colorful than I ever imagined. More *alive*. I couldn't have just made that all up." He pops another sushi roll into his mouth and talks through the bites. "It was weird, though, because it was still cold. Like, we were still in Michigan but just *seeing* Velmyra, almost like we were wearing a VR headset."

"I don't remember feeling anything around me, either," I confirm. "It felt like I was running straight across pavement, not over uneven ground and tall grass."

He puts his hand around his chin, tapping his pointer finger on his nose as he thinks. "Was it snowing when you went out the first time?"

I stop and think. "Actually, yeah."

Eddie claps his hands together. "Fuck, this is amazing! This is straight out of the guide!" Scooting his chair in closer, he leans forward and assumes his high school teacher pose, emphatically gesturing as he talks. "So, the Crystalline Mage has this ability where she can use her control over ice and snow to send—"

"Send people visions. Yeah, I know."

"Well, what if that's what happened to us? What if the Mage wanted to send us a vision? To let us know that this wasn't just a game."

"Why would she want to do that? She doesn't know who we are."

Eddie spreads his hands in front of him. "Your guess is as good as mine. It's the best explanation I've got."

I stare at my plate of nearly untouched spicy tuna, and suddenly, the pieces put themselves together. "Holy fuck," I whisper.

"What?" Eddie asks.

I look him straight in the eye. "What if she knows where May is?"

"Vi," he says, cautiously.

"I'm not being overly optimistic here, Eddie. It makes sense," I say. "May and I were attacked by those creatures, and she was dragged away into some sort of doorway. What if that doorway was to Velmyra? The whole reason I know everything about the Crystalline Mage arc in the game is because she has a girl with her. She's described just like May. Hair color, eye color. She even has a split earlobe on the same side as May."

He shakes his head at me, almost as if he hasn't comprehended what I said. "God, I wish you would have told me this before," he says.

I get sheepish now, jabbing one of my rolls with a chopstick. "I just thought it was a coincidence," I confess. "It was just something innocuously comforting. I didn't actually think it was her. Not until now."

"Yeah, but still. I would have liked to know."

"Listen, the point," I say, changing the subject, "is that those creatures might have taken May through the doorway into

Velmyra. Why, I don't know. But if that's where she went, she might still be there. She might still be *alive*, Eddie."

Saying the words out loud feels kind of like saying the tooth fairy might exist. For so long, I have been told that past the first forty-eight hours, it's unlikely that a teenage girl who went missing would be coming home alive. The fact that she could be out there still is hard to wrap my head around, like the idea that I could walk down the street and find a suitcase full of a million dollars. Though, at this point, I'm willing to believe anything.

Eddie presses his hands together and places them under his chin, breathing out. "Goddamn. This is heavy."

"You said it."

We let uncertainty and the scent of ginger hang in the air between us. Eventually, Eddie asks, "Well, what do you want to do?"

"You're asking me?"

He shrugs again. "Dude, you know me," he says. "We just found out *Mages* is real. I'm ready to go out and buy a chainmail onesie and leap glaive-first into whatever door we have to go through. But this is your thing. Your friend. I think you should make the rules."

My heart picks up. The thought of me making the rules for anything sounds like a terrible idea. I blink down at my plate. "I don't even know where to begin," I say, shaking my head. "I mean, how do you find a portal to another dimension? That's not exactly something you can just Google the directions to."

"Well, the world knows about Velmyra somehow." Eddie pauses, his brow furrowed until they fly up in realization. I can practically see the light bulb going off above his head. "Fucking of course." Digging in his coat pocket that's draped on the chair behind him, he takes out his phone, running his fingers frantically over the cracked screen. After a moment of mumbling to himself, he exclaims, "Ha, there he is." He sets the phone down and slides it across the table toward me. "If anyone knows anything, it's this guy."

I pull the phone closer. His internet browser is open to a Wikipedia page—short and all text, not a picture in sight. The title of the page reads "Hikari Inoue." I'm the one furrowing my brow now. "Who is this?" I ask him.

"That," Eddie says, "is the creator of *Mages of Velmyra*. Co-creator, anyway. There were two guys who made the original sourcebook and founded Magicka Games: Anthony Nakamura and Hikari Inoue. Anthony has always been the face of Magicka Games—he's the one you see on all the press conferences and Comic-Con panels. But Inoue has always been private. So private, in fact, that no one has seen his actual face at any public event, and when the game started getting too big and branching out beyond the original rulebook, he bailed on the company. Gave up all the IP rights and fucked off to who knows where."

I scroll through the Wiki page, and it says about all the same things Eddie is saying. "That's certainly weird…"

"I've always thought so," he says.

"Well, what about this Anthony guy? If no one knows where Inoue is, we can at least try him."

Eddie scratches his chin. "I mean, aside from the fact that he's super famous in the TTRPG community, and we probably wouldn't even get a response back from his PR manager let alone him, I don't think he's our guy."

I slide his phone back to him. "And why is that?"

"Well, they're pretty open about how the game was first made," Eddie says, matter of fact. "Anthony was the mechanics and rules guy, Inoue was the lore guy. Honestly, if we want to find the source of Velmyra knowledge, my bet's on Inoue."

"The one who disappeared into the ether."

"Well, if you want to make it dramatic, sure," he says. "But realistically, unless he's dead, he's out there somewhere."

"And how would we find him?" I ask. I'm starting to think that finding this hermit is more unrealistic than traveling to a fantasy world full of magic and goblins. "Has anyone gotten close, even? I know there's some weirdo out there who's probably tried to stalk him."

Eddie's deconstructing one of his tuna rolls as he talks, unfurling the rolled up rice and seaweed with his chopstick as if he's rolling out camping gear. "Obviously. These are nerds we're talking about. There's more than a handful of toxic obsessives in the fandom. Everything that I've seen on Reddit or other message boards has only been theories, though. Nothing concrete. And if there has been an address or something, it gets taken down before it can even be confirmed."

I nod, a little disheartened. "So, a needle in one of a million haystacks then."

Smearing his wasabi into a green streak on his plate, Eddie sighs. "It's somewhere to start, anyway."

"I guess..." My eyes unfocus as the thought of it all starts coming to me in unrelenting waves. Whoever knows where May went is out there. Or could be. What if he *is* dead? Or what if he went back to Velmyra and we have no way of contacting him? Searching for him sounds daunting enough, but searching for something that's most likely a dead end...

"Hey."

I break out of my trance and look back up at Eddie. The excitement hasn't left his face, but there's that familiar look of concern that lies underneath it. "Are you sure you want to do this?"

I blink at him. I don't understand the question—I know what the words mean, of course, but they won't process correctly in my head for some reason. "What?" I ask.

"Look, when you play *Mages*, the players determine the story," Eddie explains. "The GM lays down the plot threads, but if the players don't want to go fight the dragon, they don't have to. They could just get drunk at the tavern and sleep with the barmaid instead. That's the easier route, anyway." He gives me a restrained yet empathetic smile. "Fighting the dragon is hard, Vi. I don't think anyone would blame you if you stayed at the tavern. But if you start going after the dragon, there's no going back. You have to be ready."

I look around the empty restaurant, the cheap pleather chairs cracking and the upholstery on the wall starting to come undone. That's the thing—I've *been* sitting in the tavern. For a decade now. And even that hasn't been easy. Even just sitting and watching everyone else pair off with a barmaid while I drink myself to death in the corner has been hard.

The thought of running off to fight the dragon is terrifying.

If that's the only way we get her back, though...

"I'm not ready," I say, throwing my napkin on my mostly full plate. "Let's do it anyway."

I work all weekend, so the real research doesn't start until Monday night. I have class all day, which I half-ass, my mind drifting back to Velmyra during every lecture. Between classes, I'm on my phone, Googling anything I can think of to find out more about our only lead. Beyond his name, though, there's not much anyone knows about the guy. Hikari Inoue seems to be nothing more than a name printed on a front cover. I text Eddie in the middle of the day, expressing this to him, and he responds: *Maybe it's a pseudonym?* That just makes the mounting headache I'm cultivating worse.

By the time lectures are done and I'm back home in my room, I'm running out of options. I've been sitting at my desk, eyes straining over my laptop for hours, nibbling on remnants of a cold piece of pizza, but no amount of time is making a difference. The only thing that I can glean about this guy from Reddit or Tumblr or any other backwater forum is that, based on the revenue from the game, he was probably able to retire early. To where? That's the piece of the puzzle I can't find.

Eddie checks on me every once in a while, asking if I need

anything. He says he's been researching, too, but I can hear Kingdom Hearts background music playing out in the living room. I tell him I'm fine, but I'm losing steam.

It's nearing midnight when the final piece falls into my lap. After hours of poring through forums and weeding out all other possible Hikari Inoues in the world (the name is pretty common in Japan,) I'm ready to call it quits. Just a quick glance over my email, and then I'm done for the night. I go to my inbox and discard a few coupons from stores that I've gone to once and LinkedIn notifications for an account I created ten years ago and never touched.

The last message, though, is a Google news alert.

Last year, when I first got into *Mages*, I set up a news alert that was supposed to send me an email any time a news article showed up with the term "crystalline mage." It hadn't proved very fruitful, usually showing listicles that ranked all the *Mages* campaigns from the source materials and expansions that had come out since. I doubt this one contains anything more, but in my desperation to feel like I've accomplished something today, I open it.

It's an article from a Chicago newspaper. I follow the link, and I'm brought to a "Things To Do in Chicago This Weekend" listing. I scroll through the page, and I find toward the end of the article:

February 19th: Wyland Art Gallery—*Mages of Velmyra* in Pictures (Wicker Park)

Mages of Velmyra, a massively popular tabletop role playing game, has dominated the nerd scene for nearly a decade. With this exhibition, artists from all over the world bring their own interpretations to the stories and creatures of the land of Velmyra. Commissioned by the publisher, Magicka Games, witness some of the game's most iconic scenes and characters from the world of Velmyra such as the Battle of Uver'Dun, the Crystalline Mage, and the Squalid Squire.

I click on the link for the gallery embedded in the article, quickly scrolling through their website. This showing doesn't seem to be their usual fare—most of the samples of pieces they have on their slideshow are modern art pieces that look to me more like accidental paint spillage onto an expensive canvas than art. The show is on the calendar, but it's the only one of its kind amid features on world hunger and colonialism.

I go to the contacts page, scrolling past the phone number and general email.

The gallery owner's info is there, and my eyes go wide.

Adrian H. Inoue.

I bolt up from the desk and run into the living room. "Inoue!" I shout. "Inoue! I found an Inoue!"

Eddie jumps at my surprise exclamation, and immediately, his onscreen avatar succumbs to a group of enemies. He leaves it on the "game over" screen as he sets down the controller, turning around on the couch and looking at me with anticipation. "You found him?" he asks.

I explain the gallery and the similar name. Once I do, he looks less excited than he did a moment before. "Adrian H. Inoue is close, but how can we be sure that's him?" he asks.

"I mean, I guess we can't," I admit. "But think about it. Magicka Games is commissioning the show. If the guy who created the game retired and, say, bought an art gallery somewhere as a fun hobby on the side, they might go to him first before some other gallery, right?"

"Maybe…" Eddie says, though he sounds unconvinced.

"It's something," I say firmly. "More than anything we've found in the past two days. And Chicago is close by."

"If you consider three hours away close," he grumbles.

I shake my head at him. "Look, if it ends up being a dead end, you can say 'I told you so.' It's something, so I want to check it out."

He sighs, scratching at his couple days old stubble and looking back at his "game over." I think he's about to say no, until he throws his hands up in surrender. "Fuck it. I didn't have any plans this weekend besides customer service and getting baked." Looking up at me, he gives me a grin. "It's a date."

Neither of us have a car, so we take the Amtrak Friday morning from Grand Rapids to Chicago. It takes a few hours, though it seems like less because of the time change as we cross into Indiana. Eddie's never been on an Amtrak before, so every little thing about it fascinates him, from the footrests to the fact that they serve White Castle burgers in the food car. By the time we arrive in the city around noon, he's stuffed so full of the little sliders that he can't even think about grabbing actual lunch.

I don't need to eat, anyway. I'm too focused on finding the gallery, which should be easy to do in theory since the address is right on the website and we have phones. Chicago is just so damn big, though. So much bigger than Grand Rapids, with so many neighborhoods and bus lines and subway tracks. I've been here a couple of times, but Eddie has never been. I find I have to regularly pull him along with me as we find our way. The huge scale of the buildings downtown puts him in full tourist mode— eyes wide, mouth agape, marveling at the scale of everything. My eyes aren't on the buildings, though. Mine are fixed squarely ahead of me.

It takes a few subway rides and a bus, but we finally get to the Wicker Park neighborhood. After pushing through the biting February air—which feels even colder than back home— we find our way to a shopping district clustered with stores and restaurants, all stuffed into old buildings with new façades. As I power walk down the sidewalk, the little blue line on my phone's GPS gets smaller and smaller, and my heart picks up. To think, the person with the key to everything is just a block away, a sprint, a few steps—

I stop, my GPS announcing my arrival at my destination, and the excitement dips as I look upon what I came here for.

The gallery is hardly noticeable, nestled between a twenty-four-hour diner and a trendy consignment shop. From outside, it looks like nothing more than a closed office building, nothing glaring that announces its existence. The lack of any kind of light or sign of life makes my confidence waver, but the real plummet comes when I look at the piece of paper plastered on the inside of the glass door. Bold bright red letters tell me the one thing I was dreading:

CLOSED INDEFINITELY. PLEASE VISIT OUR WEBSITE FOR DETAILS ON TICKET REFUNDS.

I cup my hands around my eyes and look inside the dark wall of windows, like all my reading comprehension has just flown out the window. There's not much inside, just a small lobby area with geometric modern art and an empty receptionist desk. I adjust my angles, thinking maybe I'm just not seeing the person I need hiding in the corner behind the potted plants. But no matter where I look, he's not there.

I sense Eddie pulling up behind me and hear him utter a *"shit"* as quiet as he can. After a moment, his hand falls on my shoulder. "Violet, I don't think anyone is in there," he says.

"No, there has to be," I say, still looking inside. "They said the exhibition was happening. This has to be a mistake."

"I don't know, dude…"

I knock on the glass, and even while I'm doing it, it feels ridiculous. I can feel Eddie's embarrassment. Even I'm embarrassed, but I can't help it. We came all this way. This can't be it. It can't just be—

Eddie's hand wraps around my fist, stopping the knocking. I pry my eyes away from the windows and look at him, and his expression gives me the one feeling I've been afraid of this whole trip: hopelessness.

"He's in there."

Shaking his head, Eddie says, "Violet."

45

"He's in there, Eddie. I'm not leaving until I see him."

"Listen, we—"

"I'm. Not. Leaving."

His grip loosens on my fist until I'm able to pull away, and my eyes go back to the wall of windows. I stare into the dark void, my heart soaring at every shadow passing across the glass until I realize it's probably just someone walking down the sidewalk behind us. Eddie doesn't try to pull me away again, standing a distance behind me in silence as I continue to stare. Minutes turn into an hour, then an hour and a half. The grey sky starts to dim into evening, and there hasn't been so much as a flicker of life inside the building.

No one is there. It's as if no one was ever there.

I pull away from the door, stepping back in a daze. The bitter cold of the breeze around me tears at my face like claws. I try not to think about actual black claws, raking across my skin. But the images rush through my head, and I can feel the horrific clip show I'm so used to start playing through in my mind—

An arm wraps around my shoulder, and my heart slows down. I lean into the weathered canvas jacket that Eddie got for Christmas three years ago, and he gives me a quick squeeze.

"What now?" he asks.

It takes me a while to answer, but the turn of my stomach makes it pretty clear. "I'm starving," I say. And as he guides me away from the empty gallery, I turn back to look at it, hoping against all hope that Hikari Inoue will step outside at last. The door stays closed, though, as we pull to the end of the block and turn the corner, our last hope disappearing from view.

CHAPTER 5

Our Airbnb isn't available for us to crash at for another couple of hours, so Eddie and I do the only thing we can think of that will help the situation: drink.

Well, Eddie drinks. I don't drink anymore. Enough nights of puking and sobbing into Eddie's lap have put me off the relentless weekends of hopping from vodka to tequila. The idea of alcohol never stops being an enticing idea. The thought of the next morning is always what makes me steer away from it.

Eddie, on the other hand, has never really lost his gills. He is deep in the cockles of a third gin and tonic now, sitting across from me at a booth in the closest bar we could find to the gallery. The place gives off an air of wanting to be an elitist bar for the obscenely wealthy but knows it's in the wrong part of town for it. There are random bits of chrome paneling on the walls and geometric light fixtures and table centerpieces, but the tables themselves seem like remnants from an older, dingier bar. Despite the weak façade, it isn't hurting for guests. We are two of dozens of people, all chatting at tables or crammed together at the bar itself.

Eddie exhales dramatically, and I can smell his breath all the way across the table, reeking of gin. "I wish I was drinking rum."

"I mean, we're in a bar," I say, stabbing at the ice in my glass weakly. "No better place to find some."

"Psh, sure. When you say it, it sounds soooo easy," he scoffs, slurping down another mouthful.

I shake my head. "Okay, so what's next? What's plan B?"

"Plan B? There is no plan B. That wasn't even plan A. It was just 'plan.'"

"Well, then we need to come up with plan B," I say as steadily as I can, even though I don't have the foggiest of what plan B is either. Adrian Inoue—or Hikari or whatever his name is—was our only lead. With that connection a bust, we might as well just start, what? Combing through Reddit more to see if anyone else has seen Velmyra? Start standing out in the freezing snow to see if we can get back there again? There's nothing I can think of that is a remotely logical next step.

"Dude, maybe we could just—you know, like—chill for a sec?" His words are starting to slur together. "Like, we're in Chicago. I've never been here before. It would be fun to, like, go see stuff. We could go be dumpy tourists and see the Bean!"

"We don't have time for the Bean," I say, trying to keep my volume down, even though I want to scream it at him. "We're not here for a vacation, Eddie."

He sighs, letting his glass clatter onto the table. "Well, the least we could do is just take a moment, Violet. Maybe there's someone we could email or call or—"

"As if it's going to be that easy."

"I just think taking a step back and doing something fun could be good, you know?" Eddie implores. "You've been obsessing about this for a week. Longer than a week. Ever since I gave you that book when…"

He trails off, his eyes unfocusing as he gets lost in the contents of his glass for a moment. It's that moment that I realize it.

We've never talked about what happened a year ago.

Not explicitly, anyway. He checks in on me, asks me if I'm doing okay, offers to watch all my favorite episodes of *X Files* with me. But he's never really acknowledged how far gone I was that he had to drive me to the hospital and leave me there. Ever since he picked me up and brought me back home, it's been an unspoken thing, candy coated with rounds of video games and late-night discussions over who played the best Spider-Man. There was never an acknowledgement of how fucked up it was that we ended up outside an ER at two in the morning at the end of winter.

And what would bringing that up even accomplish? To be fair, I've never had much of a desire to talk about it either.

"The point," Eddie says, rubbing the heels of his hands into his eyes, "is that if we hit a dead end, what else should we do? Is it really going to make things better to sit and stew over stuff we can't change?"

"We can start looking for the next step."

"And what happens when there is no next step?"

"There is."

Groaning, Eddie slumps further down into the booth. "I'm with you, all right? I am, but I don't want you to put all your hopes for this in one basket. If it doesn't work out—"

"It's going to work out," I interrupt.

"Violet—"

"It is, Eddie," I say, firmly. "It has to."

He drops his eyes again, nodding weakly, clearly defeated. He stabs the melting ice in his cup half-heartedly with a stirring straw before he says, "Okay."

We sit in silence for a moment before he announces he's going to go call us an Uber to get to our place. As he slips out of the booth and walks out the front door of the bar, I sigh, dropping my head into my hands in defeat.

This isn't right. Nothing about this is how it should have gone. This morning, I thought I was going to get answers, and now I'm left with nothing. I can't even get drunk at a hipster bar to make it more bearable. No closer to Velmyra or the Crystalline Mage or…

I stand up from the booth, grabbing my backpack and pulling it over to the bar. It's mostly cleared out now, save for one guy, dressed to the nines in a grey suit. I perch on a barstool a few seats away, and against my better judgements, I order a vodka cranberry.

I breathe in. Breathe out.

My hands are shaking, and it's not just because Chicago is cold as dick.

Breathe in. Breathe out.

God, this stupid bartender can't mix two ingredients together any faster?

Breathe in—

"Trouble in paradise?"

I look up to see the man in the suit staring at me, an eyebrow inquisitively arched in my direction.

"Uh," I say, an uneven exhale. "No, uh. He was—he was just—"

The man holds up a hand. "It's all right," he says, one side of his mouth curling upward, amused. "I don't mean to pry. You just seem upset."

There isn't a thing about him that isn't perfectly arranged, like he's more museum piece than person. His black hair is coiffed into a dramatic pompadour almost as high as his cheekbones. He's East Asian, with tan skin and deep brown eyes that bore into me like a drill. For some weird reason, I'm drawn to his nose. It's so perfect—straight and slightly pointed, delicate yet masculine. I have a thing for focusing on nice noses, unfortunately. Mine is so crooked that I can't help but compare it to everyone else's. There's really no comparing me to this guy, though. Against his pressed suit, manicured hands, and glowing complexion, I'm a frazzled dumpster rat.

"He's just a friend," I say, a phrase I'm no stranger to when referring to Eddie throughout the years. "It'll be okay. I just—we had a disagreement, is all."

The bartender brings over my vodka cranberry along with a martini glass, which he places in front of the man. He raises a gentle hand toward the bartender, the cuff of his jacket falling to reveal what looks like a Rolex—or at least some really expensive watch. I guess I don't know the difference between a Rolex and any other brand. "Put hers on mine," he instructs the bartender.

"Oh, no. You don't have to—"

"I know," he says, matter of fact. There's no flirtation to his tone, no indication that he really is just looking to get into my pants. He's charming, but there's no creepy, preying vibe I usually get from other guys who try to buy me drinks in bars. I can't quite place his accent either—I want to say it's American, but occasionally, he says a word with too refined of a sound. "It's nothing, really. I just think if you're having a bad day, you shouldn't have to pay for your drink."

He takes a sip of his martini, looking refined as hell. I'm almost disappointed he's not hitting on me. I raise my glass at him and say, "Well, thanks. That's nice of you."

The man nods as I take a sip, the vodka burning as it goes down. Christ, how long has it been since I've had a drink? A year? Two years?

"What was the disagreement?"

I clear my throat, muscling my way through the lighter fluid taste. "Uh, not important."

"It's up to you, of course," he says, casually, "but I always find the confidence of a stranger to be therapeutic. If it interests you. I won't pry any more if you don't think so."

I sigh. I drink again.

He drinks too.

"Have you ever felt like you've made so much progress in life, and then in one week, you feel like you're right back where you started again?" I ask, gazing down at my drink.

The smirk returns to his face. "More often than you'd think."

Shaking my head, the words just spill out. "Like, I thought I was fine, you know? I was actually getting on with my life. I should be back in Michigan, in class, trying to get my fucking Bachelor's degree. The one I'm supposed to already have. But I'm here. Convincing everyone I'm crazy, yet again." I choke back the hard lump again. "I'm not quite convinced I'm not crazy, myself."

"You don't seem crazy to me."

"Well, I'm not entirely sane," I snort.

"None of the best people are," he says. His hand that isn't holding the drink fidgets, but it's somehow graceful. His fingers dance absently, one at a time in a sort of ballet, as though he's passing something fluid and invisible between them, though he doesn't pay it much mind. "Honestly, I worry for anyone who doesn't have a little bit of crazy in them."

"I wish it was that easy for me to see it that way."

The man laughs, and his fingers stop, as if he's just realized they were moving. "It isn't all that easy. It's hard as hell, actually." He pulls down his jacket sleeves, checking the buttons on the cuffs. "But I have to think about it as a good thing. Otherwise, I don't think I'd ever get out of bed." He says it like a joke with a scrunched-up smile, but as he takes another sip of his martini, the humor deflates.

We drink in silence for a bit, the natural lull in conversation washing over us as it does for all strangers. I gulp down the rest of my drink, the alcohol finally taking effect as the fuzzy light-headed feeling slows down my thoughts enough for me to breathe normally again. Digging in the front pocket of my back-pack, I pull out a twenty-dollar bill and slap it on the bar counter, payment for the drinks Eddie and I had before. "I need to go, but thanks for listening to my word vomit," I say hurriedly.

"I'm a regular here, so anytime you want to pour your guts out, you'll know where to find me," the man says, raising his glass. The only thing missing from his James Bond-esque charm is an actual wink.

"Thanks...uh..."

"Adrian," he answers.

It feels like the breath has been knocked out of me.

"Adrian," I repeat.

"Yes," he confirms. "What about you?"

"Adrian," I say again.

He furrows his brow. "Ironic that we have the same first name."

"Do you work at Wyland Art Gallery? Are you Adrian Inoue?" I ask. "Hikari Inoue?"

It's like I slapped him in the face and took the enchanting persona along with it. His expression immediately morphs from amiable to dower.

"Goddammit."

"Listen, you have to let me explain."

He isn't listening, though. Already, he's standing up, fishing out a few bills from his wallet and nodding politely at the bartender. His eyes, which just moments before were fixed on me in a vise grip, are intent on settling anywhere but on me. "God, I really need to take my name off the website. It's too easy to figure out. Fuck me."

"Wait!" I call after him as he turns around and heads for the front door. I scoop up my backpack and head after him, but his legs are so long, it's hard to keep up with his gait. "I'm not just a fan of the game. I have something important I need to talk to you about."

"I swear to Christ, Reddit is the worst thing to come out of humanity," he mutters, plucking a long black peacoat off the coat rack by the door before opening the door to the frigid February air outside. "Fuck me for wanting a night out. I can't believe it."

The cold feels like it's snatching the breath from my lungs as I follow him onto the sidewalk outside. "I'm not trying to bother you, but you have information I need. You're the only one that can help."

He waves an indifferent hand at me as he keeps his stride. "There are signed books and posters online on the Magicka Games website, okay? I'm not feeling especially charitable today."

I call after him again, but someone else catches my attention from behind me. "Violet, what are you doing?" Eddie calls.

Shit, he was probably still waiting for that Uber. I don't let him distract me, though. "I don't need a poster," I say. I do the only thing my desperation tells me will help, and I reach out and grab his coat sleeve.

Hikari Inoue—or Adrian Inoue—whips around, yanking his sleeve away from me. All the light humor in his eyes is gone, leaving nothing but anger. "What is it about you fucking nerds that makes you think you can just stalk me, and I'll just be the picture of politeness? I could get a restraining order, you know."

Eddie has caught up to us and puts his hand on my arm, pulling it away. "Sir, I'm so sorry," he says. "Whatever she said, she's going through a rough time. She didn't mean any harm."

I want to scream at him, shout that he doesn't get to speak for me, but losing my cool is only going to make it worse.

"Whatever, just keep her away from me," Adrian sneers, turning and walking away from us.

I feel it slipping through my fingers again. Our only opportunity, our only plan. I need something that will keep it from falling out of my grasp completely...

"May Beaufort!" I yell.

I half expect him to keep moving and disappear around the corner forever.

But he stops.

"You've met her," I say. "She's the Crystalline Mage's ward. But before that, she was May Beaufort." I can't tell if my eyes are welling up because of the bitter cold or if saying her name just hurts that much. "She was my best friend, and she was taken by—monsters. Right in front of me. They never found her. But I did. In your game guide."

He's frozen with his back toward us still, but as long as he isn't walking away, it's something.

"I know Velmyra is real," I continue. "I saw it. I saw those monsters, too. Everyone has tried to tell me they're fake, but I know they're real. I know she's still alive somewhere. And you do too, don't you?"

I wait. It's so cold that the atmosphere seems to absorb all my words like a dishrag over spilled water. Eddie's grip on my arm tightens, but he's waiting, watching him too. Please. Believe at least part of what I'm saying.

Just as I think he isn't going to indulge me anymore, slowly, he turns around.

And under the dull glow of the streetlamps just now turning on as dusk settles in on the streets of Chicago, the look in Adrian Inoue's eyes is one I've seen all too often in the mirror.

It's the look of someone who lost a friend.

"Follow me," he says. "You tell me everything, and I'll return the favor."

CHAPTER 6

drian leads us back to the gallery in silence, through the
empty lobby and behind the partition into the gallery
itself. It's adorned with oil paintings, watercolors,
sculptures, and modern art pieces all related to *Mages*. The quick
glimpses I'm able to get as we pass are familiar, with images of
castles, battles, and forest fairies dancing across the stark white
walls. Eddie asks why the gallery was closed if all the pieces were
already set up.

"The company and I had a tiff," Adrian says. "Boring business stuff. Thought it best to just shut the place down all
together while it gets sorted."

He leads us to an innocuous-looking door, what I think is
a storage room, but he opens it to reveal a sleek studio apartment. It's industrial but modern, with exposed brick and the
same lavish hardwood floors that the gallery has. A small
kitchenette sits by the window with minimal appliances
except for a large double oven set into the wall. The living
area has a few lounge chairs and a vintage settee, with no sign
of a television or computer. The bedroom area is a minimalist
king-sized bed with plain white sheets and a couple of bare
nightstands. It's a clear bachelor pad, no other signs of a

living soul being present or welcome here for quite some time.

"Welcome to the back room," he says, letting his pea coat lazily fall off his shoulders and tossing it across the settee.

Eddie glances around the space, his open-mouthed tourist look back on his face. "This is—not what I expected."

"And what did you expect?" Adrian asks pointedly.

"Well, I don't know. You're, like, a millionaire. I expected something in a high rise downtown or something."

"I like to keep my feet on the ground, I suppose." He walks around the other side of the settee and sits, his fingers steepled under his chin. "Now, tell me what you know."

We do as he asks. It takes a while, but I tell him everything —starting from the attack all the way to now. I don't leave anything out, including my obsession with *Mages* and the Crystalline Mage. After I've divulged all of it, the air between the three of us feels thick, like humidity has returned to the atmosphere in the middle of winter. It feels good, though, to finally put it all out there. It feels good to have someone who truly believes everything I say right out of the gate.

When he's sure I'm done, Adrian unfurls his steepled fingers, sighing. "That certainly was all of it, wasn't it?"

"Everything I know," I confirm.

"And you've come to find me because you think I can get you to Velmyra?"

I hesitate but say, "Essentially."

He breathes out slowly, like he's exhaling cigarette smoke.

"Is that something you can do?" I ask tentatively.

Adrian leans back on the settee, gazing up at the ceiling. "That's a complicated question."

Trying not to sound miffed, I say, "This whole thing is complicated, but there's got to be a way. You used to be in Velmyra, right? And then you came here. So there's a way to cross between the two places."

"You're right," he says.

"Well, what's complicated about that?"

"Maybe you should make good on your promise," Eddie says. His voice is hoarse, and he looks weary from the alcohol working its way out of his system. "Tell us what you know. She told you. Time to pay up."

Adrian looks Eddie up and down, almost as if he's sizing Eddie up, determining just exactly who he's dealing with. After a moment, he gives Eddie a crooked grin. "Hm. All right. Fair's fair, I suppose." He sits up, putting his hands on his knees. "You're right, my dear. I knew May, if only for a brief time. She and I met in Velmyra, and as far as I know, she's still there."

I gape at him. "Alive?"

He nods. Something large and bright blooms in my chest. It takes me a moment to realize that it's hope.

"However," Adrian goes on, "the reason I say it's complicated isn't just to be enigmatic. She and I only knew each other for a short period of time, and that was over a decade ago. I have no reason to believe that she's been hurt or that anyone would want her dead, but I can't be sure."

I shake my head. "That doesn't matter as long as we can get over there and get her out ourselves."

Eddie leans forward in his seat. "How exactly did you know May, anyway? Is she really the Mage's ward or what? And why put them into the game at all?"

Rubbing his hands on his slacks, Adrian sighs. "I suppose I should start closer to the beginning." He stands up. "Do you kids want tea? Bourbon? Cocaine?" At our stunned faces, he laughs. "I'm kidding about that last one. Or...am I?" He winks before striding over to the kitchenette.

"Tea sounds great," I say.

Eddie flatly says, "Water."

Adrian talks as he brings out a kettle and rummages through the refrigerator. "So, where to start? Well, I was born in Velmyra, in a province called Elowen."

"In Midra," Eddie says. "I've seen it on the map." I've seen it before, too. Velmyra is a collection of nations in the world of Fractum, consisting of four countries—Extera, Midra, Undra, and Hevara. The map almost makes it look like the United Kingdom, a collection of countries that seem like one entity and separate all at once.

"Quite the expert, aren't you?" Adrian remarks, though he doesn't seem very impressed. The gas stove clicks alive, and he sets the kettle onto it. "Sorry, I ran out of gold stars from all the other 'pick me' boys that like to show me how much they know about *Mages*."

Even in the low light of the apartment, I see Eddie's face go red.

"Anyhow, my brother and I didn't have a lot tying us down growing up—classic dead parents story. We did a lot of traveling, and eventually, we ran into the Crystalline Mage in those travels. About as simple as that."

"You went all the way to Extera and met her in the mountains?" I ask. "That's where you said she was in the game, anyway."

He walks back over to us with a glass of water, handing it to Eddie unceremoniously. "We went everywhere. Even into Extera. It was cold as hell, but beautiful. We weren't the only ones. Like the game, there were always some adventuring guilds who roamed out into the middle of the frozen wilderness to find cave treasure or whatever. It isn't that outlandish of a concept."

"And that's where you met May?"

Adrian nods, looking a bit glum, before his ears perk up at the shriek of the tea kettle. He walks back to the kitchen. "Like I said, our time was brief. But Crystalline kept her, almost like a pet."

"Not because she saw a girl who was lost in a foreign land? Not because of—I don't know, compassion?" Eddie asks.

Adrian's laugh replaces the scream of the kettle as he pulls it off the heat. "The Mages aren't like regular people. They are beings imbued with pure magic." The way he pours the water into the mug and plops a tea bag into it seems angry, fueled by a frustration I don't quite understand. "With that much power, that much magical force, you lose part of yourself. You lose the capacity for things like empathy and compassion. There's only magic that courses through your veins. There's no room for anything else."

"So, are you saying the Crystalline Mage was the one that brought May there?" I ask. I feel breathless as I ask. "It was her demons that took her?"

He walks back over to the sitting area, a mug of tea in one hand and a clear glass full of amber liquid and a single, gigantic ice cube in the other. Handing me the mug, he says, "I don't know for sure."

I take the mug, but I set it immediately down on the coffee table in front of me. "What *do* you know?" I ask.

Crossing his long legs as he sits, Adrian swirls the drink around his glass, wafting it under his nose. "The Mages all have their abilities, as is outlined in the game, though it's more complicated than I made it seem. It's more than just Crystalline controlling ice and Earthen being a Disney princess who talks to forest creatures and all that. The Crystalline Mage's power is derived from the god of the Outer Realm, the realm of space. She doesn't just control ice. She controls fractals, or patterns that occur in the universe. The most common fractals happen to be ice and crystal, so that's what she generally uses. The same can be said of the other Mages, as well. The Earthen Mage doesn't control animals, they control organic matter. The Heavenly Mage doesn't control the weather, they control the happenings of the atmosphere. And the Infernal Mage doesn't control fire. They control the energies of hell itself. They can summon hellfire, along with asking Hellions to do their bidding."

The word fills me with nausea. "Hellions."

"From what you described, that's what it sounds like attacked you and May. Hellions. Creatures of the underworld," Adrian explains.

"So, you're saying that the Infernal Mage was the one who ordered May's kidnapping then?" Eddie asks.

Adrian investigates his glass thoughtfully. "I can't confirm that, but I know those creatures are usually under the Infernal's command," he says. "Maybe it wasn't the intent, but if it was anyone who ordered her to be taken, it was the Infernal."

"And Crystalline just kept her?" I question. "Why?"

He shrugs. "Like I said, it wasn't out of kindness. A benefit of some sort, but what, I'm not sure."

"And what benefits did she get keeping *you* around?" Eddie asks, an eyebrow cocked. "Doesn't sound like she would be in the business of keeping regular people close, yet you were chummy enough to get to know her and May. What was different about you?"

There is a long pause. Adrian looks at Eddie, unmoving, a tension between the two of them that is almost a palpable beam of energy. The lopsided grin returns to his face. "Again," he says. "Complicated."

Eddie grins back, but it has far less humor to it. "That's not suspicious at all."

In response, Adrian wiggles his eyebrows at him suggestively and takes another sip from his glass of mystery alcohol.

I stand. "I honestly don't care why you knew her," I say. "You were there. Now, you're here. I want to know how, and I want to learn how I can go there too."

Adrian sets down his glass on the coffee table, a decisive clunk as the glass hits the marble top. "See," he says, pointing at me, "I knew I liked you. You're no frills. He, on the other hand —" he gestures to Eddie with his thumb "is so *nosey*. How do you stand it? Is he constantly in your underwear drawer or what?"

"You're not giving me a great first impression either, dude," Eddie grumbles.

I step in between them, hoping the literal barrier will be

enough to break the tension. "How do you get to Velmyra?" I ask once more.

Sighing, Adrian stands up and walks over to his bedroom area. As he kneels by his nightstand, I glare at Eddie, trying my best to convey *"Behave yourself, you dweeb"* without actually using words. He shoots me a look back, an expression that clearly says *"He started it."*

The sound of a drawer closing brings our attention back to Adrian, and before we have time to process it, he is back at the living room area, setting something heavy on the coffee table, another hard *thunk* as glass hits marble.

Only the thing he drops in front of us isn't glass. It is a jagged hunk of a crystal about the size of a squash, like something cut from a geode, though there is no ugly brown outer exterior. Only pure, white crystal shines up at us. No, not shines. It's *glowing*, as if it has a star sitting in its center. It sparkles so brightly that there are beams of light that hit the ceiling in twinkling little spots, our own little disco ball.

"Any idea what that is?" Adrian asks, like a teacher would ask a class full of blank-faced high school students.

I shake my head mutely, but Eddie has the answer for me. "Holy shit," he whispers. "Residuum."

Oh. Of course. I've never been much into the mechanics of *Mages*, but I know what Residuum is. The Mages often leave behind stones, liquids, or other imbued objects when they cast large spells with no regard for collateral damage. Residuum is quite literally the residuals of their magic use. Those items can then be used by ordinary people to cast magic themselves. It's the only way a non-Mage can do magic. And even just being in the presence of a stone this large shifts the air in the room, like the feeling of someone opening the window in the middle of a blizzard.

"You're curious to fault, but you're not stupid," Adrian remarks to Eddie. "Residuum. Crystalline Residuum, to be more specific."

I furrow my brow. "I'm not as well versed in Residuum mechanics. What's the difference between all the types?"

"Depends on which Mage it came from," he explains, picking up the hunk of magic. As he turns it about in his hands, the lights shooting off its uneven edges dance across the ceiling like fireflies in the middle of summer. "This is Crystalline, so it gives the wielder a fraction of the power from the Crystalline Mage. Like her ability to manipulate space. With this much Residuum, it's enough to, say, allow multiple people to travel between dimensions."

"Is that how you did it, then?" I ask. "You used that to get from Velmyra to here?"

"Yes," he confirms. "Though, Residuum is finite. When you cast magic, it uses up the materials you were channeling through. This piece used to be twice its size. Enough for a round trip between worlds."

I laugh, feeling a little breathless. It's sitting right there in his palm. The way to get to Velmyra. The way to find her. Instinctively, I reach out to touch it, but Adrian pulls it back before my fingers can even skim the rough edges.

"Careful," he warns. "The inexperienced can often trigger spells inadvertently. I've used magic for years, so I can hold it without setting it off, but you two might touch it and end up in some other realm of existence."

I pull my hand away in a quick jerk, as if I nearly touched a hot stove.

"Problem solved then, right?" Eddie says, standing up and joining us. "We'll use this to get to Velmyra, find the Crystalline Mage, find May, and come back. Sounds like cake."

Adrian isn't looking at him, though. His eyes are fixed squarely on the Residuum, the glowing beams dancing across his brown eyes. He smirks, something I've noticed he's particularly good at, and sets the stone back onto the coffee table.

"Knock yourselves out."

Eddie and I somehow pry our eyes off the rock and look at

63

him, stunned, as he saunters over to the bed, taking his suit jacket off and loosening his tie.

"You're not coming with?" Eddie asks, his voice thick, as though it's traveling through pudding.

"Are you inviting me?" he asks, throwing his tie over his head and letting it fall onto the bed.

"I mean, yeah?" Eddie says. "Of course. You just said we were too stupid to use that thing, right?" He points at the Residuum on the table. "So, you have to use it. Better yet, when we get over there, what then? Everything we know about this place is from a set of game rules. We need someone who knows the place to help us. This isn't rocket science, man."

Adrian laughs. He has unbuttoned some of the buttons on his shirt, revealing a section of his tan chest, hairless and unblemished. "You're absolutely right, kid. It isn't rocket science. You two are capable enough to track me down and harass me into giving you information. I'm sure you'll be able to keep yourselves alive. Just don't go dragon hunting, and you'll be just fine."

"Bullshit!" Eddie yells. It takes me by surprise so much that I jump. "Maybe you wrote your world as a game, but this thing we're trying to do? It's not just playtime to her, okay? This has been her whole life for years, so I suggest you find it in depths of your Armani-clad heart to give a fuck about it."

"Eddie—" I start.

"Velmyra is more my life than it is either of yours," Adrian bites back, stepping toward Eddie. "That game is everything that I remember about that place. I'm not going to come with you and be your tour guide. Use the book and leave me the hell out of it."

"Fucking coward," Eddie spits.

Swiftly, Adrian reaches around me, grabbing the Residuum from the coffee table. "I don't have to give this to you," he says. My heart seizes at his words, but the anxiety softens as he says, "I will, but that's as far as my charity goes. You best appreciate what

I give you, or I might just search my 'Armani-clad heart' and come up mysteriously empty-handed."

Before Eddie can spit any more venom at him, I hold out my hand to Adrian. "It's a deal," I say. "Please, we'll leave you alone. We'll take the stone. It's more than we could have hoped for."

For a moment that seems like years, he looks at me skeptically, searching my face for some sign of insincerity. Letting out a deep sigh, he breaks his gaze and walks back to the nightstand, procuring a kerchief that he wraps the Residuum in. Walking back over, he hands me the cloth-covered stone. "Don't touch it with your bare hands until you want to go. Magic works on emotions. I'm sure it will know where you want to go when the time is right."

As the stone sits in my hand, even through the cloth, I can feel the magic the Residuum is radiating. Warmth runs up my fingers, all the way up my arms, even into my chest. There's a pulse to it, like I'm holding a beating heart in my palm rather than a stone.

I nod at Adrian gravely. "Understood."

Behind me, Eddie scoffs. He curses under his breath, and without warning, he grabs his coat off his chair and walks to the door. "I'm waiting outside, Violet," he announces before slamming the door behind him. The wall between the back room and the gallery is so thin, it shudders like a gale force wind has blown through the room.

I turn back to Adrian expecting him to be angry, but to my surprise, he's chuckling faintly. "Violet," he repeats, letting my name roll across his tongue like the too-expensive scotch he had been drinking. "So typical. It just struck me that I never asked your name. How narcissistic of me."

"It's fine," I say. "I'm sorry about him. We're both just tired and..." I don't know how to finish that sentence. There are so many thoughts running through my mind, most that I can't even put into words. "We're just tired."

"As a fellow tired person, I can tell," Adrian says, and despite everything about him being exactly as narcissistic as he says he is, there's a sympathy in his voice.

I go to gather my coat and backpack, gingerly putting the Residuum in between a cushion of my clothes inside. As I head to the door, I pause, looking back at him. His hair is starting to deflate now, and he's in the middle of taking off his perfectly polished shoes.

"It would be nice of you to reconsider," I tell him. "We could use someone who knows the area. I won't force you, but it's your home turf. You could really help us out."

Instead of getting nasty like he did toward Eddie, Adrian smiles at me. This time, it isn't a charming, lopsided one. It's exhausted, like he only has enough energy for that last one for the day. "With all due respect, Violet," he says, sounding as weary as he looks, "I'd venture a guess that you wouldn't want to return to that park where those Hellions attacked you, correct?"

A shiver runs through me at the prospect. I never have gone back there, despite detectives wanting me to walk through the crime scene with them. The thought was enough to make me want to vomit. I nod.

"That's why I don't want to go," he says. "Velmyra, that whole plane of existence, is my park."

His eyes shimmer with a pain I understand all too well. For a moment, I want to ask him what happened, but I stop myself. He mentioned a brother who he traveled with, didn't he?

There was obviously a reason he hadn't mentioned him again.

I clear my throat and hastily pull a scrap piece of paper and nearly dead pen from my backpack, leaning down on the coffee table and scrawling my address and phone number on it. I leave it sitting there as I shove the pen back. "If you change your mind," I say, gesturing down toward the scrap.

Once we offer each other awkward goodbyes, I'm back in the gallery. When we first entered, the last beams of sunlight were fading through the tall windows of the open space. Now, the whole area is shrouded in darkness, the streetlights casting eerie shadows over the paintings and statues. My footsteps sound hollow and deafening across the wood floor as I walk through the hall.

Just as I reach the archway to the front entrance, a splash of white catches my attention out of the corner of my eye. I turn to look at it and freeze.

It's a simple oil painting, composed of messy yet deliberate strokes. It's mostly a blur of crisp white, but a few dabs of black decorate the edges. Despite it going for abstract, I can clearly see what the picture is.

It's the Crystalline Mage. And in the corner, the little dark swath of black, is May.

I stare at her for longer than I should. She doesn't have a distinct face, but I know it's her. I reach out, my fingers running over the dried strokes of paint.

The tears that I've been holding in all day stream down my face. There's no stopping them, though I try to smear them out of the way, keeping my face as dry as possible, the guise of togetherness firmly in place. This isn't foreign territory, trying to hide my emotions even in an empty room. I've been here before.

But I'm not crying because of the darkness. I'm crying because for the first time in ten years, I can finally see a way out of it.

CHAPTER 7

On the train ride back home the next day, I catch a glimpse of my nose in the train window.

It always gets my attention when I see my reflection. I'm vainly drawn to it like a mosquito to a fluorescent bug zapper. I make sure Eddie is sleeping in the seat next to me before I look back at myself, pinching the knotted bridge of my nose like that's going to do anything to straighten it back out. When it first healed, I thought maybe it would. If I moved it around enough, maybe it would smooth out like clay, and I could look the way I used to.

I don't remember being in pain during the attack. I remember being overwhelmed, piled on top of by foreign little monsters—Hellions, I guess—feeling like I was going to suffocate under their weight. Their claws dug into my back and my face, razors slicing into my flesh from every angle.

I remember the burning in my lungs as I screamed out after her, watching her disappear through a hazy door, how I kept screaming until my face was shoved into the pavement. Hard.

That's the last I remember of any of it. When I opened my eyes again, it was daylight. An old woman in a jogging suit hovered over me, asking in a muffled voice if I was all right and shouting at someone I couldn't see to call an ambulance. The ambulance ride itself was a blur of people all asking my name, how many fingers they were holding up, what day I thought it was. The EMT asked me to rate my pain. I said zero. I wasn't in pain. My whole head felt like it was stuffed up with cotton, like my skin had been replaced by felt. There was no pain, I told them. Now where was my friend?

I went in and out of consciousness from there, until I could finally open my eyes for more than two minutes. I was in a tiny hospital room—the first one I had ever seen, save for movies and TV. My parents were both asleep in chairs next to me, but as soon as I stirred, they were wide awake.

There was a hazy moment of tears and hugs. I could barely register what they were doing, though. I knew I was awake. My eyes were open, and my wits were about me enough to register that I was, in fact, not dreaming. My head felt funny, like being dizzy without the room spinning. Of course, I was on every kind of painkiller imaginable. It was a wonder I could move at all with how drugged up I was.

When the doctors came in and described what happened, I started to understand why. A jogger had found me face down on the sidewalk at the park, floating in and out of lucidity. Whoever attacked me had most likely slammed my face into the ground, splitting my lip, knocking out four of my front teeth, and breaking my nose. By the time I came to, the doctors had already given me stitches on my lip and reset my nose as best as they could. My teeth, on the other hand, would have to be handled by a dentist.

I heard them explain it all to me like it was something that happened to someone else. Even as I looked in a mirror, seeing my swollen, patchwork face, the gaping holes where my teeth used to be, and my lumpy misshapen nose, I didn't feel anything.

It wasn't until I asked my mother where May was that it all hit me at once.

She looked at me, her face a mask of regret. "She's missing," she told me.

That was when the pain came.

The next year was filled with it. Stitches had to be removed, scar tissue stung and burned until it incessantly itched, like fleas had been sealed into my sutures. The worst of it was replacing my teeth, which required drills and implants. It took over a year for me to start looking and feeling like a normal human and not a talking pincushion.

Long after that, though, I hurt. Whenever I would catch a glimpse of her empty desk across the classroom, whenever I would hear whispers around the lunch tables about how she was kidnapped by a sex cult, anytime I woke from another nightmare about black and crooked limbs dragging me into a pit of black pitch. It burned across my skin, down into my flesh, tearing at my organs. The pain during the attack was nothing but a scrape on the knee. Even the healing my body went through was nothing but moderately uncomfortable.

The worst pain I experienced was when they told me I was supposed to be healed.

I pull my hand away from my face, glancing toward Eddie to make sure he hasn't noticed that I've been fixated on it for who knows how long. But as he snoozes away in his seat next to me, I let out a shaky breath, watching the people walk the aisle and yammer on their phones to their loved ones, realizing that no one was paying attention except for me.

We make it back to the apartment a little after three in the afternoon. We spend an hour or so unpacking, showering, digging snacks out of the cabinet. Eventually, I wind up taking a nap on the couch, and when I wake up, it's dark outside. That isn't saying much since it gets dark before five most winter days in Michigan. I grumble, rubbing the blur out of my eyes, looking around the apartment.

Eddie stands at the kitchen table, staring at the center. It's only when I get up and approach him that I realize it's the hunk of Residuum that he's staring at.

I pause at the edge of the table. The stone sits nestled in its cloth, a bit of its clear crystal sparkling under the light. That unnatural glow seems to hum its own tune, and as my fingers graze the table, the wood beneath it feels like it's vibrating, almost imperceptibly.

"So," Eddie says, after minutes of silence.

"So," I repeat.

He looks up at me, his brown eyes soft and anxious. "What do we do?"

I sigh. "We had a whole train ride to think about that."

"And I chose unconsciousness," he says, rubbing his jaw. Despite his train nap, he looks exhausted, dark shadows causing his already dark eyes to look close to black. "We're here and awake now, so we might as well make a plan."

"Okay," I say hesitantly. "Well, do you want to touch it or should I?"

Eddie's eyebrows shoot up. "What, like now?"

"Why not?"

He looks me up and down. "You want to travel to a magical land in your penguin pajamas?"

I roll my eyes at him. "Okay, maybe not like *right* now. But tonight could work, right?"

Scratching his head, Eddie looks hesitant. "I don't know, Vi. I have to call into work and tell them I'm going to be out and—"

"Seriously?"

"I mean, yeah?" he says with a shrug. "I want to keep my job."

"What are you going to tell them? 'Hey, Brian. Sorry I'm

going to be gone for the next two weeks because I'm going to be fighting orcs. Hope someone can cover my shift?'"

"You joke, but LARPing is a thing," he says. "That excuse has been used at the shop before, by more than one person."

"Eddie, this is a little more important than a retail job, don't you think?" I ask, trying not to sound frantic. I'm not even thinking about missing term papers or calling into the coffee shop. The mundane tasks of my life be damned. I have the key to get to Velmyra, so I'm using it.

Eddie sits at the table, leaning his head on his hands, threading his fingers through his long sandy hair. "Well, we're not going to be there forever. We have to think about what comes afterward. We find the Crystalline Mage, we find May, and then what? We're not moving to Portland to join a commune. This is a motherfucking *quest*. We have to think through stuff. We have to, like, pack and research. Showing up to the fucking Shire with no plan is just going to spell disaster."

"The longer we wait, the less chance we're coming back with her," I say.

"I get it, but the hastier we get, the less chance we come back at all."

It's the first I'm thinking about it, actually. The fact that we could go to Velmyra and—well, not come back. For a variety of reasons. If the Residuum we have is the latter part of a one-way ticket, we'll need to find more there to get back home. But I assume that isn't what Eddie is referring to. *Mages of Velmyra*, after all, is filled with goblins, dragons, leviathans, you name it. Assuming that Adrian was accurate with what he put in the game, there are a million different ways we can get ourselves in trouble.

Killed. We could get ourselves killed.

Before I really get a chance to spiral thinking about that very real possibility, a knock at our front door echoes through the apartment.

Eddie's head snaps up, eyes going wide. "Oh shit," he says, immediately standing up and rushing to the door. "I forgot."

"Forgot what?" I ask.

Ignoring my question, Eddie puts a finger to his lips before turning to the door and opening it. "Jax! Hey!" he exclaims a little too enthusiastically. "Come on in, buddy."

I hardly have time to utter my own "*fuck*" before Jackson steps through into the entryway, looking—well, pretty un-Jackson like. His normally neutral affectation is harried, his curly auburn hair tousled and his glasses fogged up from the temperature change outside. He huffs as he rushes in, catching his breath before looking at Eddie and saying, "Where have you been all weekend?"

"It's Saturday," I point out, and Jackson glares at me, not even trying to hide his disdain at this point.

"We took a trip to Chicago," Eddie explains, his tone a lot nicer.

"Fun," Jackson remarks gruffly. "I need to talk to you. It's important."

Eddie shoots a nervous look in my direction before turning back to him. "Uh, okay. Can you give us, like, two seconds?"

Hastily unbuttoning his jacket, Jackson sighs and rolls his eyes. "Yeah, sure. Whatever."

Putting his hand on my shoulder, Eddie guides me into the hallway, just out of Jackson's sight. Smoothing his hair back behind his ears, he looks me in the eye and says, "Let me just talk to him and get him out of here, and we can keep talking about it after. But we can't just go tonight."

"Eddie—"

"We'll talk about it in a bit. Just let me—"

A high-pitched screech interrupts him. It's over as quickly as it begins, singing through the air like one of those whistling fireworks that zips across the ground rather than shooting up into the sky. Eddie and I look at each other in a panic before we run out of the hallway and back into the kitchen. Instinctively, my eyes travel to the kitchen table.

The Residuum is gone. And so is Jackson.

I swear, running my hands over the table, the distinct hum of power the stone was giving off now gone. I even stupidly look underneath the table, the chairs, hoping it maybe fell or something and that the sound we heard was some horrible coincidence. It's nowhere, vanished into thin air. My chest tightens. I feel like there isn't enough air coming in even though my breaths are coming in quick bursts.

A shattering sound shoots off above me, and a flash of bright light fills my periphery before the living room goes dark.

"Violet," Eddie says, and the alarm in his voice is enough to get me on my feet and rush over to him. He's standing by the couch, looking up at the ceiling, pointing. I follow his eye line.

"What the hell," I mutter.

There is a foot sticking out of the ceiling.

It wriggles, like a worm on a hook, the loose laces of the tennis shoe it's wearing flapping in the air and slapping against the light fixture it's sticking out of. On the ground below it, shattered remnants of the wide lightbulb that used to be in the socket lay scattered. We're both immobile, watching this foot flail about out of our ceiling in abject horror. Just as I'm about to ask Eddie what we should do—though, he looks about as sure as I do—the shrieking noise comes back, this time louder and with another quick flash of light. As soon as I blink back the spots from my eyes, I look back at the ceiling.

The foot is gone, the gaping hole of the broken light fixture left behind.

"Fuck," Eddie says, wide eyed. He grabs his head, his hair sticking out at manic angles. "Did I do 'shrooms? Vi, you have to tell me if I did 'shrooms."

"If you did, so did I," I say, looking about the room, waiting for it to pop back up somewhere.

Another whistling screech, another pulse of white light. A

thunderous clatter, a moan. It all happens as quickly as it takes for me to blink.

The spots from the flash clear again, and someone is in my living room. A whole someone, not just a foot. Jackson, full body, seemingly unharmed.

"Jax!" Eddie exclaims. "Drop it!"

I don't know what he's referring to at first. All I see is Jackson sprawled on our hardwood floor, shoes crunching the shattered lightbulb, his glasses askew and his button-down shirt disheveled and untucked. His eyes are huge as he looks about the room, disoriented in a way that reminds me of how people look after getting off a roller coaster. It's only as he starts to push himself up into a sitting position that I see it. In his right hand is the Residuum.

"Jackson!" Eddie yells again. "Put the stone down."

Jackson looks down at the object in his hand, and as if it suddenly has started on fire, he drops it. The rock falls to the floor with a heavy thud. In a panic, I run over to the table and retrieve the cloth, plucking the stone up off the floor. Jackson, to his credit, looks just as shell shocked as we do, his hands shaking as he pulls himself onto the armchair, his pale skin drained of all its pink undertones.

"What the hell happened, man?" Eddie asks.

Jackson straightens out his glasses, catching his breath. "I-I don't know. I just touched it for a second," he stammers. "My fingers barely grazed it. I thought it was some new table decoration or something, but it was glowing, so I just—what the fuck even happened?"

"You got stuck up there," I say, pointing toward the ceiling. "Did anyone see you? Like the upstairs neighbors? Anyone?"

He shakes his head slowly. "No, it was dark, save for that thing glowing. And as soon as I thought 'I want out of here,' I was back in front of you guys."

He must have used the Residuum unintentionally. Adrian wasn't kidding. One touch and you're somewhere else.

A sinking feeling drops in my gut. I look at the Residuum, curled in the cloth in my hand. It looks the same as it did before, same clarity and ominous white glow shining between my fingers, but something seems different from when I held it before.

I realize it, then. It's smaller. Where it had once been the size of a squash, it's now closer to a grapefruit.

"Well," Eddie starts. "That sure was—weird, huh? What a weird thing. Sheesh, like—like so *weird*—"

"That's Residuum, isn't it?"

The question is so candid and out of nowhere. I instinctively grip the stone tighter, dipping my hands to hide it behind the couch like it's going to make him forget that it exists. Eddie, the worst liar in human history, scoffs. "What? Residuum? Like in *Mages*? Psh, no. Like—*what*? No!"

"Cut the shit, Eddie," Jackson says, intensity back in his tone. "I know Velmyra is real."

The air feels like it's sucked out of the room. Eddie glances at me, open mouthed, clearly trying to come up with something good to come back at that with, but Jackson speaks before he gets a chance to. "That's why I've been trying to get a hold of you for the past two days. Where did you guys get that?"

"What makes you think Velmyra is real?" I ask in return.

He takes his eyes off Eddie, glaring at me like I just insulted him. "Because I saw it," he answers, matter of fact.

The casual way he says it is baffling. What I couldn't spit out to Eddie, he says like it's just what he did with his Tuesday. "What do you mean?"

"What I said. I saw it. Last weekend, I was walking home, and all of a sudden, I'm in this forest clearing. It looked like the woods from that traumatizing bit in Snow White. All the gnarled branches that look like they're going to grab you and drag you away. I ran through it, and less than a minute later, it's gone." He shifts in his seat, looking at his shoes. "I thought I had too much caffeine or something. I don't know. I shrugged it off until a couple of days ago when it happened again. I was waiting for a bus, and then suddenly, I'm on some hill, looking across a plain at a castle. Like, a *castle* castle, not like that stupid apartment building they made to look like one at the edge of town." He looks up at Eddie. "I freaked out, and the first thing I could think of was to find you, because—well, nerd shit. And you weren't at Vault, but when I was there, I saw a *Mages* book with a castle. One that looked exactly like the one I saw." Jackson shakes his head. "It was a stupid irrational thought, but with that," he says, pointing toward the Residuum I'm holding, "there's really no denying it."

No. There really isn't.

Jackson looks between the both of us, expectant. "You guys want to fill me in on what you know?"

We tell him everything—the visions we had, finding the gallery, meeting Adrian, obtaining the Residuum. I have to fill in some tidbits of my own, about the Hellions and some of the lesser-known details of the attack. The entire time, Jackson is stoically silent, his elbows resting on his knees and his hands folded in front of him, staring at the fraying rug under the coffee table.

When we're all pretty sure we're on the same page, Eddie looks at Jackson with caution. During our explanation, we ended up on the couch, the remaining Residuum resting in its cloth on the coffee table in front of us. "I know this is a lot to throw at you," he says. The whole time, he's been gentle, making sure to not overwhelm him. I'm starting to notice that when it comes to Jackson, there's something careful about the way Eddie interacts with him, like he's afraid one wrong move will scare him off. "And we understand if you don't believe us. It's hard for even me to believe, honestly."

Jackson shifts in his seat, the first movement he's made in a half an hour, but he's still silent.

"We obviously don't want anyone finding out about all this," Eddie continues. "Not that I think you'll go telling anyone, but we do want to keep it secret. So, if anyone asks where Violet and I went—"

"I want in."

Eddie glances at me, as if to confirm that he just heard what he thought he did. "Uh, what?" he asks, turning back to Jackson.

Jackson shrugs. "You heard me. I want in. I'm going with you guys."

Eddie's mouth works, but no words come out. Sighing, Jackson says, "If May is over there, you can't expect me to not want to come with. Besides, do you really think you two can run a rescue mission by yourselves?"

I reach into my hoodie pocket and latch onto the twenty-sided die. I can't say it's an enticing offer. The last conversation Jackson and I had was terse, to say the least. If we're stuck with just the three of us out in the middle of unknown fantasy terrain, we either won't speak to each other or Eddie will have to constantly play mediator. Either way I spin it, it doesn't sound conducive to a good adventuring environment.

"I mean, we didn't really have a choice up until now," Eddie explains once he's finally found the right words. "I'm not saying you won't be helpful, man, but..." He trails off, and I see him throw a skittish glance in my direction.

"I saw the same things you guys did," Jackson says, firmly. "I have just as much skin in the game as you do." He gives me a pointed look, eyes narrowing to a sharpened edge. "Just as much skin as *you* do."

I shake my head, really holding back every petty teenager thought threatening to take over. "I don't know what—"

"You know exactly what I mean, Violet," Jackson interrupts, resting his elbows on his knees and leaning in toward me. "I was just as much her friend as you were. If you're going, I have the right to go, too."

I don't have enough restraint to hold back a scoff. "Well, seeing as how I'm the one who saw her get taken and you've consistently been shitty to me, forgive me if I don't want to go fantasy camping with you."

"The fact that you saw her get taken doesn't give you the right to control the whole situation."

"I'm not trying—" I cut myself off, closing my eyes and pressing the edge of the twenty-sided die into my thumb. I don't like to think I'm a selfish person. I'm not going to Velmyra because I'm looking for an interesting vacation destination. May is over there, and I'm trying to save her. But there's part of me that wants to scream at him that, yeah, I think I do have the right to control this. I was the one who saw her get taken. I'm the one who has actual physical scars to prove it. I bite my tongue, though. "Adrian gave Eddie and me the Residuum. We're going. And you haven't given a lot of reasons why you'd be a good addition to that equation."

Eddie's hand falls on my shoulder, and he squeezes it, a cue for me to back off. "I think Violet has a point, Jax," he says, in his best therapist voice. "Going to Velmyra is going to be hard enough without infighting."

"I'm an adult, okay?" Jackson says. I can tell he's trying to back off his attitude, but there's still the clear hint of snark in his tone. "I won't be an asshole. I know I have been in the past, but—this is important." His deep brown eyes lock onto mine, and although I want to awkwardly glance away, there's something that keeps me there. At first, I think it's his trademark intensity. But I think there's something softer and more vulnerable that keeps me hooked in his gaze, something I can't quite pinpoint. "Whatever petty issues we have, I'm big enough where I can set them aside. This isn't about us. It's about her."

I sigh. Can't really argue with that, can I?

Eventually, I nod. "It's about her," I repeat.

There isn't much more that he and I say to each other about it. After a little more discussion, we all agree it'll be a good idea if Jackson stays at our place for the next couple of days while we plan our strategy. I'm stuck staring at them as they chatter back and forth, trying to parse my feelings as I listen. First, we have no guide, and now we have Jackson. It's a dynamic that I didn't necessarily expect, and I can't say it's a welcome one either. But three clambering morons are better than two, right?

Jackson leaves and returns a couple hours later with a stuffed duffle bag. It's only then that I peel myself off the couch so he can hunker down and go to sleep for the night. It's going to be a long day of planning tomorrow, after all. My own personal hang ups have to take a seat, I suppose. Because this is a good thing.

We have an adventuring party.

CHAPTER 8

It's strange to wake up and see Jackson sprawled on the couch the next morning, limbs flailing and mouth hung open. It feels equally surreal to see him eating a bowl of my cereal, hear him take a shower, play a couple rounds on Eddie's Xbox. Eddie goes about as if everything is normal, but it's difficult for me to wrap my head around it and adjust. I keep worrying that Jackson will get sick of playing the charade and just leave in the middle of the day, but he sticks around, barely saying a word to me as the day breezes by.

Rather than have a big planning session to set down all the expectations of our trip, we have little discussions throughout the day before taking breaks to do our mundane tasks.

"We should leave in the next couple of days," Eddie says at breakfast between bites of a Pop Tart.

"Cool," Jackson agrees before going back to his beat-up copy of *Hitchhiker's Guide to the Galaxy*.

"We need to pack before we go, and we need to be prepared for all possible terrains and climates," I say while heating up a can of SpaghettiOs on the stove for lunch.

"Absolutely," Eddie says while scrolling through his phone

and showing Jackson a TikTok that they both cackle at like hyenas.

At this rate, we'll be ready to go by next year.

By dinner time, the sun has long since set, and our itinerary is essentially non-existent. I'm about ready to throw Eddie's Xbox out the window when there's a knock at the door. The Indian food I put in an order for has arrived. While Eddie and Jackson chatter at each other during a particularly tense round of Halo, I rush off to the door.

When I open it, it's not the delivery guy.

It's Adrian.

With a cheesy smirk, he holds up a paper grocery bag. "I caught the delivery guy on the way up. Unless you didn't order Indian food, in which case, I got you guys Indian food. You're welcome."

I'm stunned into silence, but he doesn't need an okay from me before striding into the room, taking off his polished loafers in the entryway with elegance. He doesn't look like he belongs here among the water damaged drywall and road salt-stained hardwood. He's wearing a blue suit, as opposed to the grey he was wearing last time, and his hair is slightly deflated, still flecked with snowflakes from the outside. Shrugging off his black pea coat, he calls out into the apartment, "Who's hungry?"

Eddie's head snaps up at the sound of his voice, and Jackson just looks at the perfectly put together newcomer with bemusement. "What are you doing here?" Eddie asks, standing up, throwing his shoulders back. He might not ever admit or realize it, but even when Eddie is angry, he's not intimidating in the least, no matter how hard he tries.

"Violet here gave me your address," Adrian says casually as he sets the delivery bag on the kitchen countertop. "Thought I'd stop by and check out the area. Never been to Grand Rapids. It's no Chicago, but you guys try, I suppose. I hear this is a good town to get drunk in anyway, what with the breweries-to-person ratio."

Turning his furious gaze on me, Eddie says, "You told him where we live?"

"It was just in case," I say, but I can't hide how surprised I am myself. Adrian seemed more likely to rip his toenails off than help us the last time we saw him, and now he just shows up out of nowhere?

"Look, hard as it might be to believe, I'm not actually here for craft beer and conservative sensibilities," Adrian says. "I gave your offer a little thought, and I'm in. I'll go with you to..." He peers around Eddie and narrows his gaze at Jackson. "To you-know-where to get you-know-who."

Eddie gives a clipped laugh. "Sorry, the application period for adventuring guide has officially closed. We don't need you anymore. We're fine by ourselves."

Now, it's my turn to laugh. At that, Eddie shoots me glare.

Jabbing a thumb in my direction, Adrian says, "From the sounds of it, you really aren't."

"Sorry," Jackson pipes up, "but, who the hell is this?"

Adrian clasps his hands together, cheerily proclaiming, "None of your business, random kid. The adults have to talk, so I'd appreciate it if you made yourself scarce."

At this, Jackson snorts. "Excuse me?"

"Adrian, he knows," I say. "We told him."

His expression blinks from accommodating to dread in a matter of milliseconds as he looks at me. "You *told him?*" he repeats, his tone suggesting something much worse, as if I told him Santa wasn't real.

"We didn't have a choice," Eddie jumps in. "He used the Residuum, and—"

"He *used the Residuum?*" Adrian exclaims.

"It was an accident! Calm down, Men's Wearhouse!" Eddie yells back.

"YOU THINK THIS IS FROM *MEN'S WEARHOUSE?*"

Overall, I think it goes pretty well.

After doling out food, we tell Adrian the plan. Which is to

say, there is no plan. And he reacts about how I think he will— with an eye roll. "I gave you guys a two-day head start. What have you been doing this whole time? Eating Funyons and getting high? You think we're just going to pop in to Velmyra, waltz right up to the Crystalline Mage, and take May back like it's picking a friend up from the airport?"

"Hence why we wanted your help in the first place, dude," Eddie snipes. "Considering we only had the game master's guide to go off, I think we were doing all right. It's not like you wrote down a list of shit to pack for interdimensional travel that you can just pick up at Dick's Sporting Goods."

"Well, of course not," Adrian says. "I was writing down my life experiences, not giving geeks like you a how-to guide for glamping or whatever it is white people call it. Also, half the stuff in there probably isn't even true. Anthony tweaked a lot to make it more 'marketable.'"

"What exactly are we missing, then?" I ask him. We've found ourselves around the kitchen table, take-out cartons and empty plates scattered and stacked on top of each other. It almost feels like we're playing a session of *Mages* ourselves, minus dice and miniatures and maps. "What's the best course of action?"

"In my opinion, the best course is to stay out of Velmyra entirely," Adrian muses, swilling a glass of water around like it's chardonnay. "The second best is to get a bargaining chip. That's the only way you're getting May back: if you have something the Crystalline Mage wants."

"Which is what exactly?" I ask.

Adrian shrugs, and his eyes unfocus as he stares at one of the askew take-out containers. "Power," he answers. "Subjugation. She wants everyone she comes across to know she's in charge. That they're insignificant in comparison to her."

"Got it. Add 'abject surrender' to the shopping list, then," Eddie remarks.

I sigh, kneading my forehead. We'll be lucky enough to not

get dysentery in Velmyra. Talking down a demigod is going to be a tall ask for anyone, much less a bunch of outsiders like us.

"What about the Mage's Dagger?"

All eyes land on Jackson, who is leaning back with arms folded over his chest. He's mostly been quiet, attempting to look like he's listening but his attention keeps wandering back to his phone or out the window or to his cuticles. Now, he looks between all of us like we've all been glossing over the obvious answer. Even though I have no idea what he's talking about. "What's that?" I ask.

He looks at me, eyebrow arching. "I thought you knew everything about this game."

"I know aspects," I say, my face a little warm. "Not everything."

In lieu of making some snide comment, Jackson glances at Adrian. "Well, is the Mage's Dagger a real thing, or was that added for 'marketability?'"

"Shockingly enough, that's real," Adrian says, with hesitation, "but it's also a death wish."

"What is it, exactly?" I ask again, directing the question to Adrian since Jackson isn't going to be of any help.

"Story time. Wonderful," he says. Adrian sets his glass down, the rickety wooden chair we got secondhand with the table creaking as he leans back in it. "All right, well, once upon a time, there were four gods. They were bored being the stuffy ancient fucks they were in a vast nothingness, so one day, they decided to create something to actually rule over. A world, with many lands and many people—some of them human, others not. Each of these gods ruled over a realm of their new world—the Under Realm, the Earthen Realm, the Heavenly Realm, and the Outer Realm. For a while, the gods took care of their little pet project, but the little creatures they watched over soon became boring to them. So, they left. They took off somewhere in the universe to make new worlds, ones they could make better than dull little Fractum."

His words are full of whimsy, but his tone is exasperated. It's more like he's reciting something from a textbook, less like he's telling a bedtime story. "But of course, they weren't monsters. They knew their creations needed protection. So, the Old Gods each found a mortal of their choosing—ones who they thought exemplified the best their world had to offer—and gave to them each a fraction of their power. Hence, the Mages were born. And we all know how well that went. However, there are some sects of Old Gods worshippers who believe that they left mortals with at least a small line of defense. A fail safe."

"And that fail safe is a knife?" I ask.

"Technically, it's four items that are combined to make a knife," Eddie chimes in. He glances at Adrian, raising his eyebrows with faux embarrassment. "Oh, sorry. Was I being a 'pick me boy' again?"

Adrian snorts. "If you start a sentence with 'technically' and follow it up with nerd shit, do you even have to ask?" He smirks as Eddie grumbles and crosses his arms. "But yes. The Old Gods, for centuries, were rumored by some believers to have granted mortals the custody of four items—relics of great power made in the formation of Fractum. Separately, the Mage's Relics are useless, but when brought together by a practicer of residuuism—the art of using Residuum to cast spells—they form the Mage's Dagger. Once it's formed, it's a one-time use. But it will kill a Mage, if you're able to get close enough to one."

"And it's real?" I ask. "You keep talking about it like it's just a folktale."

"Well, it is just a folktale," Adrian says. "No one has been able to confirm they exist."

"Except you?"

"So skeptical," Adrian teases, but he nods. "I know they exist."

Narrowing his gaze, Jackson asks, "And how's that?"

"The Mages know where they all are," Adrian answers. "They

can't do anything about it, of course—they can't touch them or move them from their spots, and they can't combine them, either. But they're the only ones who know exactly where they're located. And since I spent time with Crystalline, so do I." He gives a half-hearted shrug. "Well, three of them. Heavenly had been moved somehow, but the Mages didn't know where. At least Crystalline didn't."

"Do you think that's a good enough bet to go after these things?" I ask him. "I mean, it's a magic dagger, but how much leverage is that going to give us?"

The look on his face is deadly serious as he leans forward, his elbows on the table and his chin resting on his interlocking fingers. "There are only two things in existence that can kill a Mage: another Mage, and the Mage's Dagger. If we want leverage, that's the best option we have."

"Then why is it a death wish?"

"Because the Mages keep the Relics guarded," Eddie answers, flipping open the game master's guide and setting it in the center of the table. The spread is an illustration of four random bits of what seem like junk. A chunk of tree bark with a smattering of green sparkles, a porous lavender stone that branches off into reaching tendrils, a long jagged piece of broken obsidian stone, and a shard of unpolished white crystal, all drawn with swirling magic lines connecting them in the empty spaces of the page. "The Mages can't interfere with them, but if they know where they are, they can set up enchantments to keep them away from mortals who might be looking to form the Dagger. And I'd guess that's exactly what they did."

Unimpressed, Adrian nods. "You'd guess right."

"But does that mean it's impossible?" I ask.

He sighs, scratching the back of his neck. "It's not impossible, per se…"

"Then we should go for it," I say, matter of fact.

Adrian stands, pinching the bridge of his nose with one

hand and resting his other hand on his hip. "Okay, look. I get that you all think this is going to be a camping trip to the Catskills for a few days, but it's not." He looks between all of us, a mix of frustration and pity on his face. "You're all adorable for wanting to plunge headfirst into this as soon as you can, but we have a very real chance of not coming back from this if we go in half-cocked. I can do magic once I get my hands on some Residuum, but the rest of you are essentially very large toddlers when it comes to holding your own against what Velmyra has to offer. The Mage's Dagger is not a pursuit I would even recommend to semi-experienced mercenaries, much less someone who's never picked up a sword before." He holds up a finger just as Eddie opens his mouth and says, "And no, testing one out at a ren faire doesn't count."

"Then what do you suggest?" I question. I feel too insistent, too aggressive. It isn't typical for me. I would have thought I'd been the one sitting back and letting everyone else make the plans. This wishy-washy back and forth is driving me nuts, though. It's not going to get us any closer to May. "Is there a better option than that? Is there *any* other option?"

Adrian sighs again. "Maybe if we actually get there—"

"Just say 'no' if you mean 'no.'"

We lock eyes, and there's a slight pause before he says, "No. There's really not."

"There's our answer, then," I say. "We go in, get the three Relics you know of, find the fourth, and get the Dagger. We use that to kill her and get May back."

His eyebrows fly up, and he holds out a hand. "Whoa whoa," he says. "We're not jumping to that."

I glance at the other two, and even they look taken aback. All the color has drained out of Eddie's face, and Jackson even looks at me with concern. When I actually think about what I said, I have to take a second, too. I just suggested killing someone. Not in an imaginary game. For real. My stomach lurches. Jesus Christ, I need to slow down.

Adrian's hand falls on my shoulder, and he looks me in the eye, pulling me out of the thought spiral I'm about to fall down. "We use it as a bargaining chip. We give her the knife if she gives us May. That way, she and the other Mages are safe from any other mortal that tries to mess with them. If there's any advantage we have, it's going to be that."

I nod, the sourness in my gut fading. "And what about us defending ourselves?"

He drops his hand, looking between all of us like we're sad little puppies left in the rain. "I guess we figure that out when we get there."

The extraneous details are hashed out now that we know vaguely what direction we're going in. It's Sunday now. We'll spend the week preparing, making lists of what we need to bring, going shopping, taking care of anything we need looked after while we're gone. On Friday—ironically, the typical *Mages* night—we'll leave. According to Adrian, there's no way to tell what time it will be when we get there. He's only made one trip between the two planes, so he doesn't know how much time will have passed since he left. Seeing as how Velmyra and Earth's timekeeping systems are so similar, however, he doesn't think we'll come back to Earth in 2075 or anything after only a couple weeks in Velmyra.

The amount of Crystalline Residuum we have should be enough to get us all over to Velmyra safely with Adrian casting. He knows where to get more when we get there, which we'll certainly need if we're bringing back another person with us. When he says this, the thought doesn't leave my mind.

Coming back here. With May.

The picture is fuzzy, like it's been taken with a camera that was out of focus. I can't make out the details of how that will look. If I bring her back, do we tell people? Her parents? The media? How will we explain where she's been? Will people put together the connection to her and *Mages of Velmyra*? There are so many blurry details that my mind seems to almost shut down at the thought of it actually happening.

The boys continue talking plans, but my thoughts race, a computer hard drive working overtime and overheating. I've entertained the thought before. I've had daydreams about sitting in class and getting the phone call that they finally found her, that she's been kept in a cult somewhere for the past ten years, but they've rescued her and she's coming home. I imagine bursting out of the classroom, running down to her mother's house, nearly breaking the door down running into the living room and—

That's usually as far as I can get. I can't visualize anything about what comes next. What she looks like, sounds like. I imagine she smells like she used to—vanilla lipgloss and sweet pea body spray. But beyond that, the details are hazy. And when I try to visualize what I'll say to her, I have no voice.

"Did you get that, Violet?" Adrian asks, snapping me out of my stupor.

"Sorry," I say, shaking off the haze. "Repeat it for me. I was somewhere else."

His eyes on me are heavy, like he's resting a weight on my chest by just looking at me. "I can see that," he says.

Friday is the plan. Adrian is staying at a hotel across town in the meantime, while Jackson continues to couch surf. It's nearly midnight when Adrian leaves, but he says he'll text me tomorrow and to keep him updated. We send him off, Eddie mumbling a sullen "bye" as he goes.

Jackson falls asleep mere minutes after he's gone, but Eddie and I are wide awake. We sit by the open window by the kitchen table, Eddie smoking his pipe, blowing out the smoke in a paper towel tube with a dryer sheet at the end so the landlord doesn't complain to us about the stink of weed when we move out. I take a few puffs myself. It's a typical ritual for us when we can't sleep. The street below us is slowly growing quieter as the hours grow later, the golden glow of the streetlamps casting sepia tones over the snow dusted cars parked in front of the building.

The high hits me all at once, and I start to giggle uncontrollably. It's out of such carefree delight, Eddie can't help but join in. Even amidst our cackling, Jackson stays out like a light.

We're going to Velmyra. We have a plan. And out of the haze, I see a pair of brown eyes and a lipgloss-coated smile.

CHAPTER 9

It's Thursday night, and we say goodbye to our apartment.
Adrian has offered for us to stay at his hotel suite for
the night before we take off in the morning, so we've
packed and readied everything that we need for the indefinite
amount of time we'll be in Velmyra. Eddie and I made a trip
earlier in the week out to the store for some camping items—
luckily on sale, since, you know, it's fucking February. Adrian has
advised us to pack light, however. The amount of stuff we bring
might impact the accuracy and efficiency of the Residuum trans-
port. Too much stuff might make the difference between a safe
trip and one of us losing a few limbs on the way.

We also took the time to make sure no one was going to call
in any missing persons reports on us. The official story is we're
all taking a road trip out west, and that's general enough to get
everyone to nod and smile and tell us to have fun. My parents
tell me that sounds like a fun getaway when I give them a courtesy call about it. They moved out to the suburbs a couple years
ago, and even though it's only a ten minute drive to their house,
we don't see much of each other. They both worked a lot when I
was little and continue to do so to this day. They're happy that
I'm getting out and doing something, just as long as I keep in

touch. It probably doesn't even occur to them that a road trip in the middle of my last semester of college is abnormal. When you have a kid who's as back and forth between mental health episodes as I am though, it probably gets old after a while, and you have to pick your battles.

Eddie tells Vault that he's going on vacation for two weeks, a bold move considering we don't know when we'll be back. He has enough of a reputation at the shop and a rapport with the owner that they don't make a huge fuss about it. I, on the other hand, being about as attached to my job as I am to the concept of photosynthesis, just end up calling in and telling my boss I quit. Same with school. It's just early enough in the semester where I won't fail by dropping out, but my degree is obviously going to be put off again. I was supposed to finish it last year before the hospitalization. Guess I can keep waiting. May's waited long enough.

By Thursday afternoon, I have my school backpack stuffed as efficiently as possible with clothes and toiletries. Knowing we'll be out in the woods at some point or at least without indoor plumbing, shampoo and deodorant are necessities in my book. Just as I'm about to zip it closed, I pause, glancing at the desk in my bedroom. It's covered in papers, textbooks, expansions for *Mages*. Shifting through the piles, I pull the game master's guide out and stuff it in the bag. That and a few pictures of me and Eddie, my parents, and May's last school picture are all the personal items that I take with me. It seems paltry, but I don't need anything else. Everything I need to survive can be condensed down to a backpack. I don't know whether that's something to be proud of or not. The cherry on top is making sure my d20 is in my jeans pocket. There's no way I could call myself truly prepared without that.

I look around my bedroom. The bed is made for once, all the clothes picked up off the floor. I've thrown away some of the papers filled with notes about the Crystalline Mage, theories, sketches I've done. It's so strange that I've finally gotten my life somewhat put together before completely uprooting it. As I close the door behind me, I feel a pang of fear, but it's soon replaced by exhilaration.

No looking back now. This is happening.

We convene in the kitchen before we head out. Eddie has managed to keep his stuff to one bag, but it's stuffed to the brim and bigger than mine. He's put himself in charge of the tent as well, which is rolled up in a compact bundle for the time being. We haven't seen much of Jackson over the past couple of days, but he's there as prepared as we are, his worn duffel bag slung over one shoulder. We don't say much to each other as we look around the apartment, the lights dark and the heat turned off. It actually does feel like we're going on that road trip. *We'll be back*, I repeat in my head as we lock the door behind us, walk down the stairwell and take off for the hotel.

Adrian, of course, couldn't have settled for a Holiday Inn or a Motel 6. The Amway Grand Plaza is the biggest hotel in the city, in the heart of downtown. I've lived in Grand Rapids my entire life, and I've only been in the Plaza once when I was six, a reward from school for not missing any days that year. Being in here as an adult, though, makes me feel like I'm a kid again. The wide foyer is dated, probably constructed in the seventies, but the vaulted ceiling and grand staircases are a sight to behold. I don't think I've ever seen so many chandeliers in the same room before. I feel scruffy walking among the hotel residents with their Armani blazers and Gucci handbags. It's like I've walked into an F. Scott Fitzgerald novel.

We cautiously wade further into the hotel, wandering down the hall to the front desk, trying not to look so out of place that someone calls security on us. Across the hall from the front desk, there is a trendy bar, lit up with sleek lighting and refurbished grey paneling. I spot Adrian lounging across the way from the bartender, leaning languidly with a martini glass in his hand. He waves at us, mid-gulp. "You made it," he says in greeting. "Welcome to higher living, pets."

He leads us to the top floor where the suite is, and as soon as the door opens, it's like we've walked into another world. While the lobby and halls are a throwback to the seventies, the suite is distinctly modern, with tall windows, grey walls, and angular furniture. The entryway is a foyer with two plush sofas, a desk, and a full kitchen. Eddie and Jackson are like two kids who've been invited into a royal palace, immediately throwing themselves on the sofas, looking in all the drawers. Eddie, of course, goes to raid the fridge, which looks empty from where I'm standing. After setting down my bag, I go off to explore myself, venturing down the hall. The bathroom is incredible, with marble countertops, an all-glass shower, and a bathtub big enough to fit three people at a time. There are two bedrooms, one with a king size bed and one with a queen. Something tells me that Adrian isn't going to be down for sharing the king, so we're all going to have to get cool with dividing the bed and sofas between the remaining three of us.

The most incredible thing is the view from the king room. There's an entire wall that is just a window, leading out to a patio. With the sun down, the city has lit up, sparkling with a light that you can only see and appreciate from far away. I've often seen it driving down the highway at night, marveling in the way it looks so big yet so small all at once. When I was little sitting in the back seat of my parents' car, I thought it looked like a little snow globe, and I got to shrink down and live in it until I left town again, where I would grow back to normal size until I got back home.

A hard knot forms in my throat again. It's only now I realize that I'm really leaving it behind. For how long, I can't even guess. It eases when I think about what it will be like when I come back, though. My little snow globe will still be here. And May will be able to look down on it with me.

Adrian lets us order room service, which is a cavalcade of food that probably costs more than our apartment's monthly utilities bill. Tuna tartar, filet mignon, black truffle pasta. I insist on paying Adrian back for it since it's all so pricey, but he refuses. "Last night on Earth, kid," he says, as he takes a swig of pinot noir. "I might as well spoil you before we descend into Hell."

I heed his advice, locking myself in the bathroom for a good hour, soaking myself in the bathtub, reveling in the last hot bath I might have in a while. After I'm sufficiently pruney, I come out of the bathroom, towel draped around my neck. There is something so comforting about being wrapped in fleecy pajamas after taking a long bath, and I'm feeling warm and content as I walk out. Down the hall, the door to the king room is open, and through the wide window wall, I see Adrian, leaning on the patio in his devil-may-care way. Tossing the towel on the bathroom floor, I walk into the living room and grab my coat before heading back to the king room, bundling myself up before stepping out onto the patio with him.

It's freezing out on the patio, but for February, it's actually not so bad. My wet hair freezes into tendrils as soon as the air hits it. Adrian hasn't changed out of his suit, having put on his pea coat to stave off the cold. A lit cigarette dangles out of his mouth, the orange cinder glow fitting right in among the rest of the twinkling lights of the city.

"Sorry if I'm interrupting," I apologize, shoving my hands in my arm pits. I don't think I even own mittens. I should have gotten some for the trip. Shit.

"Not interrupting," Adrian says, sounding bored as he exhales. I can't tell if he's breathing out cold air or smoke as a cloud streams out of his mouth and evaporates into nothing. He holds the cigarette up between his fingers. "You smoke?"

I shrug, noncommittal. I used to smoke more, back in my binge drinking days. Now, not so much, but with the air as cold as it is, something to warm me up doesn't sound so bad. He pulls a carton out of his pocket, extending a cigarette to me. I take it, and quick as anything, he already has a lighter in his hand. As soon as it's lit and I take a breath, the shiver running through my body settles, warmth spreading through my limbs and into my fingers and toes.

We smoke in silence for a moment, taking in the sparkling view of the city below us. I eventually say, "Thanks for coming back, by the way. I don't even think we would have gotten off the couch to get this going if it weren't for you."

"Eh, I don't know if that's true," Adrian says. "Maybe it would have taken you a few years, but you're all smart. You would have survived."

"I'm not so sure."

He chuckles at that, taking another drag.

"What changed your mind, anyway?" I ask. "You seemed determined to stay here. What happened between then and now?"

Pulling himself out of his lean, Adrian stands up straight for the first time all night. He examines the cigarette between his fingers. "I'm assuming the same reason you're going: guilt."

A pang resonates in my chest at the word.

"I think about May a lot," he continues. "Maybe not every day, but a lot. I came here, and she stayed behind, still in the clutches of the Crystalline Mage. Even if there was nothing I could do, I still feel responsible, you know?"

I do know. Every time I think back to the attack, I think about what I could have done differently. I could have yelled louder, fought back harder. There could have been something. Anything. "Why did you leave in the first place?" I ask, trying to change the subject.

He pauses, looking out over the city, breathing smoke out of his nose. "I needed to get out of there," he answers. "That place had nothing but bad memories and old scars. Plus, I'd done some things I'm not necessarily proud of."

"Like what?"

He hesitates before saying, "Illegal stuff."

"Specific," I remark.

"Well, when you're homeless and starving, there isn't a lot you won't do, Violet," he says.

Instantly, I feel bad. He did mention he and his brother had set out on their own. Just not why. "Sorry, I didn't—"

"It's all right. I'm just saying, I had to survive. Not only that, but I had someone else's survival riding on my shoulders too." Grimacing, he snuffs out his cigarette into the concrete of the patio wall.

"That's why you made *Mages*, right? Survival?" I ask, expressing something I've been thinking since I've met him. "You sold your life as a game so you could make money."

"Wow, look at you, Sherlock," Adrian says slyly. "Yeah, I was a bit down on my luck when I first got here. Then I met Anthony. Told me he was trying to make a game company for tabletop RPGs, which of course I had no idea what that was. But I gave him some writing I did, sketched out some maps, and he cut me in for forty percent. Not exactly dignified, but it kept the clothes on my back. Doesn't hurt that Anthony is fantastic in bed."

"That's how Magicka Games started, huh?" I comment.

Adrian nods. "Not exactly the glamorous story everyone thinks it is. Once the game took off, I was pretty much set. First time in my life I could ever say that, sad as that is. Anthony wanted more, wanted me to write lore for other games and expansions, but he never knew that what I gave him for *Mages* was non-fiction. The well was tapped dry. I told him I couldn't do it anymore."

"That's too bad."

He shrugs it off, keeping it nonchalant, but there's something sad twinkling in his eyes. "You win some, you lose some. He wasn't an asshole about it. I still get royalties from the game, still get the credit. Used a pseudonym so big geeks like you couldn't find me. As much as that worked." He nudges me playfully on the shoulder, and I can't help but smile.

We stand in silence for a while, before I say, "I'm sorry. About him. Whatever happened to him."

"Who? Anthony? He's fine. Lives in LA with his smoking hot model wife and two kids."

"I didn't mean Anthony," I say. "I meant your brother."

Looking at me, his gaze withers. Every once in a while, when I see him, he looks far older than what he actually is, but it's always when I catch him out of the corner of my eye. This is the first time that he's appeared this way while looking at me head on. "Thank you," he hoarsely replies. "He's part of the reason I'm here. I messed up and…"

He trails off, and I can almost hear the pain through the silence.

"You don't have to explain," I tell him. "I get it."

Through the sorrow, a grin cracks onto his face. "You do, don't you?" Adrian says. He takes out the carton of cigarettes and pulls a fresh one out, lighting it as he talks. "You know, she told me what happened when we first met. All the gory details. The ruthlessness of the Hellions, seeing her friend overtaken by them as she was whisked away through a dark door." He taps at his nose. "That's how you broke that, right?"

I nod.

Shaking his head, he mutters a soft "*fuck*" under his breath.

"It's fine," I say numbly. "I don't even notice it half the time anymore."

"No, it's not fine," he says. There's a sudden anger that flares up in him that makes me take a subtle step backward. "It's them. Those fucking Mages. They're the cause of it all. May, you, me. We're all just pawns, collateral damage. All so their magic can reign free, unsupervised and unmuzzled. It's *wretched.*"

The cigarette snaps in half in his hand, and he pulls his hand back, wincing in pain as it burns him. The remains of it fall onto the cement patio, still glowing hot. In a fit of simmering anger, he stomps them out into ashes. Not knowing what I'm to do, I keep taking drags off mine, watching him flail until he calms himself. Heaving a sigh, Adrian lowers his head into his hands, wiping down the length of his face like he's washing it at the end of the day.

"That's why I'm helping you guys," Adrian says. "The thought of their wanton destruction, still tearing the continent apart. It makes my blood boil. They deserve to lose for once. She deserves it, most of all."

She. The Crystalline Mage. The simmering heat in my chest flares. I can't help but agree with him. She does deserve a loss. But more importantly, we deserve a win.

The morning comes without fanfare. Eddie and I have slept in the same bed before, so we were fine with sharing the queen. Adrian offered to share the king with Jackson with a smarmy wink, but Jackson confidently proclaimed he was good with the couch. The light of dawn is grey and cold, but anything is enough to wake us up out of our sleep. I can't speak for the others, but I hardly slept at all, the thought of knowing it was the last night's sleep I would have on Earth. It's like being five and vibrating with anticipation the night before Christmas.

We have room service for breakfast, this time with pastries, eggs, bacon, pancakes—all the nasty carbs you could imagine. Eddie and Jackson inhale it, while Adrian and I nibble politely. After breakfast, we do one last check over what we're bringing with us. Adrian gives us the final approval, making us take stuff out if he doesn't think it's necessary. Most of the stuff he tells us to leave behind are clothes. We can always get new sets while we're there. Easier to not stick out and cause any unwanted attention, anyway.

Going through Jackson's stuff, Adrian tries to toss out some of the books he's squirreled away, but he's insistent about keeping them, heaping more pairs of jeans onto the floor.

Adrian pulls out a small black plastic case, and before he can ask about it, Jackson snatches it out of his hand. "That stays. No negotiating," Jackson says, stuffing it back in between his clothes.

"What is it?" Adrian asks, arching an eyebrow.

Jackson glares back. "Meds."

I swear Adrian is going to press the issue and ask for details, but he gives a conceding nod and moves on.

Eddie is the one who's brought the most useless stuff. Adrian looks at him with dead eyes as he pulls a Nintendo Switch out of his bag.

"What?" Eddie says with a shrug. "What if I get bored?"

Adrian tosses the console onto the sofa. "Find animal shapes in the clouds or something."

"Eddie, you're not going to be able to charge it anyway," I tell him.

"I know, but I can use it before it dies," he reasons.

"And then after, you can throw it at a hydra's head as a blunt weapon," Adrian muses. "A very expensive blunt weapon."

As he goes through my bag, he sets aside a few pairs of jeans, whittling it down to just one. He sees the game master's guide and stops, looking at me with curiosity. "Do you really think we need that? You have the game master coming with you," he says, gesturing to himself in a lithe swoop.

"It's not for us," I say, shifting on my feet uncomfortably. "It's for me."

For a second, I think he's going to toss it out, setting it next to Eddie's video games, but after a long stare, he zips the bag up and hands it back to me without another word.

It takes another hour for us to get through taking turns in the bathroom, sending our final texts, making our final calls. While Eddie makes a call to his mom, I sit on the sofa, my hands folded up on my lap. The nervous energy in me is racing, settling in my stomach in a heavy, acidic knot. I wasn't a theatre kid, but I imagine this is akin to stage fright. I'm terrified of what happens if I take that first step out into the light and botch my first line.

Finally, once the phones are put away, the four of us exchange looks.

"Well," Adrian says. "Let's do this, then."

He grabs the Residuum stone from his own duffel bag. "Okay, everyone. Put a hand on me, doesn't matter where. Try to keep it above the waist, if possible."

We do as he asks, Eddie and Jackson setting their hands on either one of his arms. I end up putting my hand on his shoulder. Even through his coat, I feel a coursing energy that doesn't seem natural radiating through him. The unsettling ball of anxiety in my stomach grows, threatening to boil over up through my throat and out my mouth.

"No matter what happens," Adrian says, "keep holding onto me. Don't let go, no matter how hard it is to hold on."

All of us breathe unsteadily. I look at Eddie, only to find that he's already looking at me. He gives me a nod and a strained smile. He's terrified, but so am I. There's something to be said about being terrified together, and it eases the tension just by a hair.

"On my count," Adrian says.

I take a deep breath in.

"One."

I breathe out, closing my eyes.

"Two."

My fingers curl into the fabric on Adrian's coat.

I breathe in again.

"Three."

Before the word is completely out of his mouth, there's a tug, as if my legs are being swept out from underneath me, a high-pitched screeching sound.

And we're gone.

PART II

"There are many foes and trials you will face as you traverse Velmyra. Keep your party together. Work with each other to build something wonderful."
-*Mages of Velmyra* Players Handbooks, Page 15

CHAPTER 10

It would be foolish to hope that I land on my feet, but I at least hope that I can hold onto Adrian tight enough that I make a semi-successful landing onto solid ground.

That's a hope too far, apparently.

There's a sensation of falling, of being tossed like a ragdoll heaved off a roof. I open my eyes, expecting to find myself in some swirling starry void, somewhere in between dimensions and too beautiful for words. But I only see a blur of brown and black before there is a painful thud and a sickening crack, the force of which is enough to break my hold from Adrian's coat. I tumble on the jagged ground beneath me, feeling every jutting edge dig into my torso. My breath gets knocked out of me as pain webs out from my ribcage and down my side. By the time I stop rolling, I'm wheezing, the pain so intense it feels like I can't take enough breath in.

Breathe in. Breathe out. You're okay. You're not dead. You're fine.

I focus on the breaths. I focus on keeping my eyes shut and just breathing. After a moment, the pain starts to dissipate, like it's being sucked back into the epicenter.

I manage to pry my eyes open, putting my hands underneath me to push myself up. The ground beneath me is dirty and firm, loose soil creeping between my fingers. It takes a moment of pushing through the throbbing pain before I'm able to get onto my knees and look around at where I ended up.

It's dark, but there is a pocket of glowing light coming from somewhere that allows me to see the rough details of where I am. A cavern full of uneven rocks and boulders sprawls out in front of me, stacked in piles of varying sizes. Stalactites cascade from the ceiling, dripping and covered in limescale. I inhale and exhale in shattered breaths, but this time, breathing doesn't make the pain in my side feel better. It exacerbates it. I clutch my side as I stand up, squinting through the shadows of the open cave to see if I can find the boys.

For a split second, I think about shouting out to them, but I hold back. With how precarious some of these rocks are positioned, it feels like anything could knock them over, even sound. That's probably not even how it works, but something in my gut tells me that making too much noise might be detrimental. "Eddie," I whisper, as I take my first tentative steps forward. "Adrian. Jackson. Hello?"

The glow that illuminates my way forward gets steadily closer, and I see it's emanating from behind a wall of rocks stacked up nearby. Keeping my steps light, I make it to the formation, wondering what could be causing it. Maybe it's Infernal Residuum. The Crystalline Residuum gave off a sort of soft, white glow, so maybe Infernal gives off something orange and angry. As I round the other side of the rock formation, I expect to see something like a big glowing coal.

I stop. My breath catches in my throat.

It isn't Residuum. It's a campfire. And scattered around it are dozens of sleeping creatures.

I clap a hand around my mouth. In the dim glow of firelight, I can't tell exactly what they are, only catching random features on them. Pointed ears, grey mottled skin, long curled talons. Most of them are small, like the size of a kindergartener, but I know better than anyone that "small" doesn't mean "harmless." Hand still over my mouth, I slowly inch backward, not daring to turn my back on them—

My left foot suddenly slips from underneath me, and I clatter to the ground, the sound of shale and loose rock skittering across the ground. I land on my bad side, another sharp hit running along the right half of my body, the pain so intense that spots sparkle in front of my eyes. I blink rapidly, trying to clear my vision, but when it does, I wish it would have gone dark completely.

The creatures are all in various states of waking from their slumber, some sluggish, some immediately jumping to their feet. With some of them standing upright, I can see they're all dressed relatively the same, but not in uniforms. They wear tattered tunics made of a burlap material. As they rise, they snatch up small objects at their side, which I slowly realize are weapons. Daggers, crossbows, maces. All stuff that I've seen at comic conventions, made from craft foam and resin. Against the glint of the firelight, these aren't just props. They're grinning, malicious metal, all to match their grinning, malicious faces. All of which are focused directly on me.

All right. Fuck stealth.

Clumsy as hell, I scramble to my feet and take off into a sprint back the way I came. As I do, a rash of snarls and shouts rise up behind me, and the patter of tiny feet against stone echoes off the cavern walls. I trip along the uneven landscape as I navigate through the cavern as quickly as I can, not daring to look behind me. *Keep running*, I will myself. Just pretend they aren't there. This is high school gym class, and I have to get my mile time up or I have to take it again next semester. Just keep going.

Something whizzes by my ear, so fast that it's only a blur in the corner of my eye. The cavern gets darker the farther away from the campfire I get, but as I run, I pass by something long and glinting on the end. Crossbow bolt. As soon as that registers, more of the same zipping noise sounds off around me, though not coming nearly as close. I try my best to just focus on the beat of my heart in my ears, muscling my way around the pain in my side, the burning in my lungs, and the shouts behind me. Do they sound like they're getting closer? No, forget that. Focus on putting one foot in front of the other. Left, right, left, right, left—

Out of nowhere, I hit something. Hard. I crumple against the hard wall of rock that I've come up against, swearing under my breath. My hands paw up the surface, trying to find a gap or an opening that I could maybe climb up to get away from the onslaught, but it's flat all the way up. No hand holds or foot holds. No escape. I turn around to see dozens of little silhouettes charging at me, weapons raised and pointed in my direction. Closing my eyes, I brace for the impact of an arrow or dagger flying my way.

A small cry of pain erupts from the horde's direction, and my eyes fly open. One of the creatures falls over in its tracks, a sizeable rock bouncing next to it as it faceplants on the ground. Some of its friends slow down, checking to see if it's okay, but most look in the direction that the assault came from. Another chunk of rock flies out, hitting another in the head. The impacts aren't enough to actually draw blood or hurt them. The two that are knocked over start to gather themselves after a moment of being stunned. Their weapons, once focused on me, turn to face their assailant, a much more formidable foe than the human girl running away from them.

"Hey, you fucks! Look over here!"

Oh god. He didn't.

I follow the gaze of the creatures to see a shadowed version of Eddie standing a few yards away, another softball-sized rock in his hand, poised to be thrown. "Over here!" he shouts.

"Eddie, what the fuck are you doing?" I scream at him. The little monsters aren't paying any attention to me anymore, instead slowly approaching Eddie.

A tiny crossbow bolt goes flying, but Eddie is able to dodge out of the way just before it hits his shoulder. "I don't know," he says to me, the nerves clear in his voice. "I didn't think about it much."

The monsters gnash their teeth, more bolts flying his direction. Taking a deep breath, I clamber to my feet and take off toward him, hurtling around the crowd of creatures until I reach him. A few of them swipe at me as I go by, and slices of pain bloom across the skin of my legs, but they're nothing compared to the constant dull ache in my side. As soon as I reach Eddie's side, I put his hand in mine and pull him forward, both of us bolting away from the pack.

We don't let go of each other's hands as we power our way through the cavern. The walls narrow, and we squeeze through a much smaller shaft than the large open one I originally found myself in. Eddie's palm is slick with sweat as we run, but I know I'm probably contributing something to that too. "Where's Jackson and Adrian?" I yell at him, panting as I run.

"Was going to ask you the same thing," he screams back. "I lost them somewhere."

The growls behind us are getting closer. I try to pick up the pace, urging myself to go faster, but as soon as I do, I have to slow again. My legs only have so much power left in them. If this keeps up, they're going to cave in underneath me, and then we're monster chow. After running through the dark, attempting to ignore the approaching battle cry behind us, a shaft of light appears ahead of us. Relief runs through me and seems to do the same for Eddie, as his grip on my hand loosens. At least we aren't randomly running through darkness anymore. Maybe we'll have a fighting—

"Fuck," Eddie swears under his breath. At first, I'm not sure what he's concerned about. Then, I see it.

The shaft of light isn't hitting any ground, cascading down into an empty gorge that starts with a steep drop several yards ahead of us. We've reached a dead end.

The noise behind us doesn't stop.

"What do we do?" I ask, starting to slow but still moving forward. Where else can we go but forward, after all?

I look over at Eddie, and I can see his gears turning, glancing from the cliff peak to the creatures behind us, back to the cliff peak. "I have an idea," he says, tentatively. "Keep running, but turn off to the right before you go over."

"Really? I was going to run right off the edge, but now that you've said something—"

"Just do it, okay?" Eddie yells. "It's the only idea I have."

Sharply, I nod. It's better than anything I have. Which is nothing.

We barrel toward the cliff edge. Closer, closer. The horde is right behind us. Another arrow grazes my shoulder. Closer, closer—

"Now!" Eddie yells.

I turn right, toeing the edge of the cliff by inches as I run off along the edge. Eddie goes left with just as much precision. I halt in my tracks after sprinting a decent distance, tripping over a pile of gravel and falling to my knees. I look behind me, expecting to see the creatures descending upon me like wild dogs.

Instead, I see them flying over the cliff's edge.

They were running at us with all their speed, only thinking about catching up with us, not about the edge of the huge drop-off in front of us. One by one, they attempt to slow down, but the front half of the group can't hit the brakes fast enough before flying off into open air, plummeting with a screech into the darkness. Those who are lucky enough to stop in time are pushed over the threshold by their partners behind them, a vicious chain reaction. Their cries which were once filled with bloodlust and malice are now frantic and fearful as they tumble into the pit. I dare myself to look over the edge, expecting to see their little bodies start to pile up at the bottom of the chasm, but it's so far down that not even the shaft of moonlight above us can penetrate the thick blanket of darkness below.

Just as soon as they came, they're all gone, the last of their cries echoing around us before fading into silence.

I see Eddie a handful of yards away. He has managed to stay standing, but he's looking down to the bottom of the cavern with me, until he notices me looking at him.

We stare at each other, unsure what to say.

Until we both break out into laughter.

It's not jovial or hysterical. It's nervous and breathless, both of us still trying to catch our breath after our sprint. I throw my head back, chuckling as I exhale and close my eyes.

We're here. It's actually real. The past couple of weeks, I thought I was going to eventually wake up from my delusion that Velmyra was real. One day, I would come out into the living room and Eddie would look at me quizzically when I brought the plan up. The idea that the dream would end—that was the real nightmare for me.

But it's real. I look down at my torn jeans, reveling in the fact that I have little cuts up and down my legs, made by little green monsters we found in a cave. It's really real. I have the marks to prove it.

Eddie strides over to me, chuckling softly. "What the fuck is our life, dude," he says. "We're in fucking Velmyra."

"Yeah," I say. "We are, aren't we?"

He holds out a hand to help me to my feet, and just as I grab onto it, a quick growl echoes through the cavern. Both of us look over to the source of the noise, and I drop back to the ground, letting his hand go in surprise.

A sole green creature sprints toward us, brandishing a mace in its hands. It screams a high-pitched wail as it catapults itself toward us, mere feet away and aiming toward my head, since it's the thing closest to its reach. I flinch, waiting for spikes to connect with my skull.

The wail cuts short, and I open my eyes to see the creature sail over my head and fly off the cliff edge, joining its friends into the blackness of the pit below. Looking over at Eddie, I expect to see him wielding another rock, but he's empty handed, looking as bemused as me. My stunned gaze follows his.

Jackson stands above me, a huge stick slung over his shoulder, almost as if he just swung a baseball bat. His wavy auburn hair is plastered to his scalp, moist with sweat, his glasses sitting cockeyed on the bridge of his nose. He's panting just as much as we are, looking back and forth between us. "The hell was that thing?" he asks, letting the branch fall to his side.

Blinking the confusion away, Eddie glances back over the cliff. "Goblins, I think. They look different from the drawings in the guide, though. Didn't expect as many…teeth."

"I think a good rule of thumb when it comes to this place is 'always expect more teeth,'" Jackson says. And in a surprise showing, he extends his hand to me.

I blink at his hand, not sure if this is a trick, like he's going to pull it away and pretend to smooth his hair out as I'm left grasping at air. But he looks at me impatiently, thrusting his hand closer. "You want help or not?" he asks.

Reluctant, I put my hand in his, and he helps me to my feet. He's stronger than I expected. I hardly have to lift any of my own weight.

We check over ourselves to make sure we haven't been stabbed. Eddie has a sizeable scrape on his left cheekbone, but other than that, he seems unscathed. I let him know about my side, and he asks if he can take a look. I lift my jacket and shirt up to just below my bra line. Having lived with Eddie for years, he's seen more of my skin than that. Jackson, I notice, shifts uncomfortably, looking off into the distance as Eddie examines my skin.

"It just looks red, so far," he confirms. "When we get to civilization, we should get someone to check it out. I hope you didn't break a rib or anything."

Lowering my shirt, I say, "I think I'm okay. I can walk it off."

"Hey," Jackson says, looking back at us as soon as he knows my clothes are fully on again. "If you guys are done playing doctor, we gotta go. I know the way out."

Nodding, I follow him and Eddie. He leads us back through another craggy area of rocks, all leading up an incline this time. "I actually ended up outside," Jackson explains as we walk. "I heard you and those things yelling at each other coming from inside this cave, so I bolted in."

"And Adrian?" I ask, keeping my balance as another pile of rocks shifts underneath my feet.

"Don't know," he says. "I didn't see him."

I bite my lip, but I don't say anything as I follow the other two through the dark of the cavern.

We climb further and further upward until we reach another shaft of light. Pale light casts its rays on our faces as we climb up. The incline is steep, and I'm panting by the time we reach a level surface. The boys don't fare much better, Eddie hunched over with his hands on his knees, wheezing. Jackson, despite how sweaty he is, seems to be keeping it together the best out of all of us. How we're going to survive out in the woods for weeks is beyond me, if this is the kind of physical capability we have.

A shadow flickers across the ground in front of my feet, and I straighten up. The boys do too, Jackson brandishing his stick as imposing as he can. As we look up at the mouth of the cave, the shadow of a person stands, outlined by soft blue light, and my muscles all tense until I hear, "What took you so long? Good grief, I was about to consider you all lost causes and go on to save May in your loving memory."

Jackson drops his stance with a sigh, his stick dragging on the ground. The shadow moves forward, and Adrian's face, while still obscured by the dark, gets clearer. He isn't his put-together self, though his attitude sure makes it seem like he is. His hair has lost all its volume, hanging in front of his face, with bits of debris stuck in it. He decided to dress sensibly—by his definition, anyway—with a casual button down and sleek black denim pants, but they're both torn, the shirt missing buttons.

"Sorry, we were literally fighting off a horde of goblins. Took us a little bit to not die," Eddie grumbles.

Rather than bite back, Adrian looks him up and down and arcs an eyebrow. "Where's your bag?" he asks.

Eyes going wide, Eddie pats his shoulders, realizing that his backpack straps are no longer there. "Fuuuuuuuck!" he yells, looking around like he just casually set it down somewhere and forgot where. But I don't remember seeing it with him at all since meeting up with him during the goblin onslaught. I check my own bag, which thankfully is still strapped to my back, but—I don't know, does it feel lighter somehow?

"There was a chance that could happen," Adrian explains. "Crystalline is the most unpredictable of all types of Residuum. With the distance we traveled, we're lucky we made it with all our appendages still intact."

"But my stuff!" Eddie exclaims.

"All right, I'm all for a dramatic meltdown, trust me, but do it while we walk. We need to get a move on." A mischievous smile spreads across his face. "Plus, you guys have to see this."

My shoes go from crunching rocks and pebbles to squishing into mossy soil as we follow Adrian out of the cave. Eddie and I steady each other, holding onto one another's forearms as we emerge from the cavern, and we look out onto the world beneath us.

The breath is sucked from my lungs.

Below us sprawls a plain, dotted with trees and rocks, interrupted only by occasional lumps of mountainous hillside. Miles of lush green forest and hills are splayed out in front of us. The stars in the sky are all present, not clouded by the muddled pollution of city lights like I'm used to back home, and I can see the branches of vegetation swaying gently in the night breeze.

Above us, casting their soft light on the world, two moons—one a pale pink and one a faint blue—hang like Christmas ornaments among the constellations. It takes me by surprise, but I feel a tear roll down my cheek.

It's real. We're here.

And that means, somewhere out there, she is too.

CHAPTER 11

"Why did it have to be *my* bag?" I hear Eddie grumble behind me, to no one in particular. "My *Firefly* boxers were in there. They were comfy as hell. Now they're in some liminal space between dimensions." He scoffs. "Hope whatever alien finds them fucking enjoys them."

We've managed to descend from the cliff side and are cutting our way through the thick forest ahead of us. The task is daunting. The view was great from the cliff, but from what I saw, there was not a soul in sight for miles. Not even a little encampment or forest cottage. We're in for a long trek, on foot no less. My tennis shoes are holding up so far, but the cuts on my legs from the goblins' blades sting with every step. The pain in my side is subsiding, but whenever we hit a bumpy patch of ground or my foot slips off a log, I suck in my breath and the stabbing sensation returns. Eddie hasn't noticed yet, too busy sulking over his lost stuff. I catch Jackson sneaking a glance at me every so often, but he doesn't care enough to say anything about it. His attention is focused more on Eddie.

"Eddie, I will buy you twenty pairs of *Firefly* boxers when we get home," he groans, narrowly missing a low hanging branch.

He's pulled a long stick from the ground, peeling the bark off of it methodically as we walk along. Something to keep his hands busy, I guess. Just like *Mages* sessions back at home. "Just chill out."

"Yeah, that's easy for you to say," Eddie says. "You and Adrian have all your stuff. Vi at least has some of hers. I've got nothing."

I sigh. He's not wrong. Once we got down from the cliff, we assessed the damage. Jackson looked like he was about ready to cry realizing the contents of his bag seemed untouched, especially the case with his meds in them. Adrian looked pretty unaffected—if he was missing something, he didn't say anything about it. Aside from Eddie, I was the one with the most missing. A good portion of my clothes are gone, along with important toiletries—god, I really hope my period doesn't show up while we're here, because that'll be a whole thing. But the one thing that bothers me is that the guidebook is gone. Along with all the pictures inside. I know I should be grateful that it wasn't everything. Still, it's like losing a flashlight. It was the thing I was focusing on, hoping that it would somehow show me the way forward. Without it, it just feels harder. Not that anything in there will be able to do what Adrian can't. I think more than anything, it's the pictures that I care about...

"Stuff can be replaced. No use getting bent out of shape over underwear," Adrian says, hopping over a log. From behind him, his voice sounds casual enough, but there's a strange stiffness to his shoulders that tells a different story. Up close, he looks even rougher around the edges from his fall into Velmyra than I first gathered. His clothes are undeniable disheveled, and there's even a chunk of his shoe missing, so large that I can see part of his sock. Still, he moves forward, not impeded by any of it, moving with a purpose.

"Coming from the millionaire," Eddie snaps, "that's not exactly reassuring."

Adrian glances at him, a grin playing at the edge of his

mouth. "Are you really so poor that you can't afford underwear?" he asks, half laughing.

"They were limited run," Eddie clarifies. "I can buy underwear, all right? Just not that underwear."

"There's absolutely no more underwear on Earth that has fireflies on them?" Adrian asks.

Eddie sighs, closing his eyes. "*Firefly* the TV show, not the bug."

"I'm sure there's some pairs on eBay," I say, trying to move the conversation along. As much as I usually don't mind Eddie's fervor for his nerdy stuff, the radiating pain in my side is making me less tolerant of all the complaining. "I think the more important thing to focus on right now is where we are and where we're going."

Gesturing to Adrian with flippancy, Eddie says, "Why don't you ask genius billionaire playboy philanthropist? He's the one who's from here."

"Yeah, where exactly are we?" Jackson chimes in.

"Working on it," Adrian answers.

"Working on it?" Eddie repeats. "You mean you don't know where we are at all?"

Adrian stops in his tracks. "Hold on, let me check," he says. Glancing around at the trees like he's gathering clues of some kind, he turns around to face the three of us, shrugging with his hands in his pockets. "Yep, just as I suspected: we're in the woods."

"In what woods, jackass?"

He spreads his arms out wide. "How am I supposed to know?"

"You're supposed to know everything!" Eddie exclaims, stepping toward him. "You're supposed to be our secret weapon."

Rolling his eyes, Adrian says, "Well, your secret weapon didn't kill you. That's step one. Step two is figuring out if we got to the right spot."

That answer is clearly not good enough for Eddie, his face

bunching into a scowl. "Does that mean we might not even be in Velmyra? Or even on Fractum?"

"We're on Fractum. Calm down," Adrian sighs.

"Don't tell me to calm down when we're clearly lost."

"We're not lost!"

"Then where are we?"

"About five seconds away from an aneurysm. At least I am. Jesus Christ."

Shaking my head as Eddie lays into him about holding up his end of the deal, my eyes wander off to the trees surrounding us. All the trees we've passed look the same, and they don't look any different from the trees that I've seen on Earth. If we hadn't run into those goblins, I might not have even realized we left at all. That and the two moons that peer down between the canopy of leaves above us, their beams the only source of light that keeps us out of total darkness.

My eyes stop on a fallen log a few yards off, and my brows furrow. There's something out of place next to it, half buried in dirt and leaves. A rectangular shape with a pop of cherry red. I take a couple steps closer to it, and though it's faint, there seems to be some kind of white detailing on it. It almost looks like words...

No way. There's no way it made it.

Running over to the log, I crouch down and scrounge in the dirt, pulling the object out of the brush and mud. I exhale in relief as I brush away the refuse, revealing the laminated cover of the *Mages of Velmyra* game master's guide.

It's mostly intact, though dirty and slightly damp. I flip to the middle of the book where I stashed my photos. Aside from the exposed corners being bent, they're the same as when I put them in there. I close it and wrap it tightly against my chest, glad that it somehow survived.

When I make my way back over to the boys, the tensions have risen, which is amazing given I haven't been gone but for two minutes.

119

ASTRID KNIGHT

"You know, man, you're not exactly a messiah or anything. We could do this without you!" Eddie says, voice raised.

"That's incredibly interesting, considering you practically begged me to come along on your little excursion in the first place, *Ed*," Adrian says. The emphasis he puts on "Ed" is laced with venom.

At this, Eddie takes a step forward, getting into Adrian's face. He holds up a finger at him. "One: only Violet can call me Ed. You call me Eddie." He holds up a second finger. "Two: I didn't beg you to come along. I just thought it might have been a decent human thing to do, you know? Help a girl rescue her friend."

"All right, Eddie. Relax," I say as I walk up, trying to break the tension.

He doesn't seem to hear me. "But I guess in order to do that, you'd need to be a decent human, huh? Or human at all."

"Eddie," I say in a warning tone.

"I mean, *are* you even human? Maybe you're like our goblin friends back there!" he exclaims, waving an arm wildly in the direction of the cliff we came from. "I mean, you did fuck off into another plane of existence and leave a thirteen-year-old girl in the clutches of a megalomaniac, so that's about par for the course, right?"

"Eddie, st—"

Before I can say anything else, though, Adrian shoves him. Hard.

And before Eddie even has the opportunity to stumble backwards, he vanishes.

The same loud crack of energy in the air that went off in our apartment when Jackson had touched the Residuum bangs through the air now, the smell of burnt ether rippling through the atmosphere. My brain barely has time to process Eddie's disappearance before he reappears, thirty feet away in midair, accompanied by another zipping sound. He flies through the air

120

for a moment before hitting a tree, collapsing to the ground with a thundering groan.

I don't even have to think before I run to his side. He's a groaning lump on the ground, but he's moving, already trying to get himself onto his hands and knees. I have a hand around his shoulders and under his arm in an instant, but my eyes go back up to Adrian.

Now, I'm mad.

"What the hell was that for?" I shout.

Adrian, for how disheveled he is, looks over at us with all the poise and indifference of a ruthless monarch, his shoulders back and his slender eyebrow coldly arched. "I could say it was for him insulting my morality, but honestly, I was just getting very tired of hearing him talk."

Eddie, almost upright again, stretches out his spine and hisses through his teeth, "Yeah, right back at you, fucker."

"All right, both of you, shut up!" I say, pulling away from Eddie once I'm sure he's not going to fall over. "We can't do this if we're going to be traveling together. We had this discussion back on Earth before with me and Jackson, so the same rules apply. If anyone can't behave themselves properly, someone's going home. No more warnings. We either put all our petty shit aside or we pack it in. And we've gotten too far to pack it in." I stop, realizing that my voice is cracking, going out of control in a way I can't quite reign in without stopping. The boys are all looking at me warily, Jackson included.

I take a deep breath, and look back at Adrian, willing a steadiness into my voice. "Understood?" I ask.

Jackson and Eddie nod immediately, though Eddie's is clearly with resignation.

I wait for Adrian to agree. He stares at me, not with that same coldness as before. His eyes have softened, the coy cock of his brow now gone. The emotion on his face is a hard one for me to place, but as the corner of his mouth turns up, I finally recognize it.

He's impressed.

"Understood," he confirms. The way he says it, the only thing he's missing is a glass he can raise in amiable surrender.

We take a few moments to get ourselves together. I hand Adrian the guidebook, which he flips through lazily. "I wrote the damn thing, but it's been a few years. I might be able to find some markers to see where we're at. Give me a minute." As he and Jackson examine the book, I take Eddie aside and brush the dirt and bark off him while he quietly fumes, shooting quick glances over toward Adrian. I take his chin and move his head to look at me. "You're not helping," I say to him, pulling a large chunk of bark out of his tangled mess of hair. "And if the next words out of your mouth are 'he started it,' I'm going to punch you in the mouth."

Instead of snark, Eddie's eyes drift away from mine. "I'm sorry," he mumbles.

I sigh. "It's okay. Just—try to behave, all right? Jackson is trying, so you should too."

He nods, still looking at the ground. I don't press it further.

After Eddie is mostly put back together, we walk back over to Jackson and Adrian. At the sight of us, Adrian snaps the book shut with a decisive clap. "Well, now that we've all had a good kumbaya, I have good news: I know exactly where to go. Follow me."

There's no way of telling how long we walk through the forest, save for the moon slowly dipping behind the trees and the sky lightening with every step. By my estimation, it's been a handful of hours, which I can only tell by the aching in my legs. Eddie and Jackson have trailed far behind Adrian and I, though I know it isn't due to lack of energy. It's miraculous to me that we seem to have already split our party into factions, and we haven't even been in Velmyra a full day. Adrian seems unaffected by any of it, acting as though he's taking a leisurely stroll down the street, occasionally flipping through the guidebook for reference, but other than that, looking confident in where we're heading.

Even though I know that I'm going to hate waking up whenever we decide to rest, I can't help but be amazed by everything we pass. I grew up in Grand Rapids, and while the occasional trip to the woods for hiking or a class field trip wasn't out of the question, I'm still far more used to concrete sidewalks and a place to get coffee within a five-minute drive. I don't have a ton of experience with pure, untainted nature. But with every caw of a crow, every patch of glowing mushrooms, every gentle cool breeze that blows by, I fall in love with it a little more. There are stars in the sky! Growing up in the city, even a relatively small city like Grand Rapids, the light pollution is enough to make you forget just how vast the starry sky is. And here in Velmyra, it's *vast*. An array of lights dance in the black tar of night above us, like fireflies stuck to flypaper.

"It's beautiful here, isn't it?" Adrian says after a long drag of silence.

I take my attention off the sky and direct it toward him. His gaze is fixed squarely ahead of him, like he can see some sort of blinking sign that's invisible to the rest of us. The hours we've been walking, that stiffness in his shoulders is accompanied by a tension to his jaw, a barely noticeable furrow to his brow. It's a strange juxtaposition to his casual tone.

"It is," I agree. "I'm not used to so many stars."

Adrian chuckles. "If you think Grand Rapids is bad about light pollution, try living in Chicago. You forget stars even exist when you live there for a couple months."

"I bet," I say. I let silence linger between us for a moment before asking him, "Are you okay? I know you were nervous to come back here."

He breathes in through his nose and lets it out in a frenetic burst through his mouth. "I'm doing better than I expected," he said. "It's jarring, though. I never expected to come back here."

"Is it like you remember?" I ask.

He laughs. "Exactly like I remember. I've walked through these woods so much, it feels like I've never left." The smile on his face falters a bit as he says it, his mouth flattening out into a straight line. "It'll be different when we get into town, though. We're going to have to keep a low profile when we get around people. You all are going to stick out like sore thumbs in a big crowd."

"We'll be that obvious?"

"As obvious as a bunch of ren faire cosplayers on a city bus. And there's no comic con excuse you guys can use," Adrian says. His eyes dart off to our left at the sound of a breaking branch, but he relaxes as a rabbit hops across our path and off in the opposite direction. "The less reason to tip off the Royal Guard, the better."

I furrow my brow as I look at him. "Is the possibility of running into the Royal Guard really that bad? I mean, we haven't really done anything wrong, right?"

A yelp sounds off behind us, and we both stop and turn to see what the commotion is. Eddie straightens himself up and hops on one foot, the other foot only covered in a sock. He shouts a curse into the mostly quiet night as Jackson doubles back and retrieves Eddie's sneaker from around a tree root that must have caught him off guard. Adrian and I both let out a breath. As Eddie frustratedly shoves his shoe back on his foot, we turn back around and continue walking, a little slower to let the other two catch up. "He's not the outdoorsy type, is he?" Adrian asked, jerking his head back toward Eddie.

"Not especially," I confirm. "He tried converting to Buddhism and going vegan a few years ago. We went hiking together to 'experience what the Earth offered,' and he managed to get poison ivy *and* ticks up and down his legs in one day. That was pretty much the end of his 'embrace nature' streak."

Adrian hums thoughtfully before casually saying, "So, have you guys fucked or what?"

I laugh, a quick bark that's way too loud for our serene surroundings. It comes out of me without thought, and I can feel my face start burning with embarrassment. It's not like the question has never been asked before. To an outsider, Eddie and I have a strange relationship. It's the off-the-cuff way Adrian asked it that's taken me aback, as if he just asked how I like my eggs. "No," I answer, after a moment of choking on my words. "We've never fucked." I say the last word in a whisper, nervously glancing over my shoulder to make sure Eddie is still preoccupied with his shoe.

"Really? I swear, you guys give off heavy 'we fucked a long time ago and we just never talk about it' vibes."

The burning in my face intensifies. "I mean…"

Adrian gasps, like a kid who just got a puppy for Christmas. "There's a 'but,' isn't there? I mean, 'but' with one T." He gasps again, somehow louder and more scandalized than the first time. "Unless it was with two."

I know he can't see how utterly red my face is through the dark, but I bury my face in my hands nonetheless. "God, there's no buts, one or two T's. We just…" I bite my lip. I'm no prude, but divulging all this to a practical stranger puts a nervous twist in my stomach. I mutter under my breath, "We almost did."

His face lights up with glee, a sharp departure from his usually cool and collected demeanor. "I knew it. I totally called it. Tell me all about it."

I throw my hands up exasperated. "There's not much to tell. I was in college, I just broke up with my boyfriend at the time. I was over at his apartment, getting drunk and crying about it, and we just sort of started…making out."

"As one does."

"That's as far as it got, though. We never did it again after that," I say. "It wasn't some big dramatic thing." It's mostly the truth. Except for that last part.

"So why didn't you do it?" he asks.

I shrug. I know the reason, but I don't feel like he needs to know. It almost feels more personal to tell why we didn't have sex than it is to talk about the prospect of having sex in the first place. "I don't know. We both had our hang ups, at the time."

"What hang ups?" he asks. "You were idiot twenty-some-things with too much alcohol and no strings attached. That's the exact time you should have done it."

The memory of that night, as fuzzy as it is, comes rushing back at me. It was in a different apartment than the one we live in now—a lot filthier, the stench of cigarette smoke saturating every square inch of the place. I remember sitting on his couch, nursing a bottle of five-dollar Moscato, occasionally wiping away a pathetic tear as I word vomited the whole argument Jared—ugh, *Jared*—and I had had in my dorm room hours before. About how he couldn't deal with me breaking down every couple of weeks and closing myself up in my room, not talking to anyone or going to classes. My grades were slipping, I showered maybe once a week. His hoity-toity parents were starting to think I wasn't as promising of a young woman as I first purported to be, that didn't fit in with his overall plan of being partner at a law firm with a wife and two kids out in the suburbs within ten years of graduating. I didn't just take it, of course. I bit back, telling him he knew that the winter especially was hard for me, what with the anniversary of the attack and all the subsequent feelings that followed. His response—and I still can't help but laugh whenever I think about it—was to tell me he had bad stuff happen in his life, too, but you didn't see him crying about it all the time. That was the line for me, and he got kicked out of my room pretty damn quickly following that.

Eddie listened as I blubbered through my messy streams of tears and snot, and with every sip of wine I took, everything got clearer, not murkier like it should when you descend into a drunken stupor. I was destroying my liver over some asshole who acted like my mental state was a burden he couldn't deal with, while this guy right next to me had stuck by me for years, with no signs of growing tired of me or giving up. There was always some spark between us, I realized. We were only two years out of high school, but already our other classmates were losing touch with each other, moving onto new best friends and relationships. And yet, he and I remained, stalwart as ever. When I wasn't at Jared's dorm, I was at Eddie's apartment, playing video games and watching *Mystery Science Theatre 3000* into the wee hours of the morning. I lost track of all the nights where I fell asleep on his couch, but I slept there more than my own dorm.

But more than that, Eddie was unwavering. Each panic attack and restless night was met with an arm around my shoulder, a cup of coffee picked up on the way back from work, a comic book he spotted at Vault that he thought I would enjoy. It was more than any boyfriend of mine had ever done for me, and through the sloppy filter of alcohol, I could see it on his face clear as day. It wasn't just my imagination. He realized that there was some kind of connection between us too, one that was stronger than a run-of-the-mill friendship.

So, with one last swig of wine, I took the plunge.

My memory of it is marred by what came after, but I know factually that it was good, at first. Really good, actually. I had been surprised at how good of a kisser he really was, since Eddie hadn't been in any long term relationship since I'd known him. But he knew just how to move his tongue against mine, where the curves of our mouths fit together. We were like magnets, forcing ourselves closer together until there was no space between us at all. The wine was starting to catch up to me at that point, and I don't know exactly how I ended up straddling him, nor when exactly my shirt came off. My brain wasn't doing any of the thinking at that point, every decision delegated entirely to my body. We clung to each other, like we were adrift at sea and desperately trying to cling to something so as not to drown. My fingers found their way to his belt, hastily undoing it and ripping it out of its loops, moving onto the waistband of his jeans, his boxers—

That's when it stopped.

His hands moved from under my bra to on my shoulders faster than I could keep track of. Pushing me away, he closed his eyes, muttering that he couldn't. He couldn't do it. It came out in gasps, too airy and rapid for what we had just been doing. He shook his head, breathless and refusing to look at me, his eyes fixated on anything but me. "You have to get out. I can't. Please," he whispered between breaths.

I tried pleading with him, asking him what was wrong, if it was something I did, but it only made it worse. His whispers turned to requests, which turned into commands. "Violet, goddamnit, *please*. Leave," he said, his voice shaking.

And—well, what else was I supposed to do?

The week that followed, to date, is the longest time we've gone without talking to each other since we met. I didn't dare call him, fearing I had crossed some invisible line, and it tore me up thinking that one stupid mistake was going to ruin the only good thing I had going in my life. I only went to one class that week, merely because I had used up all my absences in that class already. Sitting in that cavernous lecture hall, listening to the professor drone on about attachment theory, I felt like a hollowed out shell. I couldn't even pass the time by texting Eddie about how bored I was.

It wasn't until Saturday night, eight days after I left his apartment, that he came to my dorm and asked me to take a walk.

His whole explanation was a blur, barely coherent at times. It was his turn to be a blubbering mess as he told me how sorry he was for how it ended, about how he thought he wanted that to happen between us, but once it got there, he froze up. He wiped his face on the sleeve of his tattered Dragon Ball Z hoodie as he told me how before he went to live with his foster mom in Grand Rapids, his older brother would ask him to do things for him. Sometimes, it would just be stealing cigarettes from their dad's toolkit in the garage. Sometimes, it would be other, far more disturbing things. I'll never shake from my mind the look of pure trauma on Eddie's normally happy-go-lucky face as he told me how, when he was eleven, he was transferred from his first foster home after having a panic attack in the middle of their doctor's office, because the nurse wanted him to undress for his physical. About how he had to opt out of gym in high school because he knew he'd have to change clothes in front of other people in the locker room. About how the year before, freshly out of the closet as pansexual, had made out with a guy at a house party, only to cut it short so he could vomit in the nearest bathroom—no alcohol involved. Listening to him describe it all was enough to make me sick. I couldn't imagine actually living through it.

The thought struck me, and I couldn't believe it was the first time it had occurred to me: that spark, that connection—that was it, wasn't it? It was the fact that we were two very broken people who somehow, in all seven billion people in the world, found the other person that was able to keep them whole, if only for the briefest of moments.

It's more than romance, more than friendship. Hell, at times, it feels more than family.

"We didn't need to," I tell Adrian, after what I'm sure has felt like ages of silence to him.

The way he's been itching for details, I expect him to keep prying. But if there's anything I've learned about this guy from the brief time I've known him, it's that he never seems to do quite what I expect. Instead, he just smirks, a tiny upturn on the corner of his mouth that I can see as he walks next to me. "Right," he says. "There's no bond stronger than damage, I suppose."

I narrow my gaze at him, and just as I open my mouth to ask how he could possibly know what I was thinking, he stops, holding a hand up to stop me too. He stares off into the forest ahead of us, like he's a deer that just heard the footsteps of a hunter ready to shoot. "Wait here," he says, and before I can protest, he strides ahead of me, disappearing into the thick copse of trees in front of us.

I nearly jump out of my skin as I hear shuffling through the brush behind me before I remember Eddie and Jackson have been following us this whole time. "Where's he going?" Eddie asks as he pulls up next to me, glaring off in Adrian's direction.

"Don't know," I answer. "He just told me to wait here."

We wait. None of us had the foresight to bring even an analog watch, so we have no way of knowing how long he's gone, how long we should wait for him before going after him. I'm about to ask that myself, before another shuffle of brush sounds off from ahead. Adrian reappears amongst the tree branches. He smiles that lopsided smile and makes a beckoning motion. "Follow me," he says.

With not much other choice, we do.

He leads us up a sloping hill, and I'm now acutely aware of how long we've been walking—each blister on my foot screams out in pain, and the muscles in my legs threaten to give out on me, especially as the hill inclines. Once we're at the top, I'm breathing heavily, on the cusp of requesting a moment to sit down and catch my breath. Adrian must sense it, because he gently takes my forearm, leading me forward. "Almost there," he says.

We push through another swath of trees, finally breaking through the dense canopy of leaves that's shielded us from the light of the double moons, the scene ahead of us illuminated now by burgeoning sunlight peeking over the horizon. We stand on top of a large hill, overlooking a cluster of sprawling buildings, ranging from tiny huts to looming stone structures three times their size. Even from this distance, I see people darting in and out between houses, carrying loads on their backs and pushing rolling carts, calling out to each other as the morning breaks.

Even farther in the distance, the buildings grow taller, until they culminate in the loftiest one—a huge fortress consisting of pointed grey spires, like needles trying to pierce the hazy blue-grey sky above it.

"Welcome," Adrian says, "to Castle's Edge. Now, the hard part begins."

CHAPTER 12

We wait outside of Castle's Edge for hours while Adrian runs into town, and just when I think he's abandoned us, he comes back to our hiding spot in the woods with a bulging satchel and brand new plush green cloak slung over his shoulders. "All right, come on," he says. "And don't get lost."

It doesn't seem like an impossible task until we actually make it into town. It quickly becomes a maze in the thick of crammed-together thatched houses and stone walls, especially with the chaos of people added in. As we follow Adrian through the throng, I keep my eye fixed on the back of his head, nearly losing him between men carrying towering packs on their backs wrapped in cloth, children zigzagging through people's legs, folks carrying dead animals between each other, and every other person you'd think to conjure up if you were creating your prototypical fantasy world. It's like walking through the center of a ren faire at the height of the busiest day. The smell is enough to knock anyone out too.

The swarms of people cluster together like ants all relegated to the same anthill, but Adrian leads us serpentine between groups without anyone even realizing that we've gone by. It's obvious that he's done this before. He must be sweltering under that cloak, because it's absolutely stifling. The cloak's hood shields his face so I can't see if he's sweating, but he moves as if unaffected. Occasionally, I glance back at Eddie and Jackson who don't hide their discomfort so easily. Jackson's head is dripping with sweat. Eddie is showing it even more, huffing and puffing as he wipes sweat off his brow. I suppose that's what happens when nerds finally get out and exercise.

I manage to keep my eye on Adrian, and he leads us up to a meager looking building cobbled together from wood and stone, but far less imposing than some of the other structures surrounding it. A wooden sign hanging by a thread above the door shows the carved image of a boar with a ring in its nose, the words "The Prickly Pig" etched underneath it. Adrian walks in through the thick oak door, and making sure the other two are still behind me, I follow him in.

The interior is just as shabby as the outside with the main floor serving as some kind of restaurant. A pub? Tavern? I'm not sure what to call it. The floor is littered with wooden tables, only a few of them occupied by sad looking old men, their beards dripping into their mugs. On the far end of the room is a bar and a surly looking woman behind it with knotted grey hair who squints at us as we walk in. At least, I think it's a squint at first glance. After a closer look, I see she's missing her right eye, shuttering her face in a permanent sneer. Adrian gives a subtle wave in her direction, and she nods in return. With nothing else exchanged, Adrian bounds over to a rickety staircase, and we follow him up. The hallways on the second floor are almost too narrow for us to fit down, but eventually he stops at a door and opens it with a brass key.

Light blazes out into the shadowed hallway, and Adrian holds out a hand toward the open door. "After you," he says.

The room is about the size of a college dorm room with two twin beds on either wall. There is a tiny table near the lone window, but that's it. No closet, no bathroom. Nothing else. I thought the room at the Amway was too much back at home, but to call this a downgrade would be putting it lightly.

Eddie flops himself on one of the beds, groaning as the mattress gives him no bounce and just causes him to thud into what I assume is a bundle of hay. Jackson stretches out onto the other one, his eyes immediately fluttering shut. I wander over to the little table, sitting on it and setting the game master's guide beside me. It's the only thing I can think of doing. Just sit and try not to be overwhelmed.

Adrian shuts the door behind him, turning the noisy lock with a heavy click. The bag that's been slung over his back clatters onto the floor. "All right, kids," he says, opening the bag. "I have wares."

"But we have no coin," Eddie smirkingly remarks, glancing over at me to see if I get the joke. I indulge him, smiling as much as I have energy for.

"I have that too, but first..." Adrian says, rummaging through the sack. After a moment of struggling, he pulls out bundles of fabric, hastily throwing them in each of our directions. "Clothes, so you all blend in a bit more. Two sets for each of you. If we get back into the woods, I think it would be safe for you to wear your Earth clothes. But while you're around people, it's best to blend in. Violet, I don't know how much of a dress person you are, but I got you one and a shirt and trouser set. I'd recommend the trousers for traveling and the dress for milling around town. Not that girls in trousers are necessarily taboo here, but some of the older people might frown upon it."

He tosses me a few bundles, and I manage to catch them. While he talks, I silently put on the dress, taking off the clothes that I'm already wearing underneath the dress in an awkward dance I perfected back in the locker room of my middle school gym class. Every wrong turn, I'm reminded of my bruised ribs, as gentle stabs run up my torso.

"I exchanged the remaining Residuum I had, so I do have some money. Crystalline is valuable as hell, so it's nothing to snort at. I can give you each some, but most of it is staying with me so we can save it for emergencies. That's going toward things like this room, food, the essentials."

I throw my old clothes to the floor and straighten out the new dress. I'm not huge on dresses, but at least this one isn't uncomfortable. It's made of a light material and isn't insanely layered with petticoats or whatever. Overall, I think I can live with it, but I'll definitely change into the pants once we head back into the wilderness. I turn back around, and the boys are midway through putting on their own clothes. Eddie throws on his flowy long sleeved tunic over his t-shirt, already wearing his pants which are too short for his long legs, exposing his ankles. Jackson has his shirt off, and I notice the two red, raised scars on his chest from his top surgery, though they're quickly hidden by his own tan tunic.

All of our outfits are a bit drab, but Adrian's shirt is a deep purple with buttons that, of course, he leaves slightly undone. His fabric is more form fitting, and the cuffs of his sleeves are embroidered with silver curving designs. He looks more like our fanciful tour guide through Narnia than anything else.

"And finally," Adrian says with a tug at his cuffs. He turns with a flourish back to the burlap bag and pulls out another cloth wrapped bundle, walking it over to Eddie's bed and undoing the twine wrapped around it. Splayed out in front of us on the mattress is an assortment of weapons. It's like the game master's guide's list of beginner weapons manifested. Daggers, a mace, a few swords of varying sizes, even a bow and a quiver of arrows. It's clear what took up most of the room in Adrian's pack.

"Choose your weapons, you hooligans," Adrian says and saunters back behind us, leaving the three of us to stare at our choices.

I'm overwhelmed by the options. I've never handled any of these. The chances of me stabbing myself trying to put one of those swords on my belt are higher than me stabbing anything coming after me. I stare down at them like I stare at the instruments they use at the dentist. Clearly, they aren't meant for me to touch. The professionals should be handling them.

Eddie doesn't have the same reservations. "Dibs!" he exclaims, taking the biggest sword from the pile. It's as long as his entire arm, and it wobbles as he tries to hold it up in his grasp. Up close, I can see that it's far from the pristine, factory-made replicas from the ren faire. The blade is as evenly shaped as it gets for handmade, but the steel is littered with hammer dents. Even so, a glare comes off the edge like it's cutting a slice out of the light.

Jackson is more casual about his weapon choice, pulling one of the daggers out of its simple leather sheath and making a few lazy swipes in the air, testing the point with the edge of his finger. It looks a lot like the sword Eddie has, only compact. He swishes it through the open air less like he's fending off unseen attackers and more like he's practicing chopping off the crown of a pineapple.

"Does that mean you're going with thief?" Eddie comments, sloppily putting the sword back into its scabbard after a few misses that nearly cause him some stitches on his thumb.

"Sure, why not," Jackson says, shrugging as he stuffs the knife back into its sheath.

"Yeah, we're not stealing anything," Adrian says, picking up a long slender blade—a rapier, I'm guessing. I know a lot of sword names but very little of what they actually look like. "We need to keep a low profile, so the less trouble we're in, the better."

"Yeah, no shit. I was just talking about the game, you know? What class we're going to be?" Eddie says.

Adrian narrows his gaze at him in confusion.

"I mean, not for real, obviously," Eddie chuckles. "But you know. It's fun to speculate."

"What are you talking about?" Adrian asks.

Eddie returns his narrowed gaze. "Classes? In *Mages of Velmyra*?

"Ah," Adrian says, gently rolling his eyes as expertly ties the blade onto his belt. "Nerd stuff."

"You fucking created the game!" Eddie exclaims.

"Co-created," Adrian corrects. "Anthony did all the mechanics. I don't know shit about how to actually play."

Eddie rests the pommel of his sword against his forehead, closing his eyes in frustration. "Jesus, if I were to tell my fifteen-year-old self that in the future, he'd be telling Hikari Inoue how to play *Mages of Velmyra*..." He trails off, taking the belt that Adrian gave him and fiddling with it to get the sheath tied onto it. "So, in the game, you have to pick a class. Kind of like your job. It determines what kind of skills you have—if you're physically strong or smart or good with people. And it determines the role you play in the party. Priests are supporting characters because they have spells that boost other characters' stats, while classes like crusaders are full of hit points and muscles, so they're usually at the front of the combat." He jabs a finger in Jackson's direction. "He picked daggers which thieves use most often. Therefore, thief. Plus, he played one in our home game."

There's a brief period of silence while Adrian looks at him, blank faced. "Sorry, I didn't hear anything you just said. I was too busy marveling at how utterly terrible you are at getting that sheath on your belt."

Eddie's mouth plateaus into a perturbed line, and he shoves the belt and sheath in Adrian's direction. Adrian takes it, smirking as he threads the leather into knots to secure the sword on it. Keeping his head bowed, I can see a little pink rising into Eddie's ears.

"What 'class' does that mean you're playing, hot stuff?" Adrian says, thrusting the secure belt and sword combo back at Eddie. "A jester, I assume."

Snatching it back, Eddie snaps, "No, dickhead." He whips the belt around his waist and buckles it in a fluid motion, one he's probably been practicing for years thinking that some potential romantic interest would find it impressive. Tightening the leather, he pulls the sword back out, and he looks at the blade like it's an extension of his own arm. "I'm a warrior."

He says it with such conviction that for a moment, he really does look as though he's been training for this. Like all roads have led here for him.

Adrian, however, only laughs. "Oh god, you're so sincere, it hurts!" he ekes out between giggles.

The sword wobbles again in Eddie's grasp, and with a sigh, he lets it drop, the blade dipping and hitting the hardwood floor with a thud. "It's just a good mindset to be in, okay?" he mutters, and defeated, he puts the sword back in the sheath, albeit with difficulty.

Adrian breathes out, getting out the last of his giggles, and looks over at me. "What about you, *m'lady*?" he asks, laying the cheese on thick. "What's your *class* going to be?"

I stare down at the weapons on the bed. I try to imagine holding any of them, but the picture won't form. Nothing seems to fit. The daggers are too precise, the rapier too long and unwieldy, the mace too forceful and strong. Maybe none of them will work for me. Is there such a thing as a classless player?

I twist to face Adrian, but a lightning bolt of pain shoots through me, and instinctively, I clutch my right side, sucking against my teeth. Fuck, I forgot about that.

All the boys—even Jackson—startle. Eddie is immediately in front of me, hand on my elbow in support, and I feel Adrian set a tentative hand on my shoulder. "What's wrong?" Adrian asks, all humor gone from his voice.

My muscles are still spasming, so I can barely open my mouth to speak. Eddie knows that's his cue. "She bruised herself wicked bad when we got here, back at the cave in the mountains."

"Does it hurt when you breathe in? Or when you cough or laugh?" Adrian asks.

I manage to nod.

He grumbles. "Probably a broken rib. Why didn't you tell

me this sooner?" he asks. With the tone he takes, it's clear he's addressing Eddie.

"What were we supposed to do? None of us are doctors and civilization was miles away. It's not like any of us could have done anything," Eddie says defensively.

The spasm subsides, and I loosen my hold on my side. "Stop fucking bickering or I'm going to have a headache too," I tell them.

With a sigh, Adrian says, "All right, lie down." He guides me over to the open bed, and I do as he says, lying down and trying not to think about how many bugs might be crawling around in the hay bed beneath me. He crouches down next to me, rustling around in a leather satchel at his side. "Now, I know you won't want to, but you have to hike up your dress and show me what we're working with."

My face flushes hot. "Are you serious?"

"Do you want to spend the next indefinite amount of time running around in the woods with a broken rib?"

I sigh and look over at Eddie and Jackson. "Turn around," I tell them, and once they do, I lift up my dress to reveal my bruised right side. The fabric moving against the skin hurts enough, but the action of twisting onto my left side to give him a better look sends another bolt of pain through me.

Adrian dumps a handful of loose crystals onto the bed beside me. These chunks are a lot smaller than the Crystalline Residuum we had used to get here. They remind me of the stones in glass containers at museum gift shops that you could just plunge your hands into, reveling in the satisfying cool feel against your skin. Only these are less refined, unpolished and jagged, glowing in an assortment of colors. Smoldering orange, bright lavender, and vibrant green. They all emanate a soft light, just like the Crystalline piece did.

"I'm assuming orange is Infernal and purple is Heavenly, then?" I ask.

"You'd assume right," he says, picking the green crystals out of the pile. "And these are Earthen."

Another breath sends a stabbing pain through my body. "What exactly are you doing?" I ask as I wince.

"Well, Earthen Residuum can be used for a lot of holistic purposes. I'm no doctor, but I think I can at least handle this. I've patched up a few broken bones in my day."

"What, ten years ago?"

"Or so."

I sigh. "You're fucking killing me, Adrian."

"No, that would be the internal bleeding," he quips. "Now, hold still."

He puts his hands on the bare skin of my ribs, colder than I expected them to be. Between my skin and his, there's a lump of something hard and sharp. Before I can ask any questions, light glares in my periphery, quick as a camera flash. I jump, and I expect Adrian to tighten his hold on me, but he backs away, his hands lifting off of me.

"There," he says, with a shaky laugh. "Good as new."

I blink, but rather than ask stupid questions, I twist to try and look back at my bruised skin.

Except it isn't bruised, from what I can see. It looks completely normal, not a scratch to be seen.

I sit myself up, no pain as I twist myself around, still marveling at my pale, untouched skin. "How did you…"

"Magic, my dear," he says, leaning down and scooping up the remaining stones on the bed next to me and shoving them back in the satchel. "I'm not nearly as talented as some of the career holistic practitioners, but I can hold my own against a broken rib."

His hands are still shaking as he closes his bag. "Really?" I ask, raising an eyebrow.

"Yeah. There was only like a twenty percent chance that you would have died instantly. It's fine."

I open my mouth to say something—how he should have

warned me about that little probability ahead of time—but Eddie interrupts me. "Uh, can we turn around now?"

I frantically pull my dress down at least over my ass and say, "Yeah, coast is clear."

The other two turn around, Eddie looking decidedly more concerned than Jackson. "Sorry, *how* much of a chance was it that she could have died instantly?" Eddie asks.

Adrian waves a hand dismissively. "Don't worry about it. Look, you guys are probably starving." He digs into his pocket, pulling out a handful of gold coins, which he holds out to me. "Why don't you go downstairs and get something to eat? This place has the best mutton stew in Castle's Edge. I just need to get stuff organized, and then I'll join you."

I let him drop the coins in my hand. They're small enough to be quarters but are gold in color and the edges are uneven and bumpy all the way around, clearly not made in a minting factory. Closing my hand, I look up at him. "You think that's a good idea?"

"What? Eating?"

"Going off on our own."

He scoffs. "Oh, you'll be fine. I'm right upstairs. How much trouble could you all get into?"

I feel my chest tighten up as I glance at the door, then at the gold coins in my hand.

"Hey," Adrian says, resting his hand on my shoulder, and we lock eyes. "Seriously, I'm right here. You guys can eat lunch without me, right?"

I hesitate. I don't know the answer to that. In theory? Of course. But we're here in a place we have no idea how to function in. And in the game, there's danger in nearly every interaction players come across. How am I supposed to relax and eat mutton stew when we're so woefully underprepared?

I don't know how to convey all that without sounding nuts, though. Instead, I nod.

Adrian gives the boys some money too, and once they're set,

we head out of the room. I stop at the door, looking back at my pile of belongings. My twenty-sided die is still in my pants pocket, crumpled up on the floor. I move to go retrieve it, but I stop myself. There's nowhere for me to put it. My stupid dress doesn't have pockets—go figure. With an uneasy weight in my stomach, I turn around and leave it where it is. Adrian is right— it's just lunch. It'll be there when I get back.

CHAPTER 13

As it turns out, mutton stew sucks.

Even so, I chew around the fat lumps of firm meat like they're candy, catching measly bits of carrot every couple of bites. It's tough and flavorless, but it's food, which is all I need after half a day without anything to eat. It's hard not to dribble it all over myself like some sort of ravenous beast. I self-consciously wipe the corner of my mouth, glancing around to make sure the other patrons of the inn aren't staring at me like I'm some feral creature.

A quick look around reminds me where I am, though. This isn't a hoity-toity hipster gastropub. Everyone here has the same lean, hungry look about them that I do. Gaunt men and women stare at their meals as they shovel it in their mouths, ale dripping out of the corners of their mouths like foam from a rabid dog. No one is here solely for an "experience," like what restaurants are meant for at home. I can tell that for some in here, this may be the only time they get to eat today.

There's a strange thud in my chest when I see the first non-human in the tavern. This isn't even the first time I've seen a non-human since being here. But it's still a shock to see a seven-foot tall, mottled green troll-looking motherfucker standing amid regular people and not hunching in some cave eating the bones of weary travelers. Seeing the hulking form of this thing standing in the back of the room near the fireplace, glancing around bored in the same way I am, it's a bit of a surprise. As I keep looking, though, there's more than just the troll that's non-human. There are people who look like cats, people with scales for skin, people who are unnaturally big and unnaturally small. It astounds me that I hadn't seen them when we walked in here initially. I must have been hungrier than I thought.

"Violet, are you paying attention?"

I shake my head, bringing my gaze away from the other patrons of the Prickly Pig and back to Eddie. "Sorry, what were you saying?" I ask.

"I was saying, if Adrian is correct, we know the official location of at least three of the Relics. They've all made their way to Midra, so at least we won't have to trek up to the mountains or down into the desert. Gah, we should have brought the book with us. But I believe, if memory serves right, Earthen is near Marwindale, a few days journey into the Midran Forest from here. Crystalline is in a cavern in the forest just north of Lake Eris. And Infernal is in the ruins of an Old Gods temple, a few dozen miles outside Magburn." He speaks like a strategist, the usual affable air about him gone and replaced by a no-nonsense tone and determined brow. He looks between Jackson and I, expectant. From Jackson's vacant expression, staring into his empty bowl, it looks like he's been paying about as much attention as I have. "Well, any input would help," Eddie says, shoving the last scraps of a bread roll into his mouth, crumbs tumbling onto his shirt. "Otherwise, I'm just a jackass in a burlap jumpsuit talking to himself."

"I guess we need to find out where the fourth Relic is first, right?" I ask. "It would be a huge hassle to trek across the countryside only to find it's in the opposite direction we were going."

"If it's not in the guide, that means Adrian doesn't know where it is either," Jackson says, dropping the crust of his roll into his dish. He wrings his hands as he talks, visibly uncomfortable with both of us staring at him while he speaks. "We have to find the location from someone else."

"I know that," I say. I want to follow it up with "*I'm not an idiot*," but I remember the "play nice" rule and keep my mouth shut.

Eddie pinches the bridge of his nose. "So, how are we going to figure it out, then? Just wave people down and ask, 'have you seen this mythical quest object?' That won't be suspicious."

"I'm not suggesting that," I say. "We just need some sort of—"

"Hear you folks say something about a Relic?"

All three of our heads turn to face the voice that's wormed its way into our conversation, and my eyes go wide as I gaze upon the giant troll who had been standing by the fireplace, looming over our table. Up close, it's apparent that this isn't some shitty Disneyland animatronic. It's real. At least the odor coming off of it is.

"Ahem, down here."

My gaze drifts down to see the actual source of the voice—a small person, leaning their elbows on the table, their hands folded underneath their chin with a half-cocked grin. They aren't a little person, not in the technical Earth sense of the term. They're literally a miniature person, like someone took their image and shrunk them down to half size.

"Holy shit, I'm looking at a hobbit," Jackson whispers, not as quiet as he probably intended.

Eddie shakes his head, slack jawed and mystified. "Not a hobbit. Kindred folk."

"That's the first thing you think looking at me? I would have thought it'd be something like 'they dress nice' or 'they have a nice backside'" the tiny person scoffs, pulling away from the table. "What, you've never seen someone shorter than four feet before?"

"No, of course I have," Eddie chuckles nervously. "Just not —you know—"

They narrow their gaze. They obviously don't know.

"We're from out of town," Eddie blurts, after a gulp.

"You don't say!" they snort, rolling their eyes up toward the troll. They are dark skinned with tightly coiled black hair and bronze-colored eyes that dart back and forth whenever they aren't speaking. They're dressed in clothes similar to ours but more colorful—a baby blue shirt that's open a few buttons with a deep purple coat overtop of it. The unavoidable piece of their ensemble, though, is the bright orange pendant that hangs around their neck, a leather cord wrapped around it. At first, it looks like an amber fashion piece, but the glass is jagged, like it had been chipped off some larger crystal. Not only that, it glows against their skin, a glow that's just barely noticeable in the dim firelit room of the tavern.

Infernal Residuum.

The kindred folk holds their hand out to Eddie. "Allow us to introduce ourselves. Kai the Calamitous and Gren the Gentle."

Eddie hesitates for a second before taking their hand. "Pleasure to meet you, Gren."

The kindred folk's mouth flattens as they pull their hand away. "I'm Kai. She's Gren."

Eddie freezes, his eyes going wide. "Oh."

The troll, in response, sniffs.

Kai laughs as they sit down in the empty chair we were saving for Adrian. "You know how I could tell you weren't from around here?" they say. "You're in the middle of a tavern in midday, running your mouth off about Mages and Relics. That kind of talk won't get you killed, but it'll certainly attract the wrong sort."

Eddie sheepishly says, "I thought we were being pretty quiet."

"Hardly," Kai says. They kick back in the chair, leaning and throwing their feet up on the table, their short legs just barely catching the edge. Further disproving Jackson's hobbit comment, they're wearing worn out leather boots, possibly once shiny and unscuffed, but now barely held together with two loose strings. "Lucky for you, we're two generous souls who happen to be looking for the exact same thing."

"You're looking for the Relics?" I ask.

Kai lopsidedly grins. "Indeed. And we might just be able to help you out."

"How's that?" Jackson asks, leaning back and crossing his arms over his chest.

Looking up at Gren, Kai says, "It was the Heavenly Relic they said they couldn't locate, right, buddy?"

Gren grunts.

"Thought so," Kai confirms. "If it's the Heavenly one you're after, we might have information on the whereabouts."

Eddie's eyes light up, and I feel an excited flutter in my chest. Before either of us can speak up, though, Jackson says, "And what's the catch?"

They lean back, feet coming off the table and landing on the floor, and they daintily place a hand on their chest, almost in offense. "Catch? What do you take me for? I think we're friends, here! We're all looking for the same things, so the least we could do is share our vast wealth of knowledge. I'm not sure what kinds of folks you've run into since coming to Midra, but rest assured, my ogre friend and I are just looking out for our fellow adventurers."

Out of the corner of my eye, I catch Eddie pushing down a smile at us being called "adventurers."

"I don't think Jackson is wrong in asking it," I say. "What are you looking for in exchange?"

Kai's eyes bounce back and forth between all three of us. "How out of town are you folks, anyway?"

Oh god. How to even answer that? I open my mouth to spit out something unconvincing along the lines of "very out of town," but Eddie swoops in and says, "Port Seliss, in

Hevara. We heard about the Relics and thought we would try our luck."

I exhale. It's times like these that I want to eat my foot for ever doubting Eddie's ability to catalog every nerdy fact into his brain for future use.

"You all came quite a way, then." Leaning their elbows on the table, they steeple their fingers in front of their face. "For such a journey, I'll only charge—let's say—thirty gold and a day's head start. All the Mages have bounties on their heads the price of that a hundred thousand times over. If you manage to get to the Relic before us and get one of them with the Dagger, we just ask we be cut in for thirty percent of your profits. We'll of course arrange how you can get us our cut once the deed is done, and with a Mage dead, we'll certainly know that the deed is in fact done. All in all, not a bad deal, yes?"

We look from the kindred folk to the troll—sorry, ogre— and they both blink at us, unwavering. Waiting.

"Uh, give us just a second to talk it over," I say.

Kai waves a hand casually. "By all means," they say, grinning with all the charm of a used car salesman. "Take your time." I give a half-hearted smile back before scooting away from them and closer to the boys. The two of them scoot in closer as well, trying to give our little conference as much privacy as possible, though with how easily they were able to overhear our conversation earlier, I have no doubt they're still listening.

"Okay, so is thirty gold, like, a lot?" I ask Eddie, whispering as best as I can. The chatter in the tavern is starting to pick up, with more people scurrying inside in the midday rush.

"It's decent," Eddie grumbles. "Do we even have thirty gold on us right now?"

All three of us shuffle through the coins Adrian gave us, trying to remember the conversion rate—silvers are ten copper, gold is ten silver, crowns are one hundred gold. All together, we have about forty and some change after our meals. "I don't know about you guys," Jackson says, "but I don't think blowing most of our money on someone who eyed us from across a bar is a wise spending decision."

"Well, what if they really do know where the fourth Relic is?" I say.

Jackson sighs, scooping his share of the money back into his hands and funneling them into his pants pocket. "We shouldn't be making this decision without Adrian here."

"Fuck that guy!" Eddie exclaims, a little too loudly for my liking. My eye wanders over to Gren, who shifts in place behind Kai, recrossing her arms and sniffing while arching a heavy brow in Eddie's direction. "We're not kids. If anything, Violet is in charge here. It's her quest."

At that, Jackson is silent. His eye roll is actually quite restrained.

"I see your point, Jackson, but Eddie is right. He gave us the money to spend. It's the only lead we have. It could make the difference between us finding May or not," I say.

Shaking his head, Jackson makes eye contact with me finally. I expect rage or even annoyance glinting in his gaze, but he mostly looks tired, with dark circles blooming underneath his eyes. "That money could also mean the difference between us eating or not. Can't exactly find May if we're starving to death."

"I get both sides here," Eddie says, looking quickly over his shoulder at Kai and Gren. "But this is exactly what you do in *Mages*, right? You have to make tough calls."

Jackson snorts. "Whatever. I know you're going to take her side. Just get on with it."

"Dude, what kind of integrity do you think I have?" Eddie says. "I'm not just going to take her side because she's Violet, okay?"

In a rare moment of synchronicity, Jackson and I both look at him, disbelieving.

"I mean, I am siding with her on this one, but not *just* because of that," Eddie says, defensively. "I think we need to take some risks. If we get too cautious, we might be edged out."

"Would it be so bad if they get the Dagger first?" Jackson speculates. "They could get the Crystalline Mage for us, in that case. May would be free to walk away."

"Apparently, that'd be a tough thing to do," Eddie says. "They're more likely to get killed, and then Crystalline keeps the Dagger. We don't have any bargaining chips that way."

"Or if they do manage to do it, they could use it on the wrong Mage," I say. "And from what Adrian said, it's one-time use. We'd be shit out of luck."

Jackson looks back and forth between the two of us and exhales, throwing his hands up in surrender. "Fine. Go ahead and pay them. Just don't blame me when we get swindled."

My heart pounds as Eddie and I count out the coins between us, Jackson glaring over at the two at the end of the table as we do. With this bit of information, we'll have all the pieces we need to get to May. The energy I'm giving off is palpable. I have to wipe my hands on my skirt a couple of times so the coins don't slip out of my grip and fall to the floor.

"Okay," Eddie says, pushing our pile toward Kai and Gren. "Thirty gold, and we'll give you guys a head start. Fair trade."

Kai, who has been silent this whole time, looks at the pile in front of them, their eyes reflecting the gold in front of them like a flint spark. Without taking their eyes off the payment, they cock their head toward the ogre and say, "Gren, put that somewhere safe, why don't you? Don't want any shady characters getting the wrong idea."

Gren sniffs in response, and as she swipes the coins off the table into a leather pouch that seems far too small for her massive hands to handle, Kai looks up at me, their teeth glinting as they grin.

"Well?" Eddie says, expectant. "Where's the Heavenly Relic?"

The smile falters as they turn to Eddie. "Hm? Oh yes, right. The Relic is by Rogue's Rock, outside of Unisgate by Lake Gy. It's a trek, but it'll be worth it, I assure you." They slip off the chair, nodding at Gren, a silent communication that I recognize comes from years of friendship or partnership—whatever it is they have together. They look back at us. "Pleasure doing business with you all. I hope this is only the beginning of our partnership, of course. Send a letter to Hermit's Hollow if you get to it first. Good day!"

They turn around, the ogre in tow behind them. The location is buzzing in my brain. Rogue's Rock. Why do I feel like I've heard that somewhere? I must have seen it while looking over the map in the guide, but why—

"Rogue's Rock? Are you sure?"

All our attention goes back to Eddie, who looks at Kai and Gren with eyes narrowed.

Having frozen in their tracks, Kai turns around to look at him, the grin back on their face, though it's pulled a little too tightly across their mouth. "Of course I'm sure!" they say. "Gren and I have been gathering this information from a lot of reliable sources. It's Rogue's Rock."

"What kind of reliable sources?" Eddie inquires.

Their smile starts to falter. "Now, if I told you that, I'd be giving away all my cards, wouldn't it?"

"Well," Eddie says with a shrug, mirroring their confident posture as he stands up from his seat. It's casual, but to me, it looks defensive, like he's squaring up to play charismatic chicken. "I just wonder how reliable they really are, because I know that Rogue's Rock isn't anywhere near Unisgate or Lake Gy. It's actually in the Verdantia Plains, near Fort Myr. The exact opposite direction you're telling us to go."

Shit. That's right. Rogue's Rock. It was the huge rock formation that Eddie saw when we glimpsed Velmyra back home.

"Whoever told you that must be mistaken, chum," Kai responds. "Rogue's Rock is nowhere near Fort Myr."

"Yes, it is," Eddie declares, an excited glint in his eye. "I've been there. I've seen it."

The kindred folk's smile falls all at once. The ogre behind them stands up just a hair straighter.

"Now," Eddie says, his hand slipping down to the hilt of his sword, "do you want to tell me where that Relic really is?"

There's a tense pause between us, the silence heavy in our contained corner of the tavern while the rest of the room is filled with rowdy drunken conversation. I don't dare move or even breathe. Beside me, Jackson follows suit.

It's Kai who makes the first move. The twitch of a smile lopsidedly twists across their face. "Gren," they say. "Let's go."

It's faster than I can register. A flash of olive green comes barreling toward us, and my body tenses, hands flying up to shield my face before I can even contemplate what's happening. A raucous scraping sound that vibrates from the floor up through my feet is followed by a swooping shadow, a wall of wood, and instinct takes over as I throw myself out of my chair and onto the splintered floor to avoid whatever it is that's coming toward me. I hit the ground hard, and I send up my silent thanks to Adrian for mending me up when he did. As I pull myself off the floor, I look down at my hands—a few splinters in them and some scrapes down my wrists, but at least nothing feels broken.

As I push myself up, catching my breath, I try to piece together what just happened as I survey what's in front of me. Our table is flipped over, leaning haphazardly against the wall, our chairs now abandoned and strewn around it. Jackson is on his feet, dazed but scowling, throwing curses toward the entrance of the tavern. A portion of the tavern patrons have paused, staring at us, though no one offers to help us out or asks what happened. A few of them only give us passing glances before turning back to the more important task of drinking their day away. From the look of it, this probably isn't even the most exciting thing to happen here all month.

Kai and Gren are gone, and I'm only able to catch a glimpse of Eddie bolting out the front door, his sword naked and gleaming in the afternoon sun.

I look at Jackson, eyes wide.

"Told you," he says.

"What the *fuck* happened?"

I look over toward the stairway leading up to the rooms. Adrian stands at the top, wide eyed and panicked as he surveys the clear chaos that has taken place. "Okay, I may have embellished about the mutton stew, but what the—"

"No time," I blurt out, pushing myself to my feet, and before either him or Adrian can protest, I'm shoving my way past tavern patrons, rushing out the door on Eddie's heels.

The light of midday is blinding as I come out in the open, squinting down the street to see which way they've gone. From the opposite direction, I hear a distinct "SHIT!" from a voice I know all too well. I follow the sound, and through shifting windows of people, I see Eddie barreling his way through the crowd. I break into a sprint in his direction, shoving my way through the fray and not sparing a glance back to see if Adrian or Jackson are following me.

The city is a maze. I move faster than I thought possible, the gap between Eddie and I closing little by little. As I run, the path in front of me starts to clear as people gasp and make way for the chase. Without rows of people in front of me, I can see clearly what we're dealing with: Kai is at the front of the line, far ahead despite their small legs. Gren is right behind them, glancing over her shoulder and snorting like an angry bull at the sight of Eddie, who clumsily sprints after them, his long limbs flailing and uncoordinated as he hurdles down the street.

"Eddie!" I shout. "Stop! It's not worth it!"

I can't tell if he hears me or not. He powers forward, nearly running into a street vendor as he does. Even from behind, I can tell he's losing steam, his gait less broad and the gap between him and Gren widening.

Cursing, I look around for any way I can get the upper hand here. The street vendor shakes his head, looking on after Eddie, his attention conveniently off his cart full of harvested vegetables.

Oh god. I'm so stupid.

As I pass by the cart, I skim my hand across the produce, grabbing the first thing I come upon. Glancing quickly down at what I've managed to get—is this corn? They have corn here?—I look back at Eddie, and without a moment's hesitation, I throw the vegetable at him.

I'm impressed by how far I throw it, watching it sail through the air, unimpeded. Maybe it'll actually hit him, and my very dumb plan won't seem so dumb after all. I watch as it soars toward him...

Over his head...

And right into the back of Gren's skull.

Of course, it doesn't hurt the ogre, merely bouncing off her head like it was a pebble. But she stops dead in her tracks, whipping around to face Eddie and I, her heavy hanging brow furrowing deeper.

Oops.

He and I stop in front of her, caught in her sights as her lips pull back revealing her pointed, uneven yellow teeth. With another snort, she reaches over her shoulder, as if to scratch her back, but pulls out a long club—unrefined and imperfect, with knots and points jutting out of it. She holds it in one hand as she roars, lurching forward to bring it down on us. I flinch, but the blow never comes.

Opening my eyes, my mouth falls open. Gren's club hovers above us, stopped in mid-swing by Eddie's sword, which digs a groove in the bumpy wood as he pushes his own weight against the ogre. His teeth gnash, heels sliding ever so slightly against the cobblestones. The fact that he's able to hold her back without instantly breaking his arms is incredible to me, but I can see he's faltering, his arms wobbling and sweat blooming into beads on his forehead.

"Gren, what's the—" a voice calls from behind the ogre, but they stop as I poke my head around to see that Kai has doubled back, looking like they've been caught in a pair of headlights. We make eye contact for a split second before they take off running again.

"No, you don't!" I yell at them, sprinting around Gren and Eddie's struggle and toward the kindred folk. I can already feel a stitch in my side and every blister I acquired on our walk into Castle's Edge, but luckily, the gap seems to be closing in faster than it was for us and Gren. Kai's tiny legs work overtime, but there's no making up for the fact that they're half my size and unable to cover as much distance as I can. With one last burst of speed, I catch up to them, almost clipping their heels as they run.

And I do the only thing I can think to do—tackle them to the ground.

I've never been athletic. It's not that I have no coordination, but I never had the desire to push myself during gym class or try out for any sports teams. I can't recall ever tackling anything in my life, and it's painfully obvious that I don't know how to do it since I more fall on top of Kai than strategically tackle them. I'm able to wrap them into a chokehold before they flail in my grasp, flipping me onto my back. It feels not right, like I'm wrestling with a child, but there's only a brief struggle before they start to worm their way out of my grasp. My arms aren't built to keep someone constricted in the kind of hold I have them in, and I can feel my muscles straining to keep them in place.

"Let go of me!" they shriek, bucking against me, knocking my head back into the cobblestone. "It's thirty gold! You're not going to die without it!"

I can't hold on much longer. If they keep squirming like this, I'll have to let go. Their hair is in my face, the top of their skull pushing into my chin, and something hits my right cheek. I manage to turn my head to see what it is, and my vision is lit up in glowing orange. The Infernal Residuum pendant that was hanging around their neck dangles next to my face, still hanging off them but tossed askew.

That's when I have my second stupid idea.

Just as my grip is about to give way, I let the hold I have on Kai go with my right arm, reaching up to the Residuum pendant and clenching it into my fist.

Our awkward dance halts, frozen in place as a forceful wave of energy rumbles through the ground below us and kicks us both into the air. I'm still wrapped around them, now holding on for dear life as we're catapulted who knows how many feet above the ground. It feels as though we're suspended, and just as I wonder if we're ever going to come back down, we plummet, my back hitting the cobblestone with a force that finally breaks my grip on Kai, letting them spill onto the hard stone next to me.

I groan. I feel as though I've been punched by twenty people all at once, but once I catch my breath, I think I'm okay. Nothing broken if my previous broken rib was any comparison. Slowly, I push myself up onto my hands. My muscles feel like pulled apart chewing gum after the strain I put them through. To my astonishment, Kai is still sitting next to me, not halfway down the street running off into the distance like I anticipated. They look past me, eyes bugged and mouth agape. "What in the Realms did you do, foreigner?" they ask, barely a whisper as they look down the street. I follow their gaze, turning around to look behind me.

A crack—no, a *gash*—runs down the street, the aligned cobblestones now broken apart as if something had burst out of the ground. I can't tell if I'm still dazed or if the high sun is giving everything around me a hazy glow, but I swear steam fizzles out of the fracture.

I look down, opening my clenched fist. The Residuum is still in my hand, the leather cord it was hanging from now split in two hanging pieces. The orange glow emanates softly from the stone in my palm, a fraction of what it was when I grabbed hold of it. Just as soon as I look at it, I bury it in my fist again, holding it to my chest, my breath catching in my throat.

What did I do?

"You two! Stay where you are!"

The voice startles me, and I jerk my head up to see a gleaming metal point leveled at my face. A suit of armor—I'm only assuming with someone in it—levels its spear at me. "Drop the stone!" they shout.

I do as they say, letting the Residuum fall out of my hand. As I hear it clink to the ground, what feels like a dozen sets of hands are on me, pinning me with my hands behind my back. My face is pushed into the stone, scraping my cheek as I instinctively try and pit my weight against those holding me.

Everything around me is a blur as I'm pulled roughly to my feet and dragged away. My senses are flooded as I catch brief glimpses of Eddie, Kai, and Gren all being pulled away—are Adrian and Jackson being pulled away too? I hear my name over a muddle of chatter, and the smell of heat and sulfur coming up from the ground is nauseating. I have no time to process any of it before I'm pushed forward, stumbling onto hard, splintering ground and encased in total darkness.

CHAPTER 14

"Whatcha reading?"

She flops onto the seat across from me, and I narrowly avoid giving myself a paper cut on the magazine I'm reading. The library is silent—no one wants to sit here during lunch except losers like me—but May has never given the atmosphere of a room much notice. She comes in, loud and bright, and it's everyone else's problem if they're disturbed by it. Casually, she props a foot up on the table we're sitting at, and behind her, the ancient librarian raises a thin eyebrow at her in disgust.

I close the magazine, subtly keeping a finger tucked between the pages I was on. "Nothing," I say, but she reaches across the table in a flash, snatching it from my hand.

May glances over the cover, her deep set brown eyes flitting over the bright images. "*Shonen Jump*. Is this anime?" she asks.

"Manga. It's like comics. Anime is cartoons." I feel the heat of shame welling up in my face. It's not as if May doesn't know I'm into that stuff. She's seen the comics I keep stuffed under my bed, the sketchpads of terrible drawings of my favorite cartoon characters, my ever-growing stack of PS2 games in the corner of my bedroom. She's never once made fun of me for it, but I still have this overwhelming urge to pull my shirt over my head and disappear as she looks over what I've been reading. Why, I can't say, but every time I expose part of myself to her that might not fit with the devil-may-care, cool persona she's been cultivating ever since we entered middle school, I feel so small and worthless, like she's finally going to wake up and realize that I'm nowhere near her level.

As she does with most things, though, she shrugs, tossing the magazine back onto the table. "Hm, neat. Didn't know you could get it in a magazine." She flips her long curtain of box dyed black hair over her shoulder, separating it into three strands and braiding it all together. "So, Ryan and some of the other guys dared me to sneak out tomorrow night and meet them in the park down the street from my house. Wanna come?"

The question is so nonchalant that I laugh without meaning to. "Are you kidding? Your parents would get so mad," I say.

Rolling her eyes, she says, "They'd be mad at me anyway. I can't take a piss in that house without someone telling me it's too loud."

I shift in my chair, kicking my sneakers into the carpet. "I don't know. What're they even going to be doing there?"

"Dunno. Stupid boy stuff, probably."

"They're not going to be doing, like, drugs or something, are they?"

Her hands have worked their way down to the last inches of her hair, but rather than leave her finished product as it is, she rakes her fingers through the intertwining strands, melding them back together. "Even if they are, you don't have to. If they try to make you, I'll kick their teeth in."

"I don't know..."

A hand clasps around mine. I look up at her, and a rush of warmth goes through me as we make eye contact. There are these moments where her casual veneer drops, and I can see the sincerity beneath it. She acts as though she doesn't care about anything, but those eyes betray more than I'm sure she intends. "Violet," she says, "I *want* you to come with."

I can't tell if her hand lingers too long or not long enough before she pulls it away, tossing her hair back over her shoulder and grinning at me like the devil. "Besides," she says. "Where's your sense of adventure?"

I'm pulled from the memory when the dark world around me jerks to a halt, my head knocking against hard wood. I blink awake—how long was I even asleep for? —but even though my eyes are open I'm still surrounded by darkness. Small shafts of light peek through the blackness around me, ribbons of gold that barely give me enough light to piece together my surroundings.

"Hey you, you're finally awake," someone says beside me in an obviously fake Nordic accent, and I turn to my left to see Eddie's shadowed face grinning at me. There's a tightness to his expression, though, like his muscles are being pulled at by fishhooks.

I shake my head at him. "Please tell me you haven't been waiting for an opportunity to quote Skyrim at me the entire time we've been here."

"I mean," Eddie says, the uneasy grin faltering, "not the *entire* time."

"What's happening?" I ask, rubbing the sleep out of my eyes.

The smile finally fades completely as Eddie glances around. "Don't know. We were rolling along for a while, but we just stopped. I'm not sure where we are."

I squint through the dark as my eyes adjust. When we were first thrown in here after the scuffle in town, I couldn't make heads or tails of where we had been taken. I resigned myself to taking a nap, since *fuck*, I was exhausted. Now, with the limited light, I can at least make out that we've all been shoved into what looks like a covered wooden cart, lined with a set of rickety benches that our sad little party now sits on. Everyone has made it here, including some that I wish hadn't. Jackson sits on Eddie's other side, his hands steepled on his forehead, elbows resting on his knees. Kai and Gren are also shoved in here with us. Kai's little legs barely skim the floor as they kick them ever so slightly, like a kid sitting in a highchair at a restaurant. Quite the opposite, Gren is huddled in the far corner, her massive shoulders hunched and head sloped to fit her entire body in here with us.

My stomach drops for a split second with the feeling that something is missing, but everything stabilizes when I turn to my right and see Adrian. Sighing with relief, I open my mouth to ask him just what the hell is happening, but I pause.

Everyone in here looks like hell—half of us have barely had any sleep, fueled by mutton stew and the grace of whatever gods are out there—but Adrian looks seconds away from collapse. Even in the dim light, his face is sallow and gaunt, dark circles under wide eyes that are staring at the floor intently, peeking from between his fingers as his hands cover his face, weighing his head in his hands as his elbows rest on his legs. He's unblinking, staring into nothing in his hunched position, his hair limp and hanging around his head like a dark cloud and his breathing shallow and quick. I can't quite place why it's so familiar at first, but once the thought occurs to me, it's clear. I don't recognize it right away, only because I've never seen myself while I'm like that.

He's having a panic attack.

I look around at the others, who have now taken to chatting —or bickering—with each other. None of them seem to pay him any mind.

"I'm sorry," Eddie says, his attention shifted away from me. "Did you just say this was *our* fault?"

Kai, crossing their arms over their chest, shrugs innocently. "I am only saying if you lot would have gracefully accepted defeat and not tried to raise literal hell in the middle of town, we would all be having a merry old time with wenches and ale right now."

"No, we wouldn't," Eddie corrects, glaring knives in Kai's direction. "Because we—the four of us over here—would be down thirty gold. Because you stole it from us."

Kai laughs, a combative chortle. "We stole nothing, my lanky friend. We came to an agreement on information in exchange for money. The only reason it didn't work out was because you didn't like the answer," they say.

"The idea was to give us correct information," Eddie says.

"I don't believe we mentioned anything about it being correct, did we, Gren?" Kai asks.

Beside them, Gren snorts in response.

"Exactly," Kai says, "so I really do not see what the issue is."

Jackson groans, setting his head back against the wooden cage. "God, would you all please stop talking? You all cocked up for different reasons, so there's no use arguing about it."

"Cocked up?" Eddie repeats. "We didn't 'cock up.' We got taken advantage of."

"After I told you how bad of an idea it was to trust the first two strangers who eyed us across a bar," Jackson retorts. "And now, we've gotten ourselves arrested on our first day in town. First day on planet, actually. Even better."

Narrowing their eyes, Kai looks from Eddie to Jackson. "What is that supposed to mean? Is that some foreigner code or something?"

"Yeah, it's code for 'none of your business,'" Eddie bites.

"Touchy touchy," Kai says. "I thought Hevarans were supposed to be easygoing and jovial from living in paradise every hour of their existence."

"We're not from Hevara," Jackson sighs. "We're not even from Fractum."

"Hey," Eddie says, eyes wide. "You want to shut up about all that? They don't need to know where we're from."

Kai leans forward, their eyes hungry. "Oh, but now I *really* want to know."

Jackson finally takes his eyes off the ceiling and glares at Eddie. "What does it matter, huh? We're all about to be put in fantasy Alcatraz. Whether they know we're from a different dimension or not won't make any difference."

"Different dimension?" Kai repeats. They pause, eyes darting back and forth, putting the few pieces that they have together. Finally, they look up at Gren, gently batting her massive arm. "We could have gotten them for a lot more than thirty gold if we'd known they were from a completely different world!"

Gren sniffs.

"Oh, for fuck's sake," Eddie says, exasperated.

The crosstalk starts to get overwhelming, and it's obviously not going to result in anything close to a resolution. I turn away and lean toward Adrian. "Hey," I whisper. "Are you all right?"

"Do I look like I'm all right?" he asks, his voice muffled as he talks between his fingers.

"Sorry, but do you know what's going on? Are we getting locked up or something?"

He drags his hands down his face as he straightens himself out, his hair hanging in his face. "We're not getting locked up. At least, not yet."

I furrow my brow. "What do you mean?"

"On the west side of Castle's Edge, there's a barracks that houses petty criminals. By the turns we made, we didn't head that way. We went for the north." Adrian looks me in the eye, his dark brown eyes hollow and morose. "Tell me: what do you think is at the edge of Castle's Edge? I'll give you one guess."

There's no way. I turn behind me to peer out between one of the gaps of the wood of the cart, but I can't make out anything, save for some grey stone and occasionally shifting outlines of people, which is followed by indiscernible conversation. "They brought us to the castle? But why? What we did couldn't have been that bad, could it?"

"Not what you all did, no."

I don't know what he's talking about at first, but then I remember. That "illegal stuff" he talked about...

How bad was it, exactly?

"Listen," I murmur to him. The bickering among everyone else in the cart has only increased, but I still don't want anyone overhearing me. "Whatever it is you did—I think now is a good time to clue me in. If we're going down for something, I think I have a right to know what it is."

He hesitates, opening his mouth and closing it again, no doubt debating with himself whether to brush it off, tell me the truth, or just come up with a bald-faced lie. But the look on his face is another one that I've seen in the mirror one too many times: the face of someone with no other facades to put up.

"Violet, I—"

We both jump as the doors to our wooden cage open, pouring orange-yellow sunlight into our dark hovel. The bickering between the others ceases. I blink against the sunlight, shielding my face to see what awaits us outside.

A row of heavily armored guards stands a distance away from us, spears and crossbows ready. Several of them hold what look like shackles, open and ready. In front of them, illuminated by sunlight is a man decked in the same dented metal armor that the others are wearing. The only difference I can see between them is the tunic underneath his breastplate is a vibrant burgundy, as opposed to the drab grey of the other guards. His helmet is off, revealing long, silky chestnut hair that flows just past his shoulders, small braids weaved in throughout framing his angular white face. His eyes are a preternatural blue, as if they're glowing, though it could be because of the waning latter day sun hitting them just right. He arches an eyebrow as he looks over us, a look of scrutiny that makes me feel like an animal in a zoo being observed for scientific purposes.

"This is all of them, yes?" the man asks, turning his head slightly to throw the question over his shoulder. I hold back a gasp. With his head turned, a pointed ear peeks out from beneath his long hair. Longer than a Vulcan's yet shorter than what you might find in a Zelda game.

One of the soldiers behind him calls back, "Yes, sir."

His gaze turns back to us. "Good. Shackle them and follow me. Her Majesty will be most interested to learn what trouble they have been causing in town today."

The soldiers file us out of the cart in mechanical fashion, clamping a set of shackles around each of our wrists as we're pulled out into daylight. I'm able to get a better look at our surroundings when my eyes adjust. Towering above us is indeed the castle we saw in the distance when first entering Castle's Edge—grey stone bricks all meticulously stacked upon each other form a menacing structure with spires that reach up higher than I can see without craning my head too far. From a distance, it looked like something out of Disneyland, but up close it appears that Cinderella's castle has been haunted for quite some time. There is no big swinging draw bridge to let us in, no moat to keep out unwanted visitors. We appear to be within another stone wall surrounding the main structure, so perhaps I missed the swarms of crocodiles on the way in.

Our shackles are connected to each other by chains, all held by one of the guards at the front of the line. If any of us trips, we'll take all the rest down with us. The guard yanks on the chain and we all take a lurch forward as we're led through an intimidating set of wooden doors into the main building. The other guards follow behind and beside, all keeping their weapons at the ready in case we try anything.

I look down at the shackles around my wrists, already feeling the chafe of tight metal against my skin. At first glance, they seem to be a plain set of manacles. Once we pass through the looming threshold, shaded by a briefly dark, low stone ceiling, the shadows tell a different story. Inlaid in the metal are glowing shards of faint purple light, set in no particular pattern underneath the surface of the metal. Heavenly Residuum. I'm only able to see their glow for the briefest moment before we're led back into the light, but the knowledge that they're there puts a nervous twist in my stomach.

As soon as we're in the light again, my jaw drops. The guards have led us into a grand open foyer, lined with huge stone columns and cascading tapestries on the walls. The windows lining the open area let in the fading sunlight, making the entryway look open and airy, yet casting shadows off enough places to make it look ominous and intimidating. I'm very aware of how dirty my shoes are as they move across the plush scarlet rug beneath me. Glancing ahead of me to Adrian at the front of the line and behind to everyone else, we all look too dirty, too scuffed up, too imperfect to be here. There's no way that common criminals—which I guess we are—come here often.

I lean forward, getting as close to Adrian's ear as possible. "Are you in any condition to talk your way out of this?" I whisper, my eyes darting forward to the front of the line to make sure Pointy Ears or the guard holding the chain aren't listening.

Head still slumped, Adrian takes an uneven, shallow breath. "Yeah, yeah, I can. Just let me talk, I guess. I'll figure—"

Mid-sentence, he stops as his body twitches in a sudden jerk, a shout involuntarily escaping out of him. He stops in place, and I run into him since I'm standing so close behind. From the startled "jeez!" coming from behind me, it sounds like Eddie nearly did the same. Adrian swears under his breath as he straightens his spine, pulling himself out the subsiding spasm.

Ahead of us, Pointy Ears and the other guard holding the head of the chain have stopped in place as well. The guard—whose scruffy bit of chin hair I can barely make out as his only discernible feature under his helmet—glares at us. Ahead of him, Pointy Ears keeps his eyebrow cocked. "Silence from the prisoners is required," he chides. He nods his head toward the scruffy guard. "Moorsfellow is a highly skilled residuuist, and I am sure at least one of you has figured out that your manacles are enchanted with Heavenly Residuum. It would behoove you speak only when spoken to, lest you receive a quite literal shock to the system."

Not waiting for any response, Pointy Ears turns on his heel and keeps moving forward. Sneering, Moorsfellow yanks on the chain, and Adrian lunges forward. The line starts moving again. I can tell by the tight set in Adrian's shoulders he's not happy, but he turns around and briefly meets my eye.

Without making a sound, he mouths the words, *"I'll handle it."*

The foyer is a long trek, but we finally stop at a set of stone doors, ten times taller than I am. "Line up!" Moorsfellow yells at us, and with a few menacing prods of threatening spears from the other guards behind us, we manage to line ourselves up in front of the entrance. The guards stand behind us, while Pointy Ears stands in front, hands formally clasped behind his back, his feet shoulder width apart. If this were home, I'd say he's in the military "at ease" position, with what little I know about military etiquette.

His head arched as he examines us, Pointy Ears speaks. "You are about to enter the presence of Queen Visandra, Her Majesty of Midra," he says, as if he is reciting from a textbook. "While in her royal throne room, you will remain silent unless directly addressed by the queen herself. If you are blessed enough to be spoken to, you will only refer to her as 'Your Majesty' or 'Queen Visandra.' You will keep your gaze averted and never meet her eyes. Failure to follow these instructions will result in something very similar to what you witnessed your friend here go through." He gracefully gestures to Adrian, and I feel him shift uncomfortably next to me. Pointy Ears looks up and down the line at all of us. "I suggest you think long and hard about how to comport yourselves in front of royalty." His gaze settles on Eddie, whose entire body stiffens beside me. "Any frivolity or japes will be swiftly handled. It will benefit you greatly to heed my words."

He turns around to face the stone doors now, pulling on a wooden lever beside it. While his back is turned to us, Eddie leans over toward me and asks, "Why did he say that looking at me?"

"Moorsfellow, if you will," Pointy Ears says, without moving.

"Gah, shit!" Eddie yelps as he jerks, flapping his bound hands to shimmy the manacles away from his wrists. He looks at the skin as the manacles slide down his forearm, and I can see pink burn marks already forming.

An intense scraping of stone starts as the doors before us start to open outward. It takes a moment for them to open completely. Beyond them is a short set of stone stairs, with two beefy guards dressed in the same grey tunics and plain armor that the guards behind us don, both standing back in place after pushing the doors open.

Pointy Ears looks back over to Eddie with his stoic blue eyes. "I said it to you because you seemed to be the one least likely to follow instructions. As exemplified."

Eddie glowers as the guards behind us step forward, forcing us to walk through the huge doorway and up the stairs.

Where the foyer was sprawling, its size pales in comparison to the throne room. We climb the short stairway and I gawk as we come up to the round room. This one is also lined with pillars, but these are made of silky marble, the sunlight glinting off of them and casting ivory light onto the walls. There is another long wine-red rug trailing down the center of the room, but the stone that makes up the surrounding floor has glittering jewels laid into it, some so small that I can barely make them out save for the tiny catches of sparkling technicolor light. They don't glow like Residuum, nor do all the colors seem to align with Residuum types. There doesn't seem to be a practical purpose to them at all. It's merely a display of opulence.

The rug leads up to a raised platform and a tall throne where a woman sits surrounded by a half dozen people dressed in purple clothes embroidered in gold, not covered with bulky armor like the guards. A few speak to her in hushed tones, gesturing emphatically. Another sits off to the side at a small writing desk, jotting notes on a stack of yellowed paper with a long-feathered quill pen. The last man, bald and short, stands off to the side, simply staring straight ahead, yet listening intently to what is happening around him.

In the middle of all this, the woman—the queen—focuses on those who speak to her, nodding and muttering back to them. As we walk closer, she doesn't look quite as regal as I thought she would. I was expecting renaissance ruffs, hoop skirts, and bejeweled crowns. But Queen Visandra, while intimidating with a sharp brow and pointed nose, looks more like a businesswoman than royalty. She is dressed in a champagne-colored long sleeved blouse and trousers that match, meticulously beaded in silver, swooping patterns that fold into each other like waves melding together. Hanging off her back is a long cape that cascades off the side of her throne and onto the floor. She wears her short, mousy grey hair slicked back, and instead of an ostentatious crown, a small silver and gold circlet rests just above her sharp eyebrows.

The queen's hazel eyes flit from the person in front of her to me, and I break my gaze immediately, heeding Pointy Ears' warning. There is only a millisecond's worth of time that our eyes truly meet, and with only that, I can feel the intense insight that emanates from them.

"My Queen," Pointy Ears declares as we walk up. The line of guards behind us stops, and Moorsfellow gives a warning tug on our chain. We halt, almost in unison. I swallow the tiny lump of fear that's gathered in my throat, chancing a fleeting glance toward Adrian. The look of dread on his face is even deeper than mine. What are we going to do if he has to make a case for us and it goes pear shaped?

The queen sweeps her gaze over us, not settling upon a specific person. She flicks her hand at the two hovering near her, and without a word of explanation, they bow and back away, retreating down the steps and past us. "Melandrich," she says, looking at Pointy Ears. "Is there a reason why you've brought me today's garbage? I am sure I have no use for it." I expect her tone to be much more refined, but she simply sounds unimpressed. Bored, even.

"My Queen," Pointy Ears—er, Melandrich, I guess—says. "Please, forgive me for the interruption, but this is a matter of utmost importance, one that I feel you personally would be interested in."

Queen Visandra looks over the rest of us again, as if we're merely a daily set of chores. "I am not usually interested in street scum, so I'm quite curious as to why you think these particular bits of gutter trash are fascinating."

"I assure you, My Queen, I shall explain." Melandrich turns to the guards behind us, motioning toward them, and without hesitation, one of the guards comes forward, producing a rolled-up piece of paper—fraying along the edges and off white, not like the computer paper we have at home.

All the while, the queen watches us, head resting on her fist, her legs languidly crossed over one another. Her gaze, as it bounces back and forth between the seven of us, is heavy. She's daring us to be worth her time. I rub my hands together, attempting to wipe the sweat off of them, hoping we're inter-esting enough to not be executed yet common enough to—well, to not be executed. I thought "stay alive" was the rule we had to follow when we were facing down monsters, not one woman.

Melandrich unfurls the scroll in his hands, clears his throat, and reads. "Just after daybreak this morning, four foreigners—"

"Sorry, actually, would you mind waiting a moment?" the queen interrupts, holding up a finger toward him. "I just realized I haven't eaten anything today, and I would *love* if someone fetched me something quick."

His mouth sets in a line, but he lowers the scroll. "Of course, My Queen."

She glances over at one of the attendants standing off to the side of the room, but without even a word of command, he is gone through one of the side doors. He isn't even gone a full minute before he skitters back into the throne room, carrying a platter of vibrant fruits. I recognize most of them—apples, bananas, pears, grapes—but there are a few lumpy shapes in there in bright blues and purples that I don't recognize. The queen briefly looks over the assortment before plucking an apple from the arrangement and waving her hand at the wiry attendant, who takes that as his cue to take his platter back to the kitchen.

She gives the apple a lazy shine on her shirt before biting into it, a line of juice running down her chin. "Continue, please," she implores Melandrich, mouth full.

He nods, clears his throat again, and picks up where he left off, going over everything. Literally. Everything. At least everything since we've been in Castle's Edge. It seems as though we hadn't been as discreet as we thought with our strange clothing and with Adrian buying a huge number of weapons and Residuum. The Royal Guard pinned us as soon as we got into town, only made worse when we caused a scene. Once Melandrich catches up to when we were apprehended, he rolls the scroll back up, handing it back to the original guard that had procured it. Politely, he stands with his arms behind his back. Unlike the rest of us in the room, he has no reservations about looking the queen directly in the eye, doing so with his head raised high. "Are there any clarifications I can make so far, My Queen?"

"As a matter of fact," the queen says, uncrossing her legs, "you have conveniently left out the bit I'm supposed to care about." Though she sounds bored, the queen looks back at Melandrich just as confidently and comfortably as he looks at her. With the rules he laid down before we walked in the throne room, I expected her to be much more of an authoritarian. But the energy between the two of them, at least, is relaxed, if not a little formal on Melandrich's end. If I didn't know any better, I'd say this was their version of friendly banter.

"All this would seem like common trouble making, of

course. However, in our investigations, we uncovered an interesting bit of information," Melandrich says.

Adrian tenses beside me, his chains clinking together. He exhales a shaky breath.

"Our witnesses indicated that they are looking for the Mage's Relics."

On the throne in front of us, the queen freezes in place, eyes still locked on Melandrich. But her bored expression shifts from irritated to suddenly attentive with just the flare of her eyes. She looks back on us, and the feeling an ant gets looking up at a boot intensifies. Her back straightens, and she leans forward. "Is this true?" she asks.

I look at Adrian again. Where he was slumped over and despondent, he is now standing pin straight, looking up at the throne in astonishment. The same thought running through my head is surely running through his right now.

They haven't figured out who he is.

And just like that, he turns on the charm.

"It is, Your Majesty," Adrian says, smooth as butter. "We are foreigners, as he said. We have heard that the Relics are located in Midra, so we traveled here seeking fortune. I do not think that is an entirely uncommon occurrence, certainly not one that's punishable."

Queen Visandra's gaze narrows at him, so slight that I barely notice it. "Not yet, anyway," she says. "Tell me: you admit to being foreigners. Where do you hail from?"

"Undra," Adrian answers, not missing a beat. "We four are just a band of misfits from Sedaris looking for a better lot in life."

He sounds so convincing that even I believe him for a moment, before Melandrich beside him clears his throat. "My Queen, that does directly contradict the information our witnesses in the tavern provided on the others' conversation with the kindred folk and the ogre. When asked about where they hail from, they claimed Port Seliss in Hevara to be their point of origin."

Mouth curling into a smile, the queen sets her head back on her fist, glancing back at Adrian with a smug satisfaction. "My, my. You all just keep getting more interesting by the second."

She stands up from the throne, and I'm struck by how tall she is. Her shoes clack against the stone as she descends the steps to draw closer to us, but they appear to be sensible, not anything ridiculously tall like stilettos. She approaches Adrian, standing only a couple of feet away from him. Adrian is half a foot taller than me, but she stands several inches over him. In my flat shoes, she feels like a giant. Up close, her furrowed brow and piercing eyes are even more intimidating. She looks him all the way up and down, assessing him. It's as though I'm invisible—as if we're all invisible as they stare each other down.

"I would like to know where you are actually from," she says. She's so close that I catch the scent of apple on her breath. "I can tell by the look of you that you are one who deals in lies. And I hope by the look of me, you understand that I do not take kindly to that."

Adrian licks his lips, a shimmer of uncertainty underneath his newfound confidence. "I'm sure I don't know what you mean, Your—"

Melandrich barely moves his head before Adrian's body jerks, a yelp escaping from him as though he's touched a hot stove.

"I'm sure you do," she purrs. I flinch as she reaches out for his face, but relax when she merely pats his cheek, though there is a roughness about it that doesn't sit right with me. "There is much that I do not know about you, but one thing I am certain of is that you are not stupid. To keep denying this is foolish."

"Your Majesty, I have told you the truth," Adrian says. There's a desperation to his voice, a pleading. For the briefest moment, his eyes dart to me, like he's looking for me to help, but he quickly looks back at her.

The queen's smile falls, and she looks at the guard beside

him. "Moorsfellow, perhaps we've been too easy on him. What do you think?"

Instantly, Adrian's body seizes, but it's different this time, not subsiding after the couple seconds Moorsfellow had given him before. It wracks his body, pushing him to his knees. I hear Eddie behind me suck in his breath. A wave of nausea rushes over me as he twitches, teeth clenched as he holds back a scream.

Reasonably, I know it only lasts for about half a minute, but it feels like an hour before he stops writhing on the floor, barely able to prop himself up on his hands and knees. He pants, sweat dripping down his face, the hair at the nape of his neck curling from the perspiration.

The queen is unbothered, still as a statue during the whole display. She can't even be bothered to crane her head down to look at him sprawled on the floor, her chin raised as she regards him. "That's more like it," she says. "Now, where are you from? The truth, this time."

Adrian sputters, pushing himself back to sit on his knees, though the effort it takes to do it is noticeable. His hair hangs in front of his eyes like a limp mop. He shakes his head. "Your Majesty, I can't tell you that."

"Can't?" she laughs. "You can't now? What a way to phrase it. Why not?"

Weakly, Adrian sighs.

"Take too long, my boy, and Moorsfellow will not be so kind this time around."

It's painful to watch him shake his head, closing his eyes in resignation.

"Perhaps you are a fool, after all. Very well." She nods her head back at Moorsfellow, whose mouth above his scraggly chin hair twists into an ugly, uneven sneer as he tightens his grip on the chain.

"Wait!"

The word comes out of me before I can think it. And to my surprise, everyone in the throne room listens. Moorsfellow is poised and ready, but Adrian makes no sound. He stares up at me, and it doesn't take long before I feel everyone's eyes fall on me.

Queen Visandra's gaze is the heaviest of all of them, those pointed hazel eyes cutting into me like razor wire.

I have to say something. I can't just say "wait" and expect them to keep doing it. But what can I say? There's no lie I could come up with that would be as solid as Adrian's, no story I could give enough details about to sound convincing.

Except, of course...

"We're not from Undra, Your Majesty," I say, my voice tiny like a cartoon mouse. "We're not from Velmyra, at all. Or Fractum. We're from somewhere—somewhere else."

The silence in the room sits over us like a weighted blanket. My back is toward Eddie but I can just imagine the look of horror he has on his face right now. Of all the ridiculous stories I could have blurted out, I decided to go with the truth. What other choice did I have, though? She wasn't going to listen to any of our other stories, since they've all conflicted each other so far. The only thing she could possibly believe was something so outlandish that it had to be true.

And given the curious arch of her brow in my direction as she and I lock eyes directly for the first time, I think my instinct is correct.

"What is your name, girl?" she asks.

I swallow. "Violet Spence."

Taking a step toward me, she asks, "Violet Spence, if you are not from Fractum, then where are you from? The Outer Realm?"

There are a few chuckles from the guards, and I think I even hear one from Kai down the line.

"No, Your Highness. We're—"

"Highness?" she repeats, seemingly taken aback but keeping her cool composure. "You would regard me as you would regard one of the Old Gods?"

"Oh, uh, no," I stammer. "I didn't mean—"

The queen holds up a hand. "Please. It is 'Your Majesty.' I do not deserve a title such as 'Highness.'"

"Yes, of course. I'm sorry, Your—Your Majesty." I inhale deeply. "We're from a realm called Earth, outside of this plane of existence. Another dimension, is probably what we would call it where we're from."

"I'm aware of what dimensions are, Violet Spence," she says. With me, she sounds much more patient than she was with Adrian. Maybe she's taking pity on me with how pathetic and terrified I must sound. "How did you manage to get here from another dimension, pray tell?"

"We used a Crystalline Residuum stone."

Her eyebrows raise. "You have Residuum where you are from? Then you must have Mages of your own."

"No," I say, shaking my head. "The Residuum came from here. We don't have magic in our world."

"That then begs the question of how it came to your world in the first place."

It takes everything in me not to look over to Adrian. The less focus on him in this situation, the better, I think. "I don't know how, but that's one of the reasons why we've traveled here. A friend of ours was taken, many years ago. From what we've gathered, we're pretty sure that she was taken by the—" I hesitate on the word before spitting it out. "H-Hellions of the Infernal Mage. We came here to rescue her."

"And what makes you so sure that they were the ones who took her?" the queen asks.

I take a breath in and let it out, quicker than I intend. "I saw them take her."

The cutting edge in her eye softens at that, her brows knitting themselves together as she searches my face. I can't look away from her, even as she reaches out her hand to touch my cheek like she did with Adrian. I don't flinch as her hand settles on my skin. Her thumb strays to underneath my nose, a strange gesture until I realize she's looking intently at the scar that sits there, her gaze traveling to the bend of my broken nose.

"Of course you did," she whispers, just low enough for me to hear. "They can't do anything without leaving victims in their wake."

She drops her hand, our intense tether on each other broken, and she takes a few steps away, looking down the line at the rest of us. "You're looking for the Mage's Relics to get back your friend, then?" she asks me.

I nod, still dazed. "Yes. We're hoping to use the Mage's Dagger as a bargaining chip. Either for information or for her to be given back to us."

"That isn't an awful plan. Although, finding the Relics is not an easy task. It's said that only the Mages themselves know their whereabouts," the queen muses.

"We've been given…" How exactly do I say this without sounding suspicious? "Reliable information. We're not certain, but we're hopeful."

"Hopeful." She mulls the word over like a sip of exquisite wine. "How fascinating. And does this information account for all of the Relics?"

I bite my lip before responding. "No. One is unaccounted for."

Queen Visandra's eyes settle back on me, and a massive grin breaks out over her face. "Just one. Hm."

She raises a hand and snaps her fingers, an echoing sound that manages to be commanding yet not insistent. "Melandrich," she says. "Fetch it for me, would you?"

Melandrich's eyebrows raise at the request. "My Queen, do we believe that is the wisest course of action? These are criminals, after all."

"Criminals with whom we share a common goal," the queen replies. "Trust me. I know what I am doing."

"As you wish," he says. With a quick nod, he strides off through the chamber doors beside the throne.

She watches him leave as he goes, and as soon as he is out of sight, she looks back at me. "You see, my sister was queen before me. She passed a few years ago. The Infernal Mage had ravaged the country to the north, and she was foolish enough to believe that she and an army would be able to destroy him." Her eyes go out of focus for a moment, a strange sight since her gaze has been so pointed. "Nothing can destroy him, of course. Or any of them, for that matter. Nothing, except possibly the Mage's Dagger. When I took the throne, I thought the rumors of the Relics were folly—nothing more than silly bedtime stories for children. But the ability to destroy the Mages—even if it was just one—was a thought too enticing to pass up. I have heard many whisperings of them, some of which sounded promising. But none ever came into my possession."

The side chamber door opens again.

"Save for one."

Melandrich treads to her side, holding in his firm grasp a box made of dark, purple hued wood. It's no bigger than an orange, but he holds it as if there is heft to it, encircling it with both his gloved hands as if it simultaneously weighs a thousand pounds and will break instantly if a swift breeze rolls by.

Queen Visandra turns to him, lifting the top of the box. As she reaches in, her grin is self-satisfied. And as she pulls out the box's contents, I can see why.

Between her fingers is a delicate piece of stone. It isn't Residuum, though there is something faintly ethereal about it, a soft lavender glow to it that can't be explained by any rational explanation. The stone isn't round—it is composed of branching tendrils, extending off each other like reaching fingers. Like branches of lightning.

"This," Queen Visandra says, "is the Heavenly Relic. The stories say it is a piece of fulgurite—a stone made of petrified sand, struck by lightning—created from the power of the god of the Heavenly Realm itself. It was actually Melandrich who procured it for me, in the far reaches of Hevara. Our first collaboration, one might say. You remember, don't you, darling?"

She smirks at him, but his face remains stony as he nods. "I do remember, My Queen," he says, and his voice has a gentleness that his face doesn't betray. "I look back upon it fondly."

The queen lingers on his face for a moment before looking back at the stone in her hand. "This was the first victory of my reign. Some days, I consider it the only victory. Midra still suffers from the plague that is the Mages. Presently, the Infernal continues his rampage across my kingdom, though it is chaotic and unpredictable. He will rain hellfire down upon towns for weeks and then disappear for months. At times, it feels much like trying to catch smoke in a jar. With this, I thought it would be a more attainable reality, but without the other three..."

She sets the stone gingerly back in the box, flipping the lid closed.

"It's useless," she concludes.

"Your Majesty?"

It's Jackson. I look in his direction, less cautious about leaning forward out of line to get a look. He stands at attention, but I can tell he's uncomfortable standing in the same place for so long by the way he shuffles on his feet. He doesn't say anything further, waiting for a go ahead.

The queen strolls toward him. "And your name?"

"Jackson, Your Majesty. Jackson King."

At this, she laughs. "King. What an auspicious name."

Jackson is silent.

"Please," she says. "Speak."

"Is it true that if a Mage in power is killed, the power is killed with them?" he asks.

She narrows her gaze at him. "Jackson King, for a foreigner, you know much about our Mages and their folklore."

He pauses for a second, and my stomach drops, worried that he won't be able to explain away how we know so much about all of this. But he soon says, "Where we're from, your world's history are fables. Stories we tell each other, tell with each other. They just happen to be based in truth."

The queen hums, thoughtfully. "Indeed. Well, then you would certainly know that no Mage has ever died while in power. Therefore, there is no way to know if that's true. The only information in regards to that is what has been divined from the Church of the Old Gods."

Even from my distance, I can tell Jackson is holding back a laugh. "So, you're willing to take bets on us collecting these magical items for something that you don't even know will solve your problem?"

"And what makes you think that is what I am proposing, Jackson King?"

He shrugs, as casual as if he were talking to a friend rather than a terrifying royal. "Why else would you show us that thing in the first place? We're nobodies. Unless, of course, you really think what we're saying has merit."

Her slender eyebrow quirks, but she merely smirks at Jackson, impressed. "How perceptive," she says. "I do not know if it is true what the Dagger can do, but I am willing to try anything, at this point. My kingdom suffers from more than just the problems these petulant children bring to it, but it is quite difficult to treat a broken foot when the patient is bleeding from the gut. The most pressing matter is the one that no ruler before me has been able to solve, unfortunately. And with the current Mages as unstable as they are, I fear we are running out of time before there are no further actions I can take."

She looks back at Melandrich and gives him a single nod, and just as he had before, he silently strides back to the side chamber, taking the box with the Relic with him.

"Which is why I must try. A ruler unwilling to seem foolish to the outside observer is no ruler at all, in my eyes. If I am wrong, then I am wrong. But I would rather say that I did all I could for my country and its people than nothing at all." Her face is as hard as granite as she speaks and doesn't lighten up as she glances back at the rest of us. "I am willing to be merciful today and offer you all a deal," the queen continues. "Considering your knowledge of the locations of the remaining Relics, if you collect them for me and return them, I will forgive your crimes. No time spent in the barracks necessary. As long as I have the weapon in my possession, all is forgiven."

I look back at Adrian, who has made it back to his feet after his stint. He looks stunned, but I can't tell if that's because he's still working off the shock or if Queen Visandra's offer is really that outlandish. It sounds outlandish to me. Like a death sentence.

The more I think about it, the more I realize that's basically what we were planning on in the first place. Only now, we'd have royal support.

"The choice is yours, of course," Queen Visandra says. "If you refuse, you may serve your appropriate term in the barracks. That won't do anything to get your friend back, however."

"We'll do it," I blurt without thinking.

Adrian laughs, strained as he stands up right again. "Now, maybe we should talk about this, Violet. I don't think Her Majesty would want us making any hasty decisions."

"Oh, believe me, I don't care how hastily you make them," the queen says.

His mouth flattens out into a line. "Right. Well, we should still talk about this."

"What's there to talk about?" I ask him. "This was the plan, anyway, and I would rather keep going with that plan than sit in jail."

He opens his mouth to argue back, but sighs, his shoulders slumping. There's a weariness on his face now, a culmination of our utter exhaustion and the effects of having electricity sent through him multiple times, no doubt. I almost feel bad, but if that's what it takes for him to shut up and let me take the reins on this, so be it.

"I, for one," Kai's voice drifts down the line, "think we

indeed need to talk about it. Namely, the fact that Gren and I have absolutely nothing to do with these vagabonds from another world. We are humble Velmyrans who have merely been tangled into the web of these foreigner's lives, so I believe we have no duty to fulfill such a task."

Gren grunts, though it's a grunt that sounds like "*keep your trap shut*" more than an agreement.

The queen doesn't even bother looking their way. "The deal extends to all of you. Again, if you wish to decline, the Guard will make sure you compensate for your crimes in another way."

"Uh, excuse me. Your Majesty?" Eddie says, raising his hand in his manacles ever so slightly. Oh god, he's raising his hand to talk. Kill me. "Hi. Edward Hughes, since we're…saying names. Uh, just thinking about logistics: if we're doing this for you, we're going to need that Relic you already have."

The queen raises an eyebrow at him. "And why would you need that, Edward Hughes? When you collect the Relics, you can simply bring them back here to me."

"We could, yeah," Eddie says with a shrug. "But chances are, the Mages aren't going to take kindly to their stuff being stolen. If that's the case, we need some sort of leverage. Some kind of protection. If we can form the Dagger, we can defend ourselves. Or, possibly, take one of them out ourselves."

She laughs, louder than she has yet. "You think you all are able to take down a Mage yourselves? Even with the Dagger, that is no small feat."

"Neither is traveling to another plane of existence," Eddie says. There's a bright shine in his eye as he says it, one that I can't help but smile at. "Yet here we are."

Her eyebrow stays raised, but eventually, she says, "Very well. You may take the Relic with you. However, that brings up another excellent point. I am not willing to just let you all run off into the wilderness unattended. Inevitably, one of you will have the bright idea to leave and not fulfill your end of the bargain. One of my guards will be joining you."

"Hopefully not Moorsfellow," Eddie mumbles under his breath.

Queen Visandra chuckles at this, and Eddie's face goes white at the realization she heard him. "No, not Moorsfellow," she confirms. "As you've already observed, he does not play well with others."

Under his helmet, Moorsfellow's mouth curls into a crooked grin.

"No, I think this is a job for you, Melandrich." She whirls around to face the stalwart guard, who has silently made his way back from the side chamber to the queen's side—a seamless transition that looks as though it has been practiced countless times. "You brought me the first of these. I think it only fitting that you bring me the rest. What say you?"

While Melandrich keeps his neutral expression, there is a small pull at the corner of his mouth, the first indication of resistance that I've noticed since I've seen him. But he soon says, "Yes, My Queen. It shall be an honor to bring them home to you."

With a nod to him, she turns back to the rest of us. "Excellent," she says, hands clasped behind her back. "I assume then that you all accept my generous proposal."

There is silence, which only seems to amuse her.

"I will take that as a collective agreement." She claps her hands together twice, before saying, "Remove their manacles and show them to the fourth floor, west wing. Tonight, they are honored guests of the throne. Tomorrow, they are warriors for the greater good of Midra."

One by one, the guards come around from behind us and remove our shackles. I rub at the chaffed skin around my wrists. Everyone else looks just as thankful as I do that they're coming off, especially Adrian, whose wrists are adorned with burn marks blossoming into blisters.

"Please, enjoy your stay at the castle tonight," Queen Visandra bellows as she clacks back up the steps to the throne, her long beaded cape draping elegantly over each individual step. "I would think it shall be your last sleep indoors for quite some time. Relish it while you are able. You will receive further instruction tomorrow morning."

She sits down, expertly draping the cape off to the side. "And please, if any of you has the bright idea of running out in the middle of the night, think twice. As they say, the Guard never sleeps."

The guards bark at us to turn around and walk back the way we came, though they are admittedly less gruff than they were before. We turn around, walking back toward the massive stone doors. Before I descend the small set of steps down onto the main floor, I glance back at the throne. While all eyes were on her, she exuded such refinement and confidence. But the queen that sits on the throne now rests her forehead between her thumb and middle finger, closing her eyes as Melandrich crouches down beside her, speaking to her quietly.

This queen is anything but grace and beauty. This queen is exhausted.

It is the only glimpse I catch of the real Queen Visandra, though, as I'm ushered down the steps, back into the grand foyer while the stone doors seal her in the room behind us.

CHAPTER 15

It's hours later that I'm led to my room for the night. I spend a long time separated from the others as a line of faceless guards ask me questions about where we came from and what we know about Velmyra. I tell them the truth. Mostly. I leave out the fact that Adrian is from here. The last thing we need is him getting in trouble for some petty theft over a decade ago. Though, with the way he reacted earlier, part of me wonders how bad that "illegal stuff" really was. In any case, I tell them he's a guy we met in Chicago who happened to find some Residuum, and I leave it at that.

When that's over, I'm brought up a grand staircase through an elaborate corridor draped with more tapestries and suits of armor. I can only guess if some are empty or have a guard stuffed inside them. After all the tall wooden doors we pass along the hall, we stop at one that opens into a gorgeous bedroom. Compared to the inn we were going to be staying at, this is like a luxury hotel. The walls are done up in blue, with intricate white molding along the floorboards. A gigantic four poster bed sits against the wall, next to a massive window with its lace curtains drawn, revealing the darkness that has fallen over the city of Castle's Edge. Off to the side, there's a painted wooden divider, and a gold-embroidered dresser sits next to it, a mirror as wide as I am tall affixed to the top.

"You are to stay in here until you are fetched tomorrow morning," the faceless guard says to me before leaving me there. "There are spare sets of clothes for you in the dresser. Try not to break anything."

Behind the divider is a metal wash tub, but it's empty. There is, however, a smaller wash basin with water on the dresser, and after a moment of searching, I'm able to locate a washcloth. It's nothing close to the bath I had back at the Amway before we left Earth, but being able to scrub the dirt off my face and under my pits at least makes me feel less grimy after rolling around in the forest and wrestling with kindred folk on the cobblestones all day. It's even more refreshing to find several new sets of clothes inside the dresser drawers, all boasting much more color than the drab garments Adrian purchased for us. I find a long white, shapeless gown that I assume—based on nothing more than HBO period dramas—I can use for pajamas. I let the dirty clothes haphazardly lay on the floor, save for my bra, which I set on top of the dresser.

I'm in the process of running a worn-down hairbrush through my tangled mess of hair when I hear a knock at the door.

I pause, mid-brush. None of the guards told me they were coming back to check on me, did they? And if that ominous warning about staying in here until tomorrow morning wasn't just a scare tactic, I doubt any of the others would be able to come see me. "Come in," I call, hesitantly.

The door creaks open, and Melandrich steps into the room.

Though it's only been a couple of hours since I last saw him, the Melandrich standing in the open doorway is not the same one I saw in the throne room, somehow. The stoic expression and sharp edge to his shoulders have disappeared, and in the place of his razor-sharp gaze is a softness to his blue eyes that I hadn't previously seen. He's changed out of his armor, instead wearing the burgundy tunic that was underneath it, a few of the top buttons undone. His hands are still clasped behind his back, but it feels more like the stance of a respectful house guest standing awkwardly in the foyer, less like a military pose. Strangest of all, he actually cracks a smile at me.

"Pardon my intrusion, Lady Spence," he says quietly, nowhere near the clipped orders he was throwing out before. "I hope I was not interrupting."

I set the hairbrush down on the bed next to me and cross my arms, suddenly very aware I'm not wearing a bra. "No, you're fine. There's not much for you to interrupt."

He nods. "I am aware that this must feel like a prison of sorts, but it is better than the barracks. Her Majesty was quite merciful toward all of you."

"Oh, I'm definitely not complaining," I say. "Compared to where we were staying before, this is heaven."

Melandrich takes a couple more cautious steps into the room. "There certainly are worse places to call home," he admits. "Even temporarily." He looks around the room, like he's marveling at the architecture, but his nerves are obvious. No amount of observing the floor molding can hide that.

"Are there other questions you had for me? I'm pretty sure I told my life story to your friends." The way he's acting has me on edge, for some reason. This has happened to me before, in college most frequently: a guy comes over to your dorm, unassuming, and then suddenly he confesses his love for you because you gave him an extra Jello cup in the cafeteria. All the mannerisms are there. But yikes. We haven't even said two words to each other. Is that how things work here? Is everything "*I saw you from across the room and knew that we were destined to be?*"

"Ah, well," Melandrich starts. "I did have some inquiries. I hoped now would be a good time to go over them."

"Uh, sure." I look around the room. There aren't any other places to sit aside from the bed. Great. "Do you want to sit or...?"

"Ah, yes. Pardon me." He walks forward and my stomach drops for a moment before he walks past me and the bed, over to the large window. I completely missed that there was a long window seat, covered in lavender cushions, and Melandrich sits himself down onto it, though he perches on the edge like he'll be standing up at any moment.

Every muscle I had clenched relaxes, and I scoot around to the side of the bed so I'm facing him. "What questions did you have?" I ask.

Melandrich folds his hands in his lap. "Well, it may not seem entirely interesting, to some. When you claimed that you were from an entirely different universe from our own, of course I found it difficult to fathom. Crystalline Residuum has been known to allow the ability to travel between space, even rumored to be capable of inter-universe travel. But many of these stories have been just that. Rumor. To see you openly professing that you are from a world entirely separate from Fractum is, well, stunning to say the least." He looks down at his fingers, which have been fidgeting as he talks. "I am simply fascinated with what a culture outside of our universe would entail. I wondered if you would be willing to share some details from your world to appease my curiosity."

"Oh," I say, taken aback. So definitely not a confession of love. "Well, sure. I'll do my best. I'm no anthropologist, I guess."

"No need to be one," he says. He somehow scooches forward in his seat, his bright blue eyes hungry and excited, and my mind must be playing tricks on me because I swear his pointed ears perk up at my willingness to talk to him. "I'm simply looking for rudimentary answers. Also, this is for my own personal interest, nothing so official as before."

I have to stifle a laugh. How is this the same steely faced man who arrested us and led us in here? He's as excited as a puppy with a new toy. "Okay, well, fire away."

The questions come at me one after the other. What are the nations of Earth? There's too many for me to list, so I give him a few of them by continent. What sort of transportation is there? I blow his mind when I tell him we have giant metal vehicles that are powered by oil and natural gas that take us from place to place. What other creatures are there besides humans? Millions, but none of them can talk or communicate the way humans can. Every answer only brings up a new question, and once I answer that for him, he devours it in one bite and spits out another. I don't have any siblings, but I feel like this is what it's like to be an older sister, spewing out answers to non-stop questions, fearing the one question that comes your way that you don't know how to answer. Despite how rapid fire it is, it's still endearing, as Melandrich nods thoughtfully at my sometimes vague, mumbled answers.

Eventually, he asks me about religion.

"Well, we have a lot of religions," I say. "Where I'm from, one of the bigger ones is—well, I suppose they believe in one big god that created everything, but then split himself into smaller parts? One of the parts was a guy who died so that sinning wouldn't send you to Hell, I guess."

"Fascinating," Melandrich says, his fingers steepled in front of his nose. "Only one god that created the entire universe? Surely that would be too daunting a task for one being."

I shrug. "Some people don't think so. But there are other religions that have multiple gods. A lot more of them, actually."

"Very interesting."

"That's what it's like here, right?" I ask. "I don't know much about Velmyra, but you believe there were multiple gods that created everything? And that's where the Mages came from?"

Melandrich's face darkens, but he nods. "That is merely one belief, mainly in Midra. Though there are several religious outlooks in Velmyra alone that try to explain our world. The Mages, mostly. The Old Gods' religion claims that there was a good purpose for them once, but..." He trails off, his face growing somber. "Well, I suppose you know that is not entirely the case."

I hesitate before speaking. "Is it—is it really true that every human who's become a Mage has been corrupted by it? There hasn't been one Mage who's used it to make the world a better place?"

Melandrich cocks his head to the side. "That is difficult to say. Historically, no. The records we have of the Mages are incomplete. Very rarely have they wanted anything to do with Midran society, therefore few of our archivists and historians have actually been able to speak with one. The record of their destruction, however, has been well documented. That is not to say that some Mage has not done good deeds in secret. There are many gaps in the histories that could allow for such a thing."

"That's pretty optimistic."

"It is not the sentiment everyone shares, to be sure." He shifts in his seat. "As you saw, Her Majesty believes them to be beings of pure self-indulgence and indifference. Though, with her history, I can see how she may think that way."

"Because of her sister?" I ask.

Melandrich nods. "Queen Veridian's death was before I came into the employ of the Royal Guard, but through my time with Queen Visandra, I know it affected her greatly. They were the cause of her death, and Her Majesty has sworn to never forget that fact. Also..." He stops, mid-sentence, closing his mouth quickly like he just realized he was talking.

"What?"

Wincing like I just pinched him, he shakes his head, "I do not know if I should be telling you everything. It is public record, but..."

"I mean," I say, "who am I going to tell?"

"Your friends, for one."

"They're harmless, trust me." I'm not sure why I care what he's trying to hide. Something about the way he's been so forthcoming and now suddenly tight-lipped has me curious. "We don't have any investment in Velmyra. As soon as we get our friend, we're going back home. Whatever it is, you can trust us."

His eyebrows knit together, worried yet soft edged. "Well," he says, after a sigh. "This is all secondhand information. Like I said before, I never met Queen Veridian. However, there is royal court record that I discovered not long ago that sheds an interesting light on her relationship with the Mages. Namely, at one point, she was able to incarcerate one."

I raise my eyebrows. "She caught one? Is that how she died?"

"No, this is a completely separate incident," Melandrich says. "From the account I read from the royal scribe, there was a major incident in the town of Tersaria, near the eastern coast. Hundreds dead, thousands injured or displaced."

"Which of them caused it?" I ask, something strange leaping up into my throat.

Shaking his head, Melandrich says, "It seemed to be at least two of them, but the accounts vary. Some witnesses say all of them were there. The one through line was the Infernal and the Crystalline. There were no doubts that they were there that day. Which makes it strangest of all that reportedly, the Infernal went to Castle's Edge days later and turned themself in to Queen Veridian."

"He just walked up and presented himself to her?"

"The records I perused did not refer to them by any gendered terms, only describing them as 'the Infernal.' There is little description of who these Mages were at the time. The witnesses in Tersaria have given reports of every gender imaginable, as far as I can tell. But that is beside the point. The mere idea of a Mage freely giving themselves to a sitting royal was unheard of, is still unheard of. I do not think it shall ever happen again in my lifetime."

"Did they say what the reason was?"

"The only details given were—and this is my recollection after reading the record over a year ago—'The Infernal gives of themself due to remorse over their actions.' Nothing else was said over motives."

I nod, kicking at the rug as I swing my legs back and

forth. A Mage with remorse. I'm not even a citizen of Velmyra, but from the little I know of them—from the game guide and from Adrian himself—such a thing seems impossible. I think of the Infernal Mage, sending their Hellions to our world for May. Of the Crystalline Mage keeping her, like a prize-winning pet. That strange something in my throat hardens into a lump.

"Any other sitting queen would have had them executed," Melandrich continues. "From my time with Queen Visandra, I know if she were given the opportunity, she would be the one to bring the blade down on their neck herself. Queen Veridian, however—all accounts I have heard and read make it clear she was never one for swift justice. Justice, of course, but tact before anything else. And her plan was admirable. I only wish it had worked. She consulted the local Church of the Old Gods and recruited a monk to take on the power of the Infernal, which the Mage willingly gave."

I frown, knowing what his grim tone implies. "And that's the current Infernal Mage, isn't it?"

Melandrich hangs his head, though still with perfect posture. "By all accounts, yes. And the one that caused the end of the late Queen Veridian's reign."

I knew that was coming, of course. I know that Visandra's sister's time ended at some point, but the fact that she gave someone the chance—a monk, of all people—to show that Mages weren't inherently corrupted, and they murdered her without a second thought...

I swallow that hard lump in my throat, forcing it down so my voice doesn't break. "Why do you still believe they can be good, then? Even if the previous Infernal showed 'remorse' or whatever they want to call it, they still killed hundreds of people. Does being sorry about it really erase that?"

Melandrich inhales deeply, furrowing his brow, taking his time before answering me. "For me, it is something much more complicated," he says. He looks back at me, lifting his hand and flicking one of his pointed ears poking out from beneath his long dark hair. "You have observed these, I am sure."

I nod.

"Since, as you have told me, your world does not have any other intelligent creatures besides humans, I am not sure how to explain this. In Velmyra, it would be common knowledge. I am half human, half fey. Have you heard of such a term?"

"Oh, yeah," I reply. "Fey, like fairies, right?"

He chuckles quietly. "That is a very old name for us, but yes. The fey mostly reside in Hevara, which is detached from the other three nations on this side of the world. That is where I grew up, and it was the Hevaran court I served until seven years ago, when—when Queen Visandra took me in as part of the Royal Guard." He clears his throat, straightening himself out before continuing. "In Hevara, we do not believe in the myth of the Old Gods. We, of course, acknowledge that the Mages exist and have been granted great power, but our culture believes that this power was manifested by them naturally, not through means of divine intervention. The fey themselves are believed to be children of the Earthen Mage, formed out of the very ground of the Hevaran wilderness by their hand. Therefore, we rely on nature for what it provides us. Midrans—the reigning royals, in particular—believe that intervention must be taken when their own are attacked. Hevarans believe that when something unfortunate falls upon them, it is the way of things. We must let nature take its course as it sees fit and adapt accordingly. For a long while, I believed this to be true of the world."

"And Queen Visandra changed your mind?"

He tilts his head as he looks back at the floor, thinking for a moment. "In ways, yes," he finally answers. "She and Midran society introduced me to new ways of thinking, yet the benefit of being of two worlds—of being me, I suppose—is that I see what both sides value, and I am able to draw conclusions from both perspectives. And I do not believe Hevara and Midra are far off from each other. I think the Mages are human and therefore easily lose themselves in something bigger than what they may be able to handle. While this is the way of things, yes, something should be done in regard to their campaign of destruction. Hevara is on the end of indifference. Midra is on the end of decisive and equal retaliation. If asked, I would say I fall in the middle." He softly laughs again, rubbing his thumb into his palm. "I have always thought if Queen Veridian and I were to have met, we would have seen eye to eye on many things."

"And what about Queen Visandra?"

The gentle smile comes back to his face. "I owe much to Queen Visandra, including my life. Were it not for her, I doubt I would be alive today." He rubs his thumb into his palm harder, an irritated redness forming along the ivory skin. "Yet, there are times where I feel—"

Melandrich stops suddenly and stands from his perch. For a moment he's still, staring at the floor frozen like a statue, his eyes ever so slightly darting back and forth. But he soon clears his throat, smoothing his tunic out and clasping his hands behind his back. "It does not matter what I feel," he says, and he strides past me back toward the door. The robotic movements of the stoic Guard captain have returned, a smoothness to his gait that doesn't seem natural. "I will do whatever Queen Visandra deems necessary, of course. That is my duty: to aid in her reign."

I crawl back over to the foot of the bed to face him. "Yes, but she trusts you, doesn't she?" I ask him. "If you think the Mages can be redeemed—or at least, if you think what Veridian was doing was on the right track—why wouldn't you try to convince her of that?"

Stopping at the door, he turns back to look at me. His mouth is a flat line on his face, and his brow sets back in place along with it. Right in front of my eyes, the excited man of a thousand questions morphs back into a hardened soldier. "Because, Lady Spence," Melandrich says, a sadness seeping through the business-like cadence in his voice. "There is no convincing the queen of anything else."

It's only a few minutes after Melandrich leaves that I douse the candles that line the room and try to sleep. The moonlight from outside seems to be providing just as much light as the candles did, though. I lay in bed, eyes wide open, able to see every corner of the room illuminated. I guess if some assassin were sent to kill me in my sleep, they'd have nowhere to hide.

I can't help but replay my conversation with Melandrich in my mind, a bigger sleep deterrent than the moonlight is proving to be. Between the way he shifted so quickly between a normal man and the head of the Royal Guard and what he said about the Mages being complicated, not just doomed to devolving into soulless monsters...

I don't know what to think of it. All this time, I believed what Adrian said. That they, with all that magic raging within them, had no room for empathy or kindness. And of course, I believed that. Why else are we here, if not for the callousness of these people with more magic than they know what to do with?

But one of them turned themselves in. They felt remorse. They gave up the magic willingly.

How am I supposed to make sense of that?

A soft knock at the door makes me jump, and I gather the sheets around me out of impulse. I open my mouth to ask who's there, but the door creaks open. Just as I think the assassins are getting lazy and skipping the formalities, Eddie appears, shutting the door behind him.

I sigh in relief, dropping the covers. "You scared the shit out of me."

"Sorry," he says. His voice is low, but it isn't in a full whisper. He doesn't seem to have changed clothes at all, wearing his simple linen shirt and too short pants. "I couldn't sleep, so I asked my guy if I could go to your room."

"And he let you?"

He shrugs. "I mean, he came with me. He's standing out there with your guy. I'm sure he doesn't mind the company."

"Still..."

"What are we going to do?" Eddie asks, walking toward the bed. A column of moonlight falls over him, and I can see his hair is down, a tousled mess probably from tossing and turning in his own bed. "We're four stories up, so we can't really escape. They probably just think we're gonna bang or something."

"I guess," I say. "Did you want to talk about something or...?"

Eddie shakes his head. "Nah," he says. "Just thought I'd stand a chance of actually falling asleep if we were together."

At this, I can't help but smile.

He crawls into bed, lying flat on his back, and I curl up on my side, facing the edge of the wool and hay-stuffed mattress. I wrap some of the covers around me tighter, but I'm sure he doesn't mind because he gets hot in the middle of night. We know the routine. It doesn't happen every night, maybe not even every month, but we've slept in the same bed enough that we know each move the other is going to make—each twitch of a foot, each toss and turn. The bed is so huge that we don't touch each other at all, but the knowledge that the other is there is all the comfort that's needed.

I don't ask him what he said about Adrian to the Guard. I don't tell him that Melandrich visited me. I wouldn't have time to, anyway—within minutes of him laying down, I hear his soft snoring. He's asleep right away, and pretty soon, so am I.

CHAPTER 16

T he morning comes at us quickly. The sun is barely
creeping across the floor when there's a bang on our
door, a thundering voice urging us to get up and
collect anything we need to take with us. It doesn't take me long
to wipe the sleep out of my eyes and put on a new set of clothes
from the dresser—a pair of loose fitting trousers and a button-up
shirt and vest. There are dresses in there which I take out and set
aside to pack for later, but given we're headed to the first Relic,
thigh chafing is not something I want to deal with in the middle
of the forest. Once I'm dressed, I try to shake Eddie awake,
pleading with him to get up so we can get food and get out of
this damn castle, but he throws the "five more minutes" bargain
at me. He gets up eventually, only after I pull all the covers
off him.

Opening the door, two guards hand me some empty ruck-
sacks, rustic but unused. While Eddie lazily throws clothes on, I
shove extra changes of clothes into my pack as well as wash-
cloths, the brush I used the night before, and other random
ribbons to tie my hair back. There isn't much in the dresser, but I
take what I can while leaving some extra room. It's better than
what we had, which was nothing.

My stomach drops while I'm closing my pack. Our other stuff is back at the inn on the other side of town. The weapons and clothes, that doesn't really matter to me, but the game guide and the twenty-sided die...

"You ready to kick some Mage ass?" Eddie asks, shaking me out of my panic. He throws his haphazardly packed bag over his shoulder and gives me a big grin, the last of the sleep finally worked out of his system.

I give him a weak smile back, forcing back the unease. I guess that stuff is just gone. "Yeah, let's go."

The guards take us downstairs, past the massive, closed doors of the throne room and through the cavernous foyer out the way we came the day before. We exit into the front courtyard, covered in the shadows of the looming stone walls that surround it. Standing off to the side is our traveling party. Adrian leans a shoulder against the wall while Jackson crosses his arms, a rucksack very similar to the ones we received slung over both his shoulders securely. Kai and Gren have formed their own faction a few feet away from them, with Kai talking excitedly and glancing over at Jackson and Adrian every once in a while, suspiciously. Gren only grunts, which I've picked up is her favorite form of communication. Melandrich is also there, speaking with some of the armored guards in his rigid, in-charge stance, though he is wearing simple leather protection over his clothes today rather than the clunky metal armor he was adorned in yesterday. Everyone else has been given a fresh change of clothes too, much more colorful and durable than the thin, bland clothes Adrian found for us.

Eddie walks right up to Jackson, already closing Adrian out of the conversation with the angle of his body as he approaches. "Quest time!" he exclaims, holding his hand up for a high five. "You excited?"

Smiling, Jackson slaps his hand. "You know it, dude." He laughs, but his face soon goes flat when his eyes land on me. Still, he manages to nod at me, at least acknowledging I'm there.

I nod back. Still keeping it civil, I guess.

"Very well. I assume we are prepared to depart?" Melandrich chimes in over our chatter.

There are various replies—some grunts, weak "yeah, I guess's" and "sure's." Obviously, we all need coffee. If that's a thing here.

Melandrich doesn't flinch at our unenthusiastic responses. "Good. Now, before anything else, the matter of weapons does need to be addressed." He takes his own unassuming rucksack off his shoulder, opening it and rummaging through it for a moment before pulling out a red leather pouch, which fits comfortably in the palm of his hand. He holds it out for us to look at. "By your slack-jawed expressions, I am to assume you do not know what this is." Giving it a little toss in the air, he says, "This may seem like a small container, but the inside is large enough to hold a cache of weapons and Residuum."

Behind me, Eddie quietly gasps. "Boundless Satchel," he whispers, punching my arm lightly. I hold back a little smile myself. In the game, Boundless Satchels are enchanted bags infused with magic from Crystalline Residuum, creating a small pocket void inside the object so that you can store a large amount of belongings on you without being encumbered or running out of space. Incredibly useful and incredibly rare. Though, this is royal resources we're talking about. Queen Visandra can afford to enchant a few objects, I suppose.

With another small toss, Melandrich puts the pouch back in his rucksack. "When we near the Relics, I will distribute them as I see fit. Any attempts to pilfer this at any point will end… poorly, shall we say. Consider that your first and final warning." Throwing the bag over his shoulder, he pauses, looking over our surely bewildered faces before saying, "Well, if there are no further queries—"

"Uh, query from me, actually," Kai pipes up. They look around the courtyard, exaggeratedly. "Don't we get horses? A wagon? Something?"

Somehow raising his nose higher, Melandrich replies, "Her Majesty believes this mission should be carried out as quietly and discreetly as possible. That means, on foot."

Kai throws their hands up, already exasperated. "Are you kidding?" they ask. They point to Adrian, who furrows his brow in their direction. "He's a residuuist, for crying out loud! Can't he just pop us to these places with a bit of Crystalline?"

"With this many people and all the distance we need to cover, we'd need a whole lot of Crystalline. More than the queen has in her stash, am I right?" Adrian asks Melandrich.

Melandrich narrows his gaze slightly, but nods.

"Un-bloody-believable," Kai sighs. They look up at Gren. "I don't suspect you'd be willing to carry me the whole way, would you?"

Gren snorts.

"Didn't think so."

"Very well," Melandrich says, a little louder than usual. "*Now*, if there are no further queries, let us be off."

As we walk across the courtyard, the large gate that leads to the outside opens, the harsh scrape of stone echoing off the walls around us. We silently follow Melandrich's lead as he guides us through the archway down the sloping path that leads back into the city.

As we pass through, Adrian pulls up beside me. "You ready for this?" he asks, still staring straight ahead. With no styling products readily available to him, he's resorted to pulling his hair back into a small knot at the back of his head.

I swallow. "As ready as I'll ever be."

"Good answer," Adrian says. Glancing at me quickly, he lowers his voice, enough so that I'm probably the only who hears him. "When we get a moment, we should talk. Just us."

I look back at him, confused, but he's already pushing forward ahead of me. My teeth instinctively clench as I stare at his back, the bustle of the city starting to swallow us whole.

It's a handful of blocks into the city when we find ourselves in the market—an entire street dedicated to food, packed to bursting in the early morning rush. Familiar smells curl underneath my nose, as well as new smells that are no less enticing. As we snake our way through the crowd, Melandrich says we can take ten minutes to purchase any food we might want before we exit the city limits, distributing a few silver coins to each of us. With money in my hand, I look around at the vendors, unsure of where to start. As I do in most crowd situations, I cling to Eddie, who eagerly bounces from booth to booth, eyes wide and mouth running about what he thinks each one is selling. I can only guess myself. Some of the foods look like things you would find on Earth—pastries and rolls are passed from vendor to customer in crinkling brown papers, apples and oranges tossed in exchange for small copper coins—but others are unfamiliar meats on sticks, vibrantly colored fruit fillings peeking out between folded baked dough. Eddie asks me what I want, and I tell him to surprise me, shoving my silver coins in his hand and squeezing myself out of the crowd and off to the side of the street near an alleyway.

I take a deep breath in through my nose, out through my mouth. *Don't let it overwhelm you*, I tell myself. *We'll be out in the woods soon, and your feet will hurt so much that you won't have time to think about anything else.*

I close my eyes, telling myself that but not really believing it. So much is taking up space in my mind right now—the fact that we're here, the fact that we're criminals, that not only does getting the Relics mean getting back May, it means staying out of prison. The conversation Melandrich and I had, the idea that Mages might not simply be power hungry monsters, but just people given too much to deal with, kind of like me—

Something grazes my shoulder, just enough to break me out of my spiral. I look to my right, but no one is standing next to me. Glancing back in the alleyway, I expect to find nothing but emptiness, more proof that my mind is playing tricks on me.

But something is there. A dark outline of something shapeless and tall. A cloaked figure, I think at first, but there's something different about it.

It's glowing.

It's getting farther away from me, but there are cracks in its dark mass that bleed orange-amber light, simmering like the light of a cinder at the bottom of a fire pit. The perfect temperature for roasting marshmallows, my dad would always say. That's what the figure reminds me of. A walking cinder.

I don't know what compels me to follow it, but I do.

I keep my distance as I follow its trail, making sure there's enough space between us where I remain unnoticed but not so much that I lose sight. It glides across the uneven cobblestones that line the narrow alley, like it isn't taking steps so much as it's hovering. My mind was so full of jumbled thoughts just a moment ago, but the steps I take aren't thought of. They just happen. It's like those shimmering cracks of orange light force my feet forward, magnetized by some unknown energy.

I dare to pick up my pace, the echoes of my footsteps growing louder. I just want to get a tiny bit closer to get few more details of the figure. There isn't anything I can see besides the fissures of light, though. I wipe my brow and find I'm sweating. Strange for how chilly it's been this morning, but now that I think about it, I'm boiling, and it's only getting hotter the closer I get—

"Violet?"

Something falls on my shoulder, and I whirl around, yanking myself away from whatever has me, my heart nearly bursting out of my chest.

It's Eddie, his hand clasped on my shoulder, his brow furrowed in concern.

My heart reluctantly slows.

"What are you doing down here?" he asks. "We're getting ready to go."

I look behind me, back into the alley.

The figure is gone.

I lick my lips, my mouth suddenly going dry. A breeze rolls by, and the exposed skin of my collarbone rises in goosebumps. Where I was sweltering a moment before, it seems to be back to its brisk early morning temperature again. "I thought I saw something."

He raises an eyebrow. "Like what?"

"Nothing," I say, shaking my head. "It was probably nothing. Let's get going."

"Okay," he says, but there's a caution in his voice. He doesn't take his eye off me as we walk side by side back to the mouth of the alley, and he hands me a paper package, still warm as it settles in my hands. "Got you this."

I unwrap it. In the center of the crinkling brown wrapping is a golden-brown pastry, the layers of it already flaking off. On the sides, a bit of bright pink jelly oozes out, brighter than any fruit jelly I've seen back on Earth.

"What is it?" I ask.

"No clue, but I already ate mine, and it's fucking delightful."

We reach the mouth of the alley, and the rest of the crew is already there. Some, like Melandrich and Adrian, are waiting patiently, while others—Jackson and Kai, mostly—look at me annoyed. I throw out some vague excuses to placate them, which they accept, and Melandrich orders us to move along.

Before we go, I look back down the alley. For a split second, I swear I see the cinder cracks. But it isn't long before my eyes adjust, and I'm looking blankly into shadow once again.

It takes a couple hours before we're out of the city. Melandrich has a map, which he consults as soon as we're out in the flat plains of farmland that lead into the forest a few miles away. "If what information you have is correct, the Earthen Relic in Marwindale will be the closest to us now. After that, we will go back into the forest to retrieve the Crystalline Relic and finally to the Old God's Temple to retrieve the Infernal." He shows us on the map the direct line we'll be making, skirting mostly on the edge of the forest as we head to Marwindale. It doesn't seem too far as just a few inches on the map, but I remind myself that those few inches are dozens of miles. I can't see a scale from the brief glimpse he gives me, but I'm guessing that we will be walking for quite a while. More than just today.

So, we walk. The flat farmlands roll on for most of the morning, the sun rising higher in the sky and heating up the air around us. As we near the edge of the forest, I take off my vest and roll up my sleeves. The cover of trees at the edge of the Midran Forest is a godsend, the canopy above us providing a perfect amount of shade just as the sun reaches its zenith. Thank god for that. I'm trying not to sweat through this shirt right away. Laundry is something that hasn't really crossed my mind until now. If it keeps up like this, we're all going to stink to high heaven.

The factions we started in mostly stay intact as we go. Melandrich is in his element at the front of the pack, Legolas-ing his way across roots and fallen tree trunks as if they were nothing more than leaves on the ground. Everyone else is mostly walking two by two: Kai and Gren, Eddie and Jackson, and Adrian trailing off by himself. I float somewhere between them all, trying to be the connective tissue between Adrian and Eddie, but failing miserably. Whenever one falls back or picks up pace, they instinctively know to widen the gap between them, like they're opposing magnets. I make conversation with both throughout the day, but it does nothing to get them to look at the other without a sneer or an eyeroll.

A little after midday—what do I want to call it? Three in the afternoon? We'll go with that—I end up trailing behind Kai and Gren. I've caught snippets of their conversations throughout the day, as one sided as they are. Kai's voice carries, though, no matter the distance.

"God, I hate the forest," they moan. "You remember how I hate the forest, Gren. There's so much dirt. I hate dirt. It's dirty."

Gren sniffs.

"I know you don't mind it, but I do. You need to respect other people's dislikes, you walking turnip."

"Maybe if you hadn't stolen thirty gold from us, you wouldn't be here," I say, trying not to say it in the sing-song tone of an elementary schooler.

They look up at me, unamused. "Yeah, maybe if you would have just taken the hit, none of us would be here. How about that, hm?"

Gren snorts, looking down at Kai, furrowing her already heavy brow.

"What, you're taking her side?" Kai asks. "After all we've been through? Traitor."

Gren rolls her eyes at the dramatics, staring straight ahead, brushing a tree branch out of her face as she passes by it.

"Be honest," I say to them. "Were you really looking for the Relics? Or was that just to get at our money?"

"Oh *gods*, no," Kai says, tripping over a tree root. They look back at the offending root, glaring at it like it just insulted their mother. "Up until—well." They gesture wildly at the rest of the group. "Up until all this, the Relics were just Old Gods drivel to me. To most people nowadays, really. So, when a bunch of suckers who were staring at everything with wide eyes and wide open pockets, going on about the damn things in the middle of the bloody day, I had to take a chance." They pause for a moment, looking up at me, almost bashful. "I suppose, since we're going to be traveling together, I should—I dunno—apologize for that."

I grin at them. "Apology accepted."

"I said 'suppose,' love," Kai corrects me, holding up a finger in my direction. "Didn't say I was actually going to do it. Just saying, a respectable person would do something like that. In theory."

"And you're not a respectable person?"

Gren snorts again, but it sounds more like a laugh. It must be, because Kai glares at the back of her head.

"If you all keep up the attitude, I definitely won't be," they say, shaking their head before going silent.

We walk. And we walk. And after that, we keep walking. Despite my shoes being fairly supportive, I can feel the blisters forming on the balls of my feet. The soreness rivals anything else that I've experienced, even after all the ren faires and comic conventions that Eddie has dragged me to. The light sifts through the trees as the evening approaches, covering us in the shadows of the looming trunks surrounding us. As the light turns a gentle gold, Melandrich stops in front of us.

"This is where we should rest for the night," he announces. "This gives us a good clearing to set up camp, but the trees are dense enough to cover us. Let us prepare everything for the evening."

He drops the rucksack from around his shoulders and rustles around in it before stopping, glancing back up at us all. Looking around, I see that I'm not the only one just staring at him, utterly confused as to what to do.

"I cannot prepare everything myself..." Melandrich says, in his polite yet firm tone.

Adrian is the first to break stance, sauntering away from the group. "I'll go find a stream and get us some extra water."

"Very well," Melandrich says. He looks at Eddie and Jackson. "I have tents, if you two would not mind setting them up."

"Uh, sure, but don't we need someone to go get food and stuff?" Eddie asks, throwing his shoulders back and crossing his arms over his chest. "You know, hunt and gather."

Even though he's usually so even keeled, I can see the twitch of Melandrich's mouth as he tries to hold back a smile. "If you are volunteering your services, I am sure there are many packs of wolves roving the area you can attempt to subdue. Otherwise, I have packed plenty of rations that will last us until we reach Marwindale. Whichever suits your fancy."

Eddie's face blanches before he nods and says, "Tents it is."

Everyone breaks off to do their own tasks. My gaze wanders back to Adrian, who slowly walks out into the forest, hands shoved in his pockets.

"Vi," Eddie calls. "You want to help us? This is literally just sticks and canvas, so I have no idea what I'm doing."

My eyes don't leave Adrian as I walk off after him. "I'm sure you've got it. I'm going to go help Adrian."

Eddie calls my name again, but when I don't answer him as I jog off to catch up with Adrian, he doesn't persist.

"Need an extra hand?" I ask Adrian, huffing as I slow my sprint to walk beside him.

He doesn't look at me, but the corner of his mouth curls into a grin. "I thought you'd never ask."

The forest rolls down into a sloping valley, concealing us from view from the rest of the party as we descend. The underbrush shifts noisily beneath our feet, leaves crunching, twigs breaking. The idea of the wolves that Melandrich mentioned does give me pause, making me wonder if we should be quieter as we walk. But Adrian strides along as though it's no big deal. I trust his judgment probably as much as I do Melandrich's at this point. I follow his lead as we weave between branches, the golden sunlight spreading across the ground behind us, the limbs of our shadows growing long and gangly, almost menacing. I rub my arm, the sight of it not uncommon but definitely not comforting.

"You're not cold, are you?" he asks, after we've been walking for a while.

I drop my arm. "Oh. No. The opposite, actually. I probably stink after all the sweating I've done today."

"Not that I've noticed, but I'm sure we're all going to be a little grimy for a while," Adrian says. "Until we get to Marwindale, we'll just have the creeks to keep us clean."

"Wonderful," I grumble.

"Hey, I warned you beforehand. This kind of thing isn't for everyone."

"No, I know," I say. "It's just—a lot has happened in the past day."

Adrian laughs. "Boy, has it."

I look at him, my gaze narrowed. He's still walking with his hands in his pockets like he has no real goal or motivation for being out here, like he just wanted to take a leisurely stroll out in the woods. It's a far cry from the anxious mess he was yesterday before we entered the castle. "What did you say to them?" I ask. "When they all took us aside and asked us questions? I'm assuming they never found out about all the 'illegal stuff.' Otherwise, you wouldn't be here."

At this, he doesn't seem to react much, but there is a muscle in his jaw that visibly tenses. "I told them basically everything that was true about my time on Earth," he says. "I was from Chicago, was a game developer. Didn't specify what game, and they didn't seem to really care much. Wasn't hard to skirt around the details."

I shake my head. "Melandrich talked to me last night. He said that Visandra is pretty new. You were probably around when her sister was in power, right? Veridian?"

It's his turn to look at me, his gaze not narrowed but wary. "Must have been some conversation."

"Oh," I say, my face immediately growing hot. "No, it wasn't —I mean, I thought he was trying to go that way, but it turned out he really just wanted to talk."

"Sure," Adrian says, with an amused raise of his eyebrows.

"I'm serious! Nothing happened!"

"Hey, if you're into the aloof, serious type, all power to you. Just use protection. I don't need the guilt of inadvertently creating Earth's first fey child." I roll my eyes, the heat intensifying in my face, but he jabs an elbow into my side, playfully.

208

"God, you really need to get laid more," he laughs. "Every time I even mention sex, you turn eight shades of pink."

I don't respond, my eyes focused on the ground.

"I swear, I didn't want to talk to you just to interrogate you about your sex life," Adrian says. "I wanted to talk to you about what happened in town yesterday."

I close my eyes, sighing. "I know. I'm sorry. We thought it was a good idea, and Jackson tried to talk us out of it, but I was going to feel super guilty if I just let them get away with a possible lead and—"

"Whoa, I'm not even talking about that," he chuckles. "That was my fault. I shouldn't have left you alone for that long. Of course some assholes tried to swindle you. You practically have 'tourist' written across your foreheads. It's okay. Really."

I furrow my brow. "What are you talking about, then?"

He laughs. "Uh, I'm talking about the fifty-yard crack you caused in the middle of town."

"Oh. That."

"Does…" he starts. "Does that not strike you as a big deal?"

I blink, not quite comprehending him. "I mean, I don't know," I finally answer. "I didn't do it on purpose. Kai had a Residuum pendant that got within my reach, so I grabbed hold of it. I knew it was going to go off, but I didn't think it would be that bad."

"That's the thing. It shouldn't have been," Adrian says. I look up at him, and he's looking at me with that impressed expression, identical to the one he gave me when I stood up to him in the woods after the marauders. "With that amount of Residuum and your inexperience, that crack shouldn't have been possible, Violet."

"You said it could go off if you touch it and don't know how to use it. That's exactly what happened."

"Yes, but with that amount of Infernal Residuum, the most danger you should be in is burning your hand or singeing Kai's

209

eyebrows off. Not anywhere near the level of power that you exerted back there."

What am I even supposed to say to that? I try to respond somehow, but words just can't come out, and I end up sputtering and shrugging instead.

"It's not a bad thing," Adrian says. "I'm not accusing you of anything. I'm saying that you have potential."

"To do what?"

"To be a residuuist."

I scoff. "And why would I need to be…that?"

He cocks his head. "What's wrong with being that?"

"Nothing, but that—that isn't what I came here to do," I say. "I came here to find May, not become some all-powerful magician."

"I said nothing about 'all-powerful,'" he says. "And that's not why I'm bringing it up. This task—collecting the Relics—it's dangerous. You need a way to defend yourself. And when I showed you those weapons back at the inn yesterday, you looked like you were about to barf. Like you were scared of them."

I glower at him. "I wasn't *scared* of them."

"Well, you certainly weren't Mr. Warrior back there," Adrian says, jerking his thumb back in the direction of camp.

"Do I need to be?"

"No, of course not. But the point is: you need something. And if you have that natural aptitude for magic, you may as well take advantage of it."

"Adrian, I don't even know how I did it in the first place," I say, my voice raising. It startles me, how defensive I'm getting. When I speak again, I'm sure to be more mindful of how loud I am. "How can you tell I'm good at something that I accidentally did?"

He looks up at the canopy of leaves above us for a moment, thinking. "What was going through your mind when you touched the pendant?" he asks, after a moment of silence. "Your approximation, of course."

I sigh. "I don't know. Something along the lines of, 'I didn't get this close to rescuing May just to be swindled by a hobbit.'"

He snaps, the cracking noise almost muffled against the soundproofing of the padded leafy ground around us. "Exactly," he says. "You had a strong emotional reaction. If that didn't work, then you wouldn't be able to find May. That was the emotion you put into your expenditure. That was the emotion that set off the Residuum and pushed it forward into the energy that caused that crack."

"So, I'm so powerful because I just—what? Feel too much?"

"'Too much' isn't the right way to phrase it," Adrian explains. "You felt strongly. And then you directed it into action."

I can't help but laugh again. "I cannot emphasize enough how much that was not my intention."

"We can work on that," he says. He strides ahead, turning around to face me, walking backwards as he talks. "If that was the kind of energy you could produce your first time using Residuum, I can't even imagine what it would look like if you had actual training to direct your magical output with your intent."

I raise an eyebrow at him. Despite not looking where he's going, he deftly avoids any protruding roots and felled branches in his path. I try to hold back a laugh. "And is that what you want to do?" I ask. "Give me actual training?"

"If you want."

"You know, I really *don't* want."

Adrian sighs, flipping back around, walking beside me again. "Look, you're not going to be an expert, but if you can at least use Residuum in a last-ditch situation, I would feel a lot better about bringing you here in the first place. If you won't pick up a dagger, then you should use something else."

"I can learn to use a dagger," I mumble.

"What about magic scares you so much?" he asks. "It's like any other weapon. If you don't know how to properly use it, bad things can happen, but if you train enough and respect what it can do, it's useful."

There's silence, save for the soft swish of leaves beneath our feet. I contemplate not answering. With Adrian, though, there's an energy that he gives off. Something about him has always exuded a feeling that he gets it. It's probably the dead brother, but I've known plenty of people with dead relatives and friends. It feels the same way as it does for Eddie. It's not just grief, but—what did he call it before?— damage. An indelible mark on the spirit that everyone with the same mark can identify. It's like they're magnetic, finding each other and pulling in closer until there is no space left between them.

I take a deep breath. "The fact that it's my emotions driving it is what bothers me," I confess. "I can barely control those when nothing stressful is happening, so entrusting me with that kind of power when I'm under attack is just asking for something terrible to happen. A knife or a sword won't rampage out of control if I get overwhelmed."

He's quiet as we keep walking, coming upon another crest of a hill. Just before we reach the slope, he stops. I do too.

"Violet," he says. "I understand the hesitation. Trust me. But if I didn't think you could do it, I wouldn't suggest it."

There's a prickle at the edges of my eyes, and I try hard to gulp the tears of frustration down. "What makes you so sure?"

Studying my face for a moment, his mouth spreads into a smile. He shrugs. "I don't know. I've got a pretty good hunch."

"A hunch?" I laugh. "You're trusting that?"

Smile still beaming, he turns toward the precipice, walking down the slanting hill before us. Furrowing my brow, I turn to follow him, before I stop.

A winding, bubbling creek sits at the bottom of the hill, water clear and rushing into tiny rapids.

Already yards ahead of me, Adrian is rustling through his bag, pulling out his canteen. He looks up at me, and though he's far away, I can see he winks at me.

"My hunches are pretty damn good."

On our way back—our own canteens and some spare ones for the others filled—Adrian pulls his rucksack off his shoulder again. "I forgot," he says. "I asked them to go back to the inn last night and get our stuff. They brought the weapons back, but I thought you'd be more interested in this."

Before I can ask what it is, he's pulled it out and extended it to me. I nearly trip over my own feet.

It's the game master's guide.

I'm shocked, stopping in my tracks. Adrian does as well, but he keeps the guide extended to me.

"I thought you needed it."

I take it from him, flipping it open to the pictures I've stuffed in the center page. They're all there—Eddie and I stuffing our faces with Denny's after ditching our senior prom early. Mom and Dad and I after graduation. And May, her hair braided, smiling with her mouth closed, just enthusiastic enough so she could get the drudgery of class picture day over with. I close the book, and before I can thank him, he extends hand, something pinched between his thumb and pointer finger. "And this."

My twenty-sided die.

I take it from him, grasping it in my hand, and without thinking, I wrap my arms around Adrian in a hug.

He doesn't really hug me back, going mostly rigid, but I do eventually feel a hesitant pat on my shoulder. It's strange—of course, he's always looked thin to me, but with my arms around him, he seems like nothing but bones. Like I could easily break him without really thinking about it at all.

Eventually, I pull away, gripping the die in my hand like a

nun might a rosary. I inhale, exhale. "I'll let you teach me. But the second it gets to be too much, we have to call it."

Adrian nods. "I think that's a fair deal."

"I mean it."

"I know you do," he says. "But it won't be too much. I believe in you."

We continue walking back up the hill, working against gravity instead of with it. My feet slip on leaves as we push onward until finally, we crest back onto the plateau our camp is set up on, the glow of the fire already beckoning us forward.

He believes in me.

That makes one of us, I guess.

CHAPTER 17

I've never been a social butterfly, but I've often taken solace in the low hum of surrounding conversation. Maybe I'm not much of a participant, but there's a comfort in other people talking around me.

I think that's why the dead silence as we sit around the fire eating our rations is so goddamn unsettling.

The sun set about an hour ago. The tents are up, fire blazing, and rations distributed evenly amongst us by Melandrich. But aside from occasional bites of jerky, crunches of hardtack, or swigs of water from a canteen, there's absolutely nothing. No mumbled side conversations between Eddie and Jackson, no one-sided banter from Gren and Kai. Melandrich has been intently inspecting every scrap of food he's put in his mouth. And for as skinny as he is, Adrian was the first to devour his rations, choosing now to lean against a log on the ground, arms cushioning his head as he stares up at the sky. I shift awkwardly in my spot, partly because I can already feel my ass going numb, but also to stir up some noise—any noise, at all. Something to get conversation started up again. But there's nothing. Only the soft chirp of crickets and chewing.

Is this what it's going to be like every night? It's going to take us days to get to Marwindale, so what about the rest of the Relics? Weeks? Months? Are we really going to be those assholes who sit in silence for that long? I think about saying something to Eddie, making some remark about finally getting to live out his favorite parts of *Lord of the Rings* (the walking in the woods, of course. Who doesn't love all that?) but he's been uncharacteristically silent since Adrian and I returned to camp, only offering me a sullen nod and a barely-there smile. At this rate, it's going to be a long hike.

Kai is the one to finally break the silence, their groan startling me as it breaks through the stillness. "Is anyone going to bloody talk? I feel like I'm sitting in a graveyard, for the gods' sake," they complain.

"I was enjoying it," Jackson mutters, flipping the page of his book he's reading without looking up.

"Yes, I bet you were," Kai says. "But it's making all the hairs on the back of my neck stand up, thinking that I can hear every rabbit in a ten-mile radius take a piss. So, conversation! Music! Something! Fuck!"

"We're barely willing to talk to each other. I doubt fucking is on the table," Adrian muses, still staring up at the sky.

"Come on, you foreigners must do something for entertainment," Kai says, ignoring Adrian's sass. They look between Eddie, Jackson, and I in desperation. "Anything. Stories, games, songs—"

Adrian perks up, leaning forward from his relaxed position. "As a matter of fact, this one," he says, jabbing a thumb in Eddie's direction, "is quite the jester."

I think that this will be the thing to break Eddie out of his uncharacteristic quiet spell, but he merely glares at Adrian, throwing him a middle finger. Adrian takes no offense, grinning like a kid at the gesture.

"If you want entertainment so bad, you come up with it," Jackson says to Kai.

"I'm no entertainer," Kai says. I swear, I see Gren's upper lip curl in disagreement, but it might also be a trick of the dim light. "I have a terrible singing voice, and all the stories I know are kindred folk tales. Mostly about living simple, boring lives out on the plains." They scoff, kicking a bit of dirt toward the crackling flames in the center of the circle. "It's enough to make me gag."

"Lady Spence, you were telling me fascinating things about your home last night," Melandrich chimes in, looking at me across the fire with his wide, voraciously curious puppy dog eyes. "Perhaps you could tell us more."

Kai claps their hands together. "There we go!" they exclaim. "Freaky stories from Alien World. Perfect."

"Oh no," I stutter, my face getting hot again. "I'm not really a storyteller, either. I was just giving Melandrich information. It wasn't entertainment."

"Love, at this point, anything is more entertaining than the dulcet sounds of crickets humping each other. Hit me with whatever you've got," Kai says.

My mouth goes instantly dry. There's got to be something I can say, right? Maybe recite one of those stupid campfire stories I heard at sleepaway camp. If I can remember any. How does the one about Bloody Mary even go again? Do you say her name three times and she just shows up? Or is that Beetlejuice? I think it's both. Or not? Ugh, why can't I remember?

A hand clamps onto my knee, patting it reassuringly. I look up. Eddie smiles at me comfortingly as he uses his hand on my knee to hoist himself onto his feet. "Don't worry," he says. "I got something."

"Ah, the jester decides to grace us with his talents after all," Adrian quips.

Eddie shoots him a glare as he stands before the circle, the glow of the campfire dancing across his face. "It's either this or listen to everyone argue for hours," he says, but he looks at me briefly before turning back to the rest of the group. I grin. That might be his excuse, but I know he's doing it to get me out of the spotlight.

He throws his shoulders back, looking from face to face. I've seen this look before when I've sat in on him GMing *Mages* sessions, and in less formal settings, when he's telling a group of people a wild (perhaps slightly exaggerated) story about his dealings with rogue customers in the retail world. It's no longer a conversation for him. It's a performance. Eddie has always had a knack for turning mundane conversation into entertainment, whether he's aware of it or not.

He smiles, his focus particularly on the native Velmyrans. "If you want a story from Earth, let me tell you a tale from a land far from where we came from. A land called Russia."

"Oh god," Jackson mutters under his breath, finally prying his eyes off his book in horror.

I bite my lip, trying not to laugh. Mostly at how dramatically he spreads his hands in front of himself, how he puts every ounce of wonder he can into the words. The Velmyrans are wide eyed, especially Kai who sits cross legged and attentive, like a kindergartener during story time.

"Over a hundred years ago, there ruled a king and a queen of this far off land. Theirs was a rule that was never destined to last," Eddie continues rapturously. "But before their downfall came to them a devil in man's clothing. Some say he was a mystical prophet and healer. Some say he was nothing but a greedy usurper. But all were fascinated by him and his influence, and that fascination continues to this very day."

It clicks for me. "Oh no," I whisper.

"His name," Eddie exclaims, "was Rasputin."

And that's when he begins to sing.

"Rasputin" by Boney M is our dishwashing song, always in the background while we're doing chores. Seeing him tell the tale of the lover of the Russian queen for a group of enamored adventurers staring at him with all the attention an audience would give a Shakespearean actor, I can't contain the giggles.

Eddie has never been the strongest singer, but he more than makes up for it in his radiating charisma. He stands in place for the first verse, but by the second, he can't stay still anymore. He prances around the fire and addresses every line to one of his "audience members," dancing during the chorus like he's one of the toy soldiers in the Nutcracker. Jackson's hand is still on his page in his paperback, but he laughs along with me now. Despite how little I've seen them hang out, I'm sure he's seen this side of Eddie before. It's probably the reason he was drawn to him, just like everyone is drawn to Eddie.

And the Velmyrans are falling under his spell as well. Kai claps along to the punctuated beats of the chorus, gasping as Russia's greatest love machine grows bolder, cheering when they put some poison into his wine. Melandrich is not quite as vocal but listens intently to the outlandish story with his ears perked the entire time. Even Gren taps her foot along to the melody. Jackson and I, by the last few choruses, are singing along and clapping at the appropriate times as Eddie's backing track.

As Eddie ends the song, arms spread out wide in a final pose, everyone around the fire erupts into applause. Kai is the most enthusiastic of the bunch. Gren's hands smash together in delight. Even Melandrich, as reserved as he usually is, gives a few resigned golf claps.

When I look at Adrian, I half expect him to be laughing at Eddie's expense, finally watching him play the part of the Fool for everyone's amusement. But the mockery I expected isn't there. He's looking at him with a strange smile that seems genuine. I might even say he's beaming.

Eddie breaks his final pose, panting. Jackson, from his spot on the ground, hands him a canteen which Eddie gladly accepts and takes a swig from. Before he can catch his breath, though, the questions start.

"Wait, so did he actually die?" Kai asks, their eyes the size of saucers. "The poison didn't work, so did they actually do him in for good?"

Between breaths, Eddie laughs. "No one knows. Some say he's unkillable, that he was the true downfall of the royal Russian family in the end."

"I think that was just the Disney movie that said that," I chime in.

He points at me. "First of all, it's not Disney. Disney *wishes* they could make a prince as hot as Dimitri. And second, shut up. I'm weaving a tale."

"Perhaps you can tell us more about this—eh, what did you call it? Rush-ha?" Melandrich asks. Across the gently licking flames of the fire, I can see he has pulled out a small notebook, crudely bound in some sort of twine. He scribbles on the small pages with something long and thin—I suppose this world's version of a pencil.

Eddie's eyes go wide at that, but he laughs. "I mean, I'm no expert on that. I just know stories."

"Then, more stories!" Kai exclaims. "Whether it's in Rush-ha or not."

"Perhaps tomorrow night, I'll tell you all of another royal—a prince," Eddie says slyly. "Instead of Russia, though, he rules in a land much closer to ours—a city of rolling hills and opulence, called Bel Air."

The Velmyrans chatter excitedly between each other and to Eddie about the possibilities of new stories. All the while, Adrian looks on, still grinning as he looks at Eddie. But something faint and melancholy crosses his face after a while. A look I empathize with. It's the look of someone who's in a crowded room of people, yet remains completely alone.

We discuss the watch. Melandrich says that someone should be awake at all times during the night, lest we get ambushed by bears or another band of robbers. He doesn't hand out weapons yet, though, stating that if there is an issue, we should just wake him. "Though," he says, "my time spent with you all makes me think, for some reason, I will be well aware of a problem before you ever make it to my tent." Goddamn. The fey boy actually has a sense of humor.

I offer to stay up first, thinking maybe some time out in the peace and quiet will help calm my nerves, which are still riled after my one on one with Adrian earlier. We only have three tents, which we've divided by our forming factions— Eddie and Jackson in one, me and Adrian in another, and Kai and Melandrich in the other. Gren can't fit in any of the tents, so she chooses to cozy up with a too-small blanket that really only covers her torso, up against one of the larger trees. With her out in the open, I don't sweat being the only one left awake.

I really try not to fall asleep, but with the crickets chirping, the fire slowly dying, and the rhythm of everyone's slowed breath as they try to find rest, my eyes droop. Soon, I'm shaken awake by Melandrich. I muddle out an apology, but he simply gives me his trademark gentle grin and tells me to go off and get rest. I slump off toward the tent, but groggily realize I have to pee.

My eyes are barely open as I stumble off into the woods, far enough where I'm fairly certain Melandrich won't see my ass as I drop my pants and squat down. I have to make a conscious effort not to fall asleep while mid-pee. The last thing I need is to fall over in a puddle of my own piss in the middle of the night. What a fun story that Eddie would never let me live down. Once everything is taken care of, I stand and pull my pants back up.

My eyes are still closed when I notice the glow, strong enough where I can see it through my eyelids. It doesn't really alarm me, at first. Until I realize I'm facing the opposite way of camp.

I crack my eyelids open, and a jolt of panic runs through me.

I see the walking cinder. The one from the market in Castle's Edge.

Adrenaline courses through me, and my eyes fly wide open. I stumble backward, and the world falls from underneath me as I trip on something, tumbling onto my back. Through the confusion, I try to keep my eye on the glow ahead of me, but so much flashes through my head. I even think I see the silhouette of another person—Adrian? I don't know why it looks like his profile but before I can parse it out, I hit the ground, the wind knocked out of me and my vision blurring.

I take a moment to catch my breath and scramble back into a sitting position, looking back in the direction I last saw the cinder.

I look out into the dark of the empty forest. There's nothing there.

Rushing back up the hill to camp, I contemplate telling Melandrich about what I saw, but I see that he's lost in concentration with his pocket notebook. Instead, I slip around to my and Adrian's tent as stealthily as possible. As I crouch down and part the canvas, Adrian's eyes are closed.

I grab hold of his foot and shake it, and his eyes fly open a little too fast. "Hey, I saw something outside."

He props himself up on his elbows and rubs at his eye, but there's an alertness to them that tells me he wasn't sleeping, or at least not deeply. "What?" he asks.

"Something outside."

"I'm sure the elk aren't coming to kill us in our sleep, Violet."

I sigh. "It wasn't an elk. It was glowing."

"Glowing?"

"Yeah. Like a campfire."

"Like the one just outside?"

"No, like a different—it wasn't actually a campfire. It was like a person, but they were glowing and—"

I stop. Because Adrian is giving me a look I'm all too familiar with. It's a look of pity, of someone who clearly doesn't believe a word I'm saying. "Violet, we're all tired. Maybe you were just…"

He trails off. But I can fill in the rest myself.

Seeing things.

I'm being fucking crazy again. What if there was no cinder in the first place, not even back in town? Eddie didn't see it, so maybe it wasn't even there.

I shake my head. "Yeah, never mind. Sorry for waking you up."

There's another emotion that crosses his face that I can't quite pinpoint as I crawl over to my bed roll and lay down, but he doesn't say anything more before turning back over with his back toward me. I stare up at the wrinkled beige canvas of the tent, waiting for the coiled knot in my chest to loosen. But I'm so exhausted, I'm asleep before I can truly call myself relaxed.

CHAPTER 18

"You gonna take all day or what? Losing daylight here, Spence. Chop chop!"

I grumble as I power my way up the hilltop that feels like it's getting taller as I'm walking it. Every blister, fresh and healing, screams at me as I climb. Adrian's cavalier voice calling to me from the top isn't helping. I mutter a few curses under my breath as I push against the strain of my already strained muscles. Doesn't help that I'm on day three of my stupid-ass period, and every tampon I brought with me disappeared from my stuff in the Crystalline jump to Velmyra. Having to ask Melandrich for more bandages to shove in my underwear later tonight will only be mildly less degrading than the first three times I've had to do it.

It's been four days of walking for us, and it's been about as exciting as the first day was. *Mages of Velmyra* made it seem like random encounters with giant mutant worms or other wild creatures would be much more prevalent than they've proven to be so far. I'm also not convinced that we haven't just been walking around in circles for days, save for the fact that Melandrich seems to know where we are, and there wouldn't be much incentive for him to lead us off the path. If he wanted to kill us and leave us to become tree fertilizer, he could have done it a hundred times over and have already been back to Castle's Edge by now. I trust him at this point.

And somehow, I think he trusts us too. He's even given a select few of us weapons when we're on watch. I'm one of them, and he seems to trust Jackson with them as well. Gren is big enough where it's an unspoken fact that if we were to get attacked in the middle of the night, she could effortlessly turn a measly passing thief into paste with her fists alone, so she doesn't need anything from him. But that's about as far as his trust extends. I get the impression he views Eddie as a toddler—amusing but not to be trusted with sharp objects. Kai is the biggest flight risk of us all, so no weapons for them. Even so, we all know that if they really wanted to, they and Gren could have taken off in the middle of the night at any point on our journey. I don't think they fancy being wanted for escaping a prison sentence, along with whatever other charges we've racked up.

Adrian hasn't been offered any weapons either, which is confusing to me. He and Melandrich haven't exchanged so much as a passing conversation over the almost-week that they've known each other, but the way Melandrich looks at Adrian is strange—always with narrowed eyes and slightly furrowed brows, as if he's constantly sizing Adrian up yet never reaching a conclusion. Adrian, however, doesn't really seem to mind that he isn't part of the circle of trust yet. On the contrary, with the way he pops up like a freshly bloomed daisy each morning, I'd say he rather enjoys the lack of responsibility he gets.

As I head up the ravine, I take my hair down, scraping some of the greasy fallen strands of hair back in place and tying them back as tight as I can with the ribbon I have. God, I can't wait to take a bath. Melandrich says it may be possible once we reach Marwindale, but they're not a particularly rich town, mostly inhabited by farmers. Even if I can stand in a back alley and dunk a few buckets of water on myself, I'll be infinitely happier than I am now. My skin feels like it's covered in a thin film of dirt, and my hair is a mess of grimy tendrils to the point where I just try to keep it out of the way as best as possible and not even acknowledge that it exists.

"There she is," Adrian smarmily says, as I crest the hill. I'm not the only one who looks ragged, though Adrian seems to be taking the inherent filthiness of travel in stride better than me. He still keeps his hair pulled back, but every day it gets less and less refined and more like a mountain man's makeshift solution to long hair. A sparse bit of facial hair has sprouted on his upper lip and chin, far patchier than what Eddie and Jackson have cultivated so far. The man in front of me is a far cry from the refined socialite that I first met back in Chicago, though his cheeky demeanor has stayed intact.

For the most part, anyway. The anxious edge he had to him when we first arrived in Velmyra is nearly non-existent—unsurprising, given how all his fear was based in getting caught for his past crimes. Once he realized Visandra had no knowledge of his past, it was like a weight was lifted off his shoulders. Even traveling with Melandrich doesn't seem to bother him too much. But every so often, I get the feeling that he's not quite rid of that paranoia. A branch will break, leaves will rustle, and he'll look over his shoulder in alarm with his muscles tense and ready for a fight. Kai and Gren might be the ones everyone expects to take off suddenly, but I can't seem to shake the uneasy feeling that Adrian should be in that category too.

"What did he give us to work with?" he asks, hands on his hips.

I dig around in my pocket and pull out the small scrap of cloth Melandrich had reluctantly handed over to me before Adrian and I walked off from camp. Adrian takes it from my open palm, pulling back the cloth to reveal the jagged lump of Earthen Residuum nestled inside. He holds it up to the dying light of the day, the fading rays of sunshine hitting the crystal just right, sending glittering green lights dancing off the sleeves of my shirt.

"This is perfect, actually," he says, inspecting the stone. "Earthen is a nice and easy beginner Residuum. A lot less opportunity for shit to go awry. Only the slimmest of chances the entire forest shrivels up and dies."

"Great," I say dryly. He knows I'm nervous about this. I can't tell if his attempt at a joke is to make me feel better or to scare me more. My hand is back in my pocket, my fingers wrapped around the d20, my nails tracing the ridges.

"Relax," he tells me. "You'll be fine. In fact, I think you can hold onto this thing bare handed, no barrier needed." Extending the stone out to me, he grins. "Go ahead. Take it."

I take an instinctive step back. "The last time I touched one with my bare hands, I destroyed a city block."

"You were also wrestling a feisty kindred folk, so your emotions were haywire," Adrian explains. He throws his arms open wide. "We're out in the middle of the peace and quiet now. Nothing out to get you or make you flustered."

I shake my head slowly. "I don't know."

He sighs and walks toward me, but before I have a chance to counter him, he gently takes my hand, setting the stone in my palm and closing my fingers around it.

Touching Residuum through a barrier is a lot like listening to a rock concert through a concrete wall. There's the thump of the bass, the raw pulse of the vibrations radiating through your body, but it's muffled and far away. Without a barrier—like touching the Infernal stone back in Castle's Edge and holding the Earthen stone in my hand now—it's like listening to the concert on the standing room floor. The way the force of it rips up my arm into my chest and into my gut is unbridled, untamed. Every inch of me pulsates with magic.

And yet, even with my fingers wrapped around the stone's hard edges, nothing happens.

I wait, looking around for some sort of eruption in the earth, some collapse of a patch of trees. But there's nothing.

And while I look around me baffled, Adrian smiles. "I told you you'd be fine," he says.

"Why…?" I start to ask, but I trail off. I open my clenched fist. The Residuum is still intact, the same shape and size it was when it hit my palm. Proof that my touch didn't trigger a reaction.

"Here's the thing," Adrian starts. He walks a few yards off, digging in his pocket before finding something small and holding it up between his pointer finger and thumb. From the distance I'm at, I have a hard time making out what it is beyond something tiny and black, about as big as a raisin. Unceremoniously, he drops it in the dirt and buries it with his foot. "I said Residuum works off emotions, which is true in a sense," he says as he kicks at the dirt. "But what's more important than the emotion is the *intent* behind it. Back in Castle's Edge, what were you feeling when you set off the stone?"

I blink at him, shaking my head. "I don't know. Frustration? What do you think? I certainly wasn't thrilled or anything."

Looking at the dirt with some modicum of satisfaction, Adrian stops grinding whatever it was he dropped into the ground. "And what was frustrating you?"

"Besides the fact that there was a hobbit sitting on me?"

He raises his eyebrows at me, unamused yet still grinning. "Come on. Play along. I swear, there's a point to it."

I sigh. "I was frustrated because we just had all our money stolen."

"And why was that frustrating?"

"Because having something stolen from you isn't fun."

"Well, yeah," Adrian says. "But that's not why you, Violet Spence, were frustrated. Why were *you* frustrated at that exact moment?"

I pause, wracking my brain before shrugging. "Because we had just gotten here and already things were going to shit, and I wanted them to work out."

"Why?"

"Because—" I catch myself. The answer is pretty obvious, isn't it? "Because—if they didn't, we might not get her back."

He snaps, pointing at me like I just guessed the million-dollar phrase. "There it is," he says. "Your frustration, anger, fear, whatever you want to call it—it came about because you want May back."

"Why exactly is that significant?"

"Because that, Violet, manifested your intent." He's looking me squarely in the eye, an intensity emitting off him the likes of which I've never seen before. "Emotions are natural, compulsory. It's what you do with them that's the difference between controlling a flame and lighting yourself on fire. That, you do have a say in. At that moment, you knew that your chances of finding May again were slipping away, so you did something about it. That's what caused that fissure. You felt an emotion and used that as fuel to push your intention forward into that stone." I open my mouth to talk, but he holds up a finger to stop me. He looks back toward where he dropped the small black object. "I buried an azurefruit seed over there."

Apprehensively, I nod. After a few days in Velmyra, I'm starting to learn some of the foreign foods. Azurefruit looks like a giant blueberry but has the texture of a peach. I've eaten a few of them as since Melandrich doled them out for breakfast a few times, and to say it's one of the best things I've ever eaten is an understatement.

"One of the most common uses for Earthen Residuum is plant growth," Adrian continues. "So, have at it. Make an azurefruit tree."

I look back down at the green gem, guilt creeping in since I've covered it in sweat from my slick palm. Breathing in through my nose and out through my mouth, I grasp it and focus on the patch of dirt that Adrian scuffed the seed into.

Emotion and intention, huh? I guess my intention is…make tree grow? What emotion is going to push that forward? Annoyance that I'm doing this in the first place? Exhaustion because I have to do this after non-stop travel for almost a week? Is exhaustion even an emotion or just a physical state?

I focus, trying to push forward that muddled mess of incoherent thought and feeling.

And unsurprisingly, nothing happens.

I drop the tension in my arms, letting them fall to my sides in defeat. "Told you," I say.

"I would say you tried, but I don't know how true that is," Adrian quips.

I sigh.

He crosses his arms for a moment, staring at the ground in thought, before looking back up at me. "Let me see your bag."

Narrowing my gaze at him, I reluctantly shrug off my bag from around my shoulders, extending it to him. Adrian takes it, searching through it quickly before pulling out a small bread roll wrapped in a cloth. We've been getting two "meals" a day, which is usually just a piece of fruit or bread in the morning and a strip of jerky in the evening. It's apparently taken us a bit longer to reach Marwindale than he anticipated, so we're down to bread and fruit. I was saving the roll for later when we got back to camp. It's going to be the last thing I eat until morning, and I've gotten pretty good at making it last.

But that's going to be a little difficult now, since Adrian takes it out of its cloth wrapping and takes a huge bite out of it.

"Hey!" I exclaim, lunging for it. I'm not quick enough, though, and he drops it on the ground, grinding it into the dirt with his heel.

"Oh my," Adrian sighs, in faux bemusement. He's still chewing around the big bite he's taken. "How did that happen? I'm so clumsy sometimes."

I crouch in the dirt, desperately wiping at the piece of bread, seeing if there's anything to be salvaged. "The fuck was that for?" I shout.

Putting a hand to his chest in fake surprise, he asks, "What? Are you mad?"

I drop the roll in a huff and stand back up, looking directly in his eyes. "Yes," I snap.

"Why?"

My fingernails dig into my palms. "You fucking know why."

"Why does me eating your food make you angry?"

"Because," I say, through gritted teeth, "now I won't be able to eat until morning."

The false shock instantly melts from his face, his shaped eyebrow arching. "Well," he says, "what are you going to do about it?"

I set my mouth in a thin line, looking over his shoulder back at the mound of earth containing the seed.

"You have options for what to do with the anger you're feeling, of course," Adrian continues. "You could punch me in the face, run back to camp and beg Melandrich for another set of rations, bargain with one of the others. You could just suck it up and go to bed hungry. Or…"

He trails off, but he doesn't need to say anything more. I move past him, stepping in direct view of the seed's resting place.

Breathe in.

Breathe out.

I'm still angry. Maybe punching him in the face isn't such a bad idea.

But I'd still be hungry, wouldn't I?

My fingers clasp tighter around the Residuum, the jagged edges threatening to cut into the flesh of my palm. *I want to eat tonight*, I think.

I take hold of the anger sitting in my gut. And I send it forward.

At first, nothing happens. I feel the energy the Residuum gives off channeling through me. I imagine this is what it feels like to be a copper wire in a power cord. But even with this energy coursing through me, there's stillness. I watch the patch of ground for five seconds, ten, fifteen…

Just as I'm about to take my eyes off it, I catch the smallest glimpse of green poking up from the dirt, rising slowly into a thin twig. I'm stunned, mouth agape as I see it grow before my eyes, but I resist the urge to look back at Adrian in approval. I keep going. The tree grows, its small trunk ascending into the air and separating into branches with expanding leaves. When it's almost as tall as me, budding blue flowers burst forth and wilt almost as soon as they came, leaving in their place round sapphire-colored spheres.

The fruits enlarge rapidly, as big as baseballs before I have time to blink. I jump as a hand falls on my shoulder. "Don't overdo it. You can let go now," Adrian says in my ear, and with that, I pull back, cutting the connection.

My limbs buzz as the magic subsides, as if I've been holding onto a vibrating washing machine for a long period of time. Everything in me is lighter. I look down at the Residuum curled in my fist. The small green crystal is now a fraction of what it once was—closer to the size of the pendant that Kai wore around their neck that day in Castle's Edge.

Giving me a reassuring pat with the hand resting on my shoulder, Adrian walks forward to the azurefruit tree now swaying above us. Standing on the tips of his toes, he grabs a low hanging fruit, shining it on his shirt for good measure before sinking his teeth into it. He chews for a moment, before raising his eyebrows and giving a nod—an indication of "*Hm, not bad.*" With his empty hand, he reaches back up, leaping to get the next closest fruit, and manages to pluck it from the tree. He raises the fruit, and I put together that he's throwing it at me just in time for him to toss it my way.

I catch it, and it barely seems real in my hands. I feel the velvet-soft skin, smell the syrupy sweet aroma coming off it. But the hazy thought of "*I made this*" makes it feel like I'm holding a mirage.

Looking back at Adrian, he smiles at me, blue azurefruit juice staining his pearly teeth. "Congratulations, Violet," he says, raising the fruit like a champagne flute. "You're a residuuist."

He takes another big bite, juice dripping down his chin. As he goes back to the tree for more, I look down at the one in my hands.

I made this.

I raise the fruit up to my lips and take a bite to hide my grin.

The next day, we make it to Marwindale.

Melandrich stops us all just as we're about to crest over a hill, looking into the distance like a hound who's just caught a scent. "Wait here, all of you," he tells us, before running up the hill and disappearing from view.

We wait, chatting casually amongst ourselves. We all look worse for wear. Eddie's stubble is starting to grow into what I would consider a short beard, a look I've never seen on him despite how long I've known him. I'm not sure how well it suits him, and with how often he seems to uncomfortably scratch at his jaw, I don't think he cares too much for it either. The scant bit of facial hair that Jackson had at the journey's start is now growing scraggly, but he seems to relish it, running his fingers through the tuft on his chin absently every once in a while.

Eddie scratches at the stubble as we wait, looking off in the direction Melandrich went anxiously.

"Stop scratching at your face," I tell him. "You're just going to irritate your skin."

Instantly, he stops, his face turning pink as he looks at me. "It itches. I haven't gone this long without a shave in years."

"You look like a dog with fleas when you scratch at it like that," I say.

"Okay, yeesh. Sorry." Looking back up the hill, he crosses his arms, a tense edge to his shoulders.

"Are you all right?" I ask.

He doesn't look at me as he says, "Yeah, I'm good."

"No, you're not."

Sighing, Eddie says, "Well, if you were going to tell me how I feel anyway, why did you ask?"

"Jesus, what crawled up your ass and died?"

He opens his mouth to answer, but he is interrupted by Melandrich's voice shouting over the hill. "Everyone! Come up here!"

Eddie and I look at each other with concern, setting our spat aside in an instant. Melandrich doesn't sound like he's been attacked or anything, but something about the tone of his voice gets my hackles raised. We stride up the hill, the rest of the group following behind.

At the top, Melandrich has his back toward us, looking out over the horizon. Just as I'm about to ask him what's wrong, I freeze. Because the problem is clear.

The village of Marwindale sits just below us. The houses and gravel-paved streets closest to our vantage point look similar to the humble, more rural outskirts of Castle's Edge. But midway through town, there's an eerie change. The buildings, the street posts, even the odd abandoned wagon or pushcart is engulfed by gnarled tree roots and twisted black branches, devoid of any greenery or sign of life. Only a fraction of the town is left unscathed by the dead, encroaching forest that sprawls off in the distance into a mess of prickly black thorns and petrified wood.

Kai exhales in astonishment. "Well, chums," they say. "Safe to say, I think we found the Earthen Relic."

CHAPTER 19

"Well, I rolled a nat one on my persuasion."

I look up at Eddie to ask what he's talking about, but the answer is spilled over the front of his shirt, the stench of beer emanating off his damp clothes. He swipes a hand across his face, pushing wet strands of hair away from his forehead.

We descended into town about an hour ago, and so far, we haven't managed to do much except find the local tavern. Most of us revel in the fact that we're getting a full meal for the first time in days, no regard of what our next steps are. Kai and Gren stuff their faces—Gren's eaten a whole chicken by herself. And while Jackson has been mostly pacing himself, I catch him getting carried away a couple of times, consciously slowing his chewing before taking in more. Adrian, the quick eater he is, has already finished his plate of chicken thighs and miscellaneous green paste—what I can only assume used to be a vegetable of some sort before it was boiled into mush—by the time Eddie slumps back over to the table with beer dripping down his face.

"You know you're supposed to drink the beer, right?" Adrian asks with a half-cocked grin.

Flopping down on the bench next to me, Eddie grumbles,

"It wasn't mine. I thought I'd ask the barmaid about the overgrowth taking over the town."

"And?" Adrian asks.

Eddie's cheeks flush bright red. "I guess the flirty approach wasn't the right way to go," he mutters.

"Oh god," I groan. "You didn't."

"It works in the game!" Eddie says defensively. "Turns out she's married, and she and her wife are very happy together."

Jackson sets down his fork, staring at Eddie in disbelief. "Did you try just talking to her?" he asks. "You know, without making it sound like you wanted to sleep with her?"

"Well, it's a little late for that now," Eddie says, peeling his wet shirt away from the skin of his clavicle.

Jackson sighs and stands up. "Guess I'll throw my hat in the ring then. Anyone want to come with?"

I look up and down the table. Kai and Gren are still too preoccupied with their meals to be listening. Melandrich is poring over his map while taking occasional bites. No one seems especially eager to get going on this next step in the plan.

I roll my eyes. "I will," I say as I begrudgingly stand.

Managing to keep his expression neutral, Jackson nods and looks to Adrian. "What about you?"

Adrian's eyebrows raise. "What about me?"

"You're Mr. Silver Tongue, aren't you?"

"In Miami? Definitely. Here?" Adrian glances around at the room, which is pitifully populated with only a smattering of dirty farm hands finishing up their lunch. "Not so much."

"Adrian, come on," I say.

"You crazy kids go on without me," he says, waving a hand while he takes a sip from his tankard. "I'll keep an eye on Casanova here." Still wringing out his shirt, Eddie glares in his direction, but Adrian merely smirks.

I roll my eyes at him subtly. I'm sure he's figured out I don't entirely care for Jackson or vice versa. In his mind, he's probably forcing us together in our metaphorical Get Along Shirt so that we focus on the more life-threatening matters at hand, not the petty bullshit we have between us. Or maybe he's still convinced I just need to get laid more and is trying to set us up. Either way, the thought's not entirely appreciated, and I slump along next to Jackson away from the table.

A group of dirt-ridden townsfolk are leaving just as we pull up to the bar, and before we can even say a word, the bartender says, "Tell your friend I'm not interested." The barmaid looks as human as we do—her curly black hair is pulled into a messy knot at the back of her head, with sharp green eyes that size us up one at a time with careful analysis. It's the fact that she has to be over seven feet tall with biceps larger than my head that gives me a hint that perhaps she's something else. "I woulda thought I'd made myself clear already with the—ahem—house special, but seems to have a skull thicker than stone, that one."

Nervously, I clear my throat. "Um, yeah sorry about that. He's just a little—overzealous? He really didn't mean any harm by it."

"Harm or not, it doesn't change my mind," she says.

"Oh, no," I say. "We didn't come over here to change your mind or anything. We just had a few questions about the town and—"

"I'm not answerin' any more questions from you lot today," the barmaid says, bluntly. "You can tell me your drink orders, and that's about all I'll be providin' you."

I clear my throat again, trying to ignore the sweat building up under my armpits. "Look, I'm sorry about him. I think we started off on the wrong foot. We're—"

"Is that rose quartz?"

I look at Jackson, eyes narrowed. He looks at the barmaid with genuine curiosity, his eyes settling not on her face but around her neck. I follow his gaze to a small pendant around her throat, peeking out beneath the folds of her slightly unbuttoned shirt. Absently, her hand flies up to the pendant, pulling it into better view. It appears to be in the shape of a four-pointed star, wrapped in place with a plain black leather cord that loops around her neck.

She clutches at it, a wary look in her eyes as she looks at Jackson. "Yes, it is."

Jackson's brows knit together, but his expression isn't confused—it's somber. "I'm sorry for your loss."

The wall of a woman, who has looked like she's wanted to throttle us since the moment we walked up to her, now gapes at Jackson, a shimmer coming into her eye that she tries to blink away. "O-Oh. Ah, thank you," she stammers.

"How long has it been? If you don't mind me asking, of course," Jackson says. I'm so used to the smooth-as-butter nature of Adrian's deflections and advances. With him, the goal is to say whatever you can to get the result you need. But Jackson's approach is different. He oozes sincerity, looking directly into the barmaid's eyes, keeping charisma and ego out of the picture. It isn't the fake, put-upon questioning one does to be polite. I actually think he wants to know.

The barmaid smiles, though the glistening in her eye makes that smile complicated. "Two years last month," she answers.

Jackson nods. "That must have been very difficult."

"The most difficult thing I've had to endure, yes," she says.

"My condolences," Jackson says. "I'm sure whatever Realm her spirit has found its home in, she's watching after you, even still."

The barmaid takes it to heart, her grip on the pendant tightening. "Thank you. I believe she is." She blinks rapidly and clears her throat. "Tell your friend over there that I'm sorry for bein' out of sorts with him. Still a sore spot for me."

"Understandable," Jackson says. "And really, he meant well. None of us are trying to intrude. We actually noticed the overgrowth coming into town and wondered what that could be about. Do you know what's causing it?"

Her grip around the pendant loosens, and she leans on the

bar toward us, the tenseness in her body now gone. "Oh, that? What about that is interestin' to you all, anyway?"

Shrugging, Jackson says, "We're just travelers passing through, but we thought if we could help, we should."

The barmaid chuckles, cynicism clear in her tone. "No one's been able to help with that in the decade since it started. You can certainly try, but I won't be holdin' my breath for it."

"It's been doing this for a decade?" he asks.

"Just about," the barmaid confirms. "It's slow growth. We didn't much notice until the houses on the edge of the wood started gettin' overtaken. Even then, the families that lived there had time enough to pack up their things and find a new place to live, no panic to it."

Jackson exhales, nodding. "At least it hasn't forced anyone out of their home overnight."

"It hasn't," she says, "but that doesn't mean the town isn't dyin'. Over half of us have moved on since the roots started comin' up through the ground and the branches started takin' over everythin' they could. In another ten years, Marwindale isn't gonna be around anymore, I can guarantee you."

"Do you know what's causing it?" I ask, feeling slightly intrusive given the rapport she and Jackson have had so far.

"Not necessarily," the barmaid says. "There have been a few reports—mostly from drunkards makin' mischief out in the forest to the north—of something glowin' green in the thicker parts of the growth. At first, we all thought it was a bit of nonsense, but more and more folks got curious and explored for themselves. There's something out there, covered in a mess of roots and branches."

"Has no one used Residuum on it to pull the growth back?"

She looks at me deadpanned—not necessarily with the same hostility as earlier, but a hint of annoyance is obviously there. "Of course, some tried," she answers. "That's the first thing you think of it, isn't it? But nothing works on it. You can take an axe to any part of the overgrowth from the forest, and you'd sooner break the axe than clear any of it away."

"Where's this green glow?" Jackson interjects.

The barmaid jerks her head forward, her black curls bouncing. "A few miles northeast. Follow the path until you can't anymore and then keep walkin'."

I look over at Jackson, and to my surprise, he makes direct eye-contact with me. He nods, and looking back at the barmaid, he says, "Well, thank you for your help. We'll do what we can."

"Godspeed to you," she says. As we pull away from the bar and walk back over to our table, I catch a glimpse of her hand traveling back up to her pendant before we fully turn our backs on her.

At the table, we get everyone's attention and tell the group what we learned. With newfound information, Melandrich snaps into leader mode, folding up the map and straightening his spine. "There is no time to waste, then. We must move, preferably before the sun goes down."

We trek out of the tavern, some dragging their feet more than others. The sun hangs high above us but is already trending westward. If we still have a few miles to walk, it's a good thing we're going now.

As we reach the edge of town, the houses covered in decaying fauna fading behind us and the forest of rot looming ahead, I pull up beside Jackson. "Hey," I murmur to him. "What was up with the pendant?"

Jackson looks at me with an eyebrow cocked. "What, you don't know?"

I resist the urge to roll my eyes at the condescension. "Sorry, I don't know everything about Velmyran culture."

"It's not Velmyran," he says, though he doesn't sound as know-it-all as I expect. "It's giant culture, specifically. At least, I assumed she was a giant. Maybe half, since she seemed on the smaller side. But as soon as I saw the pendant, it was obvious. When they get married, giants give each other tokens carved out of rose quartz—it's a symbol of love and undying devotion. They keep it hidden on them. No one can see it except them and their spouse. When their spouse dies, the one who's passed is buried with theirs, and the remaining partner wears their token in the open as a sign of their loyalty, even in death. It was a fifty-fifty shot whether she would take me commenting on it as genuine sympathy or just complete disrespect, but we didn't have much to lose."

"Where did you learn all that?"

"The guide," he says. "You know, the one you have with you that I haven't seen you open once since we got here. I thought you were supposed to be obsessed with the game or something."

My face burns a little, though it could be because of the sun beating down on us. Unlike the previous parts of the forest we've traveled in, there is no leaf cover to shade us from direct sunlight. "Aspects of it," I correct him. "Apparently, giant culture isn't something I thought to focus on."

"Apparently."

"When did you read that, anyway?" I ask, furrowing my brow. "You're not going through my stuff or anything, are you?"

"God, don't flatter yourself. I don't want to go through your stuff," he grumbles. "I read it a long time ago. When Eddie first asked me to play with him."

"You read...the whole guidebook?"

Jackson shrugs. "Yeah? What of it?"

"I don't know. Most people don't sit down and just *read* the rulebook, you know?"

And at this, though I never thought it was possible, I see Jackson go a little pink in the face as his head slumps down. The guy who never seems ashamed of how right he is—he actually seems embarrassed at this. "I guess I just like knowing the rules," he mutters under his breath, and abruptly, he takes a couple strides ahead of me, his head still dipped low.

As he walks ahead of me, I find it almost funny. The way his head slumps reminds of him back in middle school—head on his desk, buried in his arms, not bothering to listen to what was happening in class.

I never would have pinned him for the guy who would sit down and read the rules for fun. But then, I guess, I haven't really pinned him for anything up until now.

As the path in the dead forest narrows, Melandrich hands out weapons.

The wood is a knotted mess of intertwining roots and branches, curling into each other in such a cacophonous pile that I can't tell what's coming from the trees and what's coming from the ground. There is no rhyme or reason to the overgrowth, it seems. Except for, of course, the pathway through the gnarled wood. There is a distinct earthen path straight through the middle of the forest for the few miles that we walk. Each out-of-control branch seems to know that the trail is off limits, like the forest is creating a Red Sea of sorts straight down its center. But while it started wide enough for us to walk down in rows of two or three, it now narrows, so much so that we can only fit single file.

As soon as he recognizes this, Melandrich stops us, pulling out his Boundless Satchel and distributing the means to defend ourselves. We all get our picks—Eddie has opted for a sword (of course), and I can tell he hasn't had any practice with it since we've been out here, the blade wavering in his hand as he struggles to hold it upright in front of him. Kai has gone for a hand crossbow, one that looks more deadly in their grip given the size of it compared to their small frame. The massive club that Gren had wielded back in Castle's Edge is returned to her, a wide smile exposing her uneven, splotchy teeth spreading across her face as she grips it in hand. Jackson takes his daggers unenthusiastically, shoving them with no care into his belt.

Adrian and I get Residuum. Adrian perks up as the stones are set into his hands, inspecting each crystal by holding it up to the waning sunlight. He's been given a variety of types, mostly Heavenly and Earthen. A few Infernal stones have made it into the mix, though Adrian doesn't take as much care with them as he does some of the other stones, hastily throwing them in his pocket without examining them too closely.

When Melandrich gets to me, he asks what type I prefer. I initially say Earthen, but Adrian doesn't even look up from the inspection of his stones while saying, "Give her some Heavenly too."

I start to protest, but Melandrich gives me a few of the lavender-colored stones anyway, moving on to check on the rest of the group before I can refuse. Panicked, I look over at Adrian. "I haven't used Heavenly yet," I say. "I've barely used Earthen."

"It's the same concept," he says, shoving the remainder of his stones in his pocket. Putting a hand on my shoulder, he grins at me. "You've been getting the hang of it quickly. You got this."

"I could electrocute someone."

"That's the point, isn't it?" He pats me on the shoulder as Melandrich calls for us to move forward down the path. "Just make sure it's none of us."

The path winds, narrowing and darkening as we maneuver through the twisting branches. They curl and intertwine so thickly that barely a shard of sunlight can break through the woven canopy above us. With the path tapering down, the occasional branch scrapes and claws at my clothes. Out of the corner of my eye, they almost look like long black fingers, reaching out their claws to rip into my skin—

I close my eyes, forcing the image of the elongated, black fingers of Hellions out of my head. I can't panic now. Not here. Panic later. The Relic comes first.

We step forward out of the tunnel of branches, a burst of orange-yellow light illuminating our way forward, and when my eyes adjust, I know for sure we've reached our destination. The branches have parted to make a wide clearing of matted dirt and dead grass beneath our feet, a glade about a half-mile wide ringed with the same tangled branches we passed through. There is nothing in this clearing save for a strange pillar-like structure in the center. As we approach it with Melandrich still at the helm of the group, I can see it's a taller pile of roots bursting from the ground, twirled into an intertwining helix that stands about waist height for most of us. It comes to a knotted point at the top, looking as though it was consciously shaped, not as organically wild as the rest of the forest.

From within the contorted pile of roots, a faint green light pulses.

We stop, staring at the pedestal in front of us.

I close my eyes again. Breathe in. Breathe out.

I try to latch onto something else sensory, anything. But in the center of our little clearing, there is nothing. No breeze that rolls by, no insects singing as the day fades. Like there's nothing alive in here save for us.

Breathe in. Breathe—

"All right, are we going to cut that bugger out of there or what?" Kai asks, smacking their hands together like they're about to dig into a Thanksgiving meal. I jump, my eyes flicking open and my exhaled breath coming out uneven and faster than I anticipated. There's still a tense ball sitting in the pit of my stomach as the others talk.

"According to Master King, the locals have tried their hand with force and magic," Melandrich muses. "This may be a dilemma we need to puzzle out for—"

"Oi, Gren!" Kai exclaims. Before anyone has time to react, Gren rushes over to the pedestal, furiously banging on the construction of roots with her club, grunting and yelling as she does. The club cracks against the structure over and over, though the sound seems to be absorbed by all the dead trees around us. Finally, once she's given it several whacks, she stops and lets the club rest on the ground, panting like she just sprinted a mile.

The pedestal still stands. Unblemished.

Melandrich's mouth flattens into an unamused line. "As I was saying, this will most likely require patience and erudite thinking rather than brute strength."

Kai mutters under their breath, and the only thing I can catch is a high pitched, mocking "*erudite thinking.*" Gren snorts at the pedestal in front of her, flopping down to sit in front of it, dropping her club and crossing her meaty green arms over each other in frustration.

Turning to Adrian, Melandrich says, "Master Inoue, you seem to be the one with the most knowledge of this place. In your discoveries of the location, did you receive any other information regarding how to retrieve the Relic?" There's a strange twitch to his eyebrow as he says this, an extra sharpness that I can quite discern the meaning of.

Adrian doesn't seem to take notice, however. "I just knew the approximate location," he says, hands on his hips as he stares at the structure. "Nothing mentioned this. I'm as clueless as the rest of you."

"You said Residuum did not have an effect on it?" Melandrich inquires, walking over to the roots and examining them closer.

Jackson shakes his head. "From what she told me, no. Otherwise, I'm sure someone would have taken care of all of this, by now."

"There must be some enchantment upon it that does not rely upon Residuum as an answer, then," Melandrich says, putting a hand to his chin. "Though, if the Mages were the ones to put them in place, perhaps mortals such as us do not have the means to solve it."

"No," Adrian says. "The Relics supposedly were created by the Old Gods as a way for mortals to have a leverage point against the Mages, in case of—well, in case of them abusing their power. They were designed for people like us to be able to retrieve them. As a matter of fact, the Mages can't retrieve them by themselves. This should be solvable for us." He looks over at Melandrich. "You should know. You found the Heavenly Relic, right? You retrieved it on your own."

"The way the Heavenly Relic came into my possession was— a chance event," Melandrich says after a pause.

Adrian cocks his head to the side in consideration. "Okay, fine. The guy who you stole it from retrieved it on his own."

In the days that I've known Melandrich, I wouldn't say much throws him off. But with the way his blue eyes go wide, blinking repeatedly in Adrian's direction, I would say this did. "I beg your pardon, but I did not *steal* the Relic."

"Well, I beg *your* pardon," Adrian snaps in Melandrich's ostentatious accent, "but I don't really care. The point is, we don't need magic and we don't need force, so what do we need?"

"A sword."

Everyone's gaze turns to Eddie, whose eyes have not left the pedestal since we stepped into the clearing.

Adrian sighs, pinching the bridge of his nose. "All right, apparently we need to take this from the top. Weapons won't work—"

"I'm not saying we use a sword against it, asshole," Eddie says, sounding less interested in insulting Adrian and more interested on the structure as he strides closer toward it. "I'm saying it looks like it *is* a sword."

Adrian rolls his eyes, and Melandrich looks at Eddie with the expression one might save for a three-year-old who is trying their best to accurately recite the ABCs but keeps failing somewhere in the middle. Kai sneers up at Eddie. "What the hell are you on about, mate?" they ask. "I don't know what swords look like on 'Earth' or whatever it is you call it, but that looks nothing like any sword I've seen."

Eyes laser focused on the pedestal, Eddie steps closer, moving past Kai. "It's not the whole thing," he says. "The top part is what tipped me off. You see the smaller part that sticks up at the top with the knot at the end? Pommel and grip. And the parts that are flayed out on the sides? That could be the guard."

I step closer, too, getting a better look at the shapes he's talking about. The pommel, the grip, the guard…

Holy shit. He might have something here.

"Are you saying it's stuck in there or something, then?" Kai asks, crossing their arms.

"Maybe," Eddie says. He walks around to the other side of the pedestal, the hilt of the supposed sword coming up to his waist. He examines it as he stands behind it, gaze fixated on it.

Melandrich, still stroking his chin, says, "If we remove the sword, perhaps we can then retrieve the Relic inside."

Tilting his head back and forth and rounding his shoulders, Eddie grins, wrapping his hands around the grip. "There's only one way to find out," he says.

With a deep breath, he pulls.

At first, I wonder if he's pulling the sword out slowly just to be dramatic. I'm surprised he didn't let his hair down so he could flip it dramatically in the wind as he does. He *really* seems to be milking it as we all watch him. It's like it's not moving at all.

But as the veins start to pop out on his forehead, his skin going pink, I realize it seems that way because it isn't. Eddie lets out a breath, his grip on the hilt slackening for just a moment before he goes back in for another attempt. He grunts as he pulls upward, the muscles in his neck tensing as he strains.

Nothing. It doesn't budge.

"Fucking *balls*," Eddie exhales as he lets go of the hilt, stumbling backwards but catching himself before he slips.

"How majestic," Adrian comments.

Shooting him a glare, Eddie says to Adrian, "Okay, you want to try, tough guy?"

Adrian sighs, but strolls over to the pedestal, taking Eddie's place in front of the protruding hilt, grabbing hold of it and pulling.

Nothing. Adrian tugs at the hilt (albeit with less force than

Eddie seemed to have exerted), but the thing stays stuck in place. Letting go, he flails his arms out dramatically and drops them to his sides in a huff. "Well, that wasn't much of a plan, was it?"

"Maybe it's just really jammed in there," Eddie muses.

"Or maybe, it's not a sword at all, and we need to use a little more brain power for this."

"Come on," Eddie groans. "We haven't even given it a fair shot yet." He looks over the pedestal at Gren, who is still sulking on the ground on the other side of it. "Gren, you got big guns. You should give it a go."

Gren raises one heavy eyebrow.

"Guns, you know," Eddie says. He flexes an arm and pats his scrawny bicep. "Muscles. You're a perfect fit for the job."

She furrows her brow again, but this time, it's set squarely in determination. Pulling herself off the ground, she lumbers over to the pedestal again, wraps a meaty hand around the hilt and yanks, letting out a vibrating roar as she strains against it.

Nothing.

It's a sad sight to watch her let go, snorting like a bull at the immovable object and kicking at the dead grass beneath her massive bare feet. Kai gives her a gentle pat on the knee once they realize they're out of punting range.

Off to the side, Adrian crosses his arms. "Once again, brilliant plan, jester."

Glaring, Eddie says, "At least I came up with a plan. You're just standing there, acting like you're smarter than everyone."

At this, Adrian returns Eddie's glare. "No, Ed. Just smarter than you."

I barely see the red rise into Eddie's face before he lunges in Adrian's direction. Instinctively, I call out his name and move forward, knowing I'll have to break them up again. But Melandrich is between them in a split second, a long sword in his hand but not raised. Still, the sharp, no-nonsense expression on his face is enough to stop both Eddie and Adrian in place.

"That is enough!" he exclaims, his voice more commanding and forceful than I've ever heard it. "We have a singular mission between the seven of us, and I will not tolerate petty squabbling impeding our success."

"I was trying to help!" Eddie yells. He points at Adrian. "He's the one being petty."

Adrian hardly moved from his position, arms still crossed and hip still cocked. "I was helping too. I told you it was a waste of time. Which it was. See? Helping."

There's the briefest of moments where I hear it. Where the sound of arguing is absent just long enough for me to catch it drifting through the air—something low but muffled. I jerk my head to the side (east, if I've kept my directions straight), staring off into the sea of thick, dark branches. With the sun still falling, shadows play across the stale brown grass and into the over-growth, so tightly wound together that at first, I feel as though I'm hallucinating the subtle movement between the branches.

The sound comes again, but closer. Guttural and deep.

Through the bickering, I say, "Guys."

A massive shadow, too large and too smooth to be part of the forest, moves.

"Guys?"

It rumbles. A resonating snarl.

And the shadow charges forward through the dead growth.

My mind is on a delay from my body. I realize about a half second after the fact that I'm running toward the shadow, hand in my pocket and grabbing at any loose Residuum I can wrap my fingers around. Behind me, the arguing finally dies, and someone calls out my name, but it doesn't stop me. The emotion runs through me, sifting the energy of the stone up my arm and into my chest, into my gut.

The intention, now.

Protect, I think.

As the last barrier of branches crumbles away, letting loose the shadowy figure into the clearing, I let it fly into the air.

My heart skips a beat as I let it go, a different sensation than I've felt any other time using Residuum. It isn't the climbing, spreading Earthen energy coming from the ground, nor the booming, gut-pounding Infernal energy that comes from further below. This comes from the air around me, crackling and effervescent, the hairs on my arms raised as lines of lilac-hued electricity shoot off of my fingertips toward the figure that charges at me in a blur. The violet light shoots forward and collides with the figure, the deep growl I heard before cutting off into a shrill yelp. The smell of burnt hair curls under my nose as the electricity courses through my limbs until I feel a phantom something on my shoulder—almost like a hand coming down, Adrian's words whispered in my ear, "*Don't overdo it. You can let go now.*"

I break the connection.

Even after the stream of sparking energy stops, a tingle runs through my arms and down into the tips of my fingers. I gasp for breath, trying to shake off the feeling that both my arms fell asleep. Curled up in my right hand, I see a small sliver of purple crystal, only about the size of my pinky now. So, that's what Heavenly Residuum feels like, huh?

Multiple voices call out my name, and I turn to see the whole group rushing toward me, Eddie and Adrian at the front of the pack with Melandrich close behind. "I'm fine," I say, holding up a hand in assurance.

Adrian strides straight up to me. He looks over my shoulder and, though he's still breathless, he smiles. "Not bad for your first go at Heavenly."

"Good Earth," Melandrich says, following Adrian's gaze. "What sort of creature is that?"

I turn back to the shadowy figure, now lying in a motionless heap on the ground. I take a few steps forward to get a better look at it, but since it isn't charging at me anymore, the details are clearer. Black fur covers its body, though it's patchy in certain areas, exposing raw pink skin underneath like the hair has been lasered away. It's splayed on its side, four long, digitigrade legs flailing in all directions. A long snout juts from its face with a mouth hanging slack to reveal a row of stained canine teeth.

The most startling thing about it, though, is its size. This isn't a common dog or even a coyote. It has to be the size of a horse. Maybe even bigger than that.

"Is that—?" Eddie starts.

"Direwolf," Adrian confirms.

"Shit," Eddie says.

I straighten up as I look at the still wolf in front of us, guilt rising up into my chest. I definitely don't feel right hurting an animal, but—I mean, if it's a massive fucking animal that was poised to swallow me whole, I suppose I shouldn't feel too bad. "Well, it doesn't look like it's breathing. I think we're safe," I say dubiously.

A morose shadow falling across his face, Adrian shakes his head. "That isn't the problem."

That's when the sound hits me. That same rumbling roar that rattled through my chest before. Only this time, it's coming from all sides, deeper and more resonant than before.

My hand is back in my pocket, a crystal in my hand, and I square my shoulders as I look around me into the rotten forest.

The shadows have returned at the edge of the glade, but this time, the wolves expose themselves for what they are. At least a dozen pairs of reflective emerald eyes shine at us as the massive wolves skulk out from the cover of the knotted branches, their teeth bared and saliva dripping from their lips as they stare at their targets.

"The problem," Adrian says, amidst the sound of unsheathing swords and bracing weapons, "is that they travel in packs."

CHAPTER 20

I n tabletop games like *Mages of Velmyra*, fighting can be—
well, frankly, it can be boring.

See, in order for everyone to get an equal amount of
fighting time, a player's turn is broken up into a ten-second
window of bullet time. The player says how far they move (often
limited by their character's skill set or size), what action they take
(usually some sort of attack, but it can be something else if they
desire), and if they have the ability to do so, something for extra
flair before their turn ends. These ten seconds of time in game
often take more like three to five minutes in the real world, after
the player and the GM have talked it all out, rolled the dice, and
added the descriptors to give it that cinematic flavor every nerd
plays the game for. It shouldn't take long, in theory. But when
it's multiplied by seven players, all with their own skill levels and
varying degrees of argumentative tendencies, there's a lot of
downtime. Often, when I would listen in on sessions at the
apartment, this is about the time I would get up to get a snack
or check my email, maybe even sneak in a bathroom break.
Most of the other players would also check their phones and
show each other memes. After all, it's just a lot of rule checking
and math.

This is nothing like that. This is chaos.

The direwolves are upon us in seconds. I barely have time to think before I'm hurling magic at them. I'm not even sure what type of Residuum I have curled in my fist until the ground explodes underneath one of the gargantuan wolves, spraying rocks into the air that pummel the grey-black dog as it flies through the air and thuds onto the ground. Even as I'm doing that, another wolf barrels forward, its haunting green eyes focused on me as it sneers and snaps its teeth. I throw something else out, and a cluster of roots spring up from the dirt, wrapping around its paws so it collapses onto the ground, yelping as it attempts to free its paws from the tangle.

I push harder, trying to get the vines to crawl further up its legs, but they don't budge. Glancing down at the Residuum I have in my hand, I curse. The green crystal has been shaved down to the size of a toothpick. Useless. I toss it to the ground, pulling out another green stone and throwing the magic forward. While the dog hacks away at some of the roots with its teeth, more roots shoot up through the ground, clamping down on its legs and pinning it in place.

That's the first ten seconds.

I use the next ten to catch my breath, steadying myself on my feet as I look around the clearing, the sound of snapping jaws and shouts of attack ripping through the air. It's become utter madness—direwolves bear down on each of us, some two at a time. It takes me a hazy second to pick out who the blurs are amidst the clashing and confusion. Gren rakes her club through the air, pummeling an auburn-furred wolf in the snout with a sickening crack that I can hear clear across the glade. Standing on Gren's shoulders, wielding their crossbow, is Kai, screeching as they unload a bolt into another wolf's eye socket and reload with a fluidity that's obviously practiced. Eddie and Melandrich are back to back, hacking and slashing at a couple of wolves themselves. Melandrich is clearly more adept, taking swings at an assailant of his own before rushing over to Eddie's side to assist. I search for Jackson amid the chaos, but he's missing from my view.

A few yards from Eddie and Melandrich, Adrian works his literal magic. His fingers dexterously curl in the air as he rips the ground up into sharpened spikes in front of a sandy-colored wolf, not as weapons but instead crisscrossing them to create a spiked cage that the wolf—as huge as it is—can't penetrate without getting stabbed. The way he reaches into his pocket and pulls out another stone, shooting more magical energy into the air without a second thought, is as fluid as a dance.

Watching him is like seeing an entirely new person—like witnessing a weapon forged in fire returning to the flame, lique-fying back into molten metal. I try to see him as that suit-wear-ing, martini-drinking high roller he was playing back on Earth, but that façade is gone completely. This is Adrian's true state.

"Violet!" a voice cries.

And now, for the next ten seconds

I absently turn to see who's calling for me, and my stomach drops as a haze of teeth and fur streaks toward me. I close my eyes and throw my hands up in front of me, trying to push some magic out along with it, but there's no spreading feeling of magic rushing through my nerves that accompanies it. I'm not defending myself—there's no time for it. At this point, I'm bracing myself for the inevitable hit.

There's a piercing canine whine. I open my eyes, and I see Eddie standing mere feet away from a midnight-black wolf who shakes its head back and forth in distress, pawing feebly at an angry red cut across its face that spans from its left eye down its snout and to its nose. The dog snorts blood onto the bare dirt, and Eddie holds his sword with both hands, pointing it at the wolf with menacing conviction. Though his face is set in a scowl, Eddie pants, breaths heavy and shattered. His sword falters as he calls out to the wolf, "Back off, Cujo!"

Lips pulled back showing its rows of jagged teeth, the wolf barks at Eddie through the blood running down its face and lunges. Eddie's scowl falls, and he trips backward onto the ground, the sword falling out of his grasp.

But the wolf is still in midair as I throw the intention forward. *Protect.*

A wall of rock rises between the two, and the wolf hits it with bone-cracking force—quite literally. It screeches as it bounces off the rock with a nasty sounding snap, writhing as it hits the ground, its snout now crooked and bleeding profusely. It whimpers in the dirt, and I have enough time to run around to Eddie's side of the wall, helping him onto his feet.

He's dripping in sweat, the front of his shirt plastered to his chest. As I get a better look at him, a weighty pit hits the bottom of my gut. He's not just sweaty—he's beat up. His face is smeared with dirt and littered with scrapes and scratches, a bruise already forming on his cheekbone. "Thanks," he gasps, shakily picking the sword up off the ground.

I don't release my death grip on his arm. "Shit," I breathe. "We can't do this. There's too many of them. We're not going to make it out of here alive."

"Hey, hey. Look at me," Eddie says, putting his free hand on the side of my face and forcing my head up to meet his eyes. "You can do this, all right? You're kicking ass. You got this."

"And what about you?" I ask.

Letting go of my face, Eddie's eyes are wide. "Good question," he laughs.

I want to do the same for him that he did for me—grab him by the face and tell him it'll be all right—but another deafening roar pierces through the air. We both turn to see another pair of wolves charging us, and suddenly, our fears are inconsequential. We leap back into the fray.

The fight goes on. Wolves keep coming, all just as big and just as nasty as the ones before them. We throw what we can at them, but after what feels like hours of fighting (which has probably only been a few minutes), it doesn't seem like enough. From the quick looks I'm able to get in brief moments of respite, it seems we really aren't killing a lot of them. Adrian has done well enough, taking a handful of them out, and Kai and Gren have even gotten a few of their own. But aside from that first one I hit before the onslaught, I haven't killed any of them. Just kept them at bay. And they just. Keep. Coming.

I've lost track of how many sets of ten seconds have passed. I reach into my pocket for another Residuum stone after I toss a useless scrap of Heavenly to the side, only to find that my pocket is empty.

Fuck.

I wipe the sweat out of my eyes with the back of my sleeve and look back across the glade, searching for a flurry of magic amid the skirmish. The sun is now fully hiding below the trees, but the sky is still lit up. Even so, light shadows shroud the clearing, and with us wearing such neutral clothing and some of the wolves having such dark fur, it's making it harder for me to distinguish everyone's position.

A shower of sparks erupts not far away from me, and I flinch at the light it gives off. Underneath the waterfall of lightning, Adrian stands with arms extended toward a white wolf that collapses on the ground in front of him. The intense light dies off, and I sprint forward to Adrian's outline that's been burned into my vision. I stumble across the ground, uneven and rocky after being torn up from so much Earthen Residuum. Eventually, I reach him, clasping a hand on his shoulder like he's a life raft. He jumps as he turns to me but soon relaxes when he realizes I'm not a giant dog looking to wrap my jaws around his head.

"I'm tapped out," I sputter between breaths. God, when's the last time I got this much exercise? "Do you have any more?"

Adrian looks about as ragged as I do, his hair falling out of its tie at the back of his head and sticking to his forehead. His face doesn't look as beat up as Eddie's does, but it's just as dirty. Frantically digging in his pocket, he pulls out a handful of stones and thrusts them into my hands. "That's about all I can spare at the moment," he says.

Looking down at what he's given me, I freeze, my grip on his shoulder tightening. It's all Infernal, the orange glow radiating in my palm like hot coals. I glance back up at Adrian, shaking my head. "I haven't used Infernal before."

He's not looking at me, pulling out another couple bits of Heavenly. "You did back in Castle's Edge," he corrects.

"Okay, well I haven't used it properly."

"You hadn't used Heavenly properly until about five minutes ago."

"I can't just—"

"Violet, not to be insensitive, but can we do this when we're not about to be turned into mulch?" I open my mouth to reply, but looking over my shoulder, his eyes go wide and he screams, "Duck!"

I do as he says, dropping to my knees as he hurls a bolt of lightning over my head. My hair is damp with sweat, but I still feel the bits of fluff on my arms and the back of my neck raise as the streak of purple light strikes another wolf in the face, driving it into the ground. The streak disperses, and without another word, he runs off in Melandrich's direction as he fights off another wolf by himself.

Pulling out of my crouch, I run after him, still unsure of using Infernal, but my foot catches on something, and I fall to the ground, splayed out in the dirt. The Residuum flies out of my hand, the stones scattering in different directions. Pushing myself up on my hands and knees, I tell myself "*get up, get up, get up*" as if it will make me move faster, but before I can stand, there's a furry blur in my peripheral vision. The closest stone is too far out of my reach, even if I scrambled in a crawl over to it. Curling up in a ball, I brace for impact.

The sound of clanging metal rings out, followed by an intense growl.

I cautiously pry my eyes open. Slowly, at first. But soon, they open wide, disbelieving.

Standing above me is Jackson, his back toward me in a defensive stance. A wolf gnashes its teeth at him but doesn't move any closer. Because tenuously wrapped in Jackson's grasp is a long, dark-bladed broadsword. A hilt of twisted black wood winds over his white-knuckled hands as he holds the sword out, angling it across his body in defense.

He stares down the wolf in silence, the last rays of sunlight catching off the dark steel of the glinting blade. He doesn't give any quippy one liners like Eddie does. That's not Jackson. No, Jackson King glares at the wolf with dripping fangs in front of him, daring it to make him speak.

This ten seconds is tense. Jackson and the wolf stare each other down with unbreakable resolve. The wolf's impenetrable green eyes are fixed on Jackson's face, unflinching.

They stare. They wait.

But after what feels like ages, the wolf throws back its head and howls.

A shot of adrenaline runs through me, unsure what the wolf is trying to signal with the call. But as I look around the clearing, I'm astonished to see the wolves—some of them with their teeth poised to clamp down on limbs or their claws ready to rake across faces—stop mid-action and back down, howling low in response to the main call. With the sound of baleful yowls echoing in the glade, one by one, the wolves back away, retreating back into the tangle of branches around us. The rest of the group looks just as surprised as I do—Eddie's mouth hangs open in bewilderment as a brindle-patterned wolf calmly trots past him, taking no notice of him as it passes by. With the remaining wolves vacating the clearing, the howling wolf in front of Jackson cuts its song short and canters off, back into the wild.

I let myself breathe. It takes me a moment to grasp the fact that I'm not dead.

"Is everyone all right?" Melandrich calls out across the clearing.

There's a muttered back confirmation as we all dust ourselves off. Through the fading light, I can see that no one is too bad off, at least not for what we just went up against. Kai leaps off Gren's shoulders—they seem to have staved off injury from being so high up, but Gren has some long scratches down her arm. Adrian looks worn out, but he doesn't appear to have any glaring wounds. Melandrich doesn't even look that dirty somehow, with hardly a smudge running across his face. The worst one off is without a doubt Eddie, who in addition to the previous scrapes and bruises he had before, is squinting an eye as he walks in my and Jackson's direction, dragging his sword along the ground limply.

I clamber to my feet, brushing the dirt off my pants as I instinctively walk toward Eddie. "You still have two eyes, right?" I ask him.

Chuckling as he presses the heel of his hand against his bad eye, he says, "Somehow, but this one's going to be black and blue for a little bit. What about you? Are you in one piece?"

"I think so," I say.

"Master King," Melandrich says as he approaches Jackson. "Did you pull that blade from the pedestal?"

With the threat of the wolves gone, Jackson nods and lets the blade fall, holding it up just enough so it doesn't rest on the ground. "My daggers got lost somewhere," he says. "It was either try to pull that thing out or be eaten alive. I took a chance."

"It was good that you did," Melandrich says. He stares at the sword in Jackson's hand in awe, inspecting every inch of the blade. "I am curious, though, as to why you were able to pull it from the pedestal when the others struggled to do so."

"Gren obviously loosened it up for him," Adrian says with a smirk as he pushes his sweaty hair out of his eyes.

Far less sensitive than Eddie, Jackson shrugs off Adrian's comment. "Probably. I don't know."

"That means we can get to the Relic then, right?" Kai asks, trotting over to the group.

"In theory," Adrian says. "We should do it quickly. I don't know why the wolves left, but there's nothing to say they might not come back. So we should grab the Relic and—"

It's something so small. The brush of my pant leg against my ankle that seems just too out of place for it to be the wind passing by. I look down.

My heart stops mid-beat.

Because a Hellion is clutching onto the hem of my trousers.

Time slows, like I'm watching it grin up at me with its toothy mouth at half speed. It's the same as it was back then— teeth too big for its small jaw, bulging black eyes so fathomless that I see my own terrified face reflected back in them...

The air around me freezes into a February chill. The light fades into instant pitch darkness.

I hear my name, a shriek I can't ignore through the dozens of fingers raking across my scalp.

I scream.

I pull away, hard, kicking at the monster in flailing impotence. I tumble to the ground, catching a mouthful of dirt as I do, clawing my way away from it with every ounce of coherence I have. Pulling myself across the ground, I urge myself forward with my eyes closed. Get away from it. That's it. That's all you have to do. You just have to survive.

Breathe in.

Breathe—

My chest feels like it's being squeezed in a vise.

Breathe in.

Breathe—

Breathe in.

Breathe in.

Breathe in breathe in breathe in breathe in breathe in breathe—

Something grips me on the shoulders, and I jerk away from

it with a shout. It doesn't let go, though, spinning me around onto my back. "Vi, Vi! Stop! It's me!"

Breathe out.

The fading light returns. The monster's face is gone. Hovering over me is Eddie, his hands planted on my shoulders, his face plastered in an expression of deep worry. I push myself up and into him, wrapping my arms around him as he clutches me. I'm able to breathe again. It's only now that I realize my face is streaming with tears.

My face is buried in his chest, and I try to focus on nothing but the warmth he provides and the low thump of his heartbeat against my forehead. Outside of us, I hear shouts. Not the echoing cries of May screaming my name. It's the rest of the group, shouting at something. There is a scuffling of feet, a metallic *shink*, and then silence.

Eddie puts his hands on either side of my face, pulling my head up to meet his eyes. "Hey, you're all right. You're safe."

I nod, my breath still coming out in ragged heaves.

"What was that thing? I didn't get a good look at it before you started screaming."

I freeze, blinking at him. "You saw it?"

I don't wait for him to answer, looking around him toward where the rest of the group stands. They're clustered in a group, all looking at a tiny mound in the dirt, shoulders tensed and weapons in hand. Just catching the last rays of sun glinting from above the dead branches, there is a wet gleam on Jackson's black-bladed sword, errant black drops sloughing off onto the ground.

As I look closer, I see that the mound is the Hellion. I curl my fingers into Eddie's shirt, but after a moment of stillness, I realize that there isn't any danger. Sitting just a few feet away from its crumpled body is its severed head, soulless orbs for eyes clouding over grey and staring up into the quickly darkening sky.

My fingers loosen their grip. "That was one of them," I tell

Eddie. My voice is so small. It's a wonder I found it at all. "One of the Hellions."

Eddie pales at the word. "Fuck." He pauses, looking over his shoulder at the others. His eyes grow wide. "Wait, does that mean—?"

"Good show, all."

Eddie's grip around me tightens with his left arm, but the other reaches to his side, pulling his sword back out as he looks over my head toward the unfamiliar voice that's carried across the glade. I look in the same direction, and my muscles tense again, my breath catching in my throat.

One Hellion, I couldn't handle. Clearly. But at least twenty of them emerge from the dead forest now, some hanging from branches, while others simply creep across the ground on all fours. Their teeth drip with saliva as they hiss, feral beastly children that inch closer to us in crouching menace. I push myself back into Eddie as far as I can, and even then, I try to push further, hoping I can bury myself again.

In the center of the pack of Hellions is a larger figure. That's why I don't look away.

The figure glides through the clearing, almost hovering as it draws closer to us. The swarm of Hellions parts instinctually as it slips forward toward us. Their face is covered by the hood of their cloak—a draping swath that hides them head to toe, dragging across the ground behind them in a trail. The thing about it that makes it hard to look away, however, is that the cloak doesn't seem to be made of any fabric I've ever seen. It has the consistency of half molten rock, falling over the figure's shoulders in a dark, uneven cascade of black with cracks of bright orange and red shot through it, like the surface of a crusting over lava flow.

Like cracks in a cinder.

My grip on Eddie's sleeve tightens.

The figure pulls past the monsters escorting them, stopping a handful of yards away from us. The rest of the group is behind us, but I hear weapons being braced. "State your name and purpose!" Melandrich calls out. "By order of Queen Visandra!"

For a moment, the figure is motionless, but hands appear from inside the cloak, reaching up and drawing the hood back to reveal what looks like a man beneath a messy mane of dark black hair streaked through with silver. It hangs limply in front of wide, glowing orange and yellow eyes that flicker like the flame of a candle. They burn as he stares over Eddie and me, and his grin is unhinged—simultaneously ecstatic and harboring something furious. Running along his unnaturally pale skin are the same glowing orange cinder cracks that his cloak is composed of, fracturing his cheeks and forehead like he's a moment away from exploding.

He looks past us. "Name?" He mulls over the word like it has a taste he didn't quite expect. "I don't suppose I really have one of those anymore. Purpose?" The menacing grin spreads wider across his face. "Now, that's a complicated question."

Eddie's arm tightens around me. "The Infernal Mage," he whispers, astonished.

The man's smile remains pulled tight across his mouth. "You all did so well!" he exclaims, brightly like an excited child. "I've followed many before you to this place, but none have retrieved the sword. All eaten by wolves. So sad. I almost shed a tear watching as their limbs were torn from their bodies." He snickers to himself. "But not you, my friends. I knew you could do it."

The Infernal Mage takes another step forward, and Eddie awkwardly scooches us backward in the dirt, still holding onto me with one arm and holding out his wavering sword in the other hand. The cinder man stops before he gets too close. "It would be oh-so kind of you if you handed over the Relic. Oh-so kind."

"You mean this Relic?"

I look over Eddie's arm toward the voice, which is coming from the direction of the pedestal. My heart jumps into my throat as I see Adrian standing at the pillar of knotted branches, extending an arm toward the Mage. In his hand is a piece of long bark, almost identical to the branches of the pedestal, but it glows green in the soft evening light with scattered emerald sparkles running across its surface.

Somehow, the Infernal's grin pulls tighter. "You present it to me? How generous."

Adrian gives a single laugh. "Not to be dramatic," he says, "but you'll have to quite literally pry it from my cold, dead hands."

"That can easily be arranged," The Infernal says. Behind him, as if on cue, the Hellions hiss, gnashing their dripping teeth.

If I were in his position, I would throw the Relic at him, start running, and never look back. But Adrian simply cocks his head to the side and asks, "Can it?"

I now realize how dark it's gotten in the clearing as the Infernal and Adrian stare each other down, Adrian's whole body awash in the bright light the Mage gives off. Their tension has sucked the warmth from the air around us. I shiver, waiting for one of them to make a move.

The Infernal's smile, which has remained so tight and sure, twitches ever so slightly.

"Hold on to it for me, will you?" the Mage asks. He pulls up the hood of malleable rock around his head, shielding his eyes but leaving his unnatural grin exposed. "Keep it safe. I'll see you at the next one."

And with no other word, the Infernal Mage sinks into the ground, his molten cloak melting into the dirt around him, swallowing him up into the earth. As he melts, the Hellions retreat into the black branches, blending into the crooked darkness as they flee. Just as soon as he appeared, the Infernal Mage disappears into a smoldering stain on the ground, the only trace that he was ever here at all.

I let myself exhale, and Eddie drops the sword down into the dirt. He gives me pat on my shoulder as he stands me up.

The rest of the group stands behind us in awe, staring at the dark scorch mark the Infernal Mage left behind, eyes wide and mouths open.

"Someone want to explain just what the bloody hell happened there?" Kai asks, murmuring the question in a somber tone, a stark difference from their trademark animation.

"I believe," Melandrich says, slowly sheathing his sword, "we have someone following our quest. Someone quite dangerous."

"Splendid," Kai says flatly.

Striding over to Adrian, Melandrich extends a hand. "Master Inoue. The Relic, if you will."

Adrian doesn't look at Melandrich. His eyes stay fixed on the black stain left behind by the Mage, his jaw set in some burning thought that I can't read.

"Master Inoue?"

Adrian blinks, breaking his gaze on the burn mark. He looks up at Melandrich, brow still furrowed.

Melandrich reaches his hand out again, palm up.

Like he's moving through molasses, Adrian extends the Earthen Relic toward Melandrich, setting it in his open palm. His fingers linger on the bark for a fleeting moment as he lets go of it and leaves it in Melandrich's possession. In turn, Melandrich nods, but there is nothing appreciative in his eyes— their coldness is fit for a business transaction. Perhaps even colder than that.

Through their tense exchange, I hear Eddie say, "Well, I'll be damned."

I don't have to ask what he's talking about. Before Adrian, the pedestal that used to sit at waist height on him slowly shrinks, the cluster of branches retreating and unwinding from their knot, slipping back into the dirt that they were embedded in.

And as I look out across the glade, the entire forest follows suit, the menacing black limbs pulling back and uncoiling as they return to the earth they sprung from. Brown barked trees are exposed, some of them still growing greenery after being enveloped for god knows how long. It only takes a moment for the forest to morph back into the lush, vibrant environment it was meant to be.

We check in with each other, showing off scrapes and bruises, some chattering excitedly about their battle prowess while others simply look like they want a nap. Gren looks out at the now healing forest in reverence, and I catch the edges of her mouth curling upward around her jutting tusks.

Everyone rides the high of our first victory. I wish could. But amid the retracting forest and the celebratory chatter, I wander over to the small black heap that was the Hellion that had latched onto my pant leg. My vision fuzzes over as I stare down at its two parts: the limp body covered with protruding spikes and scales, and the detached head, staring up at me with its permanent grin.

I look into its cloudy eyes, and I don't look away. Not until Adrian's hand falls on my shoulder, shaking me out of my stupor.

"Come on," he says in my ear. "Let's go get a drink."

CHAPTER 21

N ews spreads quickly in a town as small as
Marwindale. The dead branches of the forest that
encased the village continue their retreat, so quickly
that by the time we make it back into town, the overtaken
houses are clear, save for the remnants of moss and water damage
leftover from the months and years of being encased in
overgrowth.

And an event like that doesn't go unnoticed. As we walk
back through the village, baffled mine workers and perplexed
farmers stand in the street, staring at us and whispering as we
come back through. It's hard to catch anything specific as we
meander back to the inn, but I get the sense that they know it
was us—after all, we're the outsiders who blatantly asked about
the forest earlier today. The fact that these unbreakable branches
are now gone after our arrival couldn't be coincidence.

The crowd gathering in the street is nothing compared to the
one waiting for us at the inn. As the door opens, we're hit with a
wall of applause. Hands are thrust forward to be shaken, and
pats on the back are shared as we pass through. The villagers
greet us like we've been friends for years, expressing their gratitude that the forest has been cleared. The barmaid from earlier

comes around, hugging us all (she even spares a kiss on the cheek for Jackson), telling us the tavern owner is giving us free rooms for the night. Our own individual rooms. I could cry out of happiness at the prospect of not having to hear at least four of us simultaneously snore into the wee hours of the morning, even if it is just for one night.

I actually do shed a tear when I go up to my prepared room and find a huge wash basin filled with water, steam curling off its surface. The room isn't fancy by any means—nothing as ornate and lavish as the room in the castle that I stayed at in Castle's Edge—but when I sink myself into the hot water and close my eyes, I feel like I'm back at the Amway. Back on Earth. The only thing that shakes me out of my daydream is when the water inevitably goes cold, and I reach for the faucet to replenish it, only to realize there's no knob there to turn.

I think about turning in early. My joints ache, and the soles of my feet scream at me, reminding me we've been traveling on foot for days. But Eddie knocks on my door, the excited grin on his face made only slightly lopsided by his swollen eye. "It's party time!" he exclaims, grabbing me by the wrists and dragging me out of the room.

It doesn't take me long to figure out what he means. Downstairs, what looks like the entire town has filled the barroom floor, every table packed shoulder to shoulder with celebrating townsfolk clinking ale tankards together, laughing, and singing songs. In the corner, a small person with scaled skin and a pointed reptilian face plays a fiddle, an energizing ditty that fills the room. For a moment, I don't think we'll be able to find a place to sit, but a group of drunken, dirty-faced men spot us and stand up from their table, imploring us to take their places.

Eventually, the rest of our group joins us, all having taken advantage of their own wash basins—even Gren's olive green skin has been scrubbed down, though there are a few splotches of dirt on her arms that one cleaning won't be able to take care of. Everyone else looks fresh as ever. The last one to come down is Adrian, and he makes sure it's an entrance. He's changed into a crisp lavender shirt (where he even found it, I don't know), undone almost down to his navel. His hair is back to coiffed perfection, curling back into the pompadour that he sported on Earth. What did he even use as product to get it up that high? I shudder to think about the possibilities.

The seven of us gladly accept free drinks. We all handle it with relative grace, besides maybe Kai who grabs onto their tankard like it's about to save their life. We mostly stay silent as we watch the townsfolk jovially eat and dance, celebrating their rejuvenated town.

It doesn't take long before Melandrich clears his throat. "I suppose," he says, "we should discuss what happened."

Setting his tankard down onto the table, Adrian leans back in his chair, resting his elbow on the backrest. Despite the dark circles under his eyes, the rest of his face is bright, looking at the rest of us with no concern. "What's there to discuss?" he asks. "We got the Relic. Two more to go."

Jackson looks at him flatly. The rest of the group seems to have found a change of clothes, but he's thrown on the same dirt-stained shirt he was wearing when we arrived here. "Did you miss the part where—" He stops, looking around before dropping his voice to a murmur. "The part where the goddamn Infernal Mage showed up? You don't think that's something to discuss?"

"Did you think that a Mage showing up was some outlandish impossibility?" Adrian asks back. "We're looking for the only things in the world that can kill them. Of course they're going to take notice."

"Which is, arguably, a big deal," Jackson says. "We need to be prepared."

Adrian merely shrugs, taking another drink.

"What? Is preparation something we don't need to worry about either?" Jackson scoffs. "I'm sorry we aren't all seasoned masochists who relish almost being torn apart by demigods."

"For fuck's sake, kid," Adrian laughs over the rim of his tankard. "I thought the jester was the dramatic one, but apparently, I underestimated you."

"I do not think that Master King is wrong for being concerned, Master Inoue," Melandrich says. "This Mage is after the Relics just as we are. He also declared that he would be meeting us at the next Relic location. From what you have told us, these Mages are aware of the locations but simply lack the ability to retrieve them, correct?"

His brow knitting together, Adrian nods.

"Perhaps he caught wind of our expedition early on and has been following us," Melandrich muses. "Perhaps he means to take the Relics from us so we are unable to use the Mage's Dagger once it is formed with all four."

I clear my throat. "Uh, I may know something about that."

All eyes drift over to me, and I nervously grip my tankard in front of me. Taking a breath, I say, "I think I saw him in Castle's Edge, right before we left."

Most everyone's eyes grow wide. Gren's expression doesn't change much besides a twitch of her eyebrow. But everyone else looks taken aback as I describe following a figure with the same glowing patterns on his cloak. I don't mention seeing him in the woods that first night. Honestly, I'm still not sure that wasn't my mind playing tricks on me.

"That certainly confirms it, then," Melandrich says solemnly.

Something warms in my chest, something I can't quite pinpoint at first, but I soon realize: it feels so good to be believed. After a decade of telling cops and therapists and parents and friends about what happened to me, after watching nearly every one of them look at me with condescension and pity, Melandrich just *believing* what I tell him is incomprehensible. The telltale lump forms in my throat again, and I look down into my mug of ale, hoping nobody notices that I'm holding back tears.

"So, what then? He wants to destroy them all once he gets a

hold of them?" Kai asks after a long swig from their tankard. "That doesn't make an ounce of sense. If he wants to prevent the Dagger from being formed, couldn't he have just taken one of the Relics and destroyed it? You can't make it without all four, right?"

"Correct," Melandrich says. "That is curious."

"Unless he *does* want the Dagger to be formed," Jackson says.

Adrian looks at him from the corner of his eye. "And why do you think he'd want that?"

Jackson shrugs. "Maybe he wants one of the other Mages taken out. They can't all love each other. That much power in four individuals spells 'drama,' no way around it."

Circling the rim of his tankard with his index finger, Adrian says, "I don't think you're wrong, but they also have enough power to take each other on. The Dagger was for mortals to use, not Mages. If he wants one of the others dead, he could go toe to toe with one of them."

"If he wants to be messy about it," Jackson says, "but stabbing one of them with a knife is a lot quicker with a lot less collateral damage than setting the countryside on fire and hoping they burn."

"Since when do they care about that?" Kai asks with a snort.

Adrian flicks his tankard, a hollow metal ring floating into the air. "They don't."

Melandrich shifts uncomfortably in his chair, his blue eyes briefly flicking in my direction before settling back on the table.

"That brings up another question." Eddie leans forward in his seat, his eyes fixed on Adrian. "Why didn't he kill you when he asked for the Relic?"

Raising an eyebrow, Adrian says, "Well, if he needs us to get the Relics for him, it wouldn't be very smart to slaughter all of us before we can do it."

Eddie shakes his head. "He could have killed you and taken the Relic, made an example out of you so the rest of us would keep on the path to retrieve the others and give them to him under threat of death. Like you said, they don't care about collateral, so one dead human isn't anything to them."

"And you would just love that, wouldn't you?"

I can almost feel the intensity in their gazes as they stay locked on each other's eyes. I resist the urge to smack Eddie on the shoulder and tell him to play nice, because something about the seriousness of his expression stops me. This isn't him just trying to push Adrian's buttons. He actually wants an explanation. Almost like he's accusing Adrian of something.

Adrian, however, isn't playing along, spreading his arms wide. "I'm not a mind reader, kid."

"No, but you have experience with the Mages."

"I have experience with the Crystalline Mage."

"So you didn't know him?"

"No." The word is decisive, definitive. No room for any "howevers."

Eddie lets the word linger for a moment, and I wonder if he's going to push back on it. But he sighs, shaking his head, directing his one good eye back to his tankard.

Grabbing his own mug, Adrian breaks the tension by flashing that dazzling grin at all of us. "You know, for a bunch of heroes, you all need to loosen up," he says, standing up. "They're throwing us a victory party! Get up and dance, for fuck's sake!" Before any of us can object, he strides away, melting into the crowd surrounding us. Most of the group simply goes back to drinking, but Eddie stares in Adrian's direction, his gaze pointed and unbroken.

Idle chatter picks up before Melandrich's eyes widen and he turns to Jackson. "Master King, I meant to ask," he says, his pointed ears perking up. "What did you do with the sword?"

Casual as ever, Jackson jerks his head toward Eddie. "I gave it to him."

Tilting his head like a perplexed kitten, Melandrich asks, "To Master Hughes? Why?"

Eddie holds up his hands in protest. "Why not? He's the dagger guy. I'm the sword guy!"

I can tell Melandrich is holding back a sigh as he talks. "Yes, but Master King is the one who pulled the sword from the pedestal. Rightfully, it would belong to him."

"Is that how sword ownership works around here?" I ask. "You retrieve it from the magical stump, and it's yours?"

"Not necessarily," Melandrich says. "To be frank, I have never come across an artifact before that is particular about who retrieves it. But with how much we struggled with it beforehand, I cannot help but wonder if it was meant for the wielder, specifically." He looks at Jackson, his bright blue eyes somehow brighter, alight with curiosity. "Master King, I cannot confirm this, but I believe that sword *belongs* to you. You and you alone. For what purpose, that remains mysterious, but it should stay with you."

It's silent as we look at Jackson, expectantly. As he switches his gaze between our eager faces, though, he looks the least excited out of any of us. "It's like Eddie said," he finally answers. "I'm the dagger guy. He's the sword guy. It makes sense for it to stay with him. I don't want it." He looks off to the side, something sullen in his dark brown eyes that hides well behind his large-framed glasses.

"Master King," Melandrich says. His voice is soft but clearly heard, even over the raucous noise of the tavern. "Power is not something to shy away from. It is something to respect yet embrace. Daggers may be easier to wield, but the sword can be just as much about finesse as it is force."

Abruptly, Jackson says, "I need a refill. Eddie?"

Eddie nods and stands up in time with Jackson. Without another word, they head off into the crowd, the slump of Jackson's shoulders obvious as he weaves his way around bar patrons. Melandrich looks crestfallen, but once Kai starts babbling about how watery the ale is here, he turns his attention to them and tries to make polite conversation.

The night rages on. As the hours pass, there's no sign of the party slowing. The music only gets faster, the drunken stories told around us only get louder, and the laughter only grows more jovial. We all leave the table eventually to get refills, receive thanks from locals, and generally mingle. Kai and Gren show off a clearly rehearsed jig as the fiddle plays, which Eddie tries to mimic with disastrous results. Eventually, he grabs my hand, pulling me in for a dance, though it ends up being more of a spin-around-in-a-circle-like-that-one-scene-in-*Titanic* mess than an actual dance. At some point, Gren gets roped into an arm wrestling contest with some of the burlier mine workers. While she seems hesitant to participate, after some coaxing from Kai, she swiftly defeats all the opponents, generous enough to leave all their shoulders safely in their sockets.

After a while, some of the patrons trickle out, thinning out the crowd and leaving only the most drunk and rowdy. Eddie, obviously deep in his cups, somehow finds his way into a card game which Jackson assists him in since—even after being shown a few times by some of the other tavern goers—he clearly has no idea how to play. Gren moseys over to spectate, only occasionally snorting when Eddie makes a bad play. From our designated heroes' table, I watch the game with Melandrich and Kai.

"That idiot's going to lose all our money," Kai comments as they watch Eddie sloppily lean into Jackson to talk strategy on the card game.

"No need to worry," Melandrich says. While his words are clear, there is a bright red flush to his cheeks that indicate he's had more than he's used to. "I only gave him a few coins. He will only lose the equivalent of a child's allowance."

With a swig from their mug, Kai looks at me. "What is it you see in that fool?" they ask. "Sure, he's entertaining enough, but the bastard runs around acting like he's Gedron the Great." They pause, before their face lights up in realization. "Oh, folk hero from ages ago. Sorry, I forget you lot aren't from here, sometimes."

"Well, you're one to talk, Kai the Calamitous," I say, smirking.

"Hey, I have to go by that name!" they exclaim. "Being an adventurer is tough business, even tougher for kindred folk. Most bandits take one look at me and decide that I'd be a nice side dish for their ogre stew." They nod toward Gren, who is still enraptured with the game Eddie and Jackson are playing. "She's at least got the size to back up the reputation. I have the name out of self-preservation."

Melandrich reaches out an unsteady hand and drops it on Kai's shoulder. "You have no reason to feel inadequate, Mezzir Tenderfoot. Your performance in today's battle was proof enough of that."

Kai's face morphs into an expression of dread, and they bat Melandrich's hand off their shoulder. "For gods' sake, Melandrich!" they cry. "I told you to keep quiet about that!"

I giggle. "Tenderfoot? Your name is Kai Tenderfoot?"

Their head slumps as they look at me, sheepish. "It's a kindred folk name," they say. "They're all soft and dainty like that. It's embarrassing."

"No need for embarrassment," Melandrich says reassuringly. "The kindred folk are very proudly rooted in a culture of tradition. You should be proud of your origins."

Kai scoffs. "Yes, well those 'traditions' are nothing more than getting fat, having children, and dying of old age. No kindred folk I've ever met has done anything with their life otherwise. I don't find much pride in that."

I shift in my chair before saying, "To answer your question, he's the kindest and most supportive person I know. If it weren't for him, I don't—" I stop before I finish the sentence. *I don't even know if I'd be here.* It's a true statement, but one that brings up feelings that I can't parse out through this much alcohol. I clear my throat. "He's a big part of my life. One of the biggest. He's my family."

A roar of delight comes from Eddie and Jackson's direction, and I look over to see them clutching each other in an excited hug, while Eddie uses a hand to pull a pile of coins in the center of the table toward him. Behind them, Gren claps her huge hands together in glee.

Kai hums thoughtfully. "I suppose I get that," they say. "Gren's like that for me. Ever since she and I met in prison—" They look over at Melandrich, whose back has straightened slightly at the mention of the word, and they hold out a hand. "Don't worry, we served our term. We didn't break out or anything, so don't get your ears in a twist. But ever since then, she's the one I can count on being there, no matter what shit we've gotten ourselves into." Awkwardly, Kai shrugs, looking at their lap. "I don't know. I don't like monotony, but I like having a constant. I suppose that's what she is, for me."

Melandrich nods, looking on at the trio feverishly scooping coins into Gren's bag. "That is one thing that I have come to appreciate about Midran culture," he says. "Family extending beyond the bounds of blood. Hevarans value nature. Therefore, those who bore us take precedent above all else. I cannot help but look upon those of you who have forged such strong bonds despite being of different lineage and be impressed, though. It is…" As he trails off, his trademark mild smile returns. "It is, dare I say, beautiful."

I can't help but smile as well, watching Eddie get pat on the shoulder, another flagon of ale thrust into his hand, smiling through his swollen eye like he didn't almost die today. Honestly, I think it's pretty beautiful too.

276

It only takes another hour for Eddie to pass out. And it's abrupt. One minute, he's telling some of the villagers the tale of how we slayed a pack of direwolves, and the next, he's face down on the table. Melandrich and Jackson offer to bring him up to his room, and he's just with it enough to work his legs up the stairs as they support him on either side. As soon as he's gone, the crowd starts to considerably disperse, the main source of the party's entertainment turned in for the evening. Kai and Gren retreat as well, accepting accolades all the way up the stairs.

Across the room, I spot Adrian leaning against the wall near the far window. I can't tell from the distance at first, but as I walk over to him, I confirm he indeed has another button undone. Somehow. At this point, he might as well just skip the formalities and take the whole thing off.

"Are you turning in soon?" I ask as I approach him.

He tilts his head, noncommittal. "In some way, I'm sure." He gently nudges my shoulder with his hand that isn't occupied by a tankard. "Hey. You did great work today."

I scoff. "I hardly did anything. If it weren't for Jackson, I'd be puppy chow right now."

"That's not true, and you know it," Adrian says firmly. "Give yourself some credit. You used two new types of Residuum in the heat of battle."

"One," I correct. "I didn't end up using the Infernal."

"I guess we'll have something new to practice in the weeks it takes us to get to the Crystalline Relic," he says.

I raise my eyebrows. "Weeks?"

"Yep. It's three times as far as it was to get from Castle's Edge to here. We have a long road ahead of us."

I groan. My feet are going to be nothing but callouses by then. Guess it's a good thing I never had any desire to be a foot model.

"Adrian, are you ready?"

I turn to see a tall, slender yet muscular man with deep set blue eyes, looking directly at Adrian. His mess of blonde hair hangs just below his ears, and he ruffles it with one hand as he looks at Adrian with an eagerness that is all too easy to read.

"I'll be up in a second," Adrian says. "Go on ahead."

The tall man smiles and nods, turning around and heading up the main stairway to the top floor.

I smirk at him. "So, you're not turning in yet."

"I told you: in some way, I am." He winks at me. "Honestly, you should take the opportunity, yourself. Like I said, it's a long trek to the second Relic."

Forcing the heat out of my face at the idea, I say, "I think I'm good."

"Sure you are." Downing the rest of his drink, Adrian sets the tankard on the table in front of us. "Keep telling yourself that, you sad, horny little girl. Goodnight."

I'm only a few minutes behind him going back upstairs—it takes me a minute to fend off the last congratulators and well-wishers. As I ascend the stairs and make it up to my door, Melandrich emerges from the room next to mine, shutting the door behind him. As he turns to the hallway, he smiles when he sees me. "Lady Spence," he says. "I am glad you have found your way up here by yourself."

"He's okay, right?" I ask. "Like, he's not going to choke on his own vomit or anything."

"Master King has volunteered to keep an eye on him," Melandrich confirms. "He will feel terrible tomorrow morning, but I am sure he will make it through the night."

Something strange shifts in my stomach when he smiles at me, something that I haven't experienced before while looking at him. I tell myself to knock it off—it's just Adrian's obsession with sex weaseling its way into my mind. Plus, I've been drinking, and while I'm not bad enough to really consider myself drunk, it's enough where maybe I'm not thinking as straight as I should be. I smile back at him, a friendly smile. A smile that friends give each other. Because they're friends. "Well, good," I say. "Thank you for helping him."

"My pleasure," Melandrich says. He strides past me, walking to the door on the opposite side of mine. "Have a pleasant rest of your evening." As he passes by, I catch a faint whiff of rosewater, and a warmth washes over me as the scent curls in my nose.

Motherfucker. Why not.

"Melandrich," I say.

He stops, his hand already on the doorknob. He looks at me, his vivid blue eyes still eerily visible through the dim candlelight of the hallway.

"Uh," I stammer. God, I'm so bad at this. "Um, someone down there said they were sending up a bottle of wine to my room. I don't know if that's something you can do or if he was just saying it because he was plastered, but if there is a bottle there—I mean, if I start it now, I can't really take it with me on the road, and I can't drink it all myself. So—I don't know." I swallow hard. This is going so poorly. Fuck, I wish the wolves had eaten me. "I don't know. Maybe you can split it. With me, that is."

And Adrian wonders why I can't get laid.

Melandrich warily listens as I sputter my way through my attempt at flirting. But his furrowed brow flattens out, and the tender smile comes back onto his face as he realizes what I'm saying. Slowly, he let's go of the doorknob and walks over to me.

My stomach plummets. Shit, did that actually *work*? There's no way he heard that and thought "*Take me now, you beautiful, awkward creature.*" No way in hell.

Stopping in front of me, with only a couple of feet in between us, Melandrich takes my hand. I'm acutely aware of how sweaty my palms have gotten, but as he holds my right hand in both of his, he says, "Lady Spence, I hope you do not take this the wrong way."

All the nervous tension in me dissipates. Oh.

"You are a very beautiful woman, as well as intelligent and charming," he says. I resist the urge to look around behind me, wondering if maybe the intelligent, charming, beautiful woman he's referring to is standing just behind me. "I am very flattered by your request. However…" He trails off, his eyes flitting down to my hand in his. "We spoke of chosen family earlier—family not restrained by blood, yes?"

I nod.

Smiling again, he says, "I am afraid I do not experience physical attraction to almost anyone. You must be a much closer part of my chosen family for that to even be a possibility."

"Oh," I say, a little breathless.

A rush of pink flourishes through his cheeks. "I know it is odd," he says hurriedly. "For a long time, I thought it impossible altogether. But one person—the one I considered my closest family, not bound by blood—she proved that was not true."

"I understand," I say. The nervous knot in my stomach is gone. Even with him holding my hand like this, I'm far less anxious than I was a moment ago when sex was on the table. "It's not odd, Melandrich. Trust me. I've met plenty of people from Earth who feel exactly like you do."

At this he smiles again, not letting go of my hand. "Every time you speak of Earth, I think I like it a little bit more."

There's a pause before I say, "What happened to her? The one who proved it was possible."

Melandrich tries to maintain the smile, but it quickly falters. "She decided that I was not part of her chosen family anymore. And I had to acquiesce." His voice quavers on the last word, but he clears his throat, straightening out his back, showing more of the formal guard captain that I had first met within him. "It was long ago. I am not quite sure I will ever find anything like that again in my lifetime. Again, I hope you do not take it as a personal slight."

I shake my head, still giving him a reassuring smile. "It's fine. I don't take any offense."

He gives a single nod before lifting my hand up to his lips, giving it a quick, gentlemanly kiss. "Goodnight." He drops it and turns away, walking back to his door, and I turn back to mine, only slightly dejected but mostly relieved. As I open my own door, Melandrich calls out, "Lady Spence?"

I stop.

The light from his open door illuminates his face, set in a serene expression, though as he talks, a hint of concern creeps its way into his eyes. "I hope whatever you were looking for in a possible tryst you find in some other way." With another modest smile, he slips into his room and shuts the door behind him.

My own room is cold, even with the fire still burning in the hearth. I shiver as I put on the nightgown I packed from the castle, laying on my back on a bed that feels too big and too small all at the same time. Closing my eyes, I think about what he said. About what I was looking for by proposing such a thing to him, insinuating that it wasn't just the possibility of getting laid at all. I try to prove him wrong, hiking up my nightgown and exploring some parts of myself that haven't been explored in a while—thank god my period stopped this afternoon. But as I try to lose myself in the warmth that rushes down my legs and up into my stomach, images flash through my mind. The beheaded Hellion, the Infernal's cracked face, May dragging across frost-covered ground...

It doesn't take long before I give up, wrapping myself up in a cocoon of thin blankets. Perhaps it isn't an impossibility for Melandrich, but with every passing day, it feels more and more like it is for me.

CHAPTER 22

The next two weeks look a little like this:

We wake up in the morning, some earlier to rise than others. Melandrich is always the first one up—he seems to be pretty alert after only four or five hours of sleep, and he always takes the last watch, so he has usually been up for hours before any of us are even considering consciousness. Jackson is typically next, though he spends his morning lying in his tent sighing loudly or slumped next to the fire reading one of the three books he's brought with him. The rest of us—well, it's a toss-up. Kai and Gren seem to have a pretty synced up circadian rhythm, so whenever one is up, the other is awake soon after. Eddie has never been a morning person, and at twenty-four years old, he probably never will be. I fall in various spots in the line-up—some days, I don't wake up until I hear everyone chattering over shared rations. Other days, I wake from a dream before the sun is up, and despite my best efforts, I can't seem to fall back asleep.

After we've been sufficiently fed and given enough time to be coherent, we walk for about eight hours, like it's an hourly job. By the end of the first week, there is no more pain in my feet. As a matter of fact, if someone were to jab a knife through my heel,

I doubt I would feel it. We stop for the night when the sun is about three quarters of the way through the sky. It's easier to set up camp, gather food or water, and do anything else we need to before the sun sets. We've been following the Mid River, which runs through the center of the forest. According to Adrian, it's basically a direct shot to the second Relic. Where we had to wait four days for a bath from Castle's Edge to Marwindale, I can at least rinse myself off after a particularly sweaty day of walking in the early evening. That doesn't solve the shampoo issue, of course, but after a while, my greasy hair is just something I throw back into a ponytail and forget about. I can tolerate it for now, but fuck, I'm going to kiss my bottle of Suave when I get back home.

It's in this downtime that Adrian and I practice residuuism. We stick to Earthen and Heavenly, working on mastering them outside of the life-or-death chaos of a wolf attack. Throughout the weeks, I get a better feel for how they differ. I describe to Adrian how it feels to use each of them—Earthen feels like it comes from beneath my feet, while Heavenly feels collected from the air around me—and he corrects me. "It doesn't come from those places. It comes from you. Your own energy, your own intention is amplified by the Residuum you use. That's all you, being pushed out into the ground or into the air, not the other way around." It takes effort not to laugh at that. What I feel when I make vines burst forth from the ground or shoot a bolt of lightning from my hands, that can't be me. It has to come from somewhere else. But I nod and keep working on it, becoming less sloppy every time I use it.

When it's finally dark, we sit around and eat our rations and listen to Eddie go through his nightly tale. My personal favorite is his story about a boy bitten by a monster and altered into a hero that swings from buildings by webs and clings to walls named Peter Parker. I hold back a laugh as Kai marvels at the possibility of a human-spider hybrid. Even in a world where fey and scaled folk exist, that's apparently still a novel concept. Once everyone is tuckered out, we decide who's on watch that night. Melandrich almost always takes a shift, but the rest of us rotate. I like to take the earlier shift, just so I don't have to wake up in the middle of the night. I usually take it with either Eddie or Adrian, but one night, Jackson volunteers to stick it out with me.

With everyone tucked in their tents and Gren propped against her tree, things slowly settle into place, the quiet hum of the night providing the backing track for the simmering flames of the campfire. Jackson, propped against a felled log, stares intently at his paperback, lost in concentration as the flames provide him the barest source of light. After a moment, he pulls the book closer to his face, his brows knitting together like laces in a boot pulled too tight.

"How can you read like that?" I ask him. I shift, suddenly feeling every stick I've been sitting on for the past two hours. I had fully resigned myself to just sitting here quietly—albeit awkwardly—for the next couple hours until I switched shifts with someone, but the fact that he seems so insistent upon reading this book with hardly any light is too strange for me to just ignore.

He doesn't bother glancing up at me before answering, "Practice. My dad would always catch me with a flashlight in bed, so he took it away from me. I learned to read with just the hall light on." He taps his glasses. "Probably why I have these."

"You're just going to ruin your eyesight more."

Eyes still on the page, Jackson shrugs. "If that means I read all I could before I couldn't anymore, I think it's worth it."

I nod, even though he isn't looking at me. Silence settles over us again, save for the soft crackling of the fire. After a moment, I really do think I start to hear—what was it Kai said that first night?—the crickets humping each other off in the distance.

Don't say anything. It'll just piss him off. We're trying to be cordial, remember?

"Do you remember the last thing she said to you?" I ask.

So much for that, I guess.

It's enough to pull his face away from the book to look up at me, the furrowed brow staying intact, though as his gaze focuses on me, it's less in concentration and more in confusion. "What?" he asks.

I raise and lower a shoulder, looking down at my hands in my lap. "I don't know," I say. "Sorry, I just—just didn't want the silence, is all."

"Right," Jackson says, obviously suspicious.

I roll my eyes. "We promised we would do the 'get along' thing, right?" I ask. "So, I'm making conversation."

"About our kidnapped friend? Just skipping right over 'some weather we're having' and going straight into the dark stuff?"

Shaking my head, I say, "It was stupid. Sorry."

I keep my head down, focusing all my energy on examining my cuticles by the dim orange flicker in front of me. He's silent, and I don't blame him. I half expect him to just get up and walk back to the tents, leaving me alone with Gren softly snoring up against her tree.

"We had algebra together, so it was then."

I pry my eyes away from my nails. He folds the corner down on the top page of his book, closing it and grasping it between both his hands. The dancing yellow light reflects off his freckled skin, highlighting his high cheekbones. Through the flare off the lenses of his glasses, his brown eyes are flecked with firelight. He looks into the simmering pit like it's miles away.

"It was the class right after lunch," he explains. "We sat next to each other. She had a—what do you call those paper things again?" He scans his memory for a moment before laughing to himself. "Oh, a cootie catcher, yeah. She had one of those. When Ms. Davis had us all work on assignments in partners, we basically spent the whole class period messing around with that thing. According to that, I was going to be a millionaire with a mansion in Malibu." He laughs, though there's a bitterness to it. "Anyway, the bell rang, we picked up our stuff and went out into the hall. She looked at me like she did every other Friday, and said, 'See you on Monday, King.'" He exhales—not a sigh, but there is a resignation to the way he lets out his breath. "And—well, that didn't happen."

I nod. "Yeah."

He takes his eyes off the fire and looks at me, and for the first time that I can remember, it doesn't feel like he's staring knives into me. His expression is soft as he studies my face. "I'm sorry," he finally says. "I'm sorry that you had to go through that. Even without what they did to your face, I'm sure it was…" He trails off, searching for the right word to qualify it.

"Awful?" I finish for him.

Jackson nods.

"Thanks," I say, forcing a smile on my face. I know when people say they're sorry that they really don't know what else to say. Apologizing is just a space filler so they can move on from the awkwardness of talking about tragedy. It's then my unspoken duty to make them feel like they've done a good deed in comforting me, and once they've gotten confirmation of that, they can move on like we never talked about it in the first place.

But I should have known that Jackson isn't like that.

"What was the last thing she said to you? Or the last thing you remember, anyway?"

I remember it all. Every rake of long dark claws against my scalp, every shriek of discord in her voice as she was dragged away. Every last detail is seared into the grooves of my brain like a brand. He asks the question, and it flashes through my head all at once, images layered over each other in a split second. Even that feels too much to glimpse.

I hear my name, screamed in panic and confusion.

I close my eyes, hoping to blot it out. I feel my throat closing up. "Uh," I stutter. "I—I'd rather not—"

"Sorry," Jackson stammers, a flustered tone to his voice that makes it clear he's realized his mistake.

"It's fine," I say, shaking my head.

"I didn't mean to—you just asked me, so I thought I'd ask you."

"It's really—"

"I'm an idiot. I shouldn't have said—"

"Jackson, just drop it, all right?" I snap.

I can't tell if it's the firelight, but his face morphs from soft curves to hard edges in an instant. His eyes dart back and forth across my face for a moment before he abruptly stands up, wringing his paperback in his hands. Before I can say anything else, he walks off and disappears into his tent.

The fire crackles in front of me. I can feel the warmth it gives off. But I still shiver in its presence as I'm left alone, only the sound of Gren snoring left to keep me company.

One day, Adrian has me go off by myself to practice.

We're running low on rations again, even after stocking up in Marwindale. Melandrich suggests that we take a party out to hunt. We've seen plenty of deer and elk roaming the forests as we've gone on. Even if we can only catch squirrels or rabbits, it'll be better than what we've been subsisting on. Adrian and I can make fruit trees, but protein is running dangerously low, and it's reflecting in our sluggish pace as we trudge through the woods each day.

Eddie is the first to volunteer for the trip, which should only be about a day if they're able to find anything substantial early on. To my surprise, Adrian also offers up his services, much to Eddie's chagrin. It bothers him so much that he pesters Jackson the entire evening before about coming along. I hear him whisper a couple of times that if he comes with, Eddie will buy him take out for a week straight once we get home. Eventually, Jackson concedes, though he doesn't hold back any of his innumerable sighs.

Adrian asks why I don't come along, but Eddie answers for me. "Vi doesn't like seeing her food before it's food. Wigs her out." I feel my face turning red, but I don't deny it. He's right.

The next day, they head out before the sun is even up. Melandrich makes sure we all have weapons, emphasizing that if anything catastrophic were to happen, that we're to flee. No worrying about them, only moving forward onto the next Relic. As long as we follow the river south, we can find it and meet back up with them. Our safety, he says, is more important than anything.

"Rule number one of *Mages*," I mutter to Eddie as he slings his pack over his back, "Never split the party."

Shrugging, he looks over to Melandrich and Adrian, who are casually conversing. "It's been quiet so far," he says, scratching at his face but quickly stopping once he realizes he's doing it. He was able to get a shave in Marwindale, but a week and a half out, his stubbly beard has grown back in. "I think you'll be okay. Besides, you don't need us. He gave you Residuum."

"That doesn't mean we can take on the Infernal Mage by ourselves," I say.

"We already determined he doesn't want us dead. He needs us." Eddie shifts in place, eyes darting over to the group. It's an odd, out of character tic that I'm unfamiliar with. It's almost as if he's waiting for the conversation to end. Like I'm bothering him, holding him back.

I look down at the ground. "I guess."

Gently, he pats me on the shoulder. "It'll be fine. We'll be back before nightfall. Just take care of yourself."

I nod, but before I can say anything else, he's already moved over to the others, ready to take off.

Before they hike off into the forest, Adrian calls to me across camp, "Practice casting while I'm gone! I expect you to be better at Heavenly than I am by the end of the day!"

It takes me the morning and a good chunk of the afternoon to do anything but stare at the dead fire pit at the center of camp and listen to Kai bicker one-sidedly with Gren about what sort of card games they should play to pass the time. While I work up the nerve to go off on my own, I rifle around in my own pack, pulling out the game master's guide. He's not even here but Jackson's judgmental remark about me not studying the book still irritates me, even a week and a half later. Now's the time to get reading, I guess, since we don't have a day where we're endlessly walking.

I nibble on a piece of azurefruit as I skim the glossy pages, but reading it feels strange now. What used to bring me such comfort has a completely new and uncomfortable connotation now that I'm actually in Velmyra. Just flipping through the modules with actual "story," I can tell they're made up. And the actual information about the world that doesn't seem fictitious is dry to say the least. It's written out like a history book, all prescriptive terms and dates and locations. The only thing that makes it remotely interesting is the fact that it occasionally talks about magic and fey creatures and goblins.

At the beginning of the book is a map of Velmyra. We, of course, are only on one continent on one side of the world of Fractum, but I'm assuming Adrian doesn't have much knowledge of anything outside of this slice of the world.

Where did he say he and his brother were from? Elowen. My eyes scan the map and find the dot that indicates Elowen on the complete opposite side of Midra from Castle's Edge. There are so many places that I've never even heard mentioned on here, too. Zaliadon, Lakeside, Oberin, Kazden...

What was that town Melandrich mentioned? The one attacked by the Mage who turned themself in?

Tersaria. I scan the map, all along the coasts, in the forests, even into the borders of Extera and Undra. Even after I search and re-search, though, I can't find any indication of it.

"Hey, Kai?" I call across camp, not taking my eyes off the page. "Do you know where Tersaria is?"

Their incessant chatter comes to a halt at the question. "Tersaria?" they ask. "Hm, it sounds familiar." There's a moment of silence, long enough where I think maybe they'll end it there, but they soon exclaim, "Oh! That's right. We passed through there once, didn't we?"

Gren sniffs.

"Yeah, it was that town that was half in shambles. About six or seven years ago, I'd say. It was attacked by a Mage a few years before that. Miserable fucking place."

I'm finally able to pry my eyes off the book and look over at them. They each have a handful of cards fanned out in their grasps, Gren's looking comically small and Kai's looking laughably large. "Do you know where it would be on a map?"

"Just south of Kazden."

I shake my head. "I don't see it here."

Narrowing their gaze, Kai slides off the log they're sitting on and walks over to where I'm seated on the ground. They hold out a hand, and I give them the book. Their eyes flit over the page quickly, and their eyebrows raise in surprise. "Well, it should be right here. But there's nothing."

Kai lowers the book enough that I can see where their finger rests on the page, but it's sitting in the middle of a blank space.

"That's weird, right?" I ask.

Their eyebrows knit together in confusion. "I mean, this map has some missing towns. Mostly small ones, like little farming communities. It is odd, because Elowen is nothing special, but it's indicated here…" They shake their head, still scanning the page, like they're just missing the one detail they're looking for. "The big cities all seem to be on here, but Tersaria—it's not small by any means. Even after they were attacked, it's a major city. Thousands of people live there. I can't see why this mapmaker would include something like Elowen but leave out godsdamned Tersaria."

I wouldn't see why either if I didn't know who the mapmaker was.

Kai hands me back the book, and I thank them for the

information as they trot back over to their card game. I look back at the book, but my eyes aren't focused on anything. I can see why he included Elowen. He grew up there. But Tersaria...

When was it he left Velmyra? About ten years ago, right? Around the time Tersaria was attacked...

I can feel the air practically snatched from my lungs.

His brother died in Tersaria.

Fuck.

That explains it, right? The fact that he didn't ever seem to want to talk about it. The fact that he left Tersaria off the map. The fact that he hates the Mages so much. He wanted to forget it all happened. The game was his way to survive in a world he didn't know, but he had no interest in reliving the things that caused him that pain. He erased the place where it all ended entirely. And he made those who got his brother killed the villains of the story on Earth, just like they were in Velmyra.

I snap the book closed, my brain fuzzy. It's going to do me no good to speculate on it. He's not even here for me to ask. Standing up, I call out to Kai and Gren, "I'm going to go practice. I'll be back before dark."

I stop walking a couple of miles out from the campsite after I realize that I've been aimlessly wandering without really thinking for almost an hour. The pieces of Adrian's story are all there, but it's like they won't fit together for me. There's something I'm missing. Something that connects all of them.

As I slow to a halt in a clearing near the edge of the river, I close my eyes and shake my head. What am I doing? Why does it matter if I figure him out or not? He's kept his stuff secret for a reason, and I should respect that.

Distracting myself, I pull out the handful of Residuum stones that Melandrich gave to me before he left. He's told me to be sparing, since he's unsure if we'll pass through Magburn or just outside of it to get to the Crystalline Relic. If we can't make it to the city, we won't be able to replenish what Residuum we have stored up. We've been running low on Earthen, so I only have a couple. Heavenly is more plentiful. Most of what he's given me, though, is Infernal.

I ignore the amber-orange stones for as long as I can. I practice pulling up pointed spikes of dirt with the Earthen stones, creating swirling cones of controlled wind with Heavenly. After an hour or so, though, I'm out of both. I stare down at the pile of a dozen glowing ember-like crystals on the ground, simmering like hot coals after a fire has died down.

I glance up at the sky. The sun still sits high. It'll be a few hours before dusk.

I shouldn't even touch those things. Not until I can work with Adrian on it.

Although, I tried Heavenly without his instruction before, and it turned out fine. What's to say this could be any different? Besides, I *have* used Infernal already.

I flex my hands, shaking them out to dry the sweat from my palms before reaching down and grabbing one of the larger stones.

The familiar resonance of coursing energy passes through me, coming from much further below the ground than Earthen and vibrating up through the soles of my shoes. Earthen always manages to spread up to my limbs, but Infernal energy stays rooted in the pit of my gut, settling in my core. I hold onto the stone, letting it gather, but it's so uncomfortably *much*. When I used Infernal in Castle's Edge, it went off so fast that I couldn't let it build. With no distractions, though, holding onto the energy without letting go of it immediately is painful. Like my stomach is filled with hot coals.

Frantically, I glance around me, looking for a way to release it. A long-fallen branch on the ground catches my eye, and before I can consider any other options, I reach my free hand out to it. I don't even have to think about the intention. My body does it for me.

Release.

And it does. The branch bursts into flame, and the hot pit of energy within me eases.

I stand over the burning branch, breaths coming out of me in gasps. I feel lighter somehow. Looser. Every muscle in my body feels like it's been worked out at the gym after a long period of inactivity. It was so painful in the moment, but now that the tension has been released, it's almost euphoric. As I pant, a laugh shudders out of me, catching me off guard.

It takes me longer than it should to realize that a smoldering branch just sitting on the forest floor is probably a good way to start a wildfire. I scramble back over to the pile of Infernal Residuum. That little bit of flame used up the smaller stone like it was nothing. This time, I grab a bigger one off the pile, turning back to the blaze with my hand out.

Except I don't know how to stop it. How do you call back a fire that's already been lit?

My hand stays extended toward the flame, and my intention is out there. *Stop*, I think. *Stop*. It should be so goddamn simple. It's one four-letter word. But as much as I think it over and over, casting my intention forward, it doesn't pull itself back. In fact, it spreads. The flames of the branch lick at the ground, grabbing onto the dead leaves sitting amongst the brush and instantly igniting. I'm no longer throwing my intention forward—I'm catapulting, hurling, desperately propelling it at the spreading flames in front of me. But the fire doesn't hear my pleas. It does what it's meant to do—it consumes.

I only have to blink, and the entire forest surrounding me is engulfed.

Flames crawl up the nearby trees, even the bright green leaves succumbing to their power. Smoke gathers into the air, looming over me in a suffocating miasma. I back up into a patch of bare dirt, the only thing that won't catch amid the inferno. The river is next to me, and I think for a moment about running over and hurling water onto the flames, but using what? My hands? It would be just as good as spitting on it. My knees give out, my hands clawing at my hair as I look on helplessly in horror at the mess I made.

Because I did make this mess. It was me. Me and my malfunctioning emotions, my weak intentions. I knew this would happen. Adrian was convinced I could do it, but he was wrong. All wrong. This is all wrong. Wrong. Wrong. Wrong.

Breathe in.

Breathe in breathe in breathe in—

It's so hot, I feel like the air I'm pulling into my lungs has been set on fire too. I close my eyes against the heat, feeling like the fluid in my eyeballs will boil if I keep them open too long.

Breathe in breathe in breathe in breathe in breathe in—

"Violet!"

I hear it over the intense crackling of the surrounding flames, and something hot and calloused sets itself on my cheek. I open my eyes.

Adrian's face is in front of me, a wall of yellow flame blazing behind him. It takes me a moment of blinking back the blinding light and muscling through the intense heat to realize that his hand is resting on the left side of my face. Through the light, I can just barely make out his wide-eyed panic.

"You have to call it back," he says to me, his voice elevated over the discordant snaps of the fire around us.

I shake my head. "I tried," I cry. "You have to. I can't."

"I—" He stops himself for a moment, his eyes scanning my face. "I know you can do it, Violet."

His hand stays on my face, but the other thrusts something into my palms and closes in around my fingers, keeping the jagged object enclosed in my grasp. "You can do it," he says again. "But you need to calm down first. Take a second to breathe."

I open my mouth to say something, but nothing comes out. Just a sputtering gasp.

His grip on my hand tightens, his nails digging into my knuckles. "Breathe. Come on."

For a moment, with my whole world around me immersed in flickering orange light, raging heat licking at my skin, I feel like I'll never breathe again.

Until I do.

The breath I've been holding in explodes out of me, and it clears my head just enough for me to feel the Infernal energy gathering within me again.

Breathe in.

Breathe out.

Stop, I think. No, not think. Plead. Beg.

My eyes closed, nothing seems to change at first. The magic within me slowly wanes, like it's being used and released. The heat is still there, the light given off by the flames still piercing through my eyelids.

But the burning air around me eventually cools—hot, but bearable. The light fades, and as I open my eyes, I see the wall of fire slowly recede, like someone is gradually turning the knob down on a gas stove.

And the sheer panic on Adrian's face subsides, his nails pulling themselves out of my skin. He takes his own advice and breathes, looking around at the quickly fading ring of fire around us. With the last bits of flame trickling out, he looks down at my now empty hand, a faltering smile pulling at the corners of his mouth. "Told you you could do it."

The hand that rests on my cheek gives it a little pat before dropping. As he stands up and walks away, the extent of exactly what I caused shows itself. Surrounding us is a ring of scorched trees, some with still-simmering leaves and charred bark. The ground around us is covered in ashes, and a thick layer of dissipating smoke settles in among the rubble. The sea of bright orange flame has died, leaving in its wake seared desolation.

As I finally allow myself to cry, the thought won't leave my head.

I made this.

Adrian goes around the site with the Heavenly Residuum he has on him, using the scant moisture in the air to put out any of the other smaller flames that haven't already been extinguished. He leads me over to a tree that's managed to stay undamaged by the fire, telling me to relax while he runs back to camp to let everyone know what's going on. I'm alone for a while. How long, I don't know. Even if I had some way of checking time, I have no energy left in me to do anything other than stare blankly into the slow-moving water of the river in front of me. Its sluggish pace reflects how spent I feel after all that. Even without the loose, stretched out feeling of having used Infernal Residuum, I barely have enough energy to keep my eyes open, much less think.

It isn't an unfamiliar feeling. There have been so many nights that I've stayed up, writhing in my knotted bed sheets, willing myself to keep my suffering quiet so as to not wake Eddie. Too many times, I've held my breath until I've almost passed out, tears tracked across my face, wishing for the fist of pain reaching into my gut to loosen its hold on my insides and let me rest, only to feel too used up to sleep hours afterward.

This isn't a new magic user's feeling. This feeling is an old friend. An old, terrible, selfish friend.

Eventually, I hear footsteps crunching through the brush. There's no energy left in me to turn my head to see who it is, but Adrian lets out a familiar sigh as he sits down next to me in the dirt. Glancing out of the corner of my eye, I see him cross his legs and gaze out over the lazy river. His face is flecked with dark soot, his hair unruly and falling out of its tie. I can imagine I look much the same, but I can't seem to muster the energy to care. I just want to sink into the tree I'm leaning against and become one with its bark and branches so I never have to think about anything but photosynthesizing ever again.

"I told everyone back at camp what happened," he says, his voice quiet and raspy from smoke inhalation. "Not the full extent. Just that it was a Residuum thing gone wrong."

I close my eyes, sighing weakly.

"I know," Adrian says. "I wouldn't have told them anything, but we got back to camp, and we could see the smoke and you were missing. They all thought the worst. I had to go back to reassure them you were okay." He snickers to himself. "Eddie looked like he was going to pass out when I got over there. He was so worried, it was almost precious."

Opening my eyes again, I look up at the singed leaves dangling in the canopy above me, barely holding onto their branches. "Do you think we can fix—this?" I ask, pointing up to the burned flora surrounding us. "If we had Earthen Residuum, maybe..."

Adrian shakes his head as I trail off. "Earthen Residuum can enhance and encourage growth. It can't bring dead things back to life. I don't even know if the Earthen Mage can do that."

Another errant tear rolls down my cheek, and I swipe it away before he can see. "I told you," I whisper, my own voice hoarse from everything that just happened. "I told you this would happen. It always does. Eventually."

"Violet, it happens to everyone."

"No, it doesn't."

He laughs, a harsh sound that's probably louder than he meant it to be. "You think this has never happened to me? That I've never lost control, not once? I started using magic when I was a teenager, Violet. Of course I lost control. Even as an adult, I lost control. It's part of the process."

"Then when does it stop?" I ask. I don't prevent the tears from pouring down my cheeks this time, finding odd comfort in the soft breeze that rolls over my face as they streak. "When does it get easier? It can't be like this forever. When will it finally—"

I stop. Because the next words out of my mouth would have been, "*When will it finally end?*"

I don't think I'm talking about magic anymore.

Sighing again, Adrian says, "I wish I had a good answer for you. I wish I could say 'this many years and it's over,' but I can't." His voice catches on the last word, like he ran out of breath to say it all. He clears his throat. "Truth be told, I struggle with it myself. No matter how put together I seem, I'm always wary of that other shoe dropping. Always worrying about when I—when I lose control again too."

I look over at him. He stares straight ahead, not quite at the water but not quite at the trees on the other side of the river-bank. There's a subtle glimmer in his deep brown eyes, one that I barely catch before he blinks, and it's gone.

I don't think he's talking about magic anymore, either.

"How do you do it?" I ask him. "How do you—live like this? How does it not terrify you that you could shatter into a million pieces at the drop of a hat?"

He sits motionless, still staring at something I can't quite see. Just as I think he's going to leave my question unanswered, he says, "I think the difference between us, Violet, is that I've spent time accepting that these emotions aren't ever going away. They're part of me, just like the experiences that caused them. I can pretend they aren't there, but that just makes it hurt more when they do get out of control." He turns his head and looks directly at me, his ash-smeared face awash in the quickly fading sunlight. "You're still trying to convince yourself you don't have those emotions. That you've recovered, or that you're back to 'normal,' whatever that's supposed to mean. And when you can't deny it anymore, it overwhelms you. I know. I've been there."

I smile a bitter, strained smile. "So, your advice is, what? Feel my feelings?"

"As absolutely fucking hokey as that sounds, yeah." He smiles back at me, but there's no hint of malice in it. "My emotions can absolutely destroy me if I let them. But they're also the things that allow me to make magic." He looks down at the patch of bare dirt in front of him and wordlessly raises a hand in front of him, as if he were cupping someone's chin and lifting their face to meet his eyes.

A tiny hint of green pushes its way out of the dirt in front of his crossed legs, stems spreading and eventually blooming into a small white flower, hanging downward like a delicate bell. Adrian drops his hand, and the flower stops with it, a perfect tiny thing in the midst of ruin and wreckage.

He smiles again. "My thoughts and feelings are the things that allow me to create. Why would I ever deny myself that?"

The sight of the little white flower is almost enough to make me grin, no irony. But I look around us at the ring of charred trees. "They also cause this," I say.

Adrian looks around, taking a deep breath. "We can work on tearing the dead ones down and planting new seeds. It'll take time, of course. We can't bring the dead trees back to life, but new ones can certainly grow. And fire can help a forest thrive, as counterproductive as that sounds. It brings nutrients to the ground, clears out dead things so the living ones can flourish." Looking back at me, he grins. "We don't have to start that today. Maybe tomorrow morning, before we set off?"

I try not to roll my eyes at him. I'm so wiped, I can hardly comprehend the work we would have to do to get rid of all this and lay the groundwork for new growth. Feebly, though, I nod. "Sure. Tomorrow."

He nods back, his shoulders slumping, releasing the tension in them. "It's a date," he says. He uncrosses his legs and leans back on his elbows, mindful to keep the small flower undisturbed by his feet as his legs uncurl. "Let me know when you want to head back. Take all the time you need."

And as he lays stretched out in the dirt and I stay sprawled out against my tree, I think of all the thoughts and emotions that compile the both of us—the girl with demons in her head and the man with the long-lost brother. I can feel his energy. Even though he smiles as he looks up at the peeking blue of the sky through the green and black of the leaves above us, I feel how fragile he is. Because it's exactly how I feel right now.

I wonder, as I look back at the river, how right he is. If these messy bits of myself could ever amount to anything worthwhile. If they could ever do more than just decimate.

I lean my head back and close my eyes. Maybe that isn't for me to figure out right now. Maybe right now, I should just exist and be satisfied with that. And be satisfied that I'm not alone. Next to me, Adrian patiently waits, doing little more than breathing in the afternoon, the last hints of smoke finally starting to fade from the air.

It takes a while before I speak again, but I have to know. "What was his name?" I ask.

"Hm?" Adrian asks.

"Your brother. What was his name?"

It shows itself on his face then. That indelible mark. That damage. "Wyland," he answers, faint as a whisper.

I nod. "It's a nice name. I like it."

"Me too," he says, voice wavering before going quiet again.

We sit together silently, two remnants of an extinguished blaze still simmering and blackened, ready to disintegrate at the gentlest of touches.

CHAPTER 23

Nearing the end of week two, we come across the cabin.

Kai is in the middle of telling us a story as we pass the five billionth tree that looks like all the other trees we've seen for the past two weeks. Eddie is running low on lyrical stories—he's already cycled through all the TV theme songs he knows and was working again on pop songs. "Jolene" by Dolly Parton was just as big a hit as the bardcore version back on Earth. "Bohemian Rhapsody" was at least energetic, if not a little avant-garde and confusing for the Velmyrans. He really started losing them when he dipped his toe into the Weird Al repertoire. "Trapped in the Drive Thru" introduced a lot of heady concepts that I don't know they were ready for, like TVs and cars and—well, drive-thrus.

To give him a break, Kai tells a tale of their own as we walk. And they swear on their life, it's true.

Everyone else calls bullshit.

"You don't have to lie, Kai," Jackson says with a sigh, his hands shoved in his pockets as he hops over a fallen tree trunk.

"I'm not lying! Besides, I'm certain half the stories Eddie has told us aren't real."

"Hey," Eddie says defensively. "Rasputin was real."

Looking at him with a flat expression, Kai says, "Really. And what about the devil that traveled to the gorge? Was he real?"

Eddie rubs his temples. "He didn't *travel to the gorge*. He *went down to Georgia*. It's a place on Earth," he explains.

"Georgia," Kai says, mulling it over in their mouth like it's a piece of rotten fruit. "Sounds fake to me. But *this* is true!" They center themself in the middle of our group, trotting to keep up with everyone else's lazy gait. "I witnessed it myself. Gren did too, didn't you?"

Gren, who has been picking at her teeth for the past ten minutes, just sniffs.

Arms crossed, Kai grumbles, "Some help you are, you overgrown onion."

"Mezzir Kai," Melandrich, at the head of the group, says gently. "Not that I believe it to have any bearing on the entertainment value of the story, but what you are speaking of seems far-fetched at best."

Kai rolls their eyes, throwing their whole tiny body into the action. "I'm not making this up. We actually did see a former Mage! Saw his head get cut clean off his body in the middle of town by the Royal Guard when we were up north in Unisgate eight years ago."

Jackson cranes his head up, adjusting his glasses as he looks at Melandrich. "That sound familiar to you at all?" he asks.

"I only came under the kingdom's employ six years ago," Melandrich explains. "Even so, with something as—ahem, violent as that, I would think I should have heard about it in my years as guard captain."

"Well, listen up then, Tree Boy. You can tell this one to the boys back at the palace," Kai says. Ignoring Melandrich's bemused expression at his new nickname, they continue. "So Gren and I were up in Unisgate. Cold as tits, but there was a tavern on every fucking corner, so easy enough to get so drunk you can't feel your tongue, much less the wind chill. We were on day three of—" They side-eye Melandrich. "Nothing we say out here can be used as incriminating evidence for an eight-year-old crime, can it?"

Melandrich narrows his gaze at them. "I cannot guarantee that."

"Wonderful," Kai says, clapping their hands together and turning back to the group. "So, we were on our third straight day of having nice chats with the locals and them being so grateful for our company that they just gave us money without our asking. We were milling about the town square when all of a sudden, we heard this ruckus coming from down the way. Now, Gren and I, being the humble travelers that we were, thought we could offer our assistance in a fraught situation."

"So, you wanted to be nosy," Jackson says.

Kai glares at him. "Beg your pardon, O Mighty Sword Wielder, but this is my story, not yours, so hush up. Anyway, we quickly followed the noise of a crowd forming, and lo and behold, a group of at least twenty guardsmen were standing outside an unassuming Unisgatien home."

Next to them, Gren growls lowly in her throat.

"All right, all right, it was five guardsmen," Kai sighs. "Stickler for details today, aren't you? Anyhow, five guardsmen stood outside this home, pounding on the door, being awfully dramatic. 'Open up, in the name of Queen Veridian!' and all that. Eventually, some poor sap does answer. Real reedy looking fellow, thin enough where a stiff breeze could knock him over, top of his head bald as a baby's buttocks. And without a word, they throw this petrified looking sod out into the open, center of the crowd. Behind him, his wife and three children come running out the door, and they all just start wailing. I mean, it was *insufferable*. All the kids, just screaming, 'Mummy! Mummy! What are they doing to daddy?' Enough to give you a bloody headache."

"Wow, what empathy," Jackson remarks.

"So, they go up to this shivering bastard in the middle of the street, and to my surprise, they don't rough him up right there. No, they just throw a pile of purple crystals down in front of him. I wasn't terribly versed in magic back in those days, but I know now that it was Heavenly Residuum. And these guards start screaming at the man, 'Cast something! Cast something now!' And this man is blubbering, his wife is weeping, his kids are screeching. He picks up a handful of these rocks." Kai, demonstrating for us all, cups their hands together. "And he just stares at them, face screwed up like he's trying to take a shit, like he's begging these things to do something."

They splay their hands out, scattering the invisible stones they had cupped in their hands onto the ground. "Nothing. Couldn't make a single spark," they say.

"Why not?" I ask.

Kai cocks their head. "Well, it's rumor, mostly. But they say that if someone takes on the power of a Mage and then passes it off to someone else, they can never use that type of Residuum again."

Just behind Melandrich, I see Adrian kick at a loose stone, launching it off into the brush without missing a step.

Kai continues. "He starts pleading with them, literally groveling. Talking about how he gave it all up and he was trying to change, and please don't kill him because he has a family to think of." They trail off, their initial excitement as they told the tale waning, their smarmy smirk fading. "That wasn't good enough for the guardsmen, I suppose. One of them took their glaive and brought it down upon his neck. Couldn't even utter a last 'I love you' to his wife and children."

The group falls silent, nothing but the crunch of leaves underfoot passing between us as we let the somber end of the story sink in.

"I still don't think it happened," Jackson says, after what feels like an hour.

"Everyone, halt!" Melandrich says, commanding but hushed, holding up his left hand while his right goes toward his blade.

The hairs on the back of my neck stand up, and I shove my hand in my pocket, grasping onto whatever Residuum I have. Everyone else takes the same cue. We all stop where we are, tensing and reaching for whatever we have at our disposal, ready for a fight. But as Melandrich unsheathes his sword, I follow his gaze down the glen, and my shoulders relax.

Below us in a sloping valley, almost imperceptible among the thick trees, is a house. A cabin, to be more precise. It blends in perfectly with the surrounding brown bark of the trees, as if it's camouflaging itself. Simmering in front of the house is a low-burning fire pit with a sturdy black pot hung above it, though it's too far away for me to see what might be inside of it.

"Someone lives out here?" Eddie asks Melandrich, pulling up beside him with the black bladed sword Jackson wielded in Marwindale prepped and ready to go.

"It certainly seems that way," Melandrich replies, still speaking in barely more than a murmur. "That fire is freshly maintained."

"Is there a reason we have to concern ourselves with whoever's down there?" Jackson asks softly, taking a cue from Melandrich. "We can just move past, can't we?"

At this, Melandrich lowers his sword but only slightly. "We can, but we must proceed with caution. In Midra, it is not custom to live in an untamed wood such as this. Whoever resides here may be formidable."

"I'll be takin' that as a compliment."

Melandrich's sword is back at attention as we whirl around to face the unfamiliar voice behind us, weapons raised. The breath is momentarily knocked out of me as I brace myself to see the cracked face of the Infernal Mage again, even though the voice we heard was high pitched and airy, not low and lilting like the one we heard before.

It is not, in fact, the Mage we see before us. Standing a few yards off is a woman, stark and surreal with how sharp her image is against the drab forest backdrop. Aside from her vibrant red cloak and shock of bright orange-red hair falling past her shoulders, everything about her is pure white—her floor-length dress, her skin. Even her eyes appear to be white at first glance, but as I focus in more, I see they are actually a shocking pale blue. The intensity of her appearance almost makes her difficult to look at against her surroundings.

As she glances over us, she grins, her pale lips barely more than a line on her face. "You're early. Makin' good time, I see."

No one has time to question her before Melandrich strides forward, sword raised. "We are delegates of Queen Visandra passing through on official royal business. We mean no harm and ask for safe passage through this area," he declares.

The woman, however, merely giggles at him—a high-pitched, almost childlike laugh. "You're much more serious in person! Somehow!" she says, maintaining her grin. "No wonder Aletheia is so fond of you. It's intense but endearin', I suppose."

I expect Melandrich to question what she said, but he stands stationary in front of her, silent.

"Who exactly are you?" Eddie asks, stepping up behind Melandrich. "What do you mean by 'we're early?' Did someone tell you we were coming?"

"If you're worried about the Infernal Mage, no," the woman says, taking a couple casual steps toward us. Hanging in the crook of her elbow is a basket filled with wildflowers and other assorted plants, some with the roots still attached. Even as the lingering dirt brushes against her clothes, the bright red cloak and pristine dress don't seem to retain any of it. Not a smudge. "We've never been acquainted. Though, he is waiting for you. The Crystalline Relic is not far from here. He'll certainly be there to greet you when you get there."

"And how do you know that?" Eddie asks, his grip around the black sword tightening.

"She's a seer," Adrian chimes in from the back. I glance over at him, and he stares at the woman almost in awe, mouth open but eyes narrowed and cautious. "Isn't that right?"

Her grin broadens as she and Adrian lock eyes. "You would recognize all too well, wouldn't you, Mister Inoue. Or is it Hightower again? I can't seem to keep track."

Adrian's eyebrows raise, his skin paling.

Laughing again, the woman looks at the rest of us, amicably smiling. "My name is Orla," she says. "I am, like he said, a seer. A dealer in futures, if you will. I've been expectin' you all for quite some time. I'm happy to finally be of help."

Shaking out of his statue-like stance, Melandrich slowly lets his sword drop. "How precisely do you intend to be of help to us, Lady Orla?" he asks.

"Residuum, of course," Orla states, a cheer in her tone that seems misplaced amongst our wary group. "If I'm not mistaken, you lot are runnin' low, yes?"

Only briefly looking over at Adrian, Melandrich nods. "Our supply is limited, indeed."

"Well, you're in luck. I have plenty myself. It's just me out here, so I don't go through it as quickly as two of you surely do. Especially with little Violet over there still learnin'."

My gut instantly sinks as she says my name, and it plunges even further as she turns her gaze to me. Her eyes are penetrating, like she can see every thought thrashing about inside my head. I can't blame Melandrich and Adrian for being petrified in her presence.

"But we can work out the details of that exchange in time," Orla says, adjusting the basket hanging off her arm. She skips past Melandrich and Eddie while paying no mind to their swords. "Come! You all must be starvin' after such lengthy travel. A home-cooked meal will do you wonders. Follow me." Moving past us, she starts down the ravine toward the tiny cabin, not bothering to make sure we follow. And with only a few confused exchanged glances between the seven of us, we do eventually follow.

As we carefully scale the glen, I pull up next to Adrian. "What exactly is a seer?" I ask him, careful to keep my voice down. "Can she just see the future or can she, like, read our minds or something?"

He shakes his head but doesn't look at me. His gaze has not left Orla since she appeared. "No, just futures. Seers are the closest you can get to being god-touched without being a Mage."

"How exactly do you come across powers like that?" I ask. "I thought the gods were supposed to have abandoned Velmyra. That's why the Mages were even created, right?"

"No one really knows, but..." Adrian trails off, looking around him, taking particular stock of Melandrich and his proximity to both of us. With him far out of our earshot, Adrian says, "The prevailing theory is that they are children conceived by Mages in power. And honestly, I think that's more than theory. There's no other explanation besides children just coincidentally being born with the ability to see futures. And I'm not a big believer in coincidence."

"Are they—are they dangerous?"

Eyes firmly fixed on Orla's bouncing red and white figure ahead of us, Adrian shrugs, half-hearted. "I guess we'll find out."

The cabin is bigger than I first thought without the cover of dense trees, though it could not house more than one person. It looks sturdy enough, with a thickly thatched roof and a strong foundation amongst the otherwise uneven terrain of the forest, but it does appear to be sagging beneath its own weight, most likely due to age. The exterior is covered in flowers, some situated in pots while others hang off ribbons and ties from the porch beams, dancing in the soft breeze that has somehow made it through the surrounding tree cover. Orla stops by a collection of open silken ribbons to tie a few of the plants from her basket into them, not bothering to remove any of the excess roots.

As I pass by her, I see that her house is not the only thing she decorates with random odds and ends. Hidden within her knotted red hair are an assortment of objects, tied up into her strands like the plants that hang off her house. There are flowers, yes, but also plain twigs, bundles of long grass, even small glass beads and shining crystal stones.

No. Not just stones. Wrapped up in the tendrils, I see the glow of green Earthen Residuum and the smallest sliver of Heavenly. I can only just make out the orange hum of Infernal as her hair catches a shadow off a tree, emphasizing the natural radiating light coming off the crystal.

I try not to gape as she leads us all to sit down by the fire. With a flourish of her hand, the steady flame beneath the cast iron pot flaring. As we settle in, she walks back to the house, returning with a stack of wooden bowls and scooping out mysterious chunky contents from the pot into each individual bowl. She hands out the food, and when I receive mine, I can't quite make out what it is. Is it stew? Are there vegetables? A meat of some kind? It's all mashed together in some sludgy brown substance that masks any discernable features of the contents, but the smell is incredible. So incredible that I don't hesitate in taking a bite. It has a flavor more intense than anything I've eaten in my entire time in this world—savory with just a hint of something sweet lingering in the aftertaste. I waste no time devouring everything in the bowl in an embarrassingly short period of time. From the unholy noises coming from Eddie sitting next to me and Kai arguing with Gren about what the ogre is going to finish off of her portion, I'm guessing it's a shared sentiment.

Orla doesn't take a portion for herself, sitting on a nearby tree stump within our circle and crossing her legs while resting her elbow on her knee. She happily watches us slurp down our food with her head in her hand, amused. Kai, once they're done bothering Gren about her portion, huffs and looks over across the way at her, a wary arch to their eyebrow. "Aren't you going to eat anything?" they ask.

"Hm?" Orla wonders, as if she's been shaken out of a daydream. "Oh, no. I've eaten already. Don't you worry. I'm not one of those sticklers about eatin' only when everyone has food.

I say if you're hungry, you eat. Plain and simple." Her amused little grin widens as she looks at Kai. "I know that's hard for kindred folk to understand sometimes. Those manners are really drilled into you at a young age, aren't they?"

As if she had just gotten right up into their face, Kai recoils at the sentiment. "And what would you know about that?" they ask.

"Oh, quite literally nothin'," Orla admits. "Only what I've seen of you. And others like you, of course. Though kindred folk aren't normally ones to wander upon me themselves. Except you, Kai the Calamitous. Nice name, by the way. I don't think your mother will hate it as much as you think she would. You should pay her a visit one of these days. Just to let her know you're still alive."

Narrowing their gaze at her, Kai says, "Beg your pardon, but I thought you said you were a dealer in futures, not pasts. I'd appreciate it if you stayed out of mine." They straighten their shoulders, puffing their chest out, but there's an uneasiness to their expression that doesn't quite go away.

"Well, in my experience, futures often become pasts." Orla gives a wrinkle-nosed grin. "My apologies. I've seen things about you folks for quite a while now. I know things that might have already come to pass. That's the trick with time—doesn't seem to know how to stop. Just keeps on goin'."

"What kinds of things have you seen?" Eddie asks, leaning forward hungrily.

"Many things," Orla answers, mimicking his intensity. "Things that are important.

Things that probably aren't. For instance, I don't think your love of—pardon if I get this wrong—Pokémon trading cards is goin' to come much in handy for anything fate has in store for you, Eddie. My condolences."

Eddie comes back out of his lean, his shoulders slumping. "Well, I guess that YouTube channel is never gonna work out, then," he mutters.

"Well, there are certainly more pertinent things I can inform you about. For one thing, that sword doesn't belong to you." Orla motions her head fluidly to the black sword hanging off Eddie's belt. "And it never will."

Out of instinct, Eddie's left hand clasps the hilt of the sword, as if protecting it. "Why do you say that?" he asks.

"Because," Orla says, matter of fact. "It belongs to him."

Everyone's gaze follows Orla's gentle head nod, landing on Jackson's stunned face.

It's quiet for a tense moment. The only thing I hear is Melandrich next to me softly mumbling, "I knew it."

Jackson looks between our stunned faces, shaking his head and pushing the bridge of his glasses up his nose nervously. "No," he says. "I just pulled it out of the stump. It doesn't mean anything. It's not mine."

"It's yours *because* you pulled it from the stump," Orla says. "The Earthen Relic could only be retrieved if the owner of the sword decided to wield it. And apparently, you decided."

"Bullshit," Jackson spits, the consonants hard and vicious. "I didn't decide anything. I just needed to help my friends."

Orla's gaze turns curious as she stares at him. "Why does it scare you so much, Jackson?" she asks him. "It's only metal and wood." She arcs her head subtly. "Or is it just what it represents that frightens you?"

Jackson's jaw tenses as he stares at her. For a moment, I think he might lash out at her with the way his mouth is pulled so tight across his face. When he does speak, though, his voice is small. "I'm not a hero. I have no desire to be one, either."

Her smile remains as she says, "I'm not sure how much of a choice you'll have in that. After all, you have a big name to live up to."

Jackson says nothing, staring at her across the fire pit, too tired to fight her on the matter.

As if shaking out of a daydream, Orla's smile fades, and she looks around at us in a daze. "Oh, I'm sorry. I may not be a stickler for manners, but I sometimes forget how—eh, what's the word for it—off-puttin' I can be with my brand of conversation," she explains. "Not many folks come see me all the way out here, and when they do, it's typically regardin' their own futures. Don't have a lot of experience in idle chatter."

"I'll say," Eddie murmurs.

Clearing his throat again, Melandrich says, "Lady Orla, I believe I speak for the entire group when I say we have no interest in learning what fate has in store for us."

No one chimes in to disagree.

But only because I bite my tongue.

"Of course, of course," Orla says. "You're all in the Residuum business, not the fortune business. Like I said, I'm more than willin' to give up part of my collection. As you can see…" Searching through her wild hair as if it was some sort of filing cabinet, Orla sifts through the strands and pulls up one with a rather large chunk of Heavenly Residuum wrapped in it. "I've got plenty to spare. Mostly use it for odd jobs around here. But you all are goin' up against a Mage. Can't in good conscience say that you don't need it more."

"I am sure you are well aware we have the means to compensate you for any materials you would be willing to part with," Melandrich says.

She flips the strand over her shoulder. "See, the thing about that is that I don't have much need for money out here. I very rarely make it out to town, so currency really isn't of much value."

Hesitantly, Melandrich nods. "Oh. Well, I'm not sure what else we can provide…"

"Tell you what," she says, clapping her hands together and standing up off her stump. "You're all close by to the Crystalline Relic here—about half a day's walk. I'll get you whatever Residuum you need and a place to stay for the night in exchange for helpin' me around the property. It's hard to take care of the place myself sometimes. Plenty to be done, and I'll consider us more than even after that. Sound like a fair trade?"

We glance at each other across the circle, exchanging nods. "Wonderful!" she exclaims. And as her gaze turns toward me, her massive smile seems to grow even wider somehow. "Who knows? If you do a good job, I might even be able to get you some Crystalline." And with her eyes locked squarely on mine, she winks.

My insides churn.

As we casually finish our food and start wandering off to find odd jobs around the homestead, I'm cleaning out the last morsels at the bottom of my bowl when I see Adrian stand up out of the corner of my eye, striding past me and toward the house. Before he can make it too far, though, Orla intercepts him and says something low under her breath. They probably think everyone is too far off to hear. But I catch it, just barely.

"Those flames are closin' in on you," she murmurs. "How long, do you think, until you catch fire?"

If he answers, I don't hear it. I wait just long enough to turn around so if I'm caught, it won't seem as if I was eavesdropping. But when I look back over my shoulder, they're both gone.

Orla advises us on everything that needs work around the property, and it's no small list. Being self-sufficient, she has a garden and even a small barn of livestock about a quarter mile away from the house. Eddie and Jackson volunteer to run out in that direction and tend to the animals (Eddie is far too excited about the prospect of petting goats) while Kai and Gren tag along to help with some of the crops. Melandrich offers to take Orla's bow and catch some smaller animals for dinner and hide tanning, leaving Adrian and me on the property itself.

Part of the roof needs to be re-thatched, and Adrian sullenly admits he has experience with that. As for me, I end up on dish duty. At first, I think I prefer that to shoveling goat shit, but Orla's kitchen is a nightmare. The counters are covered in wooden dishes and other odds and ends—some might be trash and others might be components for some holistic spell I don't quite know how to cast, so I'm not sure what I can throw out and what I should keep. The dishes, at least, are a safe bet, and I gather them up into the cramped sink which is mostly just an open barrel with a hand pump perched over top of it. Through the clutter, I find a coarse-haired scrubbing brush. With all the strength I can muster, I'm able to get the hand pump working, softening some of the dried bits of food and possibly mud so I can start scraping everything clean. My legs have been the ones to get a workout for the past two weeks. Might as well start on my arms.

After about an hour, Orla comes into the kitchen, glancing over the freshly cleaned wooden bowls and cups stacked on top of each other on the counters with an impressed smile. "Look at you! Busy little worker bee," she delightfully cries. "I can't tell you how long most of those have been sitting there."

I wipe a bit of sweat off my brow, leaning against the sink and holding the dripping brush in a fist on my hip. "From the burning in my shoulders, I'd say a while."

"You're not wrong." Like she's half paying attention to where she's walking, Orla wanders to the plain table, perching on the edge rather than actually sitting in one of the chairs arranged next to it. "I can't help it, I'm afraid. I'm so often caught up in futures that I can't quite seem to make myself care about the present."

Hesitant, I say, "I know the feeling. Sometimes, I feel like I'm too caught up in the past."

Orla directs her wistful gaze toward me, her sharp blue eyes a scalpel digging into my skin. "That's understandable, given what you've been through," she says, absently throwing her tangled nest of hair over one shoulder. "Out of all of them, yours is the story I've been most interested in. Sure, we have the smooth talker and their muscle, the storyteller who wants to be the hero, the hero who wants to be invisible, the disgraced fey, the..." She trails off, before coming back with, "Well, I'll suppose you'll know all that soon enough. Despite all that, the girl who witnessed demons has to be the most fascinatin' part about it all. And to think that's only a fraction of what you end up bein'."

She twirls a strand of orange hair around her finger, as if I'm not staring at her like she just grew a second head off her shoulder. "I don't—" I start, but I clamp my mouth shut, shaking my head before trying again. "I don't even know where to start with that."

Giggling, she uncoils her hair from her finger. "Oh, I know you've been dyin' to ask me about it all. What the future has in store for you. For her. If she even has a future."

I bite my lip, setting the brush in the sink, knowing full well the "she" she's referring to.

"I can't tell you much, but I can at least tell you that, yes," Orla says, brightly yet with a sympathetic tone, "she is alive."

My jaw goes slack for a moment. There had always been the possibility, of course, that May was dead. That we came here only to find out we were years too late, that we might be risking everything for a false hope. All this time, though, I hadn't allowed myself to turn it into a fully formed thought, letting it remain a wisp of an idea floating in the back of my mind. Hearing Orla confirm she really is out there—it's as if an invisible yoke has been taken off my shoulders. I nod, pushing the sting of tears back as I do.

"She's different, of course," Orla continues. "But so are you. You'll be far more different than you are even now when you eventually find her."

I blink, pushing the emotion away for a time. Now's not the time for crying. There's business to attend to. "So, you know where she is then?"

Shrugging, non-committal, Orla says, "I know approximately. There's any number of places she could be. Again, I see futures, not presents."

"But you know where she *will* be?"

"Violet, I know where you're goin' with this." This time, the sympathy in her voice is front and center. "But I can't tell you anythin' specific."

I laugh at her, harsh and cynical. I think for a moment that I feel bad about it, but I don't think I actually do. "What do you mean?" I ask her. "If you tell me where she is now, we don't need the Relics. We don't need to even worry about the Infernal Mage."

"Believe me, you still will," Orla says, crossing her legs and shaking out her bright white skirt. "You see, futures aren't set in stone. The decisions you make will lead you down certain paths. And those decisions are made with the knowledge that you have at the time. If I were to tell you what decisions you were to make to get to May, all the little decisions that were made in between might prevent you from bigger decisions down the line. Step on a butterfly and all that." Her seemingly perpetual cheeky grin fades as she looks at me. "I've made the mistake before of letting someone know of their future, and I had to then sit back and watch in an instant how that future changed to another. One of sorrow and woe."

Her bright, luminous eyes center on me once again. "I don't want that for you," she says. "I've seen the end, Violet. It isn't perfect, but you get her back. Isn't that the most important thing?"

"If it can be changed, how am I supposed to know I'm making the right decisions, then?" I ask. "I could walk out the door and do something totally different than what you've seen me do. How do I know I'm on the right track?"

"How would you know if you had never come across me out here?" Orla retorts.

Crossing my arms, I lean against the sink. "I guess I wouldn't."

The smile returns to her pale face. "Hate to say it, but the only thing I can offer as far as that is 'have faith.' And not in fate or the universe or the gods or whatever else might be keepin' creation spinnin'. Faith in yourself, Violet. Faith that your choices, whether or not they're perfect, are the right ones for you as you are right now."

I laugh again, though it doesn't come out as cruel. "You obviously don't know me very well. That's the thing I have the least faith in."

This time, though, her smile doesn't falter. "Well, tomorrow is another day, isn't it?"

I'm about to ask if that's supposed to be some sort of hint, if I'm merely supposed to start inferring her winks now. But just as I start to speak, Eddie clomps into the kitchen covered in dirt—it's dirt, one hundred percent. I refuse to believe it's anything else but that. "Hope I'm not interrupting," he says between pants, "but Jackson and I cleaned out the barn, fed the animals. It looks like that's all taken care of."

Clapping her hands together, Orla stands up, practically skipping over to him. "Excellent!" she exclaims. "I'm sure those little piggies are going to love sleepin' on a fresh bed tonight. As a matter of fact, Violet here just finished up in the kitchen. Why don't you two run off to go get some extra kindlin' for the fire tonight? I haven't been out to gather any in a while, and we'll need a good bit to keep the pit burnin' for supper and whatever merry makin' you all get up to."

The both of us agree, and I spend a couple minutes stacking bowls and cups on the countertop. As I go to follow Eddie out the door, however, Orla grabs me by the crook of the arm. The look in her eyes intensifies as she looks right at me. "I'll give you one for free," she whispers as she pulls me closer. "When he asks you the question, you'll want to say no. You should say yes."

Before I can ask for any clarification, though, she lets go and saunters down the hallway into the back room, closing the door with a decisive click.

The sun slants itself directly into my eyeline as Eddie and I wander into a thicker part of the forest, both of us grabbing random branches and cradling them in our arms as we walk along. Being from Michigan, we're not all that unused to the woods. What we've been doing the past couple weeks is far more intense than anything I've experienced, but we're not unfamiliar with class field trips to the local wildlife preserves or even the occasional party at the rich kid's house with sprawling woods that encroach upon their backyard. Eddie and I have taken our fair share of walks in the woods, but normally, they're filled with chatter and inside jokes, laughing and reminiscing.

Not today, though. Today, we're silent. Which isn't all that uncommon for me, but for Eddie, it's concerning. He has small talk to share with everyone in some capacity, but when it comes to me, talking has always been as easy as breathing for him, a constant flow of words and thoughts uninhibited by awkwardness or self-doubt. The fact that he's so tight-lipped now creates an uneasy energy that bounces between the two of us, a strange Pong game of tension. I hoist another sizeable branch onto my pile, thinking of what I could possibly say to dispel this weird vibe we've established.

A breeze rolls by and carries the gnarliest stench of barn that I've ever smelled in my life with it. "Holy shit, you stink," I gasp, moving out of downwind range.

He doesn't look at me as he shrugs, shifting the mounting stack of wood in his arms. "Well, that's what happens when you shovel animal dung out of a barn."

"What, did you roll around in it?"

"No."

"It's just—fuck, it's intense."

"Better get used to it, I guess. If there's one thing I know about Velmyra, it's that there's a distinct lack of baths."

I shrug. "I could use some Heavenly and make it rain on you. Nature's bath."

"You certainly could, couldn't you."

I stop, dropping the pathetic bundle of branches I've half-heartedly gathered so far at my feet. "Okay," I sigh. "What's up with you?"

Eddie stops with me, but he keeps his pile together in his arms. "What?"

"Don't 'what' me. You know what," I say, crossing my arms. "You've hardly said two words to me since Marwindale, and you were acting weird before then too. So, what's your deal?"

Accepting that he won't be able to feign ignorance to get out of this one, Eddie subtly rolls his eyes and sets his own pile down with more care than I bothered to use. "There's no deal, Vi," he says as he straightens himself out. "It's been two weeks of non-stop travel. We're all tired and short with each other at this point."

"No, don't give me that," I say, shaking my head. "I know you well enough to know when something is bothering you."

"It's not that big of a—"

"Ed."

"Okay, fine!" Eddie shouts, loud enough where a bird scatters out of a nearby tree, taking off into the air behind him. He barely seems to notice, though. "I'm having a terrible time! There! I thought I was going to live out my nerd dreams and play *Mages* in real life, but ever since we got here, it's been fucking awful. I haven't showered in almost two weeks, I have mosquito bites the size of golf balls on my ass. I've lost ten pounds I probably couldn't afford to lose in the first place. I nearly got my arm ripped off by an ogre, my eye ripped out by a direwolf, and everyone and their sister seems real keen on telling me that goddamn sword doesn't belong to me." He looks up into the sky, running a hand over his stubble in frustration. "I came here thinking I was going to live out something people only dream of experiencing, but this whole stupid-ass country is just rejecting me like a bad skin graft or something. I'm useless."

"You're not useless," I weakly offer up.

"Yeah, and what have I done besides teach a halfling the Macarena?" Eddie asks. "I'm a fucking clown, Violet. A *jester*."

"And what's wrong with that?"

He laughs at me, the same sardonic laugh I gave Orla back at the house not even an hour ago. "That's easy for you to say."

"What's that supposed to mean?" I ask him, narrowing my gaze.

"Violet, come on," Eddie says. "You're a fucking residuuist. I watched you in Marwindale. You're not perfect, but you're able to do *something*. Of course you don't get it. You're doing what you're supposed to do in *Mages*: kick ass and take names."

I splay my hands out. "And you think it's been easy?" I ask. "It's been brutal, okay? It's exhausting, mentally and emotionally, even physically. I don't just pick up Residuum and cast."

"I know you don't," he says, closing his eyes.

"Then don't act like it's easy for me!"

"Jesus Christ, this isn't even about you! Fuck, Jackson was right."

Oh. So that's what this is about.

It takes a moment for his face to fall, realizing what he's said, putting a hand up to his forehead in embarrassment. I try to keep the anger that's boiling in my gut in check as I ask, "What are you talking about? Right about what? What did he say?"

"Forget I said anything."

"No, I want to know. What did he say?"

Eddie sighs, shifting in place and not looking me in the eye. "He just said that you tend to—I don't know—you focus too much on how shit affects you rather than, you know, other people," he mutters.

"And you agree with him?"

Raising and lowering a shoulder as he looks at the ground, he says, "Not usually."

"I told you I didn't like him," I say. "I *told* you."

"Don't make this some high school bullshit, Vi."

"Well, that's what it is, isn't it?" I snap. "He hates me for some reason, but you obviously want to fuck him, so you spend all your time with him on this trip and listen to whatever he says about me, so now I'm the bad guy. All because you're thinking with your dick."

"That's a low blow," he says, glaring at me. Even in the low light of dying day, I catch the faintest hint of red creeping into his face.

"So is saying I'm a self-obsessed bitch."

"I didn't say that!" he exclaims. "And I'm not just hanging out with him because I want to—god—he's nice, okay? He's just a chill dude. And how the hell is that any different from what you've been doing with Adrian?"

"Adrian? What do you mean? That's totally different."

"Really? Because I clearly don't like him, but you're still spending every waking moment with him."

"So he can teach me residuuism!" I yell.

"That isn't the only reason."

"And what if it isn't? That's not a reason to take Jackson's side over mine."

Eddie scoffs, kicking at a patch of dirt. "At least Jackson's not shady as shit." He must notice my face, because he shakes his head as he looks at me, almost in pity. "Come on, you're not stupid, Violet. There's something he's hiding. Everyone knows it. Melandrich can hardly look away from him, he's so suspicious of him. I've talked to Kai and Gren—well, Kai, mostly—and even the career criminals agree that there's something off. Something about his whole involvement with this is wrong, and I know you're not dumb. You have to have noticed."

It's my turn to look away, focusing on the scuffed leather of my boots as I inhale. "We all have things we don't want to talk about," I say after a couple deep breaths. "He's no different than you or me."

"It's not just that."

"Why do you care so much?" I snap. My patience is running thin, and there's a heat rumbling in my core that rivals anything that I felt using Infernal Residuum. "He's helping us. He's helping *me*."

"Violet, I'm trying to help you too. I'm trying to protect you from—"

The heat is too unbearable. I have to let it go.

"Protect me?" I yell. I nearly scare myself as I hear my own words echo off the dense trees surrounding us, taken aback by how vitriolic they sound. But it's too late to stop them. "Like when you threw me in the hospital and forgot about me for a week? Were you protecting me then?"

Even in the fading light of early evening, most of the sun now hidden behind the canopy of trees, I can see Eddie has gone sheet white.

The rage isn't through with me yet, though. "I don't want you to be my knight in shining armor or whatever!" I scream. "Adrian is teaching me to protect myself, not to just play video games and forget that my problems exist. I don't need you to be a fucking hero, Eddie. Because, given your track record, you actually do fucking suck at it!"

That's the moment when all the anger within me extinguishes. Now, I'm only left with what I said.

My face uncoils from its scowl, but Eddie's remains fixed in a pale grimace as he stares at the ground, unblinking and nodding, as if he's listening to what I said on delay. In the low light, it's hard to catch the glimmer in his eye. I've only seen Eddie cry a handful of times in the years we've known each other, and I'm afraid I'm about to add another instance to the list.

He doesn't cry, though. Instead, he sniffs, fixing his jaw and quickly running his thumb across the tip of his nose, refusing to look at me. "Cool. I'm out," he murmurs, and he walks past me, back in the direction of Orla's cabin.

"Eddie—" I call out as he walks by.

"Don't forget the firewood," he responds lifelessly, not turning around as he stomps through the trees. I watch, helpless to stop him, until he disappears.

I grind the heels of my hands into my eyes, begging the sting of angry tears to stop. I replay it all over and over in my head, thinking of all the better things I could have said—that one thing I could have held back to keep that look off his face, from sulking away like that...

As I pull my hands away from my eyes, I look around me. I'm alone.

I stand frozen in place for a few minutes that feel like a few hours. Before I muster up enough strength to walk back to the cabin, I pick up a few bundles of pathetic sticks, carrying them through the brush back to the cabin, just so I can say I did something out in the woods besides create my own misery.

CHAPTER 24

We take off for the second Relic in the morning.

I'd say Melandrich wakes us up bright and early, but the sun isn't even up when he makes the rounds and shakes everyone awake—so, just early, I guess. We groggily put on our gear, secure our weapons, and fill up on mystery stew in the dark of early morning with hardly a mumbled "morning" passed between any of us.

Before we take off, Orla makes good on her promise. She gives us more Residuum that we can possibly fit in our pockets. The remainders that are too cumbersome for us to carry with us, she gives to Melandrich to put in his bigger-on-the-inside bag. It's all about what we've seen before—jagged hunks of stones, all varying in size and in differing shades of purple and green and orange. But the *pièce de résistance* is a massive, cantaloupe-sized chunk of clear Crystalline Residuum, which she holds out to Melandrich nonchalantly, like he's about to merely go play volleyball with it. "With the size of your group, this is probably good for a couple of trips out of some sticky situations. Use it sparingly, yes?"

Melandrich nods but handles the stone much more delicately than she does, placing it in the bag with care. Once it's secured, he looks at Adrian. "Master Inoue, if I hand that to you in a predicament, I trust you will know what to do with it?"

Adrian, too tired for words, gives him a thumbs up.

"I do not know what that means," Melandrich says, brow furrowed. It's only after we take off that I explain to him it's a positive affirmation where we come from. Even though he says he understands, the baffled look stays on his face as we plunge forward into the thick trees.

We're so much quieter than usual that it's eerie, like we've found ourselves in a horror movie. The smallest extraneous sounds of the forest make me jump, and the racing of my heart doesn't go away when I see it's just a squirrel or a dead branch falling off a nearby tree. It takes me a bit to realize what exactly has changed: Eddie isn't talking. Not at all, even as he walks beside Jackson. Despite the fact that he's been miserable, he's at least tried to maintain that he's his usual chipper self. After our fight last night, though, all pretense is gone. The circles under his eyes have darkened, and he stares at his feet as he trudges along, mouth firmly closed.

As if I didn't feel like shit before.

"What'd you do, rip his tongue out?" Adrian whispers in my ear after an hour of unsettling silence.

I glare at him. "None of your business."

Shrugging with one shoulder, he says, "It's just disturbingly quiet. I feel like I'm at a wake."

"We'll see how accurate that is once we find that Relic…"

"Oh, calm down," he says, clasping a hand on my shoulder and giving it a playful squeeze. "This'll be a cake walk. We got the last one just fine."

"You have a weird definition of 'just fine.'"

"My definition is 'no fatalities,' so yes. Just fine."

I shrug off his hand on my shoulder. "I'm serious, Adrian," I say. "All the Mages have their own thing that prevents mortals from getting the Relics, right? And this is Crystalline's. What kind of weird thing is she going to spring on us?"

A shadow falls across his face, more noticeable now that the sun is finally rising. "I wish I knew. As much time as I spent with her, I can't say what she has up her sleeve."

I swallow hard. That's what I was afraid of.

We walk well into the morning. The sky is overcast, the mist of the forest never quite dissipating as we go forward. I can't tell where the sun hangs in the sky, and without anyone making conversation, the hours creep by sluggishly. My mind is consumed by replays of my fight with Eddie and the possibilities of what horrors wait ahead of us. It has to be at least midday when Melandrich holds up a hand, a silent signal for us to halt. We stop, following his gaze forward.

Amidst the still-clinging fog, a gaping cavern appears less than half a mile away, wide open like the toothless maw of a giant monster, waiting for an unsuspecting creature to wander in and make itself dinner.

Melandrich glances at Adrian. "I am assuming that is the cave you spoke of."

"Pretty sure," Adrian confirms. "I've never been here, but how many other caves do you see?"

Giving a half nod, Melandrich says, "Fair enough." He turns to the rest of us, digging in his Satchel as he does and pulling out a long stick. Strips of fabric are wrapped around the top of it, and as he pulls it closer to me, I get a distinct whiff of kerosene. "Keep a watchful eye, everyone. We know not what lies ahead."

It doesn't take him long to ignite the torch into a blazing light with a knife and flint. It would probably be easier to use Infernal, but I don't want to chance using it again. Not yet. Adrian is the only other one who can use it, but he's hardly paying attention, eyes wandering off into the forest surrounding us. The torch soon lights anyway, and we follow its flame into the demanding dark of the cave.

The silence on our walk here would almost be preferable to the jarring echoes sounding off around us as we push forward into the dripping cavern. Every movement catches on the cave walls and is thrown back at us at twice the volume. The tinny sound is almost too much on my eardrums, and the utter darkness that envelops us doesn't help my unease. Melandrich's torch at the front of our line is insufficient at banishing the darkness. The only thing that indicates that we aren't uselessly walking through a void is the occasional glisten of the cave walls, moisture lining the craggy rocks beside us. It doesn't help my irrational fear that we just walked into the mouth of a space slug with no Millennium Falcon to help us escape.

I'm just barely getting used to the crushing darkness when I hear a yelp behind me, followed by the click of a mechanism. I whirl around, my hand in my pocket grabbing onto whatever piece of Residuum it happens to land on, only relaxing when I see Kai's startled expression. Their crossbow is aimed yet empty of a bolt, and they pant as they stare at the cave wall next to them. Following their gaze, I see what the arrow struck. Pinned against the stone wall is a massive reptile, almost as big as a monitor lizard. Its long body hangs limply by its head, the crossbow bolt holding it in place through its eye socket. The salamander-like creature would be incredibly difficult to make out were it not for the ribbons of luminous aqua blue scales that run across its back, pulsing slightly before eventually fading as the last bits of life leave its body.

"Fuck!" they exclaim. "Bloody bastard about had my head. Son of a fucking…" They trail off as they load another bolt into the crossbow.

"What is that?" I ask, looking back at the lizard, the light emanating off of it now completely doused.

"Lumilander," Kai says, their breath evening out. "Nasty buggers. They love dark, wet places and snacking on unsuspecting explorers." They point at the lizard carcass with their loaded crossbow. "That one is small. A baby, I'd wager. Which means Mum is probably nearby."

Curiously, Gren jabs at the dead lumilander with the end of her club, but Kai smacks at her arm.

"Don't even think about eating that, you donkey!" Kai exclaims. "You know they're poisonous."

Dismayed, Gren huffs, slinging her club back to rest on her shoulder.

With far more caution, we continue, the smallest of disturbances now cause for alarm. As my vision focuses on the bright torch light ahead of me, the cave walls in my periphery seem to undulate like the skin of a snake. Every paranoid glance, though, proves that I'm just seeing things. My hand never leaves my pocket, the sharpened edge of a Residuum stone digging into my palm like a knife. I need that pinprick of pain, though. It's keeping me grounded as we descend further into the cavern, further into the unrelenting dark.

Or at least, it seems unrelenting. Until the light finally shows itself.

It's abrupt—one moment, it's as though we'll never see light again. The next, we're standing in an open area filled with gloomy grey light coming from a natural skylight in a straight beam, like the sun peeking through dense clouds after a rainstorm. We slow down, looking among our other party members with a quick glance to verify we all made it in one piece. For the most part, it looks like we did. No one has a massive, lumilander-sized bite taken out of them, at least. Melandrich lowers the torch. "Everyone is accounted for, yes?" he inquires, and we all respond back with varying confirmations.

The open cavern around us is wider than the claustrophobic tunnel we just emerged from, though not by much. The ceiling is, by my estimation, maybe twenty feet high. The ground is uneven but, for the most part, walkable. It also seems less moist, the opening in the ceiling likely providing some much needed ventilation. I glance around, wondering if this is where the Relic is supposed to be, but nothing stands out—no pedestal or dais to indicate where the Relic might be stored—

No, that's not entirely true. On the far end of the cavern, there's an archway. As everyone collects themselves, I draw closer to it. There's a strange fuzz over the naturally formed arch, reminding me of static on an old television. As I get closer, though, I see it's not static.

It's a curtain. Faintly billowing from a breeze I can't feel, it hangs between a sandwich of boulders, most likely too heavy for anyone to move by themselves—I'd be willing to bet even Gren can't budge them. The material is indistinct and gauzy, its borders undefined, no matter how hard I try to find a clear edge on it. It's thick enough that when I try to see through it into whatever part of the cave the arch leads to, I can't make out anything distinct. But I can tell that there's something back there. It's as though the material is censoring whatever's beyond the arch, a motion blur in real life.

"Melandrich?" I call out, not taking my eyes off the arch.

Without hesitation, Melandrich strides over to my side, pausing in front of the arch. "This is—strange."

"I think that's putting it mildly."

He thoughtfully examines it before looking at the torch in his hand and extending it forward, putting the flame against the hazy edge of the fabric. Even as he does so, the silvery wafting fabric doesn't catch fire.

"That is even stranger," Melandrich mutters. By now, the rest of the group has gathered behind us, and he turns to look at Adrian. "Did your information indicate what this may be? It appears to be an enchanted veil of some sort."

Adrian shakes his head, staring at the veil with just as much intrigue as the rest of us.

"Is there a way we can pull the curtain out from under those rocks?" Jackson asks, arms crossed as he examines the structure himself.

Gren stomps forward, arms already outstretched to take on the task herself, but Melandrich holds a hand out to stop her. "An enchantment like this—presumably put in place by the

Crystalline Mage herself—would be too powerful for any show of physical strength." Once again defeated, Gren groans and stamps a giant foot on the ground.

"Well, what are we supposed to do?" Jackson asks. "Do we really just want to walk through it? It could come to life and strangle us or something."

"I don't think we have much of a choice in the matter, kid," Adrian says.

"I will go forward first," Melandrich says, taking a cloth from his bag and smothering the flame on the torch. Melandrich deftly puts it back in the bag before drawing his sword, gripping it tightly with both hands. "It is thin enough that if I pass through unharmed, I should be able to indicate it is safe to follow." He turns to look at all of us, and while Melandrich is usually annoyingly stalwart, his luminous blue eyes flicker with fear for the briefest of moments. "If I do not respond, do not follow. Understood?"

Morosely, we nod.

Sucking in a breath, Melandrich walks forward, his steps cautious as he holds his sword in front of him, using it to part the veil and walk through the smoke-like curtain. It's an odd phenomenon to watch him go. It only takes a blink for him to suddenly not be there, swallowed by the murky grey fabric in an instant.

We wait.

No one breathes.

We don't hear an answer.

"Melandrich?" Jackson calls out, keeping a generous distance from the veil. "Can you hear us?"

Nothing.

My stomach flips, starting to churn nervously.

"Melandrich," Jackson calls again, more insistent this time. "Are you all right?"

There's more silence, too long, I think, for there to possibly be a response to follow. But Melandrich's voice soon drifts through the veil. "I—I am all right. I am uninjured." His voice sounds ragged, like he's been sprinting, and it all sounds too far away for him to really be just on the other side of a thin piece of fabric. Even so, everyone breathes a sigh of relief at the sound of his voice.

"What happened? Should we all come through?" Jackson asks him, almost shouting now.

Panting, Melandrich says, "You may come over. It is not—it will not hurt you. But..." He trails off for a moment, the sound of his voice growing faint before coming back in to say, "Take caution. You will—see things. If my experience is any indication. And it will be—unpleasant."

"What do you mean? What did you see?" Jackson asks.

Melandrich doesn't respond. Only the occasional deep breath indicates that he's still there on the other side.

Sighing and hanging his head, Jackson looks around at the rest of us. "Well," he says, gesturing a hand toward the veil like a reluctant yet accommodating waiter at a restaurant. "Who wants to go first?"

No one jumps at the opportunity. Even Jackson anxiously eyes the veil as he leans forward on the balls of his feet, knowing that he'll have to be the one to go first if no one else volunteers. Just before it seems he's going to take that step forward, though, Kai pipes up. "All right, all right. I'll go. As long as the 'things' the creepy mystery curtain will make me see isn't one of you stark-ass naked, I think I'll survive."

Off to the side, Gren whimpers.

"Well, come on then, you gigantic grape!" Kai exclaims, grabbing Gren's finger and dragging her along with them. "If you're so scared, we can go together. Gods above." With some hesitation, the two walk forward through the curtain, Gren crouching to clear the arch. One second, they're there. The next, they're not.

Reluctantly, the rest of us follow. Jackson, then Eddie. Adrian glances at me, his normal nonchalant veneer cracking as he gives me a strained smile. "It'll be okay," he reassures me, though it also sounds partially for his benefit. "See you on the other side." With that, I blink, and he's gone, absorbed by the fuzzy grey of the veil.

And I'm left alone.

For a moment, I think about not going. If this is all there is—if this is the Crystalline's big task—do we really need seven people to do it? I think back to Marwindale, though, and how it took us everything we had to retrieve it. I sigh. It wouldn't be fair to let them do it for me, to fight my battle without me. Because that's what this is: my battle. We wouldn't be here if not for me.

Pulling in as big of a breath as I can muster, I walk forward, eyes closed. As I pass through the veil, a wave of cold washes over me, until there's nothing.

And it really does feel like nothing for a moment. No warmth or chill to the air, no sound, no scents to indicate where I might be. I don't dare open my eyes, for fear that I'll open them to see something mind-bogglingly horrific. But when I dare to crack them open, I see the smallest hint of sunlight, the dim fading of late evening. With that tiny bit of sensory input, everything else starts to fill in around it. Birds chirp around me, the wind faintly blows through my hair, the smell of damp earth and blooming flowers wafts under my nose. It's comforting enough that I force my eyes open further, fairly certain I won't be looking at dead bodies hanging off meat hooks or anything like that. Fairly.

To my surprise—and confusion—I'm not anywhere horrifying at all. I'm in a forest. A familiar one, in some way. In fact, if I didn't know any better, I'd say I'm in the forest surrounding Orla's cabin.

And standing in front of me is Eddie.

I go to open my mouth, to ask him if we made it, if this is what's on the other side of the veil and what that's even supposed to mean. But nothing comes out of my mouth. I can't even move my mouth.

I can't move anything.

I give my limbs commands—I tell my pinky to curl, my foot to tap on the ground, my head to turn. None of them listen. But I'm not paralyzed. I am moving—subtle twitches, shifts in my stance, changes in my posture. Nothing is of my own volition, though. It's like I'm watching a first-person video game cutscene. The controller is in my hand, but no matter how many times I toggle the joystick, the path and the movements are set. All I can do is watch, subjected to being a bystander through my own eyes.

In this cutscene, Eddie is talking. It takes me a hazy moment to figure out what about, but it hits me. It was so recent, how could I forget?

I'm watching our argument from last night.

"Come on, you're not stupid, Violet. There's something he's hiding. Everyone knows it. Melandrich can hardly look away from him, he's so suspicious of him. I've talked to Kai and Gren—well, Kai, mostly—and even the career criminals agree that there's something off. Something about his whole involvement with this is wrong, and I know you're not dumb. You have to have noticed."

I look down at the ground, still not in control. "We all have things we don't want to talk about," I hear myself say. "He's no different than you or me." I sound so bitter and angry, like a sullen teenager. It's embarrassing, but there's no humiliated heat that rises into my face. I don't feel anything aside from the soft breeze that rolls through the leaves.

"It's not just that," Eddie says.

"Why do you care so much?" I snap. I surprise myself with how volatile I sound. That burning anger wells up in my gut as the words spill out. "He's helping us. He's helping *me*."

Don't, I plead inside my own head. *Don't say it. You don't have to say it this time. Don't.*

"Violet, I'm trying to help you too. I'm trying to protect you from—" Eddie says.

It can be different this time, I tell myself. *You didn't mean it then, and you don't mean it now. Don't fucking say—*

"Protect me? Like when you threw me in the hospital and forgot about me for a week? Were you protecting me then?"

My body feels angry. I'm shaking, adrenaline coursing through me and blood rushing in my ears. But inside my head, I'm not angry. I'm ashamed. Ashamed as I see Eddie's expression fall, all the color rushing out of his face as he hears me bring up the one thing he's tried so hard to avoid for over a year. Ashamed of everything else coming out of my mouth, about how he's failed so miserably at being the hero he wanted to be. I'm trying so hard to get myself to say anything besides those idiotic words that it almost physically hurts.

Try as I might, though, it still happens. And I'm left staring at him, a broken mess.

"Cool. I'm out," Eddie says, casting his eyes down to the ground as he briskly moves past me. I want to reach out to him as he passes by me, grab onto him, pull him into a hug and tell him I'm sorry and that I didn't mean any of it—

Right as he moves past me, my finger twitches.

I go to reach out to him, thinking I'm finally in control of myself again, turning my head to call back out to him—

When I do, I'm not in the forest anymore. I'm in the front seat of Eddie's car.

It's instantaneous, but the shift is jarring. The fresh air of the forest is replaced by the stale smell of the heater and ancient McDonald's french fries. The warm orange glow of evening is replaced by dark early morning, the harsh unnatural light of streetlamps sifting in through dirty windows.

The biggest shift, though, is that all the energy in me has been completely drained. My limbs are heavy—not that I can move them myself, anyway—hanging off me like lead weights. My eyelids hang low, rubbed raw and stinging from exhaustion.

Even though I can't move myself, the movements that my body does make are sloth-like, as if I've been rendered in slow motion.

"Violet, can you please get out of the car?"

I look over at the open car door next to me. Eddie stands on the pavement next to it, one arm resting on the roof of the car and the other braced against the door. He's clean shaven and his hair is shorter, only just long enough for him to comfortably tuck behind his ears. He looks so young, but the redness around his eyes and the sunkeness of his face makes him look so much older than he is. He's in a ratty pair of sweats and a Zelda t-shirt under his olive green coat, threadbare sneakers just barely held together as he shifts in place leaning against his beat-up Honda Civic. "Vi, please. Please just get out of the car. Please."

That's when I notice the red glowing neon sign behind him. Blaring in large angry letters is the word "EMERGENCY."

Fuck. I know what this is now.

Again, the words come out without me thinking them. "I want to go home," I say, my voice hoarse and faint. I feel myself shift in the lumpy seat. I'm wearing flannel pajama bottoms and a zip up sweatshirt hiding a holey, coffee-stained tank top underneath. And if I thought my hair had gotten greasy in Velmyra, it's nothing compared to the matted tendrils that hang around my face. If I could feel any new sensations with my body as I am right now, I'm sure my skin would crawl.

Eddie hangs his head. "We're not going home, Vi. I can't do that."

"Yes, you can. Get in and drive me back home."

"Violet, please just—"

"No! Take me the fuck home, Eddie!"

He runs a hand down his face in frustration. In the woods outside of Orla's cabin, he was so close to crying, but he's actually crying now, wiping away tears like he hopes I won't notice it. "What am I supposed to do here, Violet? Huh? If I take you home, and you do something—"

I'm crying now too. Not the little pinpricks that sting at the corner of my eyes. It's painful, rolling tears—tears that get caught in your throat and make it hard to breathe. I suck in an uneven breath. "I'm not going to do anything. I promise. Just let me go h-home, please."

"Vi, I can't."

"I'm not going to do anything!" I scream. The version of me watching winces.

"How am I supposed to believe that?!" Eddie yells back at me. "I found the note, okay? I found it, and it scared the fuck out of me. If I take you home, how am I supposed to fucking live with myself if you…?"

He stops, and my heart splits in two as he finally breaks down sobbing, leaning against the car like he's going to collapse. I want so badly to reach for him, to tell him I'm sorry for causing him this kind of pain. I'm so goddamn weak and pathetic that I make everyone else around me miserable and that's why I wrote that stupid note in the first place and—

I don't say any of that, of course. I don't have the energy. I just want him to stop crying, so I hear myself say the only thing I have the strength for. "I'll go in," I whisper, muddled through my own tears. "Don't cry." I pathetically put my hand on his slumped head, awkwardly patting it while he sobs. "Don't cry, please. I'll go in. I will."

It takes a few minutes for him to catch his breath again, and once he's taken a few deep breaths, he moves aside for me to step out of the car. The spectator version of me wants to dig my heels in. I know what's inside, underneath those huge neon letters. It's dehumanization, doctors and nurses who don't view you as a person but simply a work-related task. It's being cut off from the outside world, having your shoelace privileges taken away, having to take meds that make you want to do nothing but lie in bed all day—and having to take meds that have far worse side effects than that.

But that's not what me from the past did. She got out of the car, and she went inside.

Just as the bright electric letters pass out of my view, it shifts again.

I'm in May's bedroom.

Her house is an old one. There's still maroon shag carpet covering the floor from window to door. I sit cross-legged on it, my *iCarly* pajama pants—the envy of all sleepovers I attend—already getting a hole worn down in the knee. I try to look around, wanting to take in all the nostalgic bits that comprised this room. Over in the corner is the karaoke machine she got for Christmas one year that had maybe three songs total loaded onto it. Next to that was her *Hannah Montana* DVD collection. Stacked on her bed were a plethora of stuffed animals, all dirty and faded from their original color over years of attention and infrequent washings. I want to soak it all in, remember exactly what it was like.

But I'm not looking at her room. I'm looking at her.

There is a pang I feel when I look at her. I know this is a memory, but it's different from just recalling it in a fit of wistfulness. It's like she's really here. Box-dyed black hair—probably a recent job, since I can still see black smudges on her ears—triple pierced ears, save for the lower lobe on her right ear, the one that's torn in half. Brown eyes with flecks of gold in them that remind me of those amber stones we'd see on field trips in the museum gift shop. This isn't just my hazy recreation of her. This is *her*.

"Dude, boys are not even that scary," May sighs. She's painting her toenails a neon shade of green, unfazed when tiny hints of green find their way onto the maroon carpet. "They're idiots. They should be scared of you. And Kyle Baker is the least scary of all of them. That guy still thinks it's impressive to squirt milk out of your eye."

I feel myself rub my arm. "I don't know," I say, my voice much higher than I ever remember it being. "What if I do something wrong and he tells all his friends about it? Like, what if I step on his foot or something?"

May dips the nail polish brush back in the bottle, blowing on her sloppy paint job. "What if he steps on *your* foot?"

I shrug.

"God, Violet," she groans. "He's so not worth the anxiety. I don't understand why everyone is so fucking worried about what dumbass boys think."

"That's easy for you to say when they ask you out all the time," I say, picking at a bit of carpet. "Kyle's the first one who's even wanted to look at me, much less take me to a school dance. I still think he did it as a dare."

"Well, when he pours pig's blood all over you, you can just use your latent psychic abilities to snap his neck," she says with a giggle. I hear myself grumble, and May looks up, rolling her eyes. "You really care what he thinks?"

I hesitate, but I nod.

"Ugh. Okay, you're setting feminism back like twenty years, but whatever. Stand up."

I arc an eyebrow. "What?"

"You heard me. Stand up, Spence."

With all the grace of a baby deer, I pick myself up off the floor, and May follows suit, walking over to me until there's only a couple feet between us. "Slow dancing is literally the easiest thing on the planet. Put your arms around my neck."

My whole body goes hot. "What? Why?"

"For fuck's sake." Without warning or hesitation, May takes my limp arms and throws them around her neck. Everything in me goes stiff, and my elbows lock up as my hands bunch up into fists behind her head. "This is all you have to do. And this," she says, setting her hands on my hips, "is all he's going to do."

Slowly, with hardly any movement at all, we sway back and forth, a song playing on her speakers that used to sound cute and romantic when we were thirteen but as I listen to it now, it sounds sad and melancholy. We move in time together, like we always have. My muscles lose their tension as the music plays on.

"See?" she says. "It's not that hard." Her finger accidentally slips off my pajama pants and brushes the skin near my hip, and I feel myself jump, a weird flush of heat running through my body. But she doesn't seem to notice. "You could literally do this in your sleep."

"I guess…" I say.

"No, you don't guess. You know."

I chew on my lip. "What if he, like, grabs my butt or something?"

She pulls me in a little closer, her eyes directly on mine. She's a couple inches taller than me so she has to look down. "Then knee him in the balls," she says with no fanfare.

We sway, and the current version of me, the one watching this unfold, wonders what I should be doing here. Why am I seeing any of this? The previous two memories were horrible, some of my worst moments. Why is this nice memory here?

"Violet?" May asks, dipping her head a little to meet my eyes since I've zoned out. "Are you okay?"

No, I want to say. *I'm not. But I don't know why.*

"I'm fine," I say.

And it shifts again.

The previous times it shifted, it took me a moment to recall exactly where and when I was.

As soon as I open my eyes to the darkness surrounding me, I know exactly where I am.

"Violet, come on," May calls out ahead of me. "Catch up."

I can barely make out her silhouette against the pitch black. For February, it's especially dark since there were a few warm days that melted everything the week before. No reflection of moonlight to shine off the usual mounds of white snow. There's a street light closer to the road, but we're so far into the park that the light from that barely reaches all the way back here. I glance over at the empty playground set May skips past. It's so much creepier than I give it credit for in the daytime, emerging in the darkness like the long-abandoned skeleton of an ancient

339

monster. We're not stopping at the playground, though. We're going up the hill toward the fenced-off dog park. That's where the boys said they would be, anyway.

Turn around, the current version of me begs. *Turn around and go home. Grab May and run back as fast as you can. There's still time. There's still—*

"I swear to god, if they're not there…" May growls as we crest the hill. I'm following nothing except the pale white of her skin, the only thing on her that sticks out through the dark.

"May," I say, in a half whisper as I try to catch up to her. "We should go back. They probably didn't even show up. They were probably just being dicks."

She finally stops, groaning as we come to a stop next to the fence around the dog area. Just as I suspected: there's no one here besides us.

"Those *bitches*," May spits as she kicks at the fence, the pathetic clang of metal on metal not as loud or satisfying as I'm sure she wanted it to be. "I'm going to kick Ryan's ass when I see him on Monday."

Something snaps in the direction of the trees behind the dog area, and my head turns instinctively in the direction of the sound.

Nothing is there. Nothing I can see, anyway.

"Look, if they're not here, there's no point in staying. Let's just go," I say, grabbing onto her jacket sleeve.

"Come on, Violet," she grumbles. "We came all this way. Least we can do is, like, swing on the swing set or something."

Another rustle comes from the trees. My stomach drops. "I don't want to. I want to go home."

"Violet, don't be—"

"May, for real." I look her directly in the eye, my grip on her arm intense now. "Let's go."

Another snap of a twig sounds off behind us. All the humor drops out of May's face, and even she looks over her shoulder now. Turning back to me, her face has somehow gone even whiter than usual. She nods. "Okay," she says. "Okay, let's go."

We walk back down the hill. At first, we walk. Until another rustle behind us forces us into a brisk walk. Then another snapping branch throws us into a sprint. The feeling of something pursuing, something chasing is palpable, sending a creeping prickle across the back of my neck. And May—normally fearless, normally invincible—has panic written across her face. This isn't just to indulge me. She knows someone is after us too. As we sprint, she grabs onto my hand. I don't have the mental capacity to be self-conscious of how sweaty my hands are. All I can think is *run*.

Keep running, current me urges thirteen-year-old me. *Run faster, faster. Maybe you can outrun them this time. Maybe you can get her to safety. Maybe—*

That's not what this is, though, is it? This is a memory.

There is no changing this.

I watch as we run. Not fast enough. They're on top of us within seconds.

I tumble, the world around me blurring as I collapse on the pavement of the main pathway of the park, burning scrapes blooming on the flesh of my exposed palms as I skid to a halt. Try as I might to hold onto May's hand—my only lifeline—the force of the blow pushes our hands apart. As soon as I stop rolling, I scramble on all fours, trying to stand back up again and call out for May.

As I look up, I see the demon. The Hellion.

It grins at me, its oversized teeth dripping with saliva and malice, and my own terrified face is reflected back in the bugged-out orbs of its eyes. It squawks at me in delight, the spikes on its back flaring, and it reaches out toward me with jagged, clawed fingers.

There's still time, current me thinks. *You can still run. You can both still escape.*

We can't. I know we can't. Because a dozen of them are

already on top of me, pulling my arms back behind me as I scream out for May, pinning me to the ground, running their fingers through my hair, across the thin skin of my neck. Their breath is hot—unnaturally so. It's almost unbearable as they breathe down on my exposed skin. I shout May's name, but it soon becomes an unintelligible cacophonous sound, more garbled and incoherent with every passing minute they sit on my back, squeezing the air out of my lungs. Under the weight of all of them, I can just barely arch my head up.

It's my last glimpse of her.

The Hellions have a hold of her too, but they drag her across the pavement by her feet, struggling against the force of her attempts to kick herself free. Her fingers dig themselves into the concrete, her nail beds going bloody as they drag impotently along, unable to find a handhold strong enough to keep her in place. A streak of blood runs from her hairline down the left side of her face. But the blood isn't the thing that disturbs me. That won't haunt me for a decade after.

It's her eyes. Those warm, fearless eyes—now cold and terrified.

She locks her gaze on mine.

Her fingers pry away from the concrete, and she reaches her hand out toward me. I hear my name, screamed in a blood-curdling shriek. I reach my hand out to her...

My head is shoved into the concrete. I feel my teeth break just before it all goes dark.

And then, it shifts.

My breath suddenly comes back into me, my vision clearing. What memory have I been forced into this time? But as I blink away the haze, something feels different. I move to wipe a hand across my face, realizing my head is pounding.

I move.

I hold my fingers out in front of me, flexing them.

I'm back in control. This isn't a memory.

A flurry of shouts and crashes rocks me out of my amazement. Adrenaline shoots through me, and I realize I'm lying on my back. I roll over, propping myself up on my hands and knees—I'm back in my Velmyran clothes, my nail beds still caked with dirt, my feet still killing me. I blink the daze out of my vision, trying to regain my coherence.

It doesn't take me long to realize I've come back to a shit show.

I'm in another open cavern, similar to the one with the archway but with a much higher ceiling. A handful of yards away is a jagged, fractaled pedestal of solid clear crystal, standing taller than even Gren. And surrounding the pedestal is pure chaos.

Everyone appears to be here, fighting non-descript blurs. At first, everything moves too quickly for me to see what exactly is attacking us, but the details of scales and blue streaks of light sharpen the harder I look. What did Kai call them? Lumilanders. Only these are far larger than the one back in the cave—closer to giant alligators. And there are at least a dozen of them, all engaged with someone. Jackson slashes at two of them with his daggers, dodging out of the way of their rows of sharpened teeth. Kai is in their familiar position on top of Gren's shoulders, unloading bolts into one's back while Gren swipes at another with her club. Melandrich, who is much closer to the pedestal, brings his sword down on another trying to bite at his leg—

I'm lightheaded, my breaths coming in too fast again for me to let them out. Breathe in, breathe in—where are Adrian and Eddie? Breathe in, breathe in, breathe—

A cry comes out close to the pedestal, and I look over to see Adrian, a lumilander's jaws wrapped around his shoulder. He's using his hands to try and pry the monster's fangs out of his flesh—why isn't he using Residuum? He grits his teeth as he writhes under the thing's hold, blood oozing out of his shoulder and down his arm.

I have to do something.

My eyes turn to the pedestal.

Well. The stupid decision has gotten me out of a jam before. Let's see if it works again.

Staggering to my feet, I sprint toward the pedestal, dodging out of the way of Melandrich fighting off another sizeable lizard, though a long streak of blood coming from his hairline is clouding his left eye. I move around his flailing blade, skidding up to the pedestal. Another painful cry comes from Adrian's direction.

Think. Think quickly. How do I stop this? I look inside the pedestal, past the distorted fractals and edges. It looks like it's composed of the same clear crystal throughout, but a dark spot catches my eye— faint, like a curl of smoke trapped in a crystal cage. I put my hand on the crystal out of instinct—

And my hand sinks into it.

It feels almost as if nothing is there, as if the crystal pillar in front of me is simply an illusion, a hologram. The only difference is my hand, now completely encased, is cold. It's as if I stuck my hand out an open window, into the chill of a mild winter day.

The sounds around me mount. Adrian no longer grits his teeth, screaming in full force in pain. I push my hand in further, and I wrap my fingers around that wisp of smoke in the center, yanking it from its place. There is no struggle as I pull it forth, breaking my arm free from the crystal pillar with one swift tug.

I look down in my hands. A lightning bolt-shaped shard of smoky quartz sits in the center of my palm.

The sounds of hissing and roaring fall quiet, and as I look up, the hairs on my arm bristle. The lumilanders have paused, turning their glowing gazes on me. Out of instinct, I reach into my pocket for Residuum, but my grip on the stones relaxes as the massive reptiles one by one crawl back up the cavern walls and slink away into the shadows.

"Well. The end is nigh, isn't it?"

I whirl around. Standing behind the pedestal with his horrid, fiery face is the Infernal Mage. The cracks of fire across his skin seem brighter, more pronounced. And looking into his gaze, webs of vibrant orange veins crawl into the whites of his eyes, reaching for the glowing coals of his irises.

A smile plays at the edges of his lips as he stares at me, his eyes flitting erratically to the Relic in my hand. "One to go, then," he says, a sing-song lilt in his voice. "Race you there." And without another word, The Infernal Mage sinks in the ground, looking like he's melting into the stone, just like he did back in Marwindale. His eyes never leave mine as he smolders into a charred pit on the cavern floor, disappearing into a wisp of smoke.

The tension in the air evaporates, and I glance around the cavern to see what kind of danger we're still in. Kai and Gren finish off the last of the lumilanders, with Gren slamming her club into a straggler's skull with a roar. Jackson and Melandrich straighten themselves out, scratched and bruised terribly, but for the most part all right. Adrian drags himself back onto his feet, though it's not without effort. He rolls his punctured shoulder, wincing against the pain as he does. I keep scanning. That isn't all of us. Where's—

Panic rises into my chest as I see his feet, peeking out from around the edge of the crystal pedestal.

I call out Eddie's name, but I can't hear my voice over the sound of my heart thrumming in my ears. Tripping over my feet, I sprint around the crystal formation, a sob climbing into my throat as I see his body lying limply next to the cave wall.

There's blood everywhere. His entire left side is caked with it, some of it fresh, but most of it already drying into a hard crust in his hair, on his shirt, even down his pants. His left arm is crushed and perforated with bite marks, swelling red and puffy, patches of skin already turning black and blue. His eyes are closed, and without thinking, I lean over him and pat his face, trying to wake him up. "Eddie, Eddie," I say softly, holding back the tears. "Come on. You're okay. Get up."

"Move," a threadbare voice says, and before I even have the

chance to react, Adrian pushes me out of the way. I lean back, trying my best to keep breathing. After a moment of looking him over, Adrian lets out a tired sigh. "He's alive. He hit his head hard, and his arm is shattered, but he'll live."

I sigh in relief. The same sigh echoes throughout the group.

"We should go back to the cabin. Orla probably knows her medical stuff better than I do. Plus, I don't have any Residuum left, besides Infernal."

I look back up at the group, who have all gathered together around us. Melandrich nods, catching Adrian's eye. "Can you take us back there, Master Inoue?"

"Close, anyway," Adrian responds.

Melandrich doesn't answer back, rifling through the bag and pulling out the Crystalline Residuum stone, thrusting it in Adrian's hands.

"All right, everyone touch someone and don't hold your breath," Adrian instructs. I fold my fingers into his shirt sleeve, closing my eyes tight, waiting for the countdown. But it doesn't come. There's no gentle lead in before the high-pitched shriek rings in my ears and the ground is swept out from under me once again.

CHAPTER 25

A drian manages to get us less than half a mile away from Orla's cabin by my estimation. It doesn't make the trek back to her cabin any less tense, with Eddie slumped in Gren's arms like a child while we all rush as fast as we can through the thick wooded grove. Even though Adrian said he'd be okay, the anxious energy amongst us hasn't been dispelled completely. We're still reeling from the attack, still banged up. And whatever that veil made me see…

Well, from the looks of everyone else's haunted faces, I imagine they all saw similar things.

I pull up next to Melandrich, whose eyes are wide and unfocused as we stride back toward the cabin. "Do you know what that was back there?" I ask him.

It's as if I startle him, though I don't know how my sloppy footsteps can be a surprise to anyone. But he blinks and looks at me as though I pulled a knife on him before realizing I'm just asking an innocuous question. "I am not sure," he breathes. "Did—did you see visions stepping through the veil as well?"

I nod.

He swallows, his nerves apparent. "I cannot say what exactly it was meant to be, but what I saw—it was as if I relived every moment I ever came to regret. Times in Midra, yes, but mostly times in Hevara. Times with…" His unnervingly blue eyes go wide again as he trails off, staring off into space again.

The word "regret" sits with me as we rush through the leaves. It makes sense. Everything I saw was something I wanted to change, something that I hoped I could alter even when I knew it was impossible. Except that one with May in her room. That one still confuses me.

But was that all it was? We just passed through the veil, fought the lumilanders, and we paid enough of a price to get the Relic? Even after all of that, for all of Adrian's talk of the Crystalline's ruthlessness, it seemed too easy. Was it really just reliving my worst moments that made it so that I could reach into the pedestal?

It isn't long before the cabin comes into view, and we sprint the rest of the way there. As we step into the clearing, it isn't a shock to see Orla standing by the fire pit, prepared and ready to spring into action. "Took you all long enough," she says, as jaunty as ever. "Quickly now. We have to get that arm of his taken care of."

Gren is too big to fit inside the house, so she passes Eddie off to me and Orla. We spread his arms across our shoulders as we half-drag him through the door and into the cabin. We hustle down the narrow hallway to the backmost room. It isn't much to speak of—the same clutter that plagues the rest of Orla's home has infected this room too—but there is at least a cleared corner that has a sunken hay-stuffed bed, which we sprawl Eddie out onto.

"You need to leave now, darlin'," Orla says casually as she rifles through jars and boxes, pulling out various herbs and plants while giving them quick sniffs and even putting a couple in her mouth.

"I'm staying with him until he wakes up," I say firmly.

"It's cramped as it is with just me in here, much less three people," she says as gently as she can. "He's goin' to be fine, but you need to let me work."

"Orla, please."

"Vi?"

A groggy voice croaks from the bed, and I push past Orla and kneel next to the bed at Eddie's side. His eyes are barely open, lolling back and forth in a daze. He tries to lift his head but groans, falling back against the hay in defeat.

"Hey, don't get up. You're okay, you're okay," I chant at him, as soothing as I can possibly be.

"Where is he?" Eddie slurs.

"Everyone else is fine. We got the second Relic," I assure him. "Don't worry about that right now."

Behind me, I hear her rustle around in more of the jars near the wall. "I should put him back to sleep," Orla remarks. "Resettin' his arm while he's conscious will be frightfully unpleasant."

"Where is he?" Eddie repeats, pawing his good hand in the air like he's trying to hold onto something.

"Eddie, just calm—"

With a force he doesn't seem capable of, Eddie grabs a fistful of my shirt, pulling me closer into him. Through the dried blood, his deep brown eyes are lit up in alarm. I'd go so far as to say there's real fear there. "He didn't use the Residuum, Vi," Eddie says, quiet and garbled. "He didn't use it. You can't trust him. He didn't use it because he couldn't. I was right. He couldn't—"

"All right, out you go," Orla perkily says, wafting a vial of strange yellow liquid underneath his nose, and mid-sentence, Eddie's eyes roll in the back of his head, the grip he has on my shirt slackening before it drops completely.

Looking up at Orla, I ask, "What was he talking about?"

Already wiping down Eddie's face with a wet cloth, Orla grins. "What's the phrase I've heard you Earth people say before? Ah yes." She turns her faint blue eyes up toward me and winks. "No spoilers." I'm about ready to clock her in her smug face and say to hell with spoilers, but she grabs me by the upper arm with a strength that her tiny frame doesn't seem capable of. "Out you go, now," she says, and I don't have much of a choice as she pushes me out the door, slamming it behind me.

For a moment, I stare at the closed door in front of me, taking a second to finally breathe. I think about storming back in and demanding Orla tell me what the hell Eddie meant. Because *come on*. She knows. And the cute little "fortune teller who knows all but won't spill the ending" schtick is getting fucking old, especially now. The look in Eddie's eyes seemed frantic, like what he was saying was of importance. And after everything that just happened…

Sighing, I press my forehead against the door. I don't know what's important or not anymore.

It takes me another minute or two to walk back outside to the rest of the group, hoping that maybe we've all calmed down enough to think rationally about what to do next.

Well, that was the hope, anyway.

"Are you fucking kidding me right now?" Jackson shouts as I walk out the front door and down the porch steps back toward the clearing where the rest of the group is all assembled, a way off from the mystery pot. Jackson is cross-armed, glaring at Adrian, his glasses gone so I can see just how pissed he really is. "We're not just going to leave him here. Are you insane?"

"No, I'm smart," Adrian snaps back.

"Beg to differ."

Melandrich steps forward, holding his hands out between them like he's trying to separate a physical fight. "Master King, Master Inoue. Now is not the time for your emotions to run high."

"Yeah, too fucking late," Jackson sneers.

"What's going on?" I ask, approaching the group. Aside from the two arguing and the referee, Kai and Gren stand off to the side spectating. Kai rubs their arm, chewing on the inside of their mouth like they have something to say but are choosing to bite their tongue.

Jackson gestures to Adrian. "Go ahead. Tell her how you want to ditch Eddie."

Rolling his eyes, Adrian says, "God, you're dramatic."

"What is he talking about?" I ask Adrian.

Looking at me, Adrian's face grows grave. "We'd come back for him, okay? I'm not saying we just abandon him here."

"But you want us to leave him behind?" I ask.

He runs a hand through his tangled mane of hair, the tie that usually keeps it pulled back long gone. "The Infernal is probably on the way to the last Relic as we speak. His Relic," he explains. "He can travel underground. That's what he's doing whenever he disappears like he did back there. He can turn himself into Infernal energy and get there faster than he can on foot."

"So, if we left right now, he'd beat us there anyway," I say.

Adrian shakes his head, holding up a glittering stone in his hand. The hunk of Crystalline Residuum is smaller now, maybe about the size of a grapefruit, but the energy humming inside of it is no less palpable. "Not if we use this," he says, with all the conviction of a riled-up lawyer. "If we go now, we can beat him there. He obviously wants the Relics in one piece, which means he wants the Dagger formed. If he gets there before us, he can be ready to take us out as soon as we form the thing. He'll have the upper hand. But if we beat him there, we can grab the Relic, form the Dagger, and when he shows up, we have the power to kill him ready to go. *We* could get the jump on *him*. *We* would have the advantage."

"You said the ritual to form the Dagger takes a lot of people," Jackson interrupts. "We'd need all the help we can get. If we leave Eddie here, we run the risk of it not working. Then, we're sitting ducks."

Groaning, Adrian pulls the satchel from around his shoulders, shoving the Crystalline Residuum into the pack with obvious annoyance. He winces as he moves his right shoulder. He must have done a little healing with the small amount of Earthen we had left, but the skin on his shoulder underneath his torn shirt is still raw and pink. "If we leave him here with Orla, we'd still have six people. That might be enough," he says, slinging the pack back over his shoulder.

"Might?" Jackson echoes. "I don't like the sound of 'might.' I want 'will.' I want you to know."

"Well, I don't know, okay!" Adrian yells, and I jump. I've never seen him this upset before. None of us have, which is why we're taken aback as he shouts. "I don't know any more than you all do! The Old Gods didn't leave a fucking instruction manual for an ancient knife formation ritual. I'm trying my goddamn best here, and in my unprofessional opinion, taking action is how we're going to get out of this. *That's* how we get May back. In case you all forgot why the fuck we're all here."

Everyone is silent amidst the discomfort. Except Jackson, who hasn't backed down at the outburst. "Taking action isn't going to mean jack shit if we're not prepared," Jackson argues, just as firm as he was seconds ago. "We can't just show up half-cocked. We need to be ready. And that means having all of us there, at our best. Or as close as we can get to it."

Adrian looks like he's ready to hurl another angry argument his way, but he doesn't. He pauses, and he looks at me. "What do you want to do?"

I furrow my brow. "Me?"

"Yes, you," he snaps. The tone that he takes flips my stomach. There has always been a care to the way Adrian has talked to me. An understanding. But he barks the words at me like they're poison. "We're here because of you, because you want May back. You decide what we do. She's your friend."

"She's *our* friend," Jackson says.

Adrian glances back at him with a sneer. "Well, it's a little different for her, isn't it?"

"So she's the only one who gets a say in it? Or are you just asking her because you know she'll agree with you?"

At this, Adrian hesitates. The sour twist in my stomach spreads.

"Lady Spence," Melandrich interrupts. "Your input would be appreciated in this matter, regardless of the motives for asking for it." The gaunt look he's worn on his face since the cavern hasn't quite shaken itself yet, but I can tell he's trying his best to look like the stoic, put-together royal delegate we've known him to be. Even with that, he still throws a side-eyed glare in Adrian's direction.

The three of them look at me expectantly. The only one who I can seem to look at, though, is Adrian, still simmering in anger but staring at me with anxious expectation.

I swallow before I say, "Eddie is part of the team. We should wait to see if he improves enough to come with us. I'm not leaving him alone."

Melandrich solemnly nods, while Jackson—even though he fucking won—still stands defensively, arms crossed over his chest in dismay. "I suppose," Melandrich says, "that decides it."

Before Melandrich even has all the words out, Adrian laughs, a cruelty to it that makes the hair on the back of my neck prickle. "Wonderful. Fucking wonderful." He shakes his head, and then looks directly at me. His gaze is sharp and cold as he stares at me.

"Congrats, Violet," he snaps. "You just chose him over May. Hope you're happy."

The vitriol he puts into her name is enough to make it feel like a sucker punch. I open my mouth to bite back at him, but he's already walking away, stalking out into the woods in a huff.

I bite my lip, hard. It feels hot again. That swelling feeling in my core, heat rising into my chest—

"I'm taking a walk, too," Jackson says, already wandering away. "Since we have time."

The anger in me flares as I watch him walk out in the opposite direction of Adrian. I watch him go, thinking about just letting it be, but the heat is just too much. I run after him, ignoring Melandrich calling out to try and stop me.

I hold myself back until we're well away from the cabin, deep into the rough terrain of uninhabited forest, roots sprouting up from the earth in chaotic intervals, branches hanging low enough where I have to dodge them as I stomp after Jackson. "Hey!" I shout when I finally can't contain it anymore.

"What?" Jackson asks, not bothering to stop or even turn to look at me, which just pisses me off even more. I crouch down, finding a loose stone on the ground, and I throw it at him. I'm not really aiming anywhere in particular, and as soon as it leaves my hand, I hope it doesn't hit him in the head. Thankfully, it collides with his shoulder, hard enough where it stops him in his tracks. He turns around, rubbing his shoulder blade. "God, what the fuck is wrong with you?" he shouts.

"I could ask you the same thing," I say, stopping in front of him, fists balled up at my sides.

He drops his arm. "I don't know what you're talking about."

"Yes, you do, asshole!" I yell. "What the hell is your problem with me?"

Jackson sighs, running his hands down his face like he's just too tired to put up with this. "Do we really have to do this right now, Violet? For fuck's sake, we almost just died, and we're going to go try to do it again in a couple of hours. Save your energy."

"No. Like you said, we have time. So, have at it. What's your issue with me?"

"God, this is so middle school."

"Jackson—"

"Okay!" Jackson says, spreading his arms out in front of him. "You want to know what my problem is with you? It's this. This whole self-obsession you have going on. The idea that everything that's happening is some kind of slight against you. That's my problem, Violet."

I shake my head. "I don't know what—"

"You know exactly what I'm talking about," he says. "Ever since we got here, you haven't given a damn about Eddie, but the moment he gets his shit wrecked, you act like the selfless best friend. Fucking forgive me for assuming you'd side with Adrian, but that's been your track record ever since we got here. Since before we got here."

"That isn't even true," I bite.

"Yeah, of course not."

"Fine," I relent. "Let's say you're right. I'm sorry if coming here with the prospect of finding May hasn't made me the perfect friend or whatever. Fuck me for being traumatized, right?"

At that, Jackson snaps his fingers, pointing directly at my face. "That, right there. That's it," he says. "You honestly think that being here is fucking you up, and you alone. We're all struggling here, all right? You don't have some weird claim to suffering."

"No offense, but I think I have a bigger claim than you."

"Why, because you saw her get taken?" he asks.

The abruptness of the question throws me off. I blink at him. "Yeah, kind of," I answer.

He laughs, a sound laced with venom. "Did you know she invited me to come with you guys that night?" he asks.

I keep blinking at him, like the words don't quite make sense to me. Slowly, I shake my head.

"Yeah," he continues. "During that algebra class I told you about. She asked me to come, and I said no. I was too scared of my parents finding out. I had to find out she was missing from the news the next day. You don't think that fucked thirteen-year-old me up, royally?"

I'm silent.

"I spent *years* dealing with that, Violet," Jackson goes on, his voice starting to break. "There were nightmares and panic attacks in the middle of class and months and years of isolating myself from people. The guilt ate me alive. I told myself if I would have gone with, maybe I could have helped. Maybe I could have fought whoever it was off. Maybe if I hadn't been so chicken shit, she'd still be here. I've been in therapy since fucking eighth grade over it. Then throw the whole 'realizing I'm a guy' thing on top of it…" He trails off, and he finally allows one of the tears welling up in his eyes to spill over, wiping it away immediately. He sniffs, the tense edge in his muscles loosening. "What you went through was awful. I would never deny that. I wouldn't want to trade places with you for anything. But she was my friend too. My only friend back then, actually. But no one cares because I'm not the one that was there. How's that for being traumatized?"

My eyes are fixated on a toppled over tree a few yards away. I can't look at him. "I…" I pathetically stammer. "I'm sorry."

He doesn't respond for a moment. But he finally speaks. "That would have been nice to hear any time in the past ten years."

I close my eyes, the fists at my side shaking. The rage that is coursing through me right now, though, isn't toward him anymore. I suck in a painful breath and look up, ready to face him. But he's gone.

I stagger through the uncharted path of the forest, tears obscuring my vision. I will myself not to cry while I walk, begging myself to take a moment to just breathe and figure out where the hell I am in relation to the cabin so I can find my way back. Everything that's happened within the past couple hours clouds my head. All the old memories, the image of Eddie's broken body, the terrified look in his eyes, Adrian's accusatory sneer, the revelation of Jackson's guilt—it's all too much. I feel like I'm choking on it. I stumble forward and brace myself against a tree, pressing my forehead against the bark and digging my nails into soggy moss clinging to it.

Breathe in.

Breathe out.

Breathe in.

Breathe out.

Why is this not making me feel better?

The sharp snap of a twig sends a jolt through me, my heartbeat picking up pace. I look around the tree in the direction of the sound, peering around it out of caution. The tree is huge, enough to hide all of me if there's a bear or—or something worse that's picked up on my scent.

The grip of fear in my chest eases, though, as I see Adrian wade through the trees. Breathing a sigh of relief, I retract my nails from the tree bark, attempting to move from around the tree to confront him. I'm still pissed at him for what he said to me back there, after all.

It's only one step in before I freeze in place. Because Adrian is talking to someone.

"The answer is the same as before: no," he says. His tone is firm, no room left for arguments.

Peeking one eye out around the tree, I think for a second that maybe he's talking to himself. But a figure follows closely after him, draped in a black cloak shimmering with streaks of pulsing burnt orange light—like pockmarks in a cinder.

A shot of cold dread runs through me as the Infernal Mage glides behind Adrian, an arm outstretched. Not in an attack. In desperation.

"Please," the Mage says. "See reason, friend."

"I'm not your friend," Adrian hisses.

From my vantage point, I can just barely make out the twitch that runs through the Mage's face. "This suffering—this anguish—it can all go away," he pleads. For the first time, I see him trip, a brief interruption in his otherwise smooth gait. "Your friends do not need to die for this. You may have the Dagger for yourselves. If only you take it from me—"

Adrian stops, whirling on the Mage and taking a threatening step toward him. To my shock, the Mage cowers from him, stepping back as he comes forward. "I will *never* take it back," Adrian barks.

Like a child being reprimanded by a parent, the Infernal Mage twists his fingers around each other, unable to look Adrian in his eye. "Please," he says, his voice tiny. "I beg of you. You gave me this agony. I want you to end it."

The hard crease of Adrian's brow unfurls, morphing from hard resolve to pity. "Brennan," he says, "I'm sorry I ever gave it to you. Really, I am. It's haunted me for a decade." He pauses, and the sharp angles to his face return, hardened in resolve. "But so have the things I did with that power. I can't go back to that."

The word "power" hits me in a way I can't quite pinpoint— like someone jabbing a finger into my chest. I cover my mouth, though I'm not sure why.

"That is why I ask you to take it, friend," the Infernal Mage implores. "We are damned, you and I. This power cannot help but corrupt whatever it touches. I understand that now. But if you take it back, it will not poison another innocent soul." His wide glowing eyes flicker in despondence. "Let it serve as your penance. I know that is what you seek. It is why you want the Dagger for yourself, is it not? You wish to destroy her. One last thing to absolve you of your sins."

Adrian doesn't answer him.

"Let me give you that absolution, friend," the Mage continues.

"Go to hell," Adrian spits.

The veins of fire running across his face flare as his face twists into an angry grimace. "If you continue on this path, I will have no choice but to end you all. Then you will never find the peace you seek. They will simply be more names to add to your body count. The dozens who were collateral damage, the hundreds in Tersaria—"

"*Don't.*"

My nails dig into my cheek.

Adrian points a finger toward the Mage, menacing. "*Don't* say that word," he warns.

A smile briefly flashes over the Infernal's face. "Or what?" he asks. "What will you, a mortal, do to me? You are not a Mage." A throaty giggle bubbles up from within him, like water overflowing from a cup. "Not anymore."

Adrian's hand falls, just as the Infernal Mage with his mangled smile sinks into the ground, melding into the earth and disappearing into a scorched circle on the forest floor.

I don't breathe as I watch him stare at the charred ground in front of him. He's as motionless as a delicate statue carved from marble. After what feels like years, he stares up into the open air ahead of him, running both his hands through his wild hair. And without fanfare, he turns on his heel and walks off into the green of the forest.

CHAPTER 26

I'm an idiot.

It's minutes after I lose sight of him that I pull the hand away from my mouth. Even when I do, I still don't breathe. I don't think I remember how to.

I'm such an idiot.

My knees give out on me. I fall back against the tree, and I slip down on the ground, my hands bracing both sides of my head like my skull is going to burst open.

I'm such a righteous *fucking* idiot.

My breath comes back to me in gasps, shattered and heaving. It all makes sense. Too much sense, in fact. So much sense that I should have seen it all before. Eddie even tried to tell me, for fuck's sake, and I didn't listen. That's what he was talking about before Orla put him out. *"He didn't use the Residuum, Vi. He didn't use it. You can't trust him. He didn't use it because he couldn't."*

He saw Adrian fighting the lumilanders. He saw that he didn't use Infernal Residuum against him when that was all he had left. *Couldn't.*

Former Mages can't use that type of Residuum once they've given up their power.

360

I squeeze my eyes shut, so tight that white spots dance in the dark behind my eyelids. It's all right there, you stupid fool. That's what I am. Because only a fool could overlook all of it—the reason he knew so much about the Mages, the location of the Relics, why Crystalline kept him around in the first place. Why he was so terrified to get found out by Visandra, why Tersaria isn't in the game master's guide...

And why May *is*.

My hands fall to the ground, and I grab a fistful of dead leaves, crushing them in my grasp, needing something to do with the rage running through me right now. I don't even know who I'm mad at more—him or me.

Me. Definitely me.

I was so willing to believe everything he said just because, what? He didn't look at me like I was crazy? He fed me the fucking dead brother story, and I didn't question it for a second. I was so desperate to connect with someone just as broken as I was that I couldn't see how much I was being duped. Couldn't see that the reason he understood my pain was because he—

No, I won't let myself think it. I can't. Not now.

I open my eyes, clambering to my feet and walking forward. That roiling anger rushes through me again, no longer content to sit at the bottom of my stomach and simmer. It rockets through my core, into my limbs and my face. I seethe as I fight my way over the bumpy terrain back to the cabin, following the direction Adrian went in. My fury is so palpable that I wonder if I set the trees behind me ablaze.

The cabin comes back into focus. A quick glance around shows that everyone has come back to camp—Jackson eats a bowl of mystery stew as he sits on a stump in front of the fire pit, while Kai and Gren silently sit across from him, neither looking particularly hungry. Melandrich scribbles something down in his small twine-bound notebook closer to the house.

And standing on the bottom step of the porch, is *him*.

The burning energy in me flares. It needs release.

I have enough sense that I don't reach into my pockets for Residuum. With how infuriated I am, I'd almost certainly burn him alive if I used magic. As I stomp toward him, I eye Melandrich's sword hanging off his belt. In as smooth a motion as I can make it, I grab hold of the sword's handle and pull it from its sheath. I don't stop even as Melandrich stumbles back startled, calling out my name as I walk toward the bastard.

Adrian's back is toward me, so he has no time to defend himself as I lunge forward and kick at the back of his knee. He collapses, flailing out onto the porch steps. More people shout my name now—I don't give a shit. All I care about is him. With a grunt, he flips himself around, his expression angry at first, but turning to shock once I stick the point of Melandrich's sword directly in his face, hovering just inches away from his nose.

There's scuffling behind me. "Violet, what the hell are you doing?" Jackson shouts.

I ignore him. "Give me your bag," I command.

"Lady Spence, this is an egregious overstep," Melandrich says, his soldier voice coming out. "Return my weapon at once."

"Bag!" I shout, jabbing the sword forward in warning. "Now!"

Eyes wary, Adrian doesn't argue, shrugging his rucksack off his shoulders, tossing it on the ground toward me.

"And your pockets," I say, trying not to sound as frantic as I feel. "Turn them out. All the Residuum you have."

He does so, without hesitation, almost as if he's been rehearsing it. The stones he casts out are mostly Infernal, a couple useless shards of Heavenly and Earthen intermixed. As he turns his pockets inside out, he doesn't break eye contact with me, a look of fear and concentration in his eyes. It's something less shocked than it should be. Something far more accepting.

"Violet, have you lost your mind?" Jackson asks. "What exactly is going on?"

My expression doesn't waver as I bore my eyes into Adrian's.

"Well," I say, quieter now. "You want to tell them what I just saw?"

He is motionless, that frightful yet resolute expression plastered across his face. Breaking from his stiff position, he cautiously shakes his head. "I don't know what you're—"

"Don't!" I scream at him, shaking the sword at him menacingly. "Don't, Adrian. Don't make me out to be the crazy one here." My eyes sting, and I try to blink back the encroaching tears. "Not anymore. Don't do it."

He sighs, nothing more than a wisp of a breath, still refusing to break eye contact with me.

"What is she speaking of, Master Inoue?" Melandrich asks, the tough tone in his voice faltering.

Adrian, however, doesn't acknowledge him. There is nothing happening outside of him and me, trapped in each other's burning gazes.

"How much did you hear?" he asks.

"All of it."

He nods, mouth bunching up in bitter acceptance.

"You almost had me fooled," I spit. The sword dips, and I have to consciously raise it back up to his face. "I ignored all of it because I wanted to believe you were—that you were just like me. That you were just suffering and wanted it to stop." I shake my head as the tears start. "But that wasn't it at all, was it?"

Adrian doesn't move, eyes glistening.

It comes out of me in barely a whisper, clogged and muddled by the lump lodged in my throat.

"You were the Infernal Mage, weren't you?"

At the words, Adrian visibly winces. A silent moment passes, his mouth working but never producing words. No one else speaks, either.

After a tense minute, he finally says, "I can explain."

The laugh that comes out of me is unnatural, painful. "Explain what? How you killed hundreds of people? Melandrich told me about Tersaria, Adrian. How do you explain that?"

At the name, he closes his eyes, sucking in a sharp breath.

"I thought it wasn't in the guide because your brother died there, and you just didn't want to think about it," I say. I stop for a moment, the thought just now coming to me and making my gut flip. "He *did* die there, didn't he?"

Adrian drops his head.

"Good Earth…" Melandrich breathes.

I laugh again, despite it all being so utterly humorless.

"Violet, I'm not denying any of this." He arches his head back up, barely able to meet my eyes. "I know how much I fucked up."

"Do you?" I exclaim. My voice is shaking, the blade in my sweating hand trembling. "Because I think you have no fucking clue! Because if you destroyed Tersaria, gave away the power right after, and then went to Earth that means—"

The blade dips, its point falling to the ground while the grip is still in my hand. I squeeze my eyes shut. I can't say it. I don't even want to think it.

Jackson does it for me. "Oh my god," he says, dazed. "You took May."

A pause. I look back up at him. He's staring at his feet. "It was an accident."

"Bullshit," I hiss.

"I swear to you, it was," Adrian says, the measured meter of his voice elevating. "I never meant to do it."

"So, what was going to happen when we found her?" Jackson demands, pulling up next to me. He has both his daggers in his hands, one pointed at Adrian slumped over on the steps. "She would have recognized you, and the jig would have been up. What was the plan, then?"

That's when he breaks.

Adrian laughs, hysterical and unhinged, streams of tears pouring down his face as he pushes his knotted hair out of his eyes. "There was never any plan!" he says between breaths. "Are you kidding me? I'm not a planner, okay? I'm a *liar*." The laughter stops, the last word said with a bitter resentment reserved only for pure disgust. "I say what I need to survive, and I fit it into a narrative later. If we found her, I knew it would have been over. I'm not dumb. It was inevitable."

"So, why'd you come with us at all?"

"He wasn't going to," I say. "He was going to let Eddie and I go by ourselves. Until he had a change of heart."

Adrian still won't meet my eyes, doing nothing to wipe away the tears streaked down his face. "I can explain everything."

"I don't want to hear it."

"Well, I do," Jackson says.

Glancing over at him, Jackson's face is stony and cold. The unbridled rage that runs through me right now isn't nearly as unsettling as the icy disdain in Jackson's shadowed brown eyes as he looks at Adrian. "I want to know why we're all here," he continues, stepping forward, dagger still leveled at him. "Why the past decade happened the way it did for us. I want an explanation. And I want you to make it a good one, motherfucker."

Adrian's lifeless gaze darts from him to Melandrich to behind me where Kai and Gren most likely stand in silent anticipation.

But he cannot look at me.

"I'll tell you," Adrian says, fixing his sights on the ground in front of the porch steps he's sprawled across. "I'll tell you everything. Keep one thing in mind, though: I said I'm a liar, but I have never once told you all that I'm a good person. That, even for me, has always been a lie too far."

THE MAN IN THE HIGH TOWER

Where I grew up, there was a well at the bottom of a hill.

It had run dry long before I was born. The active one was a mile south of it, but my brother and I passed it every day on the way to the fields in the morning and then back to the barn when the sun went down. Wyland, usually sensible, would only act like the child he was around that well. He would stop and lean over the edge of the stone ring, throwing his voice down into the empty cavern just to hear it bounce back up to him, giggling like a maniac at the sound. I would let him do it, but only until he leaned too far—if even one foot left the ground, my hand was on his shoulder, pulling him back from the stone wall. He would grumble at me, wondering with a whine why I never let him have any fun.

And I would warn him, fierce and unwavering: never be the one stuck at the bottom of the well. There was no climbing your way out of that, unless someone at the top were to help you. The man at the top of the well was the one with the power, and there was no telling what sort of man he was.

I don't know where I was born. In fact, I don't know much about my life before my brother. I know I had parents, but I don't remember what meals they made for me or what stories they told me at night. The only thing I know for certain was Wyland was born a week after my third birthday—and two years after that, we were on our own. They died somehow—I recall masks of horror on lifeless bodies, a stench that I still wake up to after nightmares—but the details have been lost. Sometimes, I think I want to go back to Elowen, run through the city archives there to see if I can find them, put an exact cause to their deaths. Maybe I could find the true reason why Wyland and I were left alone. Most of the time, though, I realize how stupid that sounds. There has never been anything tragic in my life I've ever thought I was better off remembering. I doubt that would be any different.

The local orphanage in Elowen took us in, and somehow, we made it there a couple years more. I was around six or seven when the farmer came by that day in the spring. He lived just outside the town, all alone on a large plot of land perfect for crop harvest. His wife had just died, leaving him with no children or any other family to tend to the farm. He needed farmhands. Of course, he didn't put it that way to the orphanage workers, fabricating some woeful story about wanting to honor his late wife by raising the children they were never able to have. The orphanage didn't really care—the more children adopted out, the more available beds—so Wyland and I were soon packed up and sent on our way with him, along with seven other kids. It started out as just the seven of us, but over time, it was more like twenty—twenty-five at the most. And the years that followed were brutal.

Even before the sun rose, we made our way to the fields. We clawed at the dirt—sometimes with tools, if we were lucky, but most of the time with our hands—making way for seeds to be planted. We painstakingly scattered the seeds, spreading cow manure over them afterward. We watered, we gathered and harvested, and then we did it all over again. Dawn until dusk, every day. Even in the winter months, there were tasks to complete—livestock to attend to, chores around the homestead. There was rarely a day off. By the time I was ten years old, I had broken and beaten feet, hands with calluses that would never fully disappear, and a desire to run away from that place and never look back.

I didn't, of course, because of Wyland. There, we had food and shelter guaranteed. To run off in search of something else would have been foolhardy at best—suicide at worst.

That didn't mean I couldn't dream, of course.

Huddled together in the barn we lived in, we and the other children would exchange stories late at night that we heard about far off places—the plush wilds of Hevara, the open Verdantia Plains, the frozen mountains of Extera. My favorite stories by far, though, were the ones from Castle's Edge. Tales of valiant kings and rich dukes, all manner of people who didn't need to worry about where their next meal was coming from. I envied them and their stone castles with their high towers. I got the nickname "the boy in the high tower" from the other kids because of my reverence for those stories. Many of us didn't have family names, so I took that in stride and made it ours. Adrian and Wyland Hightower.

And I never stopped wanting that life. In the early mornings before we made our way to the fields, I would climb up to the barn loft and stick my head out, looking down at the other kids walking out early, marveling at how small they were from my vantage point. Imagine if I were a prince living in Castle's Edge, watching all my subjects below me. What sort of existence that would be. What kind of bliss.

Wyland never had the same lofty ideals I did. The kid was content with his life—infuriatingly so. No matter how little we were fed, how cold we were, how many blisters on our feet, he never complained. When the younger kids would cry in the middle of the night because they were in pain or hungry or longing for their parents, Wyland would curl in next to them and say, "There's so much to be grateful for. The fact that you're alive is wonderful itself. Don't cry over what you don't have. Celebrate what you do."

I have no idea where he learned any of that. I certainly never taught him such gentle words. I was always angry, raging against the things in our lives that wouldn't relent. Hell, I would bitch about the sun shining at the wrong angle in my eyes as we worked. It never did me any good, either. The farmer didn't take well to whining, rewarding complaints with a smack in the face, a thump on the head, or worse. If you didn't learn your lesson after that, you went to bed without food. And if you didn't learn after that—well, there were always more kids at the orphanage. Some of the worst offenders would leave with him one morning and never come back, only to be replaced a couple days later. I was never subtle, but I was smart enough to know what kind of back-talk and rebellion would be tolerated and what would get me in real trouble. I always toed the line, but for Wyland's sake, I never crossed it.

I was twelve years old when I became the Infernal Mage. And I had no idea what I was getting myself into.

The farmer sometimes sent one of us off to town to pick up supplies that were running low. I was sent that day to get more feed for the chickens. I always relished the opportunity to step away from the hard work of the fields, and after I got what I needed from town, I took my time walking back—exploring different parts of the woods, climbing trees, pretending I was a famous adventurer. On any given day, the forest was empty. The worst I would usually encounter was a fox who hadn't eaten for a few days. But fate had something bigger in mind for me that day. That day, I came across him.

It was an odd clearing of trees, I thought at first—symmetrically cleared, something that shouldn't occur in nature. It took me a moment to realize the trees hadn't grown in that formation. They had been burned into a ring of charred foliage. If Wyland were with me, he would have told me to turn back, that whatever happened there could have been dangerous. But I was much stupider than he was. It didn't scare me. It intrigued me. Especially considering that in the center of the clearing sat a figure. A figure that appeared almost human.

Almost.

As I got closer, I saw he was man in shape alone—smooth head, limbs loosely hanging at his side. He sat on his knees in the center of the wide-open pit, smoldering like the remnants of a dying bonfire. He wore no clothes, his skin an ash grey, cracking and disintegrating off his body. Where his eyes should have been were smoldering pits, empty and hollow. I was afraid the mere sound of my footsteps would be enough to disturb his delicate structure and send him crumbling. He stared at the ground in front of him, but as I approached, his hollow gaze settled on me, and I felt the weight of it press on my chest.

His empty sockets for eyes blinked, over and over as we remained caught in each other's sights. When he spoke, it was a wisp of a voice. I could hardly hear it over the sound of the wind.

"Are you frightened, boy?"

It took me a second to answer, but I shook my head.

"Then you are a fool."

That put the first pangs of fear in me, but as ominous as it sounded, he did nothing but stare at me with his empty pits. It was minutes before he spoke again, his voice somehow weaker than before.

"Who do you serve, boy?"

I didn't answer. He was so strange, so off-putting. Though he was weak, I didn't want him to know where I lived, in fear that something might happen to Wyland. "No one," I replied. Out of instinct, though, my gaze briefly flickered toward the direction of the farm.

"No man who serves himself looks behind him," the shell of a man whispered. "The man truly in control of himself always casts his eyes upward."

I was silent.

"Would you like to serve only yourself, boy?" Puffs of smoke escaped his mouth as he spoke. "Would you like to keep your eyes only on the sky?"

Every smart part of myself screamed to run away. Whatever this man—this creature—was, there was an energy that radiated off him that was toxic, suffocating. I felt as though *I* would start crumbling if I got any closer. The smart thing to do would have been to turn and run as fast I could in the opposite direction.

The dumb part of me—the selfish, arrogant part—was in control that day. The part of me that wanted to be up in that high tower made me stay.

The ashen man held his cracking hand out to me. "Let me grant you that power."

And...

I was twelve years old. I was tired, beaten down, starving for more than food. And I had someone to look out for.

Of course I took his hand.

Taking on the power of a Mage is indescribable. It is to be undone—every part of you is torn apart and crudely stitched back together, the very fabric of your soul incinerated and the debris forced back into the shape of something whole. To obtain such power, you must first render yourself powerless. You have to burn.

And burn I did.

For how long, I don't know. It could have been minutes, hours. It felt like lifetimes. But when the anguish finally lifted and I was something resembling myself, the sun was still up, shining through the blackened trees. And the man—the former Infernal Mage—was a pile of soot on the ground in front of me.

As I made my way back to the farm, I convinced myself that nothing out of the ordinary had happened. I looked at my hands, my feet. I seemed to be whole. Normal. The same kid who had left the farm that morning. The only thing that was any different was the concentrated spot of searing pain in my chest. I twisted and stretched, knowing sometimes, even at age twelve, my muscles could tighten and knot themselves in ways that just needed to be stretched apart. Nothing I did worked, though. When I made it back to the barn, I found water and drank it. No matter how much I drank, that burning spot wouldn't leave. I fell asleep that night only because I was so exhausted from traveling and whatever that ashen man had done to me. If my body hadn't been physically worn down, I don't know if I would have slept at all.

For the next few days, it all seemed like a hazy daydream I had. Nothing changed. I went to work, I kept Wyland from falling down that well. I bit my tongue whenever the farmer would tell us to work faster, harder. I collapsed into hay and filth at the end of the day, too tired to do anything else. It was business as usual. But that searing feeling never left me, no matter what I did.

It was nearly a week later that the power made itself known. Wyland and I went to the active well, and he stopped by the old one while we were walking back. The well was the only thing that really seemed to allow him to act like the kid he was, so I always indulged him until he went too far. That day, he let a foot leave the ground, and I pulled him back. He complained, which was normal. But as we walked back to the fields, he wouldn't let up. He kept saying how it wasn't that dangerous and how I had done dumber stuff, going on and on and on. I snapped at him, what I thought was a harmless snipe and nothing more. As I turned around and told him to just be quiet, a tree exploded into flame, not even a few yards away.

And the pain in my chest went away.

The other children on the farm had told us stories of the

Mages, of course. There were some kids who had come from families of devout Old Gods worshippers. Their stories of the Mages were ones of reverence and fear, an acknowledgement of awe-inspiring might. I had never taken them as truth, though. Even though I had seen people in town and at the orphanage use Residuum, I never made the connection that the stones came from the Mages. The stories I heard were just that. As I experimented, though, I wondered if perhaps the man I had run into in the forest that day was someone far more terrifying than I had first given him credit for. Slowly, I started thinking maybe the stories the kids told weren't just make believe.

Wyland certainly seemed to think so. Having seen me light a tree on fire and put it out just as fast with merely a thought, he was faster to accept that I was the new Infernal Mage than I was. For those first few months, it was a fun secret we kept between the two of us. At night, when the others slept, we would sneak off to a corner of the barn, and I would practice creating a flame in the palm of my hand, singeing handfuls of hay, or incinerating an ant that passed by us. It fascinated us, and we sometimes got so caught up playing around that we would lose track of time, watching the dark sky outside the barn begin to lighten into yellows and pinks.

There were even moments when I dared sneak out of the barn and walked into the woods to try larger things on my own. The energy of the ground beneath me was something I was acutely connected to, and I soon learned I could create cracks in the earth and pull steam up from the ground. The more I pushed myself, the more confidence I gained. I found myself laughing as I created columns of fire taller than me, beaming at the fact that if one of the surrounding trees caught fire, I could put it out with a mere wave of my hand. There were moments that I would sit in silence, watching the dawn break with a grin on my face, unbothered by the fact that I would be dog tired while working that morning. This was what I had been waiting for, after all. This would be the thing that gave me at least a chance. A chance to be something more than what I was born as. A chance to climb my way up into that high tower.

That chance came two months after I had met the ashen man. And it was not the chance I had expected.

It was nearing summer, and the heat was already unbearable. Being further south, Elowen does have milder winters, but the spring until the fall can be suffocating. And when you worked in the sun every day, it was worse. If you weren't careful, it was easy to pass out from heat exhaustion. Which is what Wyland did one day. When we had lived at the orphanage, he was prone to getting sick. It left him weaker than a lot of kids his age. He normally worked through it. But that day, he couldn't anymore. With the sun beating down on us so oppressively, he collapsed into the freshly dug ground.

I panicked, of course, abandoning my own work to try and get him to at least stand back up. Laziness, while it might sting on your backside for a few days, was forgivable up to a point. Physical inability to work meant obsolescence. That, you never returned from. I begged him, tried to pull him up onto his feet myself, but he could barely move. Eventually, with enough struggle between the two of us, the farmer caught wind of it. He came around to our section of the fields, staring at us mercilessly with his beady black eyes behind curling, uncontrollable white eyebrows. It didn't take a scholar to know what he was thinking, what he was planning once he sent everyone back to the barn at the end of the day.

Once the sun started to dip below the hills on the horizon, the kids all left for the barn, lifelessly limping back down the paths in the fields and through the trees back to the barn. The farmer, however, took Wyland by the arm and dragged him back toward his home toward the opposite end of the property, towing him along like a mutt that misbehaved. I followed after them, cursing and shouting to let my brother go, that if he wanted to get rid of him, he'd have to get rid of me too. My threats did nothing to sway him. He dragged my brother along in an unwavering tread, like I was nothing more than a mosquito in his ear. Nothing I said was going to matter to him.

So I stopped speaking. I acted, instead.

It took only a foot slammed into the ground to make it shake beneath him, throwing him off balance and tripping him. He had enough sense knocked out of him that he let Wyland go. It was only then that I recognized where we were. Just a few yards away off the path we were walking was that dried up well. The farmer had been thrown against it, using it to prop himself back up onto his feet. As he struggled, he glared at me, a cruelty that's rivaled some real evil that I've come across in the decades since—both in Velmyra and Earth.

I didn't even think about putting another tremor underneath him. It just happened. And with enough force, it toppled him over the stone side of the well.

There was a yelp, then silence. For a moment, I thought perhaps the fall from such a height broke his neck. It wasn't long before a torrent of echoing coughs and curses erupted from the opening. My feet instinctively moved forward, but they stopped as I heard the desperation in the man's voice reverberating off the stones.

The patheticness.

"Wyland," I said, my eyes not leaving the stone structure. "Go back to the barn."

He protested at first. I think the intensity in my eyes might have scared him off, though. He soon padded his way back down the path toward the barn. I made sure he was out of sight before I walked over to the well and peered down into the hole.

The well was deep enough that it was almost too dark for me to make him out, but I could just barely see him—patchy white hair, wire rim spectacles now missing. Where I thought his scowl of unmatched anger would be, however, was a petrified expression. Those beady black eyes were wide and frightened. He called up to me, asked me to fetch a rope from the house and pull him back up. If I did that, he would forget about Wyland's slip up earlier.

I looked down at him, the ant that he was. I could have gotten the rope. That would have been the benevolent thing to do, I supposed.

Would he extend that same benevolence back to me and Wyland, though? If I were to help him, wouldn't he just go back to being the same tyrant he was before?

Why would I help him? I was the man at the top of the well now, after all.

I've told myself I don't regret killing him. It was for the benefit of my brother, for the sake of family. It wasn't the selfish act of a beaten down child that it appeared to be. That doesn't mean I can't remember the exact smell of his skin burning as I pulled the molten earth from beneath his feet, slowly and sadistically up above his head. That I don't hear his screaming when I find myself in too quiet of a room. That I don't remember the intensity of the heat and the rage rushing through me and how much I didn't care.

I waited until the molten earth had cooled completely, the rocketing orange fading gradually into a dull black. It was almost funny. If you looked down the well, it looked as though nothing had happened at all. From that high up, you couldn't tell that it was a grave.

I trekked back to the barn. Wyland was there waiting for me, worry plastered across his face. The rest of the kids were concerned too, especially when Wyland had miraculously reappeared back at the barn after they thought he was gone for good. They asked me what happened. That was when I cut my teeth on my first lie. I said the farmer had gotten so frustrated with the both of us that he said he was leaving us all here alone. He would travel to Hevara to live out the rest of his days, since he was too old to keep wrangling children. We were all free to go. He even left us some money at the house. He wasn't kind enough to tell us where, but it could be a fun game to play, anyway.

No one believed me. To be fair, it was a terrible lie. But it was enough to get the rest of the kids out of the barn and heading off toward the farmer's house in search of the money that supposedly existed there. I held Wyland back, and once everyone was gone, I told him to gather up his things. We were leaving. And we were never coming back.

As we walked off into the night with the farm at our backs, he asked me what really happened to the farmer. He only asked once. Only needed to ask once. The fact that I didn't say anything was answer enough.

Survival was what the next years of our lives were about. We stayed in Magburn for quite a while doing odd jobs for local artisans. It was there that I learned more about residuuism. It's a wives' tale that Mages can't use Residuum. They certainly can. Mage magic easily gets out of control, and as a teenager with emotions that can go haywire in an instant, it happened to me more than once. I was always able to recall any errant magic that got too out of hand before it caused any noticeable destruction, but there were too many close calls. I needed to know how to use magic—actually use magic, not just tread water. I found a local residuuist who worked with me. She was ancient and couldn't hear a damn thing, but she was brilliant. Earthen and Heavenly were my specialties when I worked with her. I never picked up Infernal. Using Infernal Residuum when you're the Infernal Mage is sort of like playing two songs at once in different ears. It overwhelms, makes things confusing. I tried a couple of times, only for it to end poorly. I'm sure my teacher caught on, but she was either too smart to approach me about it or too apathetic. I spent years with her before she died. And my young, stupid ass thought that meant my training was done.

We traveled after that. We went to the east and spent time in Kazden with the eventual goal of moving to Castle's Edge. But my brother grew increasingly anxious the longer we stayed near large groups of people. I told him he worried too much. But he probably worried the right amount, to be honest. There were definitely nights of drinking where I stupidly showed off my ability to snuff out candles and reignite them with just a look as a flirting tactic. The guys who I flirted with probably thought I was a good magician with some Residuum hidden in my pocket. There were plenty of lurking bounty hunters in the squalid bars I frequented, though, and we had a few close calls, narrowly slipping out of their grasps after I had been too liberal with my displays. It wasn't long before we abandoned the cities all together, taking to the woods and open plains of the north.

The forest was a dicey area, obviously. A fire magician in the woods spells nothing but disaster. There are scars all over the northern end of the Midran Forest from my magic. I would like to say they were all mistakes. But there would be days where the radiating pain in my chest was too much, and I would have to release it somehow, somewhere. And there were even days where it wasn't painful. There were some fires I started just because I could. The Verdantia Plains were much better for me, in that regard. There was less cover, but I could let the magic go without having to worry about consequences, for the most part. When I sent up a torrent of flame, it of course attracted attention from passing marauders. I was the motherfucking Infernal Mage, though. They weren't much of a challenge.

The more I used the ability—the bigger the shows of force—the more I changed. Every part of me. My hands started to glow dull pink and orange underneath my skin, my veins ignited. Patches of my skin started to char—in unnoticeable places at the beginning, but they soon sprouted up on my neck, my chest, my face. They would start at a single point and spread, like holding a piece of paper over a candle and watching the burnt center race toward the edges. Whenever I did get a look at my reflection, I would sometimes catch a glimpse of a dull glow in my eyes, flickering out fast enough where I thought maybe my mind was playing tricks on me. Given how warily Wyland started looking at me, though, it most likely wasn't just my imagination.

It wasn't just my appearance that changed. Every moment not focused on making sure we had enough food and shelter was dedicated to working on my magic. Painstakingly. I focused on how to make things bigger while also maintaining control, and every person who accosted us for any reason was just target practice. After a while, even those who didn't bother us weren't safe. We still needed supplies to stay alive. There were times where we got desperate—

God. I'm doing it even now. Trying to make myself sound better than I actually was.

Maybe sometimes we were desperate, but we were mostly comfortable. Wyland was happy for the most part—satisfied, healthier than when we were living back in Elowen. We weren't that bad off. But I still used my abilities to scare other travelers on the road. If they put up a fight, it was easy to put them in their place. I didn't kill anyone, but if they fought back, they didn't run away unscathed. They had to know who was in charge in the situation, who would come out on top. It was always going to be me.

It left me wanting more. Needing more. It was empty and desolate out in the plains, not the fast-paced excitement I hoped for when I envisioned entering adulthood. Wyland loved it, though, so there wasn't much I could do. I felt doomed to a life of mediocrity that I would never be able to escape.

I suppose I should have been careful what I wished for. Not long after I turned twenty, *she* found us. That's when everything really changed.

We naturally moved farther north, even finding ourselves as far up as Unisgate. It was an unspoken agreement to stay out of Extera, since there isn't much there besides snow and mountains—it could be mild in certain areas, but in most spots, you were sure to die a horrible, freezing cold death. The power, as I found out when we skirted the colder areas north of Unisgate, also made cold unbearable to me. If there was any bite to the air at all, it was as if I were naked in a snowstorm. Wyland's health didn't respond well to cold, either. We made plans to travel back down south eventually, but at the beginning of the winter months, she found us.

I still remember her ghostly image. It's scarred into my memory: this willowy figure draped in a colorless dress, whiter and brighter than the snow and ice surrounding her. Crystal encased her arms and her neck, all the way up to her chin. It moved with her, like it had become a second layer of skin. Her eyes were the most unsettling part. There was barely any color to them—just flawless pits of white save for faint rings around her irises and her black pupils. By looking you in the eye, she could have frozen your blood solid in your veins. For some reason, though, she didn't try it, even after I shot a column of fire at her. She just laughed, parrying whatever I threw at her with more magic than I had ever seen concentrated in one area before. And once all my bravery died down, she stopped, looking at Wyland and I like lost puppies in the snow.

"So," the Crystalline Mage said to me, cold eyes solidifying me to the core. "You're his replacement? Glad I've found you. Now, the work can begin."

The years that followed are simultaneously vivid and hazy. We stuck to the north, never crossing the mountains but staying away from civilization. Crystalline pointed out to me many times that Mages eventually looked inhuman after years of using the power. Perhaps I could make excuses in pleasant company for a while, but soon, people would figure it out. It didn't matter at all to her, though. She had been separate from society for so long, she didn't miss it. She preferred the desolation of the mountains—the peace they brought, the loneliness they guaranteed.

I wondered why she joined us at all. There were times when she would stare at Wyland like he was an alien, cocking her head to the side like he didn't quite make sense to her. It was like that with me to a lesser extent, but there was also a shared bond between us. We had something Wyland would never understand, something that only a handful of people on the planet could ever relate to.

All the time we were together, I believed us to be equals. Looking back, though, Crystalline didn't think the same way. While I knew residuuism, I didn't know how to be a Mage. That much was clear when she and I would spar against each other. My teacher in Magburn taught me how to use Residuum, but Crystalline wanted me to be more than just a cheap magician. Why, I never figured out. She was closed off and apathetic until it came to me and my training. From what I had heard—and what I know about the current Mages—they all stay solitary, never bothering with the others. She, however, took a vested interest in me for some odd reason.

I learned so much from her. Not just magic. I also learned cruelty.

My brother and I were used to hiding from oncoming travelers, staying out of their way unless they had something we needed. Crystalline didn't see the point. If they thought about crossing us, one of us by ourselves was enough to annihilate them. Wyland, of course, never wanted conflict. Even more, he didn't trust Crystalline, never wanting to agree with her for fear that might give me more incentive to tangle myself in her web. As time went on, though, it didn't matter how contrary he was. I hung on her every word. If she said to jump, I would ask how high and leap no higher nor lower. So, when she said that the band of explorers trying to traverse the mountain pass were nothing more than ants we could crush, I believed her.

I'm not proud of any of this. Even though I killed the farmer out of desperation to stay with my family, it still haunts me. These people, though—they were innocent in every way. They didn't bother us. And it didn't matter. To Crystalline, they were good practice. They were expendable to her.

To me. They were expendable to me.

Hold on. Just give me—give me a second…

Sorry. I just needed—

Doesn't matter. Sorry. I'll keep going.

It happened several times—bystanders would get too close, and we wouldn't give them a warning. We were the ones at the top of the food chain, after all. It was survival of the fittest, and they weren't fit. Wyland was sufficiently horrified. He was quiet about it around her, but whenever we were alone, he made it clear to me that he didn't like it. That's too mild of a term—he was appalled by it. Not by me. He still looked at me with empathy, like I was the victim in the situation, as if I wouldn't stoop to such depravity if she weren't pulling my strings.

I don't think he was right, though. She enabled me, sure. But it was only a matter of time before I stopped caring about people all together. Crystalline was just the excuse I needed to finally jump off the ledge into complete disregard for innocent lives.

Not complete disregard, I guess. Because I still cared about my brother—his safety and well-being, of course, but also what he thought of me. As the years in the mountains went on, I could tell that his perception of me was shifting, and the more I pressed the limits of my power and my empathy, the quicker I saw him lose faith in me. It all boiled to a head, eventually. After a couple years, he was done. And when my gentle and patient brother told me he was done, he meant it. He gave me an ultimatum: leave Crystalline behind or he was going to have to go off on his own.

I panicked. What made me panic more, though, was the fact that panicking wasn't my first thought. My first thought was indifference. Wyland and I were both adults at that point. If he didn't want to be part of this, he didn't need to. I didn't need to protect him anymore, and we clearly had two different ideas of what was important. It took me too long to realize the weight of that thought. I didn't have to dig too deep into that thought process to know that if he left, I would never see him again. This kid I practically raised, my only real connection to my humanity, would be gone. All because I wanted to get stronger. To finally climb that high tower when I had done nothing but hide in caves and cliffsides.

It was sobering. I laugh at it now, because I thought that was the moment I hit rock bottom. It certainly wasn't, but at the time, I thought I was a loathsome monster. Don't get me wrong: I *was* a monster. But I had plenty of room to keep digging my hole deeper.

And deeper I went.

I haven't mentioned the Hellions until now because—well, to be frank, they give me the fucking creeps. They always did. It was months into my tenure as the Mage that I would notice them out of the corner of my eye, always disappearing before I could ever really catch them. A year or two in, they got bolder— crouching next to me and watching me as I slept, hanging out of trees and staring at me as Wyland and I hiked through the forest. They were like curious children, always wondering what I was doing but never daring to approach. The day that Wyland gave me that ultimatum, they finally approached me as I sat alone in one of the nearby caverns by our encampment, trying desperately to keep my magic in. Weirdly, they were a calming presence. I wouldn't go so far as to say they comforted me, but they looked at me with the same reverence they always had, despite the fact that I was a goddamn mess. It was the first time I'd been around them that I wasn't unsettled.

It's fuzzy what exactly I said to them. A lot of those years are fuzzy, like I tried to delete it all. But everything that *did* get erased was inconsequential. All the worst moments stayed. I don't remember why I was ranting to myself, to them. Maybe I just needed to vent, to talk to someone who wasn't so pure of heart or so absolutely heartless. I only remember vaguely saying, "If only I had someone to give this power to. If only I could give it up and go back to the way things were."

It was stream of consciousness bullshit. I didn't actually want to give it up. I was the strongest I had ever been and only getting stronger. But in those brief windows of clarity, I thought maybe that was the key to it all. Wyland wouldn't have a reason to leave if I didn't have the power. We could go back to the way things were. I could still use Residuum. It wouldn't be so bad.

Once the Hellions left and I was alone with my thoughts again, I realized how stupid that sounded. Why would I go back to being nothing? With this ability, I was superior to the weak child I was before. I thought of the farmer, screeching as he was consumed by molten earth at the bottom of that well. That would never be me. I wouldn't allow it.

A day or two passed. I don't remember exactly how long. Wyland didn't ask for an answer to his proposition right away, but I could tell he was getting antsy. Every minute spent with Crystalline was too much for him, and I think the feeling was mutual. In her eyes, Wyland was becoming an annoyance. It was only a matter of time before she thought it not worth the effort to keep him around anymore. It was while I was hiding in one of the caverns avoiding the whole situation that the Hellions found me again.

This time, though, they weren't alone. Dragged along between a half a dozen of them was a girl.

You said you wanted to know, right? You wanted to hear it all? She's part of it all. I'm sorry.

She was young, twelve or thirteen years old at the most. Long, tangled black hair that hung down past her shoulders and a fire in her eyes that rivaled mine. She was dressed strangely, her coat and pants made of a material I had never seen before. She pulled against the restraining grasp of the Hellions with an unimaginable tenacity. I knew nothing about who she was or why she was there, but I knew one thing: she had a spirit I'd never seen before and would never see again after.

The Hellions threw her in front of me, sprawled on the ground at my feet. It didn't take long for me to see that she was smart, realizing quickly that she was surrounded with no good way out. She looked up at me, that damning scowl on her face never wavering. It was a total refusal to show fear. "Who the hell are you?" she asked me.

It was strange. Her voice was odd and alien. Not just because of my time away from other people. Her accent wasn't Velmyran—it was blunt and sharp, something I'd never heard before. The tone didn't sit right in my ears.

"I could ask you the same thing," I said to her.

The scowl only cracked for a second, the severity of the situation starting to dawn on her, but she looked back at me, teeth gritted. "Listen, my parents don't have money or anything," she said. "I'm not anybody special. Let me go back home." I must have stared at her too long, trying too hard to figure her out, because she soon said, "If you're going to kill me, just do it now. I don't like the anticipation."

I tilted my head, almost certainly looking at her like Crystalline did Wyland—a look of curious examination of a foreign species. "Where is your home?" I asked.

She quickly glanced around the cavern, shifting in place on the ground. "Grand Rapids."

I furrowed my brow. "Your home is a river?"

"It's a city," she said. "In Michigan."

I repeated the word. It felt strange having it in my mouth.

"United States? On planet Earth? Any of that ringing a bell?"

I know she was joking, now. Then, it was practically gibberish, save for the word "earth," though why she thought the whole planet was just called Earth was a little ridiculous to me. As she watched my face, though, her own defiant scowl faded, the panic finally starting to set in. I looked behind her at the row of Hellions, hunched over and watching me expectantly, wanting so badly for me to be pleased.

"What did you do?" I growled.

Of course, they don't speak, so I had to gather details from her. Her name was May Beaufort, an eighth grader in East Grand Rapids Middle School. Her parents were David and Victoria, she had two older sisters and a younger brother. She and her friend had snuck out late at night to meet some kids from school at a nearby park—apparently, that was something against the rules, though it didn't seem so crazy to me. The Hellions got the jump on them there. After a struggle, she ended up in Velmyra. As we talked more, we started to put the pieces together. She was from a completely different plane of existence, and for some reason, the Hellions found her and dragged her back to our world.

The only issue was, I didn't know if the Hellions could actually do that themselves. Capture a thirteen-year-old? Sure. But the Old Gods' stories never mentioned them being able to cross planes of reality. With no mention of any ability to travel between worlds, it puzzled me. Why May? Crystalline had told me that they follow my orders. Even if I was just ranting to myself, they could have taken my incoherent thoughts as a command. Surely, though, if they were just finding someone to host the power, they could have found someone on our plane. I knew travel between worlds was possible because she told me about it. One of the abilities of the Crystalline Mage was the ability to travel between space, and with enough power, that even meant travel between dimensions...

That's when the thought struck me: maybe she had something to do with it.

Why, I couldn't say. But how else did they make it there? May said they took her through a dark portal of some kind, a door. I had seen Crystalline slash open portals to other places before. It was possible that maybe she heard me speaking to the Hellions and helped them. The questions of why it had to be May, why it had to be a travel across realities in the first place also came to mind, but they were secondary. I was convinced that at least Crystalline had worked with the creatures and given them a way over to May's dimension. And for the sake of the terrified kid in my possession, I wasn't willing to stick around and find out why.

Wyland knew about her, of course. But if you've figured out

anything about me, I'm sure it's that truth and I don't really work well together. It was mostly the truth—she was a girl who was lost, taken from her home, and I was worried Crystalline might do something nefarious with her. Conveniently, I left out the part that she was from another plane of existence, and I may have been the cause of her kidnapping in the first place. Wyland didn't seem to care all that much about details, thankfully. The fact that I was showing interest in another human being must have been his sign that his brother wasn't completely corrupted by power. It wasn't long after making the plan that we took off in the dead of night from under Crystalline's nose, heading south where we hoped she wouldn't find us.

We traveled for a few weeks on foot. I wanted to hide in Castle's Edge, while Wyland wanted to stay away from people as much as possible. My need to protect May was proof to him I wasn't a monster, but the same couldn't be said of Crystalline. If we hid in a crowd and she found us, there would be carnage, and he didn't want to risk that. At the very least, he wasn't looking at me out of the corner of his eye anymore, terrified that I was becoming some sociopathic void. I cared about someone, and even if it was just him and one girl, that was enough for him to stay quiet.

Except...

No. I have to. I've spent so many years lying. I've got to be honest now.

I don't know if I actually cared about her, then. My need to keep her away from Crystalline was not out of some selfless desire to protect a helpless girl lost in a foreign land. It was solely because Crystalline wanted her. While she had helped me in my magical growth, there was always something suspicious about her interest in me. She wanted me more powerful for her benefit but never more powerful than her. She was the one in control of the situation. Wyland and May were merely pawns. And I was too. I was just too myopic to see that then. Once again, I was the one at the bottom of the well when I had promised myself I would never be there ever again. With May in my corner, though, I had something she wanted. I was in control. Just as it should have been.

Eventually, we reached Tersaria.

Tersaria was a pristine city—small enough where it could be maintained well, but large enough to have a sense of grandeur about it. When I pictured Castle's Edge as a child, Tersaria was closer to my image of it, not the crowded mass of buildings and people it actually was. Rather than drab gray and red brick, Tersaria's buildings were mostly made of white stone, scrubbed clean to perfection. At the very heart of the city was the Sky Spire, a massive tower that was there more for appearances than any actual purpose. It used to house royals before the capital of Midra moved to Castle's Edge hundreds of years previous. And it was there that we hid since it was abandoned and boarded up from the inside. We would have a vantage point for an attack if it came to that. May went along with it all, as much as she hated it. I'm sure you know how smart she is, though. She knew that being lost in a land she didn't know anything about meant she had to rely on us. I think she may have trusted Wyland to an extent, but not me. She could barely look me in the eye. To her, I'm sure I was nothing more than her captor. And I don't blame her for that one bit.

Wyland was the one who protested. As we set down camp in this tower, windows shuttered and unable to be opened, floors covered in rat feces and dead insects, he said enough was enough. We needed to work on getting May back home, not hide in a hovel. "Adrian, enough is enough," he told me, his sincere eyes brimming with more anger than I had ever seen in them. "She doesn't deserve this. We're taking her back." He stammered out that I was going to do it or else.

And I *laughed* at him.

Because what was he, a frail human boy, ever going to do to me? If he thought he had any say in the situation, he was mistaken. I could have lit him up like a dry leaf, and he would be helpless to stop me.

I wish I had kept that to myself. I didn't. It was exactly what I said to him. And as I did, the anger drifted out of his eyes and was replaced by horror. Fear.

My brother *feared* me.

And that was the last thing he ever thought of me. Not long after that, Crystalline found us. And to let us know of her arrival, she decimated a block of buildings across the square.

I told Wyland and May to stay put while I went out to negotiate. By negotiate, of course, I meant "lie my ass off" because I'm a fucking one-trick pony. When I stepped outside, the flawless houses of white stone were destroyed, run through by menacing spikes of crystal that glittered in the morning sunlight. It would have been beautiful if not for the screams I heard around us—people rushing out of the untouched homes, attempting to get to safety. The unlucky ones trying desperately to escape the wreckage they'd been crushed under. Crystalline stood across the square from me unflinching as panicking citizens raced around her, her colorless eyes focused on me.

"I didn't like finding you had gone, Infernal," she said, barely raising her voice above normal volume. She didn't have to for me to hear her clear as day. "I thought we trusted each other enough not to do foolish things such as that."

I shrugged, trying to keep my cool. "We needed a change. I'm grateful for your tutelage, but we needed to make our way elsewhere."

"Without a goodbye? How rude." The coy smile on her face wasn't lost on me. As if she cared about manners.

It took everything within me not to look back toward the tower, to give away their hideout. I kept my eyes firmly on her. I stupidly thought, *I can take her.*

I tried, anyway.

It was chaos. Fire and ice hurled toward each other in torrents for miles on end, the streets crystallizing and turning to lava all at once. In the moment, there was nothing to me but guarding the tower, keeping her away from May and Wyland— May, most of all. As I remember it now, all I hear are the blood-curdling screams of those caught up in our dance. All I see are women burning alive, men crushed into paste by blocks of crystal, children drowning in burning liquid earth and stone—

H-hang on. Sorry. Sorry, I—

Look, I'm *trying* here. I just need a moment…

All right. Anyway.

It went on for hours. The sky, which was so clear that morning, clouded over by midday. I was concerned that maybe she brought in Heavenly for back up, but it wasn't a change in weather. It was merely the atmosphere filling with ash and blocking out the sun. We carved our way through the city, somehow missing the tower the entire time. Strange, considering she was not careful about anything else we were destroying…

Just as I realized she knew what I was hiding in there, it didn't matter anymore. Because May stood at the tower entrance on the ground, wide-eyed at the wreckage that surrounded her, carefully keeping her gaze off the corpses strewn in the streets.

The barrage of attacks ceased. Crystalline looked at May, lips curling back into what she must have thought was a smile but looked more like the snarl of a lioness. "What a beautiful little lamb," she cooed. "This is what you have been keeping me from this whole time, Infernal?"

"You're not taking her," I spit at her. I didn't have time for any of the pretense after taking such a beating. "She's mine."

She arched her head back, not a strand of stark white hair out of place after our tussle. "You think so?" she posited.

Before I had time to answer, a mass of crystal burst up from underneath the tower.

And it fell.

I wake up in the middle of the night, and I still hear the screams of the people whose deaths I'm responsible for. The farmer, the travelers, the citizens of Tersaria. They do haunt me.

But I never heard my brother scream. The sound of crumbling stone cascading into sharpened quartz was too overpowering, drowning out anything I could have heard otherwise. The screams are enough to make me reach for an extra shot of whiskey when I'm already too drunk. The sound of the Sky Spire falling, crushing my brother to death—that's enough to make me hope I pass out and don't wake up again.

When the debris settled, I searched for him. I found him. He was—he was unrecognizable. The only way I knew it was him was because he was the only other person in that tower. At some point, I was on fire—the rage and sorrow of it all too much for me to contain. But that was the thing about being the Infernal Mage: I could set myself ablaze as much as I wanted, but I could never seem to truly burn.

When I pulled myself from the ashes of my brother's pyre, I realized how fruitless it all was. Crystalline was gone. And so was May.

I did the second easiest thing I know how to do: I ran. I left the smoldering ashes of Tersaria at my back, never wanting to see that godforsaken city ever again. I wandered for days, wrapped in my own grief and shame, mindlessly shuffling through fields and forests with no aim except to not fall apart. Because it was all hitting me—years of clarity that I had been ignoring in favor of my growing power. I wasted so much time, hurt so many people, just for a chance to get to that tower, only to have it crumble beneath me...

It only occurred to me then that I didn't deserve the tower after all I did.

Eventually, I found myself in Castle's Edge, so run through with emotion that the thought of turning myself in never presented itself fully formed. It was just something I instinctively knew I had to do. I had to attempt to make it right. As if it could ever bring Wyland back. I arrived at the gates of the palace just as the sun crested the horizon. And as soon as I said I was the Infernal Mage, I was in shackles.

I floated through the next day, hardly registering being brought in front of the queen for sentencing. Queen Veridian was shrewd yet, in a way, empathetic. Having met Visandra for the short amount of time I have, she is analytical to the core. If you don't fit her needs, she wants nothing to do with you. But Veridian listened to everything I said, and I felt understood. She looked at me with a softness to her face that I hadn't seen since my own mother—something I could only recount in feeling, not in actual memory. That didn't mean she took it easy on me, of course. I was still sentenced to death. It didn't come as a shock to me in the slightest. What did shock me was her plan for the Infernal power.

The brief moment I knew her, I knew Queen Veridian was resourceful. If she were given a fish, she would find a use for every part of it, bones and all. Putting me to death would boost morale across the kingdom and take one dangerous Mage out of the picture. It isn't known for sure, but it's believed that if a Mage is killed while in power, the power is destroyed forever. The opportunity for her to be written down in the annals of history as the ruler to solve even a fourth of Velmyra's problems was, I'm sure, tempting. Veridian, however, saw that as wasted potential. What if, she posited, there was a way to use the Mage's power for good? What if it wasn't bestowed upon some unsuspecting teenager with a god complex, but someone who was spiritually and mentally trained to resist the temptation the power would bring? With that kind of power on the throne's side, the chances of taking down the other Mages jumped exponentially. She called upon the Church of the Old Gods that served the royal court and asked them for a candidate, one who would take on the power and use it to help Midra out of the Mage's reign of terror.

It was brilliant. It was also foolish. Because I could have told her that that much power was a corruptor. No amount of piety could save you from it. I didn't say anything, though. Call it grief, call it self-preservation, whatever. People believe that when threatened with death, the power makes Mages do what they must to keep the magic within them alive, even if the host dies. It was probably that compulsion that kept me from opening my mouth as they brought the Church's selected monk who I was to give the power to.

I knew nothing about the kid whose life I ruined. I didn't know where he grew up, what his parents were like, why he joined the Church, whether or not he'd ever been in love, or what he liked to do in his free time when he wasn't being a saintly motherfucker. All I knew was he was a fresh-faced kid of maybe twenty years old, saucer-eyed and eager, a look on his face that screamed he had something to prove to someone. That, and his name was Brennan. No last name. They strip you of that when you join the brotherhood. And I was in charge of stripping him of his humanity.

The transfer wasn't nearly as traumatic for me the second time around. It was a drain, like years of my life were being plucked from me like individual hairs on my arm. By the time it was done, I hadn't wasted away like my predecessor had, but I was left raw and used up. As if they had thrown me naked in front of the entire court, nowhere to hide all my exposed and bloodied skin. It took me a moment to realize that what I was feeling was shame—all that regret, that humility that the power tried to push down throughout the years was now front and center in my mind, screaming how idiotic I was, how utterly I had failed everyone around me, failed the one person that mattered at all...

All this while Brennan howled in pain as the power incinerated him and put him back together again.

They didn't let me stay to see him after. They dragged me from the court as he burned. The only thing I recall seeing as they pulled me away down to the dungeon was Queen Veridian's face—once so confident, now flickering with the barest hint of insecurity. As if she didn't know whether she had saved her kingdom or dug its grave.

As the guards pulled me deeper below the castle, the panic set in. I hadn't been afraid of death in so long—the power wouldn't allow for it—but every human emotion I had been cut off from for years was now churning inside me like a fever. Shoved between a wall of guards, I felt claustrophobic, like the uncertain throes of death were already surrounding me. You all have been in near-death situations now. You know your mind goes to places you never thought it would go. Fight or flight.

I didn't have magic anymore, but I was still a trained residuuist, and there's more to it than just the mental aspect. On a good day, I could fight off a few guys on my own. In the feral, unhinged state I was in, I fought off six guards without any difficulty. Then, I bolted.

Sweating and panicking, I ran down the halls in the depths of the castle, clanking footsteps from the armored guards never too far behind. I tried every door that passed me by as I rushed down the way, in the hopes that one of them would miraculously be open. With every locked door, my heart raced faster. If the guards weren't going to be the death of me, my own overwhelmed body would be. Finally, one door opened, and I didn't hesitate as I pushed my way inside, slamming the door behind me and locking it.

The room I found myself in was cramped and cluttered, filled with stacks of books set into towers as high as me. On the far end of the room sat a desk, covered with papers, trinkets, and most noticeably, Residuum stones, all varying in size. The largest one was a sharp-edged white glittering crystal, almost as big as my head. Given Crystalline Residuum was so rare, I had never seen so much of it in one place before, much less in one massive piece.

I didn't have time to be curious about it. The door behind me shook as guards pounded on it, ordering me to open up and slamming themselves against it trying to break it down. Glancing back at the desk, I frantically grabbed onto a handful of stones and stuffed them into my pockets before turning my attention back toward the Crystalline piece.

I'd never used Crystalline before. It was always too expensive, too precious. My mind was so fractured that I had absolutely no destination in mind. I briefly thought "home," but where was that exactly? Not the mountains, not the farm, not the orphanage. There was no home for me. Not anymore. Not with him gone.

As the door forced itself open behind me, I laid my hand on the stone, and I was gone, off into the ether.

Landing in my destination was a bit like waking up hungover. Disoriented and reeling, it took a moment to gather myself again, but it quickly became clear that I was somewhere far from Midra. The buildings were made of materials cleaner than stone and wood, sleeker and shinier than glass. The roads were paved and painted with smoothed out, dry tar. Carriages were made out of the same shiny steel of the buildings, rolling on wheels without a horse to pull them forward. It was so completely foreign. I wasn't quite convinced I didn't hit my head and it wasn't all just some fever dream.

After the shock wore off, I slumped next to the garbage of some restaurant back alley. I still had the Crystalline Residuum in my hand, but it was about half the size it had been. Wherever I was, I could still make it back to Midra, and then—

And then what? What exactly did I have left for me back there? My Magehood, my brother—the only things in the world that ever mattered to me were gone. I would have to hide around every corner to survive, like a mangy animal.

Wherever I ended up, maybe I was better off there.

So, I stayed.

I spent the first few nights sleeping on park benches, under overpasses. It was a morning of waking up behind a dumpster that I had my first real connection with another human that wasn't just quickly averted eye contact. A grey-haired old man found me huddled in the alley as he went to take the trash out. I fully expected him to shoo me off, but he didn't. Instead, he wordlessly invited me inside. And for the first time in days, I was given a full meal and a place to sleep indoors. Granted, it was the storage room of a Japanese restaurant, but I wasn't particularly picky, at that point.

It took a few days for me to realize that not only was I in a foreign country, but I was also in an entirely different plane of reality. The old man and his wife owned the restaurant, and while they could speak Velmyran—or, as the people there called it, English—there was still a bit of a language barrier, since their first language was called Japanese. It took a while for me to piece it all together, but this place was Earth. May's home. The plane I stole her from.

The couple had a son who was about my age who also worked at the shop. He was wary of me the first day or so, but the first time we really locked eyes, he lightened up on me. I must have looked like a goddamn wounded animal. He took pity on me, gave me stuff to do around the restaurant—wiping down tables, folding napkins, washing dishes. And he would talk to me, even though I would never talk back. From him, I learned I was in a city called Los Angeles. We were in a district called Little Tokyo, which his parents had moved to from Japan, a country on the other side of the ocean. He was born in America, though. Had dreams of making games. Games that you played with dice and words. But he never had the right idea that really stuck to make it work. It didn't make much sense to me, but he had a nice smile. Even nicer when it was directed at me.

It was only a few weeks before Anthony really started to feel bad that I was sleeping in the stockroom, and he invited me to stay at his place in his spare room. And it was a few months after that when he first noticed me writing.

When I moved in with him, I still had next to nothing besides a few changes of clothes and the few Residuum stones that I still hadn't used. Anthony helped me with some of the other stuff—he had a spare mattress and sheets, and whenever he cleaned out his closet, he asked me first if I wanted anything before giving it to the thrift store. Even though I wasn't sleeping among boxes or dumpsters anymore, it didn't do much for the nightmares. Raging infernos, merciless columns of crystal, towers cascading down into dust. The first couple times I woke up screaming, Anthony ran into my room with a bat in hand, ready to fight off whoever had broken in. After a while, he realized whatever was haunting me was all up in my head. Instead of a bat, he would bring me tea and sit with me until I stopped hyperventilating. Usually, he didn't say anything, leaving me to calm down in silence until he left to go back to his room, saying he would be there if I needed him. After one such occurrence, though, he offered up a suggestion.

"Sometimes, it helps me to write thoughts down after I get overwhelmed," he said. "I put them down on the page and keep them there. At least for the time being."

It sounded foolish to me. I wasn't the most literate to begin with—I knew how to read and write, but it wasn't a skill I had kept very sharp over the years of hiding in the mountains. But a few more horrid nightmares later, I was willing to try anything to get my brain to shut up.

I started filling an old notebook that Anthony gave me, not with thoughts or feelings, but facts. Things about Velmyra that I remembered. That was the stuff I wanted to leave on the page and keep there. I wanted to forget that place ever existed. I drew maps, wrote out old poems I remembered from childhood, described what Crystalline's pointed terrible face looked like. What May looked like. Everything I wanted to forget went into that notebook, and when it was filled, I took paper from Anthony's printer and scrawled stuff on there. I wrote about what I did too. The people I killed, the cowardice of running away...

Sometimes, I wrote out in the kitchen, and Anthony eventually caught me one night. It had to have been four in the morning, but he sat with me at the kitchen table, watching me as I scratched across the page. After staying quiet for a while, he asked, "Could I read some?"

I hesitated. But eventually, I let him. It was an uncomfortable feeling. It was clear to me after almost a year of being on Earth that people didn't know what Velmyra was, so everything I wrote down would seem like fiction to him. Still, it would be divulging basically every detail about my life before. I eventually turned over my shame to the man who had shown me endless kindness, expecting him to be disgusted by it all.

Of course, he wasn't. I watched as something unexpectedly invigorated came across his face as he read through it. "I didn't know you were a storyteller," he said with a grin. I didn't say anything. I didn't know I was one, either.

Over the next few weeks, Anthony asked me questions about Velmyra, and I gave him answers. Some of them he liked, others he wanted to tweak. I let him go, not caring that he was trying to make changes to a real place. It was worth it just to see him ramble off his own ideas, the excitement on his face utterly adorable. It took him a while, but he asked if he could use the information for a game he was making. I would oversee world lore, and he could take care of stats and rules—all the boring stuff. I nearly refused, but he said we might be able to make a little money if it found the right circles. Since money was still in limited supply for me, I eventually said yes.

The rest, you can probably find on Wikipedia. The game got popular in online circles until we finally sold it, and it exploded from there. He and I dated on and off for a few years, but he wanted me to make more content for the game. Little did he know, there was nothing left for me to write. That was pretty much the nail in the coffin of our relationship, but he wasn't cruel about it. I gave him all the rights to the IP with the stipulation that I still kept getting paid, and that was that.

Once the agreement was signed, I moved out to Chicago. With my newfound money, I was suddenly able to pay for anything I wanted without worrying about the consequences. I was able to get a penthouse in a high rise downtown. Everything I ever wanted—the top floor of the high tower. Finally.

The first night there, with all my belongings stacked in boxes around me, new furniture haphazardly arranged across the massive, wide-open room, there was none of the joy or satisfaction I was anticipating. I shuffled to the wide window wall that overlooked the city. As I looked down at all the people on the sidewalk below, the cars rushing back and forth, the river only a few blocks away, there was a hollowness. A deep sense that I had worked for all of this but deserved none of it. I spent the whole night staring out into the city, fixated on how far down that sidewalk was, what kind of grizzly artwork my guts would make if I decided to open that massive window and throw myself out of it...

That was also the last night I spent there. I sold the place shortly after. Found the art space in Wicker Park instead. Wyland would have liked it, with new paintings coming in every few weeks, new sources of beauty and inspiration. I decided to turn the back room into an apartment, keeping myself at ground level.

It was where I belonged. Feet on the ground.

Then, of course, you all showed up.

And—well, here we are.

PART III

"Dark times await any who confront a Mage. But keep in mind one thing: this is not our world. In Velmyra, you can do magic too."
-*Mages of Velmyra* Players Handbook, Page 74

CHAPTER 27

No one speaks. No one moves. No one does much of anything except breathe.

A breeze rolls through the leaves above us. The overcast of the morning has cleared, and the sun has suddenly gotten too hot. It's a perfect, beautiful day for such misery.

Adrian stares at his feet. As he spoke, there were moments where he choked up and stopped because he had to compose himself before continuing. Now, he sits on the steps of Orla's cabin, a blank expression devoid of all energy on his face. He's a shriveled husk of the once suave, confident man we knew.

"If it's any consolation," he whispers, keeping his gaze down. "I wasn't going to come with you. I knew if I did, this would happen eventually. It was a bad idea from the start."

No one responds right away. It's a tense moment before Jackson croaks, "So, why did you?" His voice is ragged, like he's the one who just got done spilling his guts out. His hands are choked up on the handles of his daggers, knuckles white and straining.

Adrian keeps his hollow eyes on the ground for a moment before meeting Jackson's gaze. "I spent years regretting what I did," he says. "But I never once did anything about it. I knew

May was here and that I had a way to get back to Velmyra, but…" His hair falls in front of his eyes, and he makes no moves to brush it away. "It would be suicidal, of course. Without the Mage power, if I tried to go after Crystalline to get her back, I would be gem dust faster than I could blink."

And his eyes settle on me. "But you didn't care about that."

I'm suddenly aware that I exist again—that I have a body with nerve endings and a brain with conscious thought. Through his story, I drifted in and out of reality, Adrian's words barely registering at times. When May came into the story, it felt far away, like he was talking underwater. But as his eyes connect with mine again, I'm suddenly, acutely aware. And while I don't know what to feel, I *feel*. The rawness of my eyes, the heaviness of my arms, the rioting of my emotions. It's all so palpable, so present and insistent.

I can't bring myself to do anything about it, though. I just stare back at him, empty.

"You knew it was dangerous," Adrian says. "And you didn't care. You were going to get to Velmyra either way, hang the consequences. This place was set to chew you up and spit you out, but you didn't give a shit. Because she was here, and she wasn't supposed to be." His mouth weakly twitches into a humorless smile before fading back into its hopeless line. "What kind of a bastard would I have been if I let you run off here without even trying to help?"

He looks at me, the expectation in his eyes clear. He wants something from me. Anything.

I can't give him what he wants. I can't give anything. It's like I've been cut off from my emotions.

"I really debated it," Adrian continues, fumbling over his words. It's the nervousness of someone not sure when to stop talking, unsure if silence will make it better or worse. "This was all going to come crashing down around me at some point, I knew. I planned on just letting my good deed be giving you the Residuum and leaving town, disappearing in case you came back looking for me. But I got tired of acting like regretting my actions was going to absolve me of anything. I knew I had to do something about it. That was the only way I could make things right. I genuinely thought this would be the way to cause the least amount of harm." His eyes glisten again. "I guess I was wrong."

I should say something. I should tell him yes, he was dead wrong. Instead of letting us struggle on our own, he decided it would be better to keep close to us—to me. He wanted to gain my trust, make me think he was my friend, someone who actually believed in me, someone who didn't treat me like I was a fragile piece of glass, when he was the glassworker the entire time—

I don't say anything. There's nothing I can say that isn't going to be the last crack to shatter me completely.

"Violet—" Adrian starts.

"Master Inoue, I think you have said quite enough," Melandrich interrupts. His gruffness shocks me. Usually, he's so gentle with us. Even when he's commanding, he's direct and forceful, no emotions reflected in his powerful tone. I've never heard him angry until now. Adrian is shocked too, shutting his mouth abruptly.

"What are you going to do with him, Melandrich?" Kai chimes in, cautiously stepping forward. Their crossbow is in hand, but they point it at the ground.

Despite the rage in his voice, Melandrich's face is placid as he looks at Adrian, the same cold indifference he exhibited in our first meeting. He pauses, but says, "I do not think that is my place to decide his fate."

Kai raises their eyebrows. "What do you mean 'not your place?' This is exactly your place!" They raise the crossbow, pointing at Adrian, and he flinches as they gesture emphatically toward him. "He killed hundreds of people! Midrans! People with friends and families!"

Behind them, Gren grunts.

405

"I *do so* give a shit about that!" Kai exclaims. "And you do too. There isn't one of us here who doesn't know someone whose lives haven't been ruined by the Mages and their sick disregard for mankind. That's the whole reason the kindred folk stick to the glens and the marshes—to keep out of their line of sight." Kai's mouth is bunched into a scowl, and I'm taken aback. Even their golden eyes shine with the beginnings of angry tears. "My whole people could have had a life of freedom and adventure if they weren't so fucking afraid of him and his kind. Not only that, but he's lied his scrawny ass off about it this whole time. As the queen's right hand, it is certainly your place, Tree Boy. Punish him, for *fuck's* sake."

Closing his eyes, Melandrich says, "I will not."

"Why the bloody hell not?!" Kai yells. "He destroyed Tersaria! He wounded Midra!"

"And I am not Midran."

His gleaming blue eyes bore into Adrian, brows knit together in fury and disgust. "I know many good Midrans whose lives have been destroyed by you and yours," he growls. "Good people who have lost friends, family, livelihoods. Not one of them deserves such a fate as you've given them, Master Inoue. And were I Midran, I might be inclined to spill your entrails on the ground beneath you, the blood of a Mage nourishing the very land that he scarred." His fists ball up white-knuckled at his sides. I wonder for a brief moment if he might take back the sword I stole from him and actually do what he describes. But his tight grip relaxes as he says, "I may serve Midra and her queen, but I am also Hevaran. And their philosophy is to turn the other cheek. Forgive and move forward. You have helped us greatly in retrieving the Relics, I will not deny that. Any sort of punishment I give to you will not be justice served, in my eyes."

"Great, so we're just going to say 'bygones' and pretend he isn't a mass murderer, then?"

"I did not say that."

"Then what are you saying, Melandrich?" Kai snaps, jabbing

the crossbow at him now. "Because there is no way I'm going anywhere with this man. I'd love to rip him a new asshole too, but that wouldn't be the Hevaran spirit, I guess."

Sighing, Melandrich says, "I am a man of two worlds. Complete forgiveness in this situation would be foolhardy, but nothing would come of striking him down, either." He steps toward Jackson and me. "When there is a crime committed in Hevara, the one to decide the punishment is the one who was most hurt by the actions of the perpetrator. If not the victim themselves, then the family of the victim. Perhaps that would be a wise option for this circumstance. In which case…"

His heavy gaze falls on me. "I believe that distinction belongs to you, Lady Spence."

A pang echoes through my chest, though I'm too numb to really feel its full impact. I look from Melandrich back to Adrian, who peers at me through the strands of his loose hair, a beaten, resolute dog. While there's fear there, there's also bitter resignation that whatever comes to him is entirely deserved.

All the Residuum he had is out of his reach. He's defenseless.

It would be so easy. To extend my hand and send a bolt of lightning through him. To rip roots up through the ground to wrap around his neck and choke the life from him. To set him on fire, let him burn alive, like all the people he didn't care enough about in his mad quest to mean something.

I should want to do that, right?

Tears bite at the edges of my eyes. I don't think I know what I want any more.

I blink, and I look at Jackson. "You choose."

Jackson blinks back at me, my words not registering. "I don't…"

I open my mouth to say it. That he was right—he was just as hurt by May's disappearance, and I was too wrapped up in my own bullshit to acknowledge it. That Melandrich said I had the right out of all of us to avenge her, but he has just as much claim to it. That this fucking megalomaniac fed into the drama between us and pushed me farther away from Eddie, even farther from Jackson so that he would always seem like the bad guy, so no one would ever expect the truth...

But I can't say all that. I can't say anything. I just step back, weakly pointing my sword back at Adrian before letting it go limp back at my side.

Bewildered, Jackson looks at Adrian and swallows. Adrian looks just as surprised, staring at Jackson dead in the eye, the first time I've seen them really make direct eye contact since they've met. Jackson's jaw is tense, the skin on his knuckles pulled so tight as he grips his daggers, the bones look as though they'll break through the flesh.

I see Jackson breathe in.

Breathe out.

"I think you should just go."

Adrian stares at him, eyes still wide and unsure. He looks like he's playing at half speed as he slowly blinks, looking from Jackson to the rest of the group.

"Melandrich is right," Jackson mutters. "You've helped us. We wouldn't have gotten this far without you. But knowing what we do, you can't stay. It's best if you just get out of here."

Taking a breath in, Adrian looks like he's about to protest, but he stops himself as he looks among the group. His face falls as he looks at each of us—I don't meet his eyes as they settle on me. After a moment of quiet desperation, though, he nods. "All right."

He's shaky as he pushes himself off the steps and onto his feet, eyes shifting cautiously between us all, as if he thinks he's getting off too easy and that our kindness is about ready to run out. "If you go after the last Relic..." he starts but trails off. "Just—be prepared. I know what that power does to someone. Trust me. He won't go easy on you."

No one responds, save for the breeze that rustles through the leaves above us.

Nodding again, Adrian walks forward, passing by me as he does. My gaze is fixed on the roots arching out of the ground as he approaches, the acorn shells scattered and pressed into the dirt—

My stomach flips as he stops next to me. And against my better judgment, I look at him.

Our eyes connect.

Adrian's mouth works silently, starting and stopping a sentence multiple times. Finally, he whispers, "Don't deny yourself."

And he walks away.

I stand there for a moment, my mind being pulled in ten different directions. Melandrich's sword falls out of my hand, clattering on the ground next to my feet. And without thought, I walk in the opposite direction that Adrian took, a slow shuffle that isn't entirely of my own doing. I move past the others in a blur, hearing Melandrich call out to me as I go and Jackson stopping him.

I stumble through the forest in a haze, not paying attention to where I'm going or what's surrounding me. All I see is indistinguishable green and brown, my eyes welling up again. I try to keep it in—I cry too damn much. I'm such a weak piece of shit. Come on, stop crying, you useless idiot. You're so fucking dramatic. No one else is crying, so get it the fuck together. Get it—

My foot hits something, and I'm on the ground.

And I wail.

There is no telling myself to breathe this time. There's nothing but the overwhelming feeling of shame and failure. Of anger and frustration. I curl in on myself like a leaf being consumed by a flame, wracked by all the thoughts swarming in my head.

I was so close. So close to having it be over. To getting her back. To ending the nightmare.

Who am I kidding? I was nowhere close to that. The idea of

finding May, of going back to the way things were, of repairing all that damage—it's a fantasy. An idealized version of my life that could never be. Just like that stupid fucking game he created. All fake nonsense.

Writhing on the ground, tears rolling down my face in streams, I ram my fists into the ground, wishing it was Adrian's face. I should have taken the opportunity back there, just for the smallest fraction of payback for the past ten years of torture. I hate him so much, so goddamn fucking much—

Except I really don't.

I think I hate me more.

It isn't long until all the energy leaves me, and I'm limp on the ground, heavy and unable to move. I'm reminded of how I felt in that memory in Eddie's car—depleted of everything. A husk. Useless and hollow.

The only thing I have ever found comforting about these episodes is the aftermath. Because for once, my mind is quiet. I lay on the ground, cleaned out like a deboned fish, staring at a tiny plant sprouting out of the dirt and focusing on nothing else. The veins running through the green leaves, the perfect curl of the bud as the rest of the leaves prepare to unfurl as it grows. It's all I can see. All I care to see. I don't know how long I sit there, watching this little perfect thing, just starting its growth and taking in its first rays of sunshine, breathing its first breath.

"You can't possibly be comfortable lying like that."

I have just enough energy to lift my head up and look toward the voice, but the surprise of who I see sends a rush through me.

Eddie stands a few yards away, his silhouette illuminated against the dying light of the evening.

"What are you doing?" I ask, feebly pushing myself to sit up as he limps over to me. I'm astounded that he's in such good shape. But as he gets closer, I see he isn't even close to one hundred percent. The blood that coated the left half of his body has been cleaned up, but his face, neck, and arm are marked with cuts and bruises, some deeper and nastier than others. His left arm is wrapped in a crude splint of stiff wood and bandages, propped up by a sling of what looks like part of a bed sheet. He moves slowly, groaning like an old man as he lowers himself down onto the ground next to me. Yet, he grins at me, strained against the pain as he settles into the dirt.

"Well, they told me you ran off somewhere. Thought you couldn't have gotten too far. I can't even get you to go to the gym with me half the time," Eddie chuckles, wincing a little as he does.

"You shouldn't be out here," I say. "You look like shit."

"Eh, I'm fine. It's only every inch of my body that hurts. I also may have hit my head so hard that I have astigmatism now, but whatever. I've been told glasses are sexy."

I shake my head. I don't know if I'm holding in a laugh or on the brink of tears. "You're an idiot."

"So I've been told."

There's a pause, but I croak out, "Adrian—"

"I know." His face isn't hard or accusatory. It's sympathetic. Almost mournful. "They told me."

Tears slip out of my eyes again, just when I thought I was finished crying, and I don't have to say a word before he wraps his good arm around my shoulders. "I'm sorry I didn't listen to you," I say.

Eddie shrugs, gently as he can. "Honestly, I wouldn't have listened to me either if I were you."

"Well, you were right."

"Not for the right reasons."

I run my sleeve under my nose. "Still, I didn't even question him," I sniff. "Didn't even give all his shady shit a second thought."

"You were looking for answers, Vi," Eddie says. "I don't blame you for that. No one would."

"I do."

"Well, of course. You wouldn't be human if you didn't. We

always hold ourselves to a higher standard than everyone else around us. Doesn't mean you're right."

Another breeze rolls by. Leaves sway above us, but the chill of the wind doesn't reach us. We're encapsulated by our own private pocket of warmth and safety.

"Do you totally hate me for putting you in the hospital last year?"

I draw back from him, looking at him in surprise. "What?" I ask. "No. Of course not."

He drops his arm, immediately picking at a twig on the ground and drawing meaningless shapes into the dirt. "I don't know," he mumbles. "Yesterday you kind of threw it at me, and it was basically all my worst fears realized."

I close my eyes and sigh. "That was shitty of me."

"I mean, I get it. I was a dick too. Still, I…" He stops, breathing out slowly and looking up into the open air. "I've been scared to talk about it at all, you know? The stuff from last year." His voice wavers as he talks. "I didn't want to do it—to put you there—but I got scared, and—I thought I could be enough, you know? I thought that I could be an idiot and play video games with you, and you'd laugh at me and forget everything, and that would be enough. I mean, I have bad stuff too, and I pretend I'm fucking King Arthur for five hours a week. That's usually enough to keep my shit at bay, so I thought maybe—it sounds stupid, now that I say it out loud, but that's what I really thought. And then I found the note and—I just felt…"

He trails off, breaking the twig in his hand against the ground. It's so flimsy that it doesn't take much to crack it in half. "Helpless," he says, letting the broken pieces fall into the dirt. "I felt helpless."

I rub my hands against my pants for a moment, not sure what to say about that. After a moment, though, I pick up a shattered piece of twig, running lines of my own in the dirt next to his squiggles and squares. "It wasn't fun. But I wasn't there to have fun. I was there to survive. And I did. I would never blame you for wanting me to live when I—didn't." The last word tastes ashy on my tongue. I've never admitted out loud before that there was a time where I'd wanted—well, the end of it all. I'd been too afraid to, whether out of self-preservation or the fear of it becoming too real, too close for comfort. I don't know if that means I'm far enough away from that feeling where I feel safe admitting it or—or something else. That's a thought too far at the moment.

Eddie laughs, a bark that comes out a little too forceful since he'd probably been holding his breath. An errant tear rolls down his cheek. "I know. I knew that, deep down, but there was always part of me that was too petrified to ask. So, I just pretended nothing happened. And when we found out this place was real, I thought maybe I could make up for it by being the big hero and getting May back for you. Which was stupid, I know. It was all so asinine. We should have talked about this way beforehand. That was my bad."

"Mine too," I admit. "You don't get to take all the blame in that."

"You had other stuff to think about."

I shake my head. "You wanted to distract me, and I wanted to be distracted. And that doesn't solve anything. It just pressurizes it. Don't get me wrong—I love beating your ass at Mario Kart."

"Wow, this *was* a nice conversation," Eddie says.

I laugh. "I appreciate you being a distraction. I need that. Honestly, I prefer a jester over a knight any day."

In the fading light of the forest, I can just barely make out the red that comes into his cheeks. He opens his mouth to talk, but he closes it and smiles instead.

"But that can't be everything," I continue. "That isn't a replacement for confronting what's going on in my head. If you put it all in a box, it stays in the box. If you let it out, though, a little bit at a time…"

I don't know what else to say. I'm talking as though I have it all figured out. I don't. I'm talking out of my ass, and as I wipe my sleeve across my face again, it disturbs me how much I sound like Adrian. Still, Eddie looks at me expectantly.

That's when I remember: I still have Residuum in my pocket.

I reach in and pull out a green stone. Finding the little sprout I was watching earlier, I let the energy gather into the tips of my fingers. I point at the little plant, letting it flow out of me and into the earth. The small green thing inches up out of the soil, raising into a collection of small fanned out leaves hanging from the scrawny beginnings of a tree trunk. It pulls up and up until my hand is empty, the green stone used up, and the sapling stands taller than our heads from our spot on the ground.

I smile. The sight of something new and thriving never seems to get old to me. "I guess, you can make something of it."

Eddie runs a hand down his face, wiping away more stray tears. "If we got anything out of this, Vi," he says, "I hope you at least realize how totally badass you are."

"Oh, for fuck's sake."

"I'm serious," Eddie says, and I believe him. There's not a hint of irony in his tone as he looks at the newly formed tree in awe. "Maybe we didn't finish the big mythic quest for the legendary item, but if anything, you're a fucking *magician*." He gingerly lifts his left arm in its sling, as much as he can without wincing. "That makes this worth it in and of itself."

I want to refute him again, but I stop before I say anything. I watch the wind catch the new tree, its leaves shimmying in the air for the first time, bending and adapting to the gust that hits it with natural flexibility.

I stand up.

Eddie furrows his brow as he looks up at me, but before he can say anything, I extend my hand out to him. "Get up," I say. "We have to go."

"Where?" he asks.

"The final Relic," I answer. "We might still have time to beat the Mage there, but we need to go soon."

"You still want to get the Dagger?"

I nod, fervent and invigorated.

"Why?"

"Because," I say, "we're not helpless. Not yet."

Eddie looks from me, down at my hand, and then back at me. A smile spreads across his face, and he takes my hand in his right. Once he's on his feet, he pats my arm. "With you 'til the end of the line, Cap."

I grin at him as I walk around the new sapling, eyes focused forward. "Let's just hope everyone else feels the same way," I say.

CHAPTER 28

"Are you fucking mad?" Kai exclaims.

Unsurprisingly, not everyone feels the same way.

"Mezzir Kai, I implore you to be respectful," Melandrich says as soothing as possible, but his weariness is showing through after the draining day we've had.

"Respectful, my left buttock!" they yell. "She's looney!" They whirl back on me, pointing a finger in my direction. "You're utterly batshit if you think we're still going after that thing without him here. Absolutely daft."

The sun is still above the horizon, but the light is quickly fading. The never-ending fire glows brighter as the sky darkens, the light dancing off everyone's concerned faces as we congregate outside of Orla's cabin. Orla herself stirs the perpetual stew but otherwise doesn't intrude on the conversation. I catch her glancing up from the pot occasionally, obviously listening in on what we're saying. Not that we're being quiet about it.

I don't know how much anyone else is willing to listen, though. As soon as we announced our intentions to go after the final Relic, Kai has been adamant in their refusal to be part of it. Melandrich has been staring into the fire, unmoving, and Gren has been frowning and intermittently huffing whenever Kai gets too riled up. I knew it would be a hard sell, but I know it's necessary. The others don't seem to see it the same way, though.

Eddie holds up a hand. "Kai, just hear us out, okay?" he says.

"Oh, I've heard you loud and clear!" Kai says. "And I want absolutely no part of it."

Behind them, Gren groans from her spot on the ground, slumped over in front of the bonfire.

Kai sets their sights on her, their golden eyes flaring. "Don't you dare start, you ginormous cabbage! You know as well as I do that we have no chance of making it out of that alive. Especially without the traitor."

"We do have a chance," I say, brushing past the bit about Adrian as best as I can. "The Infernal Mage confronted Adrian here not that long ago. Using his abilities, he can only travel so fast. But with the Crystalline Residuum we have, we could still beat him there."

"All right, I'll play along," Kai says, narrowing their gaze and crossing their arms. "Let's say we do miraculously get there before he does. We're still down a person to perform the ritual to form it. Not just a person, but our best residuuist. No offense, but you've learned how to do some fun party tricks over a few weeks. You've got nothing on his years of experience. Even if we get the last one, we're stuffed like a winter goose." They unfurl from their angry stance, and to my surprise, their face falls, looking almost despondent. "It's over, love. I'm not saying this lightly, but if we go to that temple, we may as well write out our last wills and testaments."

I half expect Gren to snarl in protest, but her small ogre ears droop flat against her stringy hair, sighing as she stares at her feet.

Jackson sighs. To my surprise, he's been on my side as soon as I got back to camp. Though, us going through with this is the difference between getting May back and leaving here with nothing to show for it. Perhaps it's not that surprising after all.

"Melandrich, you're technically in charge of all this," he says. "Our job was to get all the Relics. We haven't finished our assignment for Queen Visandra yet."

"While that may be true," Melandrich says, his tone melancholy as he looks into the fire, "I am inclined to agree with Mezzir Kai. The odds in this endeavor seem to be stacked against us. As our group's coordinator, I would feel responsible if anything dire were to happen to any one of you." He sighs, wearier than he's ever sounded, closing his eyes and slumping out of his normally pin-straight posture. "She may not be happy about it, but I can attest to the danger of the situation when we return to Castle's Edge and attempt to convince Queen Visandra that what you have accomplished is enough to erase your debt to the kingdom." He looks up and between all of us, and I swear I see a shimmer in his bright blue eyes that I've never seen before. "In fact, I feel that the retrieval of two Relics far outweighs any of your crimes. In earnest, you have done more for the kingdom of Midra than many of the men I have met in my time on the Guard. Even though we did not obtain all four Relics, you all have been invaluable to our country. Sincerely."

"No offense, Melandrich," Eddie says, his voice barely a murmur, "but three Relics doesn't get us any closer to what we want to accomplish."

At this, Melandrich nods solemnly, looking back at the fire.

Despite Melandrich's malaise, Jackson rolls his eyes, glaring at Orla, who stirs her pot with a serene smile on her face. "I don't suppose you have any insight you'd like to add to this?" he asks sardonically.

Orla laughs, not taking her eye off the pot. "No, I'm not supposin' I do."

"Well, you seem to know how this all turns out," Jackson says. "You can't even give us a hint?"

Her pale eyes flit up to meet his. "Now that seems a bit like cheatin', doesn't it?"

"It's not cheating," Jackson sneers. "This isn't a game. It's the difference between going home with our friend or not."

"It's the difference between going home with your friend and ending up carrion," Kai huffs.

I glance up at the sky. It's almost dark.

"I don't care what the difference is," I interrupt. "And I don't care if you all don't want to go. I'm going, either way."

There's silence. Kai simply gapes at me in astonishment, and Gren's heavy brow raises enough where I can actually see her eyes—a forest green, brighter than her skin. Melandrich pries his gaze away from the fire too, his expression cautious and pitying. Jackson and Eddie don't seem surprised in the least bit, their faces remaining unchanged.

And with the glow of the fire illuminating her pale face, Orla smiles, broad and unrestrained.

I dig my nails into the flesh of my palms. "I came here to get her back. And I haven't done that yet. The only way I have a shot is if I go after it. I won't drag anyone along against their will. I know it's dangerous. The least I could do is get in there, get the Relic, and get out. If that's the case, then I can go back to Castle's Edge and give it to you so we can get the Dagger formed. But no matter what, we need that thing. So, I'm going." I look at Jackson, who meets my eyes with no reservation, no backing down for the first time. "And I know he is too," I say.

His jaw set, Jackson nods. "Damn right."

Eddie jerks his head toward the two of us. "And I go where they go," he says, as nonchalant as he would as if we were just talking about grabbing pizza. He lifts his slinged arm gingerly. "I may not be useful, but someone's gotta be the comedic relief, right?"

I smile at him before looking back at the rest. "Maybe with the three of us, we won't die horribly." I chuckle, going for more levity. But no one laughs in response. They all look down at the ground, fire light dancing across their morose faces. It's just then that I realize I'm witnessing the precursor to my own funeral.

"We'll be okay," I say, though not really believing it myself. "And if we're not, that's fine. I would rather run headfirst into it than spend the rest of my life wondering what would have happened if I did."

The silence returns. Even Eddie and Jackson are looking unconfident about their choice. And with every passing second, my nails dig further into my hands, the weight of what I'm committing to sinking in. I bite the inside of my cheek, wondering if I should back out or if that would make me look like an even bigger fool...

Until, on the other side of the fire pit, Gren stands up.

She hulks her way past the simmering pot, around Kai, who looks sufficiently flabbergasted, stopping in front of me with a final *thud-thud* of her feet. She looks at me, deep green eyes fixed and her mouth set in a line around her protruding tusks. And without any fanfare, she holds out a massive mottled green hand, palm extended upward toward me.

She snorts, nostrils flaring.

For the first time, I don't need Kai to translate for me.

I grin up at her and put my hand in hers, letting her powerful fingers curl around mine. I expect them to be more calloused and rough, but there is a softness to her hardy skin. The cradle of her hand is gentler than I thought possible, given how many skulls I've seen her smash in with her club. She nods, her brow furrowing again in resolution.

"Are you fucking *high*?" Kai exclaims, their fingers running through their curls in distress. "You're going *with* them?"

Gren lets my hand fall out of her grasp, turning around to look at Kai and grunting decisively in their direction.

They hold their hands out, their curls flying out in a mess of errant strands. "Do you want to die? Because that's how you die! In case you weren't aware."

Gren sniffs.

"I can't bloody believe this," they say. "I swear to the Old Gods, Melandrich and I are the only sane ones left."

"I am going as well," Melandrich says suddenly, standing up and walking toward us.

"For tits' sake!" Kai cries.

Ignoring them, Melandrich continues, "I cannot in good conscience let you all charge forth into such dangerous circumstances without my assistance. If you insist on proceeding, then I must accompany you. Besides, the more your numbers, the more likely you are to succeed."

I smile at him too. "You know it's dangerous, Melandrich."

Curtly, he nods. "I do not care."

"And what would Visandra say about that?" Jackson asks.

He pauses, but arches his head, the tiniest grin playing at the edge of his mouth. "Queen Visandra is not here. I think my say in the matter circumvents her wishes, whatever they may be."

"Wise words," Orla comments, still stirring the stew off to the side.

"Fine!" Kai yells. "Fine! Have fun getting fileted alive and served up with a garnish of dill! Apparently, I'm the only one of us who wants to keep their damn head on their shoulders."

"You don't have to come if you don't want to, Kai," Eddie says, almost amused.

"Good! Because I'm not!"

Jackson shrugs. "Okay."

"Fine!"

"Good for you," I say.

"Thank you!" With a last show of indignance, Kai stomps over to one of the seating logs near the fire pit, grabbing their satchel and throwing it over their shoulder. "Good fucking riddance to the lot of you!" they shout, and with one last huff, they turn on their heel and walk off into the forest, disappearing fairly quickly.

I look up at Gren. "How long should we give them?" I ask her.

Gren holds up a hand as if to say, "*just wait.*"

We wait. Not very long at all, because less than ten seconds later, Kai comes clomping back through the trees, swishing through the underbrush with a gait that even seems annoyed. "All right, you win!" they declare, throwing their bag back on the ground in defeat. "You happy? I'm resigning myself to being roasted like a pork cutlet because of you shits and your lost friend. Bet she's just as much of a tosser as you all are. This better be bloody worth it, or so help me gods, I will haunt everyone you have ever loved. I don't care if they're in Velmyra or whatever other alien planet you hail from. Mark my words!"

They cross their arms, still fuming, but I walk over to them and put a hand on their shoulder. "Thanks, Kai," I say.

The tense muscles in their shoulders uncoil, and their scowl softens. "Well, at least with me, you idiots stand a damn chance. Besides…" They jerk their head toward Gren. "I have to make sure that one stays out of trouble."

Around her tusks, Gren smiles.

"I suppose it is settled, then," Melandrich says. "We go to retrieve the Relic."

"And form the Dagger," I say.

Melandrich furrows his brow in concern. "Lady Spence…"

"We have enough people, now," I argue. "Maybe…"

Melandrich's face turns grim as my confidence wavers. "Lady Spence, you will be the only one with any magical knowledge. You will have to lead the ritual."

"Do you even know the ritual?" Kai asks. "Did the asshole even tell you what it involves?"

I shake my head. "No, just that a residuuist has to do it with assistance. Honestly, I don't think he knew how to do it either. I'm probably just as qualified."

"Minus the years of experience, of course," Kai murmurs under their breath.

"Listen, if we have the Dagger, we can negotiate with the Infernal," I say. "That's the whole point. We'll have a weapon against him or a bargaining chip. Win-win."

"Uh, do you really think it'll be that easy?" Eddie questions.

"Master Hughes is not wrong in his caution," Melandrich says. His eyes, almost glowing in the near darkness around us, meet mine. "Are you sure you are prepared for such an endeavor, Lady Spence? Are you sure you are willing to risk this much?"

I hesitate. It's a damn good question.

But she flashes through my mind, the memory of us practicing slow dancing in her bedroom as fresh in my mind as ever, the image of her lip gloss smile as I looped my arms around her neck burned into my brain.

As firm as ever, I nod. "And more," I respond.

We spend a hasty half hour preparing to leave. With this being the first time I'm using Crystalline Residuum, there's no guarantee that we'll be able to find our way back to Orla's place. There's no guarantee that we'll even make it to the Old Gods Temple, but I'm trying not to think about that too hard. As everyone frantically scrambles, scarfing down spoonfuls of perpetual stew and gathering provisions, I'm at the edge of the clearing, staring down at the game master's guide, fixated on the map when a voice breaks me out of my concentration.

"Hey."

I look up. Jackson stands in front of me, a wooden bowl in his hand extended toward me. "You eat?"

"No," I answer. "Not all that hungry."

"Well, you're the one leading this magical ritual," he says, almost as a mumble. "And I don't think I've seen you eat since this morning. You think running on empty is a good idea?"

I think about protesting, but he's right—it wouldn't be the smartest for me to go in there hungry. I reluctantly take the bowl, prodding at the lumps of meat at the bottom with the spoon and taking a few hesitant bites. Still so unappetizing to look at, but it tastes astounding after the whirlwind of a day we've had.

Instead of walking off, Jackson awkwardly sits on the other side of the log I'm sitting on, keeping a good distance from me as I eat. Out of the corner of my eye, I see his fingers twist over each other, going through each individual knuckle and cracking them nervously. "Uh, so…" He stops, staring back out at the camp, chewing on his lip before continuing. "Um, thanks. For—I don't know, letting me decide a mass murderer's fate?"

"What a way to put it," I snort between bites.

"You know what I mean," Jackson says, bashfully dipping his head to look at the ground. "Just—thank you."

Setting the bowl on the ground, I shrug. "You were right," I say. "She was your friend too. Everyone keeps saying this is my journey, my quest. But you hurt just as much." I pick at my cuticles as I talk, trying not to let my nerves show. "It's easy to get wrapped up in my own bullshit and not account for what other people are feeling. Especially here. I feel like I've been in mental survival mode ever since we got here."

Out of the corner of my eye, Jackson nods. "I know what you mean. And I also think I owe you an apology."

"Oh, you don't—"

"No, I do, Violet," he says, looking right at me, and I can't help but look back at his fierce brown eyes, trying so hard to hide behind the thick frames of his horn-rimmed glasses. "You did go through a lot that I didn't. I would be an idiot to say that the pain we share is identical. I think years of having mine ignored made me resent you, and…" He trails off, breaking our eye contact with a sigh. "I haven't really been that much of a saint, either, I guess."

I keep my eyes on him as he stares at the ground, and the fire illuminates a person that I feel like I haven't seen before. The prickly wall that I used to feel so inferior around is now just a boy, the years of neglect and loneliness obvious on his angular face. There's a pang in my chest as I stare at his flame-illuminated figure. "It's sad," I say.

He looks back up at me, eyebrows raised. "What is?"

"This whole time, we were the only two who could really understand what the other was going through," I say. "We spent all this time hating each other when we could have been friends."

There's a shimmer that comes into his eye—it could just be the light of the fire—but he soon swallows and shrugs a shoulder. "There's still time for that."

And Jackson King smiles, just an upturn at the corners of his mouth. But even just that is enough to show me a whole new person. I can't help but smile back.

We sit with each other for a while before he stands, but I stop him before he gets too far off. "Take that sword with you."

Despite the shadows cast by the campfire, the hesitation in his expression is clear. "I don't—"

"Do it," I say. "Orla said it's yours, after all. You should use it."

He opens his mouth to respond, and I can tell the word "*no*" is sitting just on the edges of his teeth. But heaving another sigh, he merely answers, "I'll take it with. Just in case."

Once he's gone, I focus back on the map in the guide. The tiny icon of a Parthenon-esque building off to the west end of Midra etches itself into my vision, so much so that when I close my eyes for a second, I can still see it. It's not a replacement for having been there, but it's as close as I can get. That's going to have to be enough.

"You'll make it there. You don't have to worry too much about that."

I open my eyes, and Orla stands in front of me, head cheekily cocked to the side as she looks down at me.

I sigh, closing the book and stuffing it in my pack before I stand up. "You know, for all your talk about how dangerous it is to tell me how things turn out, you sure do like telling me how they turn out."

She lopsidedly grins at me. "I can tell you the outcome," she states. "I can't tell you how you get there. That's up for you to determine."

"Great," I grumble. As I look at her, I sigh again. "I'm sorry. I don't mean to be ungrateful. You've helped us a lot. So, thank you."

For the first time, the amusement on her face fades away, and she seems taken aback. It's as if no one has ever thanked her for anything before. "I didn't do anythin' more than any other decent person would."

"That's not true," I say.

She shrugs, uncharacteristically bashful. "It's nothin'." She shuffles uneasily for a moment before taking a deep breath and letting it out, straightening back out. "Anyway!" she says, pepping back up into her normal jaunty self. "I wanted to make sure you had enough Residuum to last you an encounter with the Infernal Mage."

She hands over a couple handfuls of assorted Residuum stones from a leather bag, and once they're nestled in my pockets, she pulls out another mid-sized chunk of Crystalline Residuum. "I know you have the one piece left over, but that'll only get you there," Orla explains. "This will get you out, if you're in a pinch."

I take it with caution, the hum of energy running up my arm as I do. I've never held Crystalline bare handed before, and it's a sensation I can't quite describe. It isn't like Heavenly where the energy seems to come from the air surrounding me, nor like Earthen which seems to come from beneath my feet, and certainly not Infernal which feels even deeper than that. This comes from—outward. Further than Heavenly. Outside of the realm of what a body could possibly perceive. It's light and airy, but the weight of it seems so much more than the others. It's nearly unfathomable. I quickly stuff it in my bag. "Thank you," I say. "Hopefully we won't need it."

The edge of her mouth quirks, but she doesn't say anything. Well then. I assume we'll need it.

I secure the strap over my shoulder as Orla digs back into the pouch. "I also think this is yours. Must have fallen out of your pocket when you were cleaning the kitchen yesterday." From the bag, she pulls out something I didn't even realize I'd been missing: the red twenty-sided die.

I take it from her, letting it roll lazily into the center of my palm. "Shit," I whisper. It's now that I realize how dingey it's become since I brought it here with me. The once stark white numbers are now a dull ivory, and the shiny red resin surface is clouded and flat.

"Must mean a lot to you," Orla comments. "It looks well-used."

I laugh. "Not for what it's intended."

"What did you use it for?"

I hesitate before answering. "It was a symbol, I think. That the things that happened to me were determined by something outside of myself, and there was nothing I could do about it. It was all a roll of the dice."

Humming thoughtfully, Orla looks down at the bit of plastic in my hand. "And what do you think now?"

I pause. At first, I only look at the die with a crease to my brow. It's like looking at a foreign object. Just to make sure, I run my thumb over one of the edges, but the comfort that I've come to know from it isn't quite there.

"I don't think I was wrong. At least not completely," I say. "There are things that I don't have control of. But I have control of me. What I do, what I say. No one else has any say in that. Dice be damned."

Orla doesn't even attempt to hide her smile this time, beaming at me in full force. "You know, darlin'," she says. "I'm thinkin' I agree with you."

It isn't much longer before Melandrich calls us all together. He presents me with the remainder of the Crystalline that got us out of the cave earlier, and I take it, no hesitation. I look between everyone's faces, and while the uncertainty is palpable, I don't feel fear. Maybe it's stupid of me not to be afraid of what awaits us on the other side of this hunk of crystal. But something tells me from the way Orla stands off to the side of our huddle, giving me another wink as we briefly lock eyes, that what I'm feeling right now—the determination that races through my veins—is the right feeling to have.

Have faith. That's what she said before, right?

I close my eyes, and with all that faith, I push my intent forward.

And we're gone.

CHAPTER 29

When our feet touch the ground again, there's no give to it. My grasp on Eddie's hand breaks, and I lurch forward, but I'm able to catch myself on the firm foundation under my feet before I topple over. Some of the others aren't so lucky. I hear Kai squeal as they thud onto the ground and Jackson's daggers go scattering, the scrape of metal against stone ringing out around us. The worst is Eddie who lands next to me like a limp sack, sucking in his breath and exhaling a string of curse words. Still disoriented, I kneel next to him, hurrying out words to ask if he's okay. It takes him a moment, but he eventually spits out that he's fine—thankfully, he didn't land on his bad arm. Probably wasn't much help for his good arm, though.

Knowing that he's all right, I stand up and take account of our new surroundings amid the chorus of groans. At first, I think maybe my vision hasn't adjusted, but a few good blinks show me that my eyes are working just fine.

I was aiming for the temple. Did I expect to end up there? Of course not. Being my first time using Crystalline Residuum, I was hoping to at least not sink us into the deepest trench in the ocean or in the middle of a brick wall. I expected something in

429

the middle, closer to what happened when Adrian would get us around with Crystalline—maybe we'd end up a couple miles away in the woods surrounding the temple.

But as I look around at the white marble pillars surrounding us, a grand open hall of sprawling statues lit by a line of interspersed torches hanging on the walls, it dawns on me.

"We are...inside the Temple," From a few yards away, Melandrich pulls himself to his feet with the assistance of one of the pillars. He speaks like he's in a daze—though with how disheveled his normally pristine hair is and how unsteady he is as he pulls away from the pillar, he might be. "That is unexpected."

"That's putting it mildly," I say. As I look around at the vaulted ceiling of the temple, I have to consciously stop myself from grinning. It's become a habit now, after I manage to get Residuum to work the way I want.

The Old Gods' Temple is the strangest cross between a Catholic cathedral and Greek Parthenon that I've ever seen. Closed off by stone, the columns of marble line the longest walls leading down to a glowing dais at the head of the room. Shafts of moonlight pour in through small windows dotting the walls, but most of the light comes from the hanging torches that cast shadows across the white floor underneath us in harsh contrast. In between the pillars, chiseled statues of various people in action line the path—a woman kneels on the ground, her hands pressed together in prayer while her long hair cascades around her and onto the ground, so long that it curls around her knees. A man with a bushy beard wields a sword pointed skyward, his heavy armor so detailed that I feel as though I could reach out and undo the laces on his belt. They are all in some sort of act of defiance or reverence, as if they are protecting the sanctum either by action or pacifism.

We check in with each other, and I do a mental headcount. Six of us. I got us here in one piece. It's exhilarating to say the least, even though I know that's not what the focus should be right now. The focus should be—

The Relic.

On the far end of the temple, a marble plinth stands, the moonlight filtered through the windows hitting it in just the right angles so it's illuminated as the centerpiece of the room. Unlike the other columns that line the room, this plinth is sculpted out of grey stone, its cracks and ridges outlined in reflective golden hues, like its core is solid gold ore, just waiting for its chance to burst forth and show its true splendor. The general chatter around me dies down as everyone realizes where the Relic must be, as obvious as if there was a neon "HERE IT IS" sign pointing to it.

I take a cautious step forward, and a hand clamps on my shoulder. I look back to find Eddie clutching onto me with his good hand, his eyes stuck on the plinth at the front of the room. "Hold up, Vi. Are we sure that's it?"

"Looks pretty damn conspicuous to me," Jackson mutters behind us.

"We're really looking this gift horse in the mouth?" Kai asks. They look as calm as they possibly can, but their crossbow is raised and ready, finger on the mechanism's trigger. "The idea is to get this thing formed quickly. We don't need to question it, do we?"

"The other two Relics did have additional barriers," Melandrich says cautiously. "It would stand to reason that this should be no different."

I shake my head. "I think it is different."

"Of course you bloody do," Kai sighs.

I roll my shoulder out of Eddie's grip and take another few steps forward. Eddie makes a noise in protest but goes quiet behind me as I walk, my steps slow and measured. "He wants us to form the Dagger, right?" I say over my shoulder. "If that's the case, he'd make it as easy as possible to get. He's in charge of how this one is guarded. If you wanted someone to take it..."

Without ceremony, I walk up the steps of the dais and approach the plinth, my steps echoing loudly against the stone.

While from far away the flat surface appeared clean and bare, I see what it really holds now that I'm up close. In the center of the pedestal sits a crude, oblong black stone shaped to a wicked point that looks somehow natural and curated all at once. Gingerly, I pick it up, running my fingers along the edge just lightly enough that I don't break my skin open. Despite how sharp it is, it feels light and brittle, like I could crack it in half with ease.

This isn't just a stone. It's obsidian. Cooled down molten earth.

I turn back to the group, the Relic in hand. "You'd let them take it," I say.

The five of them look at the stone in my hand, wide-eyed and wary as I descend down the platform and walk back to them. I hold it out for everyone to see plainly. "Well, that's anti-climactic," Eddie grumbles as he examines it in my hand. "I expected something, I don't know, bigger. Deadlier. Fierier."

Kai rolls their eyes. "I don't care, personally. The less hassle, the better. Let's get this godsdamned ritual over with already."

I look at Melandrich. "You have the rest?"

He nods, pulling out his bag and rooting around in it for only a frantic moment before producing a bundle wrapped in cloth and twine. His hands tremble as he unfurls it, revealing within the cloth the three previous Relics: the sliver of bark with the slight green sparkling sheen, the long shard of smoky crystal, and the delicate piece of lavender fulgurite that was in the queen's care before we started the journey.

We have all four.

I exhale, my head swimming for a second. It doesn't seem real. It's only step one, of course, but it's one step closer to May...

Melandrich crouches and sets the cloth down on the floor, open-faced with the three Relics lined up on top of it. I kneel as well, setting the fourth down at the end of the line, my hands as steady as I can make them. I let out a shuddering breath. "Okay, um, let's form this thing. I guess."

Sinking to his knees, Eddie squeezes my shoulder again. "You got this," he whispers.

One by one, the rest of them crouch too, huddled in a circle around me and the Relics. Even on her knees, Gren towers above all of us, while Kai scoots closer to me in order to be seen. I look down at the items in front of me, wracking my brain for any bit of information Adrian might have told me about the ritual. I always figured he would take the lead in that particular area, so I never thought to ask about details. I curse my past self for not thinking about the very real fact that I was the second most experienced magic user in the group, and if anything were to happen to him, it would be all up to me.

These four random objects just seem like junk we picked up along our trip. As I stare down at them, though, the image starts to form in my brain. How they all fit in a grander picture. How they can all come together.

I look up at the others, curious faces all pointed in my direction.

There was one thing he said for sure that we needed: as much help as we could get.

"Put your hands on me," I say to them. I try to seem confident, but it sounds just as unsure as they all look.

Even so, they do it, Melandrich taking the initiative and setting his gloved hand gently on my shoulder. They all touch me somewhere, whether it be a shoulder, an arm, what have you. Gren, having the hardest time finding a spot, huffs and plops her massive hand on top of my head, as if she's attempting to ruffle my hair.

"Anyone else think this feels a little evangelical?" Eddie asks with an anxious chuckle as he grips my upper arm. No one responds, but I do see Jackson clench his jaw as he manages to get his fingers on my knee.

I'm already sweating with the six of us clustered together

swapping body heat, our breath intermingling, all connected through the shared conductor of me. I close my eyes, the Relics still visible in my mind.

This is magic, right? You only need three things for magic. Emotion, intention, and action. All through the conductor of Residuum.

That's when it starts to take shape. I'm not casting the spell at all. They are. I'm the conduit. *I* am the Residuum.

I don't do anything. I simply let their intentions flow through me.

It isn't magic like I'm used to. It's not intense and grating. It's warm and comforting, like a blanket thrown around my shoulders. And it takes a moment for me to realize that I have felt it before. I've felt it as I've played Mario Kart with Eddie, as I've listened to Melandrich speak of his fascination of Earth culture, as I've seen Jackson struggle to read just a few more pages by dim firelight, as Kai jabs at Gren in some language unknown to the rest of us. That is my contribution. That glow of a feeling is what I send forward, casting it upon the items in front of me.

The energy builds, swelling into a symphony within me and growing in intensity so quickly that it starts to overwhelm me. I feel tears well up behind my closed eyes, but just as I think it's going to be too much, it subsides. The hands on me ease up, and I hear, "Lady Spence. I believe you have done it. Good Earth, you've done it."

Gradually, I pry my eyes open, gazing back down at the spread-out cloth in front of me. It takes me a moment to process what I'm seeing, and even when it clicks, I still don't quite feel the weight of it.

In the center of the white cloth, the blue moonbeams and warm torch light illuminating it in juxtaposed ambiance, sits a dagger the length of my forearm—a completely different thing from the four separate objects we had before. But each part of the Dagger is clear in what it used to be. The pommel is rounded off, the fulgurite's once delicate spreading tendrils worn down into a polished orb on the end of the hilt, connecting to a grip made of dark bark, delicately flecked with green throughout its cracks. The crosspiece separating the grip from the blade shimmers in the light, the opaque crystal's hard edges smoothed out just like the pommel. And sitting atop it is the long piece of obsidian, stretched and filed down, the craggy pieces I nearly cut myself on before now honed into sharpened edges and a fierce point, a gleam running off its dark black surface.

"Fuck me," Eddie whispers.

"Seconded," Kai says.

The others slowly draw back from me. Hesitant, I reach out and take the Mage's Dagger in my hand, afraid that the tenuous magic we used to keep it together will give out at any moment and cause the blade to fall apart in my hand. But it holds, sturdy enough to have been put together lovingly by a craftsman. I turn it over, inspecting it for any flaws, any sign that we messed up somewhere—that I messed up. There's nothing, though. Not a seam or crack to be found, as if it were made in a factory.

Everyone's hands are off me now, but Melandrich leans back in and pats me on my arm. "Well done, Lady Spence," he murmurs. "Well done."

I breathe. That's all I can do. Breathe and keep myself from breaking out into a stupid smile.

"Well done, indeed."

My head snaps up at the voice that echoes across the temple walls, though I'm not surprised in the least to see who it belongs to. Across the expansive hall, a bright orange-red glow emanates from a mass of black robes, cracked through with the same patterns I saw in the forest clearing mere hours ago. The Infernal Mage's hood is down, and as he glides toward us in his ghost-like canter, the bright flaming lines of his face come into focus. Every time I've seen him before, the mania in his eyes has flickered just below the surface of the fire glow. Even from this distance, though, I can tell he isn't reigning in his desperation, his hunger.

Those eyes are wide and incandescent, fixed squarely on the object in my hand.

"You really have done so *well*," the Mage lilts, stopping several columns away from us. This close up, there seems to be more grey streaks in his dark unruly hair, more angry cinder cracks creeping across his strikingly white skin. "I must say, my faith did falter at the start. Being foreigners, I worried you would be unprepared for the arduous journey. But you have exceeded expectations, indeed." Out of nowhere, he cackles, the hyena-like sound hard on the ear. It goes on for longer than any joke should be funny for, but eventually he settles, his eyes still huge and menacing. "I would like to show my gratitude. As a Mage, I could never acquire the Dagger myself, so you have assisted me so greatly. As a gift, I will let you walk away from this place unscathed." He holds out a quivering hand. "As soon as you give it to me, of course."

I rise to my feet, trying to hold steady the tremors running through my own hands. I throw back my shoulders, feigning some kind of confidence. "I think we need more negotiating than that."

A twitch runs through his face, but he doesn't break eye contact. "I believe the gift of your lives is incredibly generous given your position, friend."

"That's the thing," I say. "We have the one thing in this world that can hurt you. I think that's worth listening to."

I expect this to rile him more. But his hand steadies as he drops it back at his side, and he looks at me with something akin to pity rather than anger. "You know nothing of inflicting pain, friend," he says. For a brief flash, there is something stable in his gaze, the fire glow pulling back. "For your sake, I suggest you keep it that way. It is not something you know the weight of. I am being gracious in offering you the easy end to our relationship. Believe you me."

Beside me, the others grip their weapons, not raising them but keeping them handy. I take another shaky breath before answering. "If you tell us what we want to know, we'll give you the Dagger. No fights necessary. But you need to tell the truth."

It's obviously not the answer he wants to hear, but the Mage angles his head curiously, nonetheless.

I swallow, realizing my mouth has gone dry. "The Crystalline Mage," I say. "Where is she?"

His eyes are still unblinking. "And why do you wish to know this?"

"That isn't your business," Jackson interjects, squaring his shoulders as he walks up next to me. "Just answer the question."

Another manic laugh erupts from the Mage, though he cuts it short quickly. "And what do you plan to do with that information when I give it to you? If I tell you what I know and you give me the Dagger, what will her whereabouts mean to you? You will have no way of defending yourself against her. It would mean nothing." His eyebrow spasms suddenly. "Unless, of course, you don't plan to give the Dagger to me at all. Unless you plan to run off with that Crystalline Residuum and take the Dagger with you."

My grip on the Dagger tightens, afraid it will slip out of my hand against the slick sweat of my palm. "We wouldn't do that."

"*Lies!*" the Infernal Mage bellows, orange eyes flaring, the sudden outburst a sting against the ear as it reverberates through the hall. I flinch but hold my ground, my fingers choking the grip of the blade. "Lies and obscenities!"

The tension between our clustered group winds tighter. I can feel the anxious energy radiating off of Melandrich next to me, his own long sword steady and ready to swing at a moment's notice. Kai's crossbow is poised to shoot, and even Eddie, with his one immobilized arm, stands prepped with a small dagger. We must look like kids with toy guns to the Mage, but we hold steady as his piercing cry dies down, the sound eventually swallowed up by the cavernous room.

The flare in the Mage's eyes rages for a tense moment, but soon, it settles, the furious glow ebbing. "Fools," he finally sputters, the word almost whispered. "Fools, all of you. I'm giving you the choice to live. To turn it down…" The sentence ends, abrupt and meandering all at once.

And against every thought running through my head, I step forward to the front of the group, pointing the Dagger at him. For the first time since I picked it up, it isn't an artifact in need of protecting. It's a weapon, and I'm going to use it like one.

"If you want it, you either tell us where she is," I say, "or you take it from us."

The look of pity returns as the Infernal Mage pulls his gaze from the floor and locks his flickering flame eyes on mine. I don't know what to think of it as we stare at each other. Because the fact that he's hesitating at all confuses me to no end.

That conflicted look does not waver as he raises a hand limply forward, mirroring my stance with the Dagger. "Well then," he says, almost in a sigh. "I suppose there is no other choice."

That's when the shadows pull themselves from the walls.

Creeping around the statues and their accompanying columns are dozens upon dozens of lanky black Hellions, crawling on their hands and knees across the marble and stone and into the torchlight of the open chamber. Their massive teeth snap as they charge toward us, their sharp cries earsplitting as they peel themselves from the darkness. Behind them, the Mage stares, unblinking as they scurry toward us in a frenzy.

My stomach plummets, the Dagger still pointed but my attention now on the approaching horde of monsters. I knew that they would be here. They come as a package deal with him, after all. But fuck, why don't I feel prepared?

I lower the Dagger, using my other hand to grapple whichever Residuum stone it can get a hold of—Heavenly, by the feel of it—and frantically wonder what I should do. What *should* I even be doing? Fuck, I shouldn't—

Breathe in.

It's with some hesitation, but I eventually do breathe out.

And realizing my hands are both full, I slam my foot down, unleashing a cascade of lightning across the stone floor. The web snakes its way over the ground and latches onto the closest handful of Hellions who all writhe in pain in front of us, shrieking in agony until the coursing purple light releases them, and they clatter to the floor, lifeless.

From the way the others pick up the pace, rushing toward us, I get the impression they didn't like that too much.

Ten seconds on the clock.

And it's a whirlwind of a round. The low light of the temple causes everything to blur, my baser instincts the only things guiding me as I sling magical energy toward the moving shadows. The only thing keeping me from attacking my friends is the occasional echo of steel and ogre-like snarls to let me know where they are. I use the hand holding the Residuum to push the energy forward too, which feels a bit like writing with my non-dominant hand. It's sloppy, but as the electrical energy bursts forward from my hands and rockets through the skull of one of the Hellions, I at least marvel at the fact that it gets the job done. I don't want to let go of the Dagger or even put it in my belt. I can't let them get hold of it and bring it back to him. We'd be out of bargaining chips. I grip the knife tighter and dig my nails into the heel of my hand, the pain keeping me viscerally aware that I still have it.

I catch a glimpse of the others for a split second as another Hellion folds into a smoking heap and I reach for another stone. Melandrich slashes one of the tiny beasts across the chest before sinking the pointed blade into another's stomach. Gren's club mows down another cluster of the creatures, and one that manages to cling onto it is swiftly turned into black paste as she slams the club into the stone. All the while, Kai holds onto Gren's shirt for dear life, hanging off her back and shooting bolts whenever they get the opportunity to reload. Eddie is the only one shying away from the main fray of the fight and for good reason, as he uses his one useful arm to slash at a couple of the creatures who seem less concerned about their pack tactics and more about the instinctual need to take out anyone their master wishes. He's holding his own but clearly only treading water. Once my fingers find another crystal, I lunge forward, hoping to do something to shield him against the onslaught—

A rumble emanates from beneath my feet, and I come to a halt. In fact, everyone—even the Hellions—stops in surprise at the quaking ground beneath us, the deep shudder intensifying as we all pass uneasy glances between each other. Eddie and I make bemused eye contact for the briefest of moments before a pulsing shake rattles beneath the stone, so intense that I'm nearly knocked over again.

From the center of the room comes a loud crack.

"Move back!" I hear Melandrich yell, but it is quickly drowned out as stones pry themselves up, launching across the temple hall as the center of the stone floor bubbles upward into a swelling mound of broken rock and dirt. I shuffle backward, though I'm mostly out of the line of fire. Some of the Hellions closer to the epicenter scuttle off to the sides, disengaging with whoever they're attacking and hiding behind some of the statues close by to shield themselves from the flying debris. I throw my arm over my face to defend against the chunks of rock that fly my way, but I remain mostly unscathed as the rumbling subsides, the air in the room filling with a dusty haze.

As things settle, I peer toward the center of the temple hall, wafting away the dust in the air. It doesn't take long for a shiver of intense cold to run down my spine.

A looming, nightmarish monster sits in the center of the room, smoke billowing off its emaciated form. The Temple's high ceilings extend over thirty feet high, but the creature that has emerged from the pile of rubble in the center is far larger than that, its skeletal frame crunched inward like an injured animal. While it doesn't look exactly like the Hellions, it sure does resemble a mangled, gigantic version of one. There is no flesh on its dark black bones, only a slender rib cage connected to a spine with protruding vertebrae and long haunting limbs, all positioned on the floor since it cannot stand up straight due to its sheer size. Its skull is round and squashed like a poorly bred dog, but the spiny oversized teeth of a Hellion remain, fitting into each other like a zipper made of needles. Where the normally bugged-out eyes would be are two hollow sockets, glowing with a red-orange light like two simmering embers in a dead fire pit.

Our staggered group stands silently in awe of the beast, which must be bigger than all six of us combined and doubled. And as it opens its toothy maw and lets out a roar, its empty rib cage ignites with a swirling core of bright amber light that sits where its stomach would be. As the roar vibrates through the marbled hall in ear-piercing resonance, the core of fire flares. A stream travels up its invisible esophagus and out its open mouth, a line of fire blasting through the air in a show of intense light and heat.

Well. That complicates things.

Ten more seconds.

The Hellions, seemingly overjoyed at the sight of another ally, creep out of their hiding spaces and resume their attack. They catch Kai and Gren off guard, while the giant skeletal monster stomps in its limited space, shooting a ray of fire over our heads in another torturous scream. As another of the smaller Hellions charges at me, I make use of the upended dirt from the crater the monster came out of by using Earthen to hurl missiles at them. I thank whatever it is out there running the universe that stone can't catch fire. Wait, can it? I sure fucking hope not. One of the errant flames gets a little too close to the top of my head, and I drop to the floor out of instinct. Maybe stone can't catch fire, but I sure can. That's probably the thing to worry about most.

Another Hellion goes down, a sharpened spear of stone cultivated with Earthen Residuum sent flying through its middle. But before I can breathe, a shout sounds off near the crater, and I whirl around to see Eddie cowering on the ground, propped up by one hand while his other hangs useless in its sling. Scrambling on the ground, he hobbles over to a loose dagger that must have fallen out of his hand. He doesn't see behind him that the massive skeletal beast has homed in on him. I don't know if that thing can grin, but it sure looks like it does, lifting a bony but still absurdly huge foot over Eddie's head as he limps away. I open my mouth to shout at him while scrambling for more stones, not sure how exactly I'm supposed to stop this thing.

But it turns out, I don't have to. Because the monster's foot stops midair, its body suddenly wracked with an intense spasm as lavender strands of zig-zagging lightning encase its bones.

I reach Eddie and pull him to his feet just in time to get out of the way of the monster's foot as it stamps on the ground behind us. It sends another shower of shattered stone and dirt up in its wake that hits me in the back as we run off to the side of the hall. Eddie heaves deep breaths as he leans against a column, his face pale and eyes wide. As he steadies himself, I look back up at the huge creature, shaking with residual spasms of electricity as the bright tendrils of lightning dissolve. I search at its feet for who could have cast that. I may not be the most experienced caster, but I know Heavenly lightning when I see it. It must have come from someone.

And when I see who that someone is, my breath catches.

Through the monster's scrawny legs, I see him standing on its other side, his hands encased in a still-pulsing swirl of purple electricity, arms of errant power snapping off into the air at random as it crackles. He's wearing a clean shirt, and the curling strands of hair he couldn't keep out of his face before are now pulled back in a tight knot at the back of his head. His is gaze frighteningly determined, and the reflection of the sparks he holds in his hands pulsate in his dark brown eyes.

With hardly a flick of his wrists, Adrian lets the lightning contained in his grasp loose from his hold, shooting it back at the skeletal monster with a guttural cry. The force hits the creature again, traveling across its body in leaps and sparks, and it lets out another booming roar that rattles in my ears.

I glance at Eddie, making sure he's situated in a hidden spot behind one of the statues and out of sight from the creature, before I sprint beneath the monster's legs as it shakes off the last of its electric convulsions. I clumsily dodge its stumbling feet as it attempts to steady itself again, shooting out another stray stream of flame from its burning core in Adrian's direction. Acting quicker than I can think, I grab hold of an Earthen stone in my pocket and pull up a shield of stray dirt around him. It glances off like the shield was made of metal, and I drop it as I pass on the other side of the beast, locking my fingers into Adrian's shirt and yanking him to the other side of the hall behind another set of columns.

Sure that we're out of sight, I take a chance and peek around the column protecting us. The massive monster swivels its head around, looking for where its pesky attackers have run off to. Thankfully, the rest of the Hellion horde has thinned out, and Gren and Kai take shots at the beast with Melandrich flanking it from behind, slashing at its ankles. From my vantage point, I can't see where Jackson ran off to, and Eddie seems to be safe in his hiding spot.

I whirl back around to face Adrian. "What the fuck are you doing here?"

He heaves deep breaths as he wipes away a thick line of sweat from his forehead. "What does it look like?" he asks between gasps. "Helping."

"And I thought we told you we didn't want your help."

"Well, you know how good I am at following instructions." I open my mouth to snap back at him, but he holds up a hand. "Look, I get it. You don't have to tell me. I wanted to leave you all be, but something brought me back to Orla's place. You'd already left, but she gave me some more Crystalline." The look on his face softens, morphing from his trademark snarkiness into that broken expression from back at the cabin. And I see now, while he had appeared to have pulled himself together since splitting off from us, the mess that we left him in hasn't quite been cleaned up. Deep shadows ring his eyes, and loose strands of hair are falling out of their knot. But he stares at me with a hollow resolve. "I know what you must think of me. It's every terrible thing I've thought of me over the past twenty years. But I came here to make up for what I did. To fix the shit I broke. And that starts with you. And him."

That numbness starts to creep back in. That feeling of not knowing whether to reach out and slap him or hug him. The convergence of those two feelings weighs so heavily on me that my body chooses no emotion at all.

Another roar from the creature sounds off behind us.

I can't afford no emotion. Not now.

"Do what you need to feel better about yourself, I guess. Just stay out of the way," I say, and before he can respond, I peel off from behind the column, hurling another beam of lightning at the huge creature in the center of the room.

It rages for far longer than ten seconds. I run through my stones like charcoal pencils running short in the midst of drawing a portrait. While I have plenty, each one that expends in my hand gives me a brief jolt of fear. Because the creature keeps screaming, and our attacks don't seem to be doing anything to it at all. There's no flesh or tendons to slash at with a blade or sink an arrow into. There's nothing to singe with electricity or bludgeon with a flying boulder. With every hit, it gets angrier, sending another line of fire into the air. And while the Temple isn't catching on fire, the ancient stone around it is beginning to crumble from the disruption in the foundation and the heat being pushed around the room. I dodge falling rocks as I hurl attacks, hoping that I'm not contributing to the damage to the structure.

An Earthen stone disappears in my palm, and I instinctively

reach for another. A hot ball of energy hits my core, and I pause. Infernal.

I take a deep breath. Not yet. Not ready for that.

I grab another. Infernal.

Another. Infernal.

I swear under my breath, shakily switching the Dagger to my right hand and digging in my left pocket. More Infernal. I have at least ten stones on me, but they all seem to be goddamn Infernal. I let out another uneven breath, trying not to let it overwhelm me. It'll be okay. I can control it. There's nothing here to catch fire, remember? Except my friends, of course. Which is arguably worse. No, you won't hurt them. You won't. You can't. You—

"Violet!"

It's Adrian's voice that jerks me out of my panic, and feeling a dark shadow roll across me, I look up, eyes going wide. The beast's massive front foot hovers over me, and while it's slower due to how big it is, it's coming down on top of me fast. I will myself to move, but my mind is still on what's in my pocket, and my feet can't react fast enough for me to—

A cry sounds off, a rush of air passing me by, a brief reprieve from the sweltering heat. The monster roars again, its burning belly flaring as it sends a bolt of flame up into the air. It recoils, and I stumble backward as something falls in front of me with an empty clatter. The room spins, but as I reorient myself, I see scattered across the floor what I thought had been part of the crumbling temple walls. But it isn't stone or marble. It's bones. A pile of small digits that match the dark skeletal structure of the creature. I glance back up at the bucking monster. It cradles the foot it was about to bring down on me, except where there used to be a foot, there is now the nubby stump of a femur bone.

Still dazed, I look around, and when I see what's managed to finally lay a damaging hit on this thing, I can't believe it.

Standing with his normally hunched shoulders thrown back is Jackson. His daggers are nowhere to be seen. Grasped in both hands, tensed and ready to strike, is the black-bladed sword he pulled from the stump all those weeks that seem like years ago. As the monster shoots another furious stream of fire into the air, the light glints in the lenses of his glasses. The focused furrow in his brow is something I have never seen in him before. It's not anger, not frustration. Dare I say it—it might be confidence.

"What did you do, King Wank-off?!" Kai yells as Gren shifts away from the stumbling monster. "And how do we copy it? We haven't been doing bugger all to this thing!"

The confident expression wavers as his gaze shifts. "I don't know. I just—swung the sword, I guess."

"Well, keep doing it!" Kai says, loading another bolt into their crossbow and shooting at the creature again.

Jackson opens his mouth to say something, but soon closes it, just nodding and charging forward, whipping the sword through the air and swiping it across the creature's dipped head. It screeches in pain as a glowing red line—a scorch mark— appears across its jaw. Jackson grunts as he runs on the creature's other side while it's distracted and howling.

I pull in another breath, about to sprint forward since there's nothing else I feel like I can do. I know that in order to do anything, I'll need to use Infernal Residuum. But before I can move, a shout goes up into the air, followed by a thud. I whip around, and my stomach flips.

Eddie has emerged from his hiding spot, toppled over on the floor and scrambling backward in a panic, sluggish since he's really able to only use one arm. But adrenaline and fear are the things pushing him forward, because standing over him, approaching in a menacing glide, is the Infernal Mage.

His back is to me, but the cracks in his cloak are bright and fierce, more intense than I've ever seen them. Outstretching a hand, the white skin on his arm is run through with pulsing fiery energy, the glow building and building and—

"Hey!" I shout.

The Mage takes his focus off Eddie, turning his head and

inclining it unnaturally to stare at me with his huge, blazing eyes.

Words catch in my throat, but I glance down at the Dagger, still wrapped in my grasp.

I hold it in front of me. "You want it, don't you?"

His deranged eyes flare silently, hungry.

"Then come take it."

Eddie calls my name, merely a ringing in my ear as I turn around and take off, dashing past the scattered bodies of Hellions and vaulting over fallen stone and debris, rushing toward the head of the Temple where the Relic laid on the pedestal minutes before all this. There's no strategy besides *"run."* I don't even know where I'm supposed to go once I reach the dais at the front of the room, but I spot an archway off to the side leading into a shadowy hall. I take one last purposeful breath before I charge.

Eddie screams my name as I barrel through, shadows swallowing me whole. And as I plunge into the darkened doorway, a radiating heat burning at my back, I struggle not to hear her calling out to me too.

CHAPTER 30

B reathe in. Breathe out.
That's all I can do. That's all I hear. Just my own breathing as I run, the cramped stone hallway deadening any noise from the outside and amplifying everything in. My heartbeat, my footsteps, my ragged breathing. Everything *me*.

Breathe in. Breathe out.

My fingers wiggle into my pocket, and I grab onto a piece of Infernal Residuum. I don't want to use it, but I can't see anything around me. There aren't even shadows or shapes—just darkness. The Infernal energy rushes into my gut, and I will myself to release just a little bit of it, just enough to cast light and not catch myself on fire. A small burst of orange light springs to life in my palm. It isn't even fire that I'm holding, just emanating light from the Residuum itself, enough that I can see in front of me at least a few feet. Even with that, though, there's not much I can see besides uneven jigsawing brick on top of brick. The hall is narrower than I thought, and as I rush through it with the same alternating patterns flashing by me, I feel like the tunnel is pressing in on me, getting tighter and tighter as I run.

Breathe in, breathe out. Come on. It's as simple as that.

Something echoes behind me, and I nearly trip, but I manage to stay upright as I sprint. He's not running after me. If anything, he's using his ability to travel underground. The thought should be comforting, but it isn't. Because that means he could show up anywhere. In front of me, behind me, right below my feet...

No, no. Breathe in. Breathe out. Don't get caught up. Just keep moving forward.

Ahead of me, the overlapping pattern of brick shifts, and it takes me until I'm almost on top of it to realize it's a doorway. A wave of relief washes over me as I skid across the rocky floor, rounding the corner. I half expect another enclosed hallway, but when my footsteps' echoes ring out just a little broader, I pause.

The room I find myself in is wide and open, though not nearly as majestic and sprawling as the main temple hall. Another array of statues resembling the front hall greet me, but these are different. They sit about the main area of the room in no particular arrangement, and as I step in and pass by a few, I see that they all have some kind of flaw. Some have limbs that have been knocked off, some are missing their heads. Some even have paint on them, though time has chipped away at the colorful exteriors. The quick glance I get suggests that this is a storage area for old statues that either used to or were meant to reside in the main hall.

I hold the Residuum out in front of me to cast light on the back of the room. No additional doorways. The only exit is the way I came.

Exhaling, I go to turn around to take my chances back out in the hallway, but another ringing noise clatters from the doorway. And it sounds closer.

Like a cornered deer, I frantically back up, drawing further into the room. And when a soft rumble starts up below my feet, I stumble into one of the broken statues, clawing at the stone until I slide down on the other side of it, shielding myself from the doorway. The rumbling intensifies, and I clap a hand over my mouth, holding my breath. My breathing is so loud. Maybe if I stay quiet, he won't find me. I squeeze my eyes shut. I had so much confidence before. Where did it all go?

I open my eyes again as the rumbling dies out, and a warm orange hue bursts into life against the shoddy brick walls of the room. There are no echoing footsteps, nothing to indicate that anyone is here with me. But the glow brightens to an uncomfortable glare, and I know it's him.

"This could all be over so quickly, friend."

I shut my eyes again, my stomach twisting itself into knots.

"I gave you so many opportunities." The Mage's lilting, gentle tone fills the room easily. With my eyes closed, he seems reasonable. Friendly, even. But I know he says it with his deranged face peering from statue to statue, lips pulled back in a wild sneer and eyes incendiary. "All I wanted was the Dagger. I did not think that was an unreasonable request."

I try to take a slow breath through my hand clamped around my mouth, as quiet as I can make it.

"Even with the Dagger, you're no use against a Mage. You know this, friend. I know you do. It is the only thing that can kill a Mage, yes, but that implies you can get close enough to one without meeting your untimely demise. I know you are not a fool."

I shake my head, trying so hard to push the nausea away.

There is silence, and the bright light maintains itself. Until a loud pop rings out, a sudden explosion turning into a shower of stones on the other side of the room from me. I suck in a breath suddenly but keep my hand over my mouth at the sudden outburst. I pull my grip on the Dagger tighter as the last rain of debris settles.

"You have nowhere to turn," the Mage says. "There is no scenario where you walk away from here with that Dagger, friend. I will upturn every stone in this room, and it will be as easy as lifting my hand." He's quiet for a moment, and I almost think I hear a footstep before it goes silent again. "You know, I have seen you wield your magic. I kept my eye on you and your group, ever since you arrived here. There is a special pull between Mages and their surviving—benefactors, I suppose you would call it. I knew where you were as soon as he came back to Velmyra. I saw him train you on how to use the powers that come from us Mages."

Now I definitely hear footsteps, as if he has stopped his otherworldly glide and taken to walking. Though the steps seem more like shuffling, heavy feet scraping against granite. "You are a novice, friend. What do you hope to do against us? We are so much more than what you have held in the palm of your hand. We are all-encompassing, uncageable. The power we wield is not merely something you can keep in your pocket."

I drop my hand from my mouth, letting it fall at my side.

"We consume," the Mage says. "We decimate. What do you and your stones think you can do?"

Another pop, another shower of stone raining down on me, this time from behind. I cover my head with my hands and keep tight hold of the Dagger as the flying bits of rubble fall.

"It is over, friend," The Mage says. His voice is so close, like he's saying it in my ear. "What's to say that you can face me and my betters? You cannot even keep a forest from burning."

I open my eyes.

As silently as I can, I dig into my pockets. A pile of radiating Residuum sits in my hand, giving off just enough light where I can see the sharp edges and grooves of their fragments, enough to glimpse the complexities that simmer in their center.

I can't keep the forest from burning.

But what if I want the forest to burn?

I suck in a breath through my nose as the Infernal magic builds in my gut, red hot energy racing through my body. There's not a big window of opportunity for me. I need to be deliberate. The magic rushes into my limbs from my core, and I grit my teeth as I rise, stepping out from behind my protective statue.

It all takes place in such a small sliver of time. I step out, and he's so close to me—closer than I thought. His orange eyes are filled with malice. I only focus on them for a split second, though. He isn't my target. I fix my eyes up at the ceiling.

I breathe out.

And I let it go.

Amber light flashes in front of my eyes, energy shooting from my fingers, and it takes a moment for the cacophonous sound of combustion to follow, ripping through my ears as the world upends and flips over on itself. Something hard hits me in the shoulder, and I'm forced on the ground. Everything blurs, cascades, blinks from hot bright light to darkness to shadow in such quick succession that I don't know where I am any more as the thunderous noise continues like the explosion is still happening. Huge chunks batter themselves into my body, but I can't move out of the way as they pelt me in rapid fire, jolts of pain shooting through me as they do. It's endless and disorienting.

And then, it's quiet. I pry my eyes open, my heart hammering against my ribs. There had been such intense heat, but a gentle burst of cool air rolls over me as I regain my senses. I look down.

The Mage's Dagger is still in my hand.

I sigh in relief as I shift, attempting to sit up. My entire body screams in pain—it's everywhere, but something in my left side sends a sharp jab through my torso. I lift myself up with no regard for how much it hurts. The scrapes on my hands sting as I anchor myself on my hands and knees, and I blink the haze from my eyes as I look out at what's happened.

Stone can't catch fire, at least from what I know. But something in this area must not have been stone. Flames lick at the edges of the room, illuminating an area filled with crumbled piles of rock and debris. None of the flawed statues are left standing, all demolished heaps matching their surroundings. I glance up as another rush of cool air hits me amongst the heat in the flames surrounding me. The high ceiling of the storage room is, for the most part, gone—a jagged hole of still-crumbling stone sits in its place, revealing a tarry black sky dotted in pinpricks of stars.

I swear under my breath.

I made that.

A groan comes from a couple yards away, and I follow the sound. Ahead of me, there are only shapeless blobs of debris piles, but there's a shift near one of them. My heart kicks up again, and I try to scramble to my feet. That pain in my side flares, and I suck at my teeth, hesitating. I look down at my side and hold back a gasp. Through the flickering firelight, I can't make out anything distinct, but my entire left side from ribcage to belt is soaked in something dark and wet. I paw at it, but through my brain fog, I can't tell if anything is wrong or not. Whatever. Deal with that later. I stagger to my feet, shambling over to the groaning pile.

Amidst the unceremonious grey heaps, I see him. His dark robes are stiff and plain, missing their trademark cinder cracks. His face is plain too, though the angry burn marks where the cracks once were show prominently. He lays on the ground, and I'm hesitant to approach until I see that his legs are pinned underneath a gigantic chunk of the exploded ceiling. Even so, he doesn't seem to struggle against it, simply letting out a moan as he rolls his head against the ground.

My head swims, and I only make it halfway to him on my feet before I stumble and fall back on all fours. Grunting, I crawl the rest of the way with a desperation to my movements, brandishing the Dagger with a shaking hand. I level the blade at his chest, which is partially exposed against his torn robe. And as I do, his eyes flicker to my face, a weak ring of yellow light surrounding his pupils.

"Tell me where the Crystalline Mage is," I pant, swallowing just enough to wet my parched mouth.

The Mage's eyes are wide as he stares at me. He grins, chortling low.

"Tell me! Now!" I scream at him, jabbing the point of the blade closer to his chest, the obsidian blade just barely touching the flesh.

The Infernal Mage keeps laughing, shaking his head back and forth. "My friend," he says. "I cannot thank you enough."

And before I can ask what he's talking about, the Mage wraps his hands around mine that hold the Dagger and thrusts the blade into his chest.

It's such a quick motion that I don't think to recoil until well after he's let his hands fall back limply to the floor beside him, a shallow wheeze escaping him as I pull the blade out. "No no no no," I mutter to myself, looking over the knife in disbelief and vainly using my own bloody fingers to wipe away his blood from the black obsidian. Even as I do, the integrity is deteriorating. The blood eats away at the blade like acid, and soon, it evaporates into a wispy ether until only the hilt is left in my hand.

"No!" I shout, tossing the hilt to the side. "*Fuck!*" I grab my head in my hands. This can't be happening. This is what we came here for, and just as soon as I had it, it was gone. I yell an incoherent noise of anguish, the only thing that I can think to do.

And once my throat is raw, I still hear him laughing.

It's labored and choppy, but as I look over at him, the Mage seems euphoric, staring up at the starry sky in ecstasy as the hole in his chest hemorrhages. The little ring of yellow around his eyes grows dimmer as he looks back over at me. "My apologies, friend," he says after a gasp. "But I did ask."

It suddenly dawns on me how drained I am, every inch of me getting heavier. It's as though I can see my battery gauge slowly being pulled to zero. "That was all you wanted," I mumble, the pieces finally coming together as I talk. "The only way you can die is the Dagger. And you knew we were after it. So you had us do the work for you."

"I would have let you all be," he says, and a pool of yellow-orange light gathers at the corners of his eyes. It's only when they slip down his cheek in a burning streak that I realize they're tears laced with fire. "You all do not understand what it means to be killers. I apologize for involving you at all, but—it had to be done."

Brennan's smile wavers as he gazes up into the sky, the fire in his tears slowly burning out, leaving clear wet trails down his face in their wake.

I hang my head, shoulders slumping. I open my mouth to say something, but what can I say that sums up every messy, angry feeling I have in me right now?

"If it's all the same, you never would have won against her." His breathing is still shallow and strained, but his voice is dream-like and distant, as if he were floating on a cloud. "Crystalline is the most ruthless of us all." He chuckles again, but it's weak—so weak. "The beautiful fortress. She would never have let you close enough for that knife to matter. It would be a fool's errand. Only a Mage can truly match a Mage, after all."

I close my eyes, my head floating. It's over. And I'm so tired. I wish he would stop talking so I could float away like him.

"I could give it to you, you know."

I open my eyes. His gaze is off the sky now, directed at me. With all the humanity in him slowly returning, the yellow glow still clings to his irises. "The power of the Infernal Mage does not die until I do," he says, heaving in another gasping breath. "The time is short. But until I breathe no more, I could pass the power to you."

It's my turn to laugh now. "Are you joking?"

In response, he smiles. Not the Joker-like, deranged grin. A soft, genuine look of empathy.

I shake my head. "Isn't that half the reason for all this?" I say, gesturing to the destruction surrounding us. "To rid the world of one of the Mages. Not just pass it on for it to stay alive."

"I think so," he comments. "But—the power has other

desires. It wants to live even when I do not." A sudden sputter erupts from his mouth, and blood cakes the edges of his lips. "It cannot inhabit someone unwilling, however. Also...I think I would like to die human. The way I was born. The way my mother raised me. The way the Church embraced me when she was gone."

I swallow, though there's no moisture in my mouth. I'm so thirsty. So tired.

"The choice is yours, friend," Brennan wheezes. "To become a Mage or not. But if you let this power die now, you will never defeat her. What she took from you will be gone. Forever."

Another grin flashes in front of me. One coated in lip gloss. The scent of vanilla curls under my nose, muscling past the iron scent of blood.

Gone. Forever.

Through the haze, I hear Orla's voice in the back of my mind. "*When he asks you the question, you'll want to say no. You should say yes.*"

Brennan hacks again, and my heart leaps into my throat right as I say, "Okay."

He gasps again, but deliriously grins, blood staining his teeth. "You will do it?"

I nod frantically, lightheaded as I do. "Yes. I'll do it. Give it to me."

More tears gather into his eyes, pouring down his face in clear tracks against dirt and blood, the unnatural glow slowly dying out. And this Mage—this man—smiles at me with a graciousness I've never seen from anyone before. "Thank you, friend," he gasps. "Thank you."

His smile fades, the gratitude morphing into something else. I think I would call it pity.

I don't have time to suck in another breath before he lifts his hand up and presses his palm against the exposed skin of my chest, just below my collarbone.

He takes in as deep a breath as he can, but his voice is still barely a whisper.

"I am so, *so* sorry."

The yellow light in his gaze flares.

And I burn.

I am being unmade.

I rip at the seams, the minute stitches that make up the fabric of my being crudely splitting into frayed feathers that edge deep, unfathomable gashes. Everything within me goes up like dry grass in high summer. What I know, what I was, what I could be. The fire comes for it all. Undiscerning. Ruthless.

And it is *pain*. Visceral and inscrutable. My flesh bubbles and blackens, but it isn't my body that hurts. It eviscerates everything surface, burning down to my core and igniting what's left. A wick too short lived. Candle wax laced with gasoline.

Wrapped in its vise grip, I age decades. Everything I have experienced before is a flash lost in a sea of incomprehensible suffering. I am reduced to nothing in the course of minutes, days, years, decades, lifetimes. Ashes and smoldering dust.

Until it reaches out and shapes me into something else.

Something that resembles who I used to be, yet something alien. The soot and refuse that once was me is forced into a new skin, the folds of fresh cloth sutured together over the remnants of what the fire took and tore. I am reforged by the fire that destroyed me. As the agony subsides, my first emotion is gratitude. But why should I feel grateful for the thing that incinerated me?

As the presence comes back to me—the feeling in my fingers, toes, spine, neck—I do not think I have the capacity to answer that question.

For now, I open my new eyes to see what I've become.

CHAPTER 31

I t's not as hot as I remember.

That's the first thing that comes to mind as I crack my eyes open once the overwhelming pain subsides. It was so overbearingly hot before, as the flames around the edges of the room grew. But that sweltering heat is gone. It's actually pleasant. Like a fair day in June in Michigan, before the humidity rears its ugly head. As I blink, I wonder if maybe the fires have died out after however long I was out—it could have been minutes or years. But as my vision adjusts, the bright orange glow of the flames flicker just as fiercely, if not more so than they did before.

I look at them without fear or panic. I remember the last time I was surrounded by flame with no way out. How I saw it as a prison that I would never escape. But these flames don't seem so bad. I bask in their warmth, embrace them like comforting friends.

I glance around me, and as the afterglow of the intense pain wears off, I realize that I'm completely naked, crouched on the ground in the same spot I was when the Mage laid his hands on me. There aren't even remnants of clothes left. I hold up my hands, stretching my fingers in front of me. My skin is tight, pink and raw like the fresh skin underneath a scab that's fallen off. I marvel at the fact that I've seemed to have lost some freckles, and moles that have dotted my arms for as far as my memory reaches back have vanished. It's as if I shed like a snake. I am fresh. Unblemished.

But my eyes wander from my skin to the husk of a person in front of me, still pinned beneath a pile of rubble. Everything in the Infernal Mage's—Brennan's—body has been drained. The cinder cracks of his robe have all cooled into dark black, and the lines on his face are nothing but burn scars. His eyes are open, staring lifelessly up into the void of night. The faint yellow rings around his pupils are gone, leaving a beautiful sea green in its place.

I don't take my eyes off him as I wobble to my feet.

He looks so…young.

Not that much older than me…

A curious squawk comes from behind me, and I turn around, my hair falling around my shoulders as I move. I don't know what I expect to see behind me besides more of the demolished statues from the explosion.

I definitely don't expect to see a swarm of dozens of Hellions.

My heart leaps into my throat as I stumble backward. The fire surrounding the room dances in their bulbous, reflective eyes as they gaze at me, clutching onto each other and inching forward like a curious herd of deer—one false move and they'll scatter. But they're interested. In me. I hold my breath, hoping this is like T-Rex rules—if I stay still long enough, they won't realize I'm here.

We stare at each other. I'm useless against them. I have no more Residuum. Is that how it works still? What's even happened here, I don't—

They move, and I tense, waiting for them to descend upon me.

But they don't rush at me. They stay in place, crouching low and flattening themselves down onto the stone with their bodies still turned toward me. They brace their hands on the floor, their spindly black clawed fingers splayed out in front of them. For a moment, I wonder if they're all in pain for some reason, until it dawns on me.

They're bowing.

To me.

I let go of the breath I've been holding, shaky and uneven.

"Violet."

The voice startles me, but I don't react as quickly as I feel I should. Slowly, I turn toward the entrance of the statue room that I came through only a few minutes ago. Has it only been that long? It could have been hours. Weeks. I could have always been here. But the person standing in the archway reminds me that I haven't, that there was a life I had—do have.

Standing in the doorway, surveying everything in the room in wide-eyed horror, is Adrian. I can barely make him out through the gore and dirt covering his face. His skin is coated in wounds, blood pouring out of his nose which is crooked and bruised—I know a broken nose when I see one. He glances from Brennan's body to the flames on the wall, to the prone Hellions behind me, and finally to me. And through the grime on his face, I can't tell if he's relieved or terrified.

"What the hell did you do?" he whispers.

A loud rumble shakes the ground beneath us, an uproar of sound coming from off in the distance.

Adrian's eyes flit down the hallway, panicked. "Fuck," he says. He extends a hand out to me. "That monster's dead, but it damaged the structure too much. It's about to come down. We have to get out of here. Now."

I nod, but I still don't quite know how to respond. All my instincts are coming back to me too slowly. I glance over my shoulder at the horde of Hellions, but I do a double take.

They've all vanished. Not one remains.

"Violet! Now! Come on!"

Another loud rumble, the ground beneath us vibrating.

Nodding, I sprint toward Adrian. As I join him at the doorway, I notice he's barely looking at me. From the way we've spoken with each other these past few hours, I can imagine why. But when I pull up next to him, he hastily takes his shirt off, handing it to me. "Here," he says, out of breath as he glances nervously back down the hall. "Put that on. Quick."

Oh yeah. I'm naked. I take the shirt, awkwardly putting it on. It's just long enough to cover everything important. Once I have it on, he grabs me by the wrist, and I instinctively want to pull away. I don't want him touching me. But the thunder of more crumbling stone indicates that that isn't the battle I need to fight right now. I let him hold on to me as we take off down the hall.

We run, the pinprick of light coming from the main hall's entrance growing as we speed toward it. The noise of the collapsing structure gets louder the faster we go. The hallway seems so much shorter now, less foreboding and suffocating. It isn't long before we burst into the hall, and I'm blinded by the chaos that surrounds us. The flames are ten times higher in here—though it still seems like it should be so much hotter. Stone and marble cascade onto the floor around us in chunks twice the size of me. A heap of burning bones sits in the center of the room, motionless as one of the marble columns falls on top of it and crushes it with a sick succession of cracks and snaps. Another column teeters threateningly above Adrian and I, and he pulls me out of the way as it falls, a deafening crash echoing in the hall as it clatters to the floor and explodes into a pile.

I hear a faint cry over the sound, and I look toward the center of the room. A bit of that hope rises up into my chest again. It's hard to parse out, but I see Eddie, his hand outstretched to us. There are others behind him, but they're mere shadows against the bright plumes of flame and falling rock. They huddle behind him, and I finally see why—nestled in Eddie's grasp is the Crystalline Residuum I had in my bag.

I don't wait for Adrian to pull me along now. I wrap my fingers around his wrist, my once limp hand now firm in its grasp as I push forward, dragging him along with me as we dodge the Temple falling around us, pushing through the hot light of the fire around us. It's hard to see anything but light and the staggering approaching shadow of crumbling walls. But I see Eddie's hand outstretched. That's what I aim for. I reach back—stretching, pulling, craving. For the briefest of moments, the world dims, and another hand reaches out for me, dragged further away as I keep reaching in vain.

But I push farther.

Our fingers brush.

And the world is pulled from under me.

We tumble in a void, a familiar feeling to me now. The feeling of being pulled into an in between space. I don't let go of Adrian's wrist or Eddie's hand. They're the only things that feel real right now. Even I don't.

Until it's like gravity is suddenly turned back on, and I slam into something that shudders, hitting the ground hard and pelted by a number of objects that clatter around me. The force is enough to break my grip on the boys' hands, and they scatter somewhere in the confusion, though I hear their groans close by. There's a moment of messy noise and motion. Then, silence.

I moan as I push myself onto my knees. It's so much darker here than where we came from, though grey light filters in through—somewhere. Where are we even? It just smells different. Not the earthy, fresh smell that I've become accustomed to in the woods. It's too clean, too stale. I stretch, ignoring the bruise that I'm sure is already forming along my spine, and as I straighten, one of the objects that fell on me rolls off my back and onto the floor. I'm still in a haze as I grab the flat, rectangular thing in my hand, and as my eyes finally adjust, straining in the dull light, my stomach sinks.

It's a video game. The Legend of Zelda: Breath of the Wild. One of Eddie's favorites.

My mind has been moving so slowly since Brennan put his hand on me. But something finally clicks.

I look around. I'm not just holding a video game Eddie loves. I'm holding *his* copy. We're in the apartment, in our living room.

My chest tightens. It's all just like we left it. It's freezing in here—fuck, it's cold as hell, and all the blinds are closed. The couch, the TV, our empty cabinets. All exactly as we left it.

"I didn't mean to."

I frantically look over to the far wall underneath the window by the couch. Eddie is huddled in a ball on the floor—my mind wants to put him in Marvel pajama bottoms and a ratty hoodie, but he's wearing his Velmyra clothes still. He clasps his hands together, the injured one still bruised and swollen. His eyes find me, wide and panicked. "I didn't mean to," he repeats. "I'm sorry. I swear, I didn't mean to."

No. No, this can't be happening.

Adrian grunts behind me, pulling himself up on our ottoman, still shirtless and wounded all to hell. And coming around the other end of the couch is Kai, their hair a mess of curls and their clothes a tattered mess of fabric, soot covered and barely kept together.

I glance around—there should be more, right? There were more of us. But as I stand up and look around, there's no one. Nothing.

"I'm sorry," Eddie says again.

I look back at him and walk over to him, crouching down. "What do you mean? What are you talking about?" I ask.

His eyes are flitting back and forth a mile a minute, as if he can't settle on one thing to focus on. "I-I don't know. I never used Residuum before," Eddie shakily says. "He told me he was going to get you and that I should be in charge of it so we could get out if you didn't come back in time. And I kept picturing Orla's house—I did, I really tried—I just thought it for a split second. I didn't think it would matter that much. It was only a second."

"What? What did you think?" I ask him.

His gaze finally settles on me. As the words leave his mouth, I don't even know why I asked the question. "I thought, 'I want to go home,'" he admits.

I shake my head, a numbness spreading through me again. This can't be it. It can't.

"Where are the others?" Kai chimes in, looking around the apartment in wide-eyed terror. "Jackson? Melandrich? Gren. Where's Gren? They were holding onto us too."

"Crystalline Residuum is unpredictable," Adrian drones, empty of all emotion. "Especially if you've never used it before."

"The fuck is that supposed to mean?" Kai yells. "Did they make it out of there or not?"

No one answers. Because no one knows.

I turn back to Eddie. "You can take us back, right? There's got to be some left. Maybe even one of us—"

He cuts me short with a shake of his head, holding out what's cupped between his hands. Sitting in the center of his palms is a sliver of clear crystal, no more than a couple inches long. "I don't think that's going to work, Vi," he says. And the disappointment in his voice is clear. Not for him—he told me before how much he hated being in Velmyra.

It's for me.

I sit back on the floor, gingerly taking the shard of Residuum from his hands in between my two fingers, twisting it around to see its different chambers and fractals, realizing that it was my chance at finding her again. My one shot at fixing a lifetime of misery. And I'm holding it, a broken fragment of so much possibility.

I think I want to cry. I think I should.

Instead, I laugh.

Maybe it turns into crying at some point. I'm not sure. No one makes a move to do anything about it. Eddie closes his eyes, resting his head on the wall behind him, while Kai paces from room to room, calling into each of the bedrooms for Gren. I don't see Adrian. I don't really care what he does. They all probably think I'm losing my mind, knowing that we fucked up so epically, knowing that half of our party is missing, and the one thing we went there for was forever out of reach. Maybe they're just letting me have my moment of madness.

I don't laugh because I'm losing it, though.

Because I feel it already building—the heat in my core.

I've never been crazy. And especially not now, knowing that I hold within me a power that the world outside this room could never possibly fathom.

I'm not crazy. As a matter of fact, I have never been saner.

EPILOGUE

I am different.

Maybe not at a surface glance—I don't think even Eddie has noticed anything, but he has been preoccupied since we've been back. He made a trip to the ER to get his arm set and put in a sling that isn't made of bed sheets, and he was sent home with some stellar pain killers that have kept him well sedated. But as I step out of the first hot shower I've had in weeks and wipe the condensation off the bathroom mirror, I see it. It's striking. Like I'm looking at a new person entirely.

It isn't just my physical features, though those have changed. Freckles I've had since childhood have vanished, the divot above my eyebrow from when I had chicken pox as a kid is smoothed over. I'm disappointed that my nose is still crooked from when the Hellions broke it a decade ago, and that scar above my lip is still there. Still, it's faded considerably, like someone photoshopped it off of a picture of me but didn't quite have the skills to get all of it. Someone as close to me as Eddie might brush those things off as markers of time passing without really realizing it.

There's something more that's changed, though. I stare at myself for a while—too long, I conclude, as I notice the pruning of my fingertips smooth after a while. I study every inch of my face, something that in the past, I've often been too afraid to do. I look for exactly what it is, something that I can point to and say, "*There. That's what's different. That's what I am now.*"

My hair is nearly dry by the time I give up. Maybe it'll come to me tomorrow.

The others must not have made it back to Earth. Jackson, at least, didn't. He's savvy enough to have waved down someone with a cell phone to get a hold of us. Melandrich and Gren, we can't say. Maybe they actually did make it to Orla's cabin. To put us all at ease, that's what we choose to believe happened. Any other option seems—well, Eddie doesn't even want to consider it. Every time I bring it up, he changes the subject, sometimes leaves the room altogether. I keep the fact that there's a very real chance they were crushed in the crumbling ruins of the Old Gods' Temple to myself.

I ask if we should contact someone about Jackson, give his family some kind of excuse as to why he's not answering calls or texts. He only shakes his head at that. "He and his family—they're not all that close. I don't think him not talking to them for a while is going to set off any alarms."

Kai is in the same boat as Eddie—they refuse to talk about possibilities of where the others are. In fact, they refuse to talk most of the time. Eddie gives them his bedroom and resigns himself to sleeping on the couch, so Kai mostly spends their time locked away in there, only coming out every few hours for food. When they do emerge from their hole to hang around us, all it takes is one joke, one hint of a smile, an instinctive look over their shoulder, and their face falls. Eddie wants to get them out in the world, familiarize them with Grand Rapids a little bit at a time so they get less overwhelmed, but I think it's best to leave them be for the moment. Coming from experience, even without being in a completely different world, it's tough going from a duo to solo in such a jarring way.

Inch by inch, we acclimate to life back in the real world. Our appetites have dwindled after weeks of subsisting on rations. I remember thinking in the thick of the Midran Forest that the first thing I would do when I got home would be to order Taco Bell. But I never seem to be hungry enough now that I'm here. Eddie started off that way, but by the second day back, he's already caved and gotten himself a Big Mac. The biggest shift, though, is stepping outside onto the street for the first time. Grand Rapids isn't massive, but it's *loud*. With every car that rushes by with its bass blaring, I wish I were back beneath the familiar canopy of trees. What was once so foreign is now the familiarity I crave amidst the chaos of life on Earth.

Eddie and I eventually go out to Big O's again, just to feel some sense of normalcy. It's smaller than I remember, and the sticky floors feel too clean. We order half pepperoni, half ham and mushroom, staring at the checkered laminate tablecloth in silence before it arrives. I catch glances of him. His wounds are mostly gone, the last remnants of bruises fading into sickly green. When the pizza gets to our table, we eat a slice or two, but we bring most of it home in a box for Kai. Eddie doesn't even mind that they eat the pepperoni half.

Friday night comes and goes. Eddie's canceled the weekly *Mages* game. He gives his players the excuse that he's burnt out and has a lot on his plate. Some of them are bummed, but there are other game masters and other groups. They'll survive.

Vault has him start back up work on the fifth day back. I guess I'm still out of a job. I briefly glance at job postings online in the mornings, but I can't seem to put my heart into it for more than a few minutes. Going back to making coffee for bland businessmen rushing to their first meeting of the day sounds so menial, so flavorless. I could focus more on school—except I dropped all my classes. March is nearly over, the semester more than halfway done. I officially have nothing I can do, nothing to set my sights on.

Well, not nothing.

Eddie and Kai don't say it in so many words, but it's the way they don't talk about it that I know they're not making any plans to head back to Velmyra any time soon. How can we? Adrian was the only person on Earth with Residuum that we knew of. We have no way of getting back. The only option we have is hoping that one of the others survived, gets a hold of some Crystalline Residuum, and knows enough of residuuism to get back here and bring us back. Which isn't a plan at all. There's also all the things that I'm still wrapping my head around, the questions I can't answer—if Crystalline was really behind May's disappearance and why she wanted May in the first place. How I was able to pull the Crystalline Relic from the pedestal without any resistance. Why those visions of Velmyra came to us in the first place. What those regrets I saw back at the veil really meant…

I'm back to scouring the game master's guide to see if there might be some other way to get back, some loophole. My copy somehow survived since Eddie was holding onto it when we passed back into our world. I take the measly bit of savings I do have and buy all the source material that I'm missing, knowing most of it is fiction since it was made after Adrian left Magicka Games. But I still look, retreating into my late nights of reading. Of obsessing. Because what else can I do?

I am different. We are different. But I suppose not everything has changed.

I see the man who was once a demon sitting at the bar before he sees me.

We've been back for a week, so I'm surprised he's still in town. It was a long shot texting him and asking to meet up. I take an Uber to the Amway and meet him at the bar just outside the main lobby. It isn't unlike the bar where we first met—polished, modern, trying way too hard to distract from how shabby it is beneath the renovations.

He's back to his usual attire, but there's something much less put together about him now—his half-tucked shirt hides beneath a dark blue blazer, and his pants have creases in them that don't look decorative. His hair has gotten so long now that there is no styling it. He has it pulled back from his face by a hair tie again, a few strands flying out. There's also, of course, the massive purple and black bruise across his nose and underneath his eyes. It must've been set by a doctor since the last time I saw him, but even with that, it's crooked now. And it will most likely stay that way.

It's the first time that I feel almost as put together as he does, and I'm not in anything fancy—a flowy pastel orange blouse that I wore to a job interview once and a pair of khakis. I felt like I should look some kind of appropriate for such a nice place. I can't seem to sacrifice my tennis shoes, though. After wearing tough leather boots for weeks, I never want to take them off again.

Staring down into his drink, he doesn't see me until I'm nearly next to him. When he does spot me, he looks alarmed, his body going rigid like a deer at the sound of a snapping twig. He shuffles onto his feet, nodding in acknowledgement. I nod back, trying to keep my face placid. By just a tick, the heat within me increases. I'd say I've gotten used to it, but it doesn't really go away. It only builds. I know I'll have to release it when it gets too much to handle. There's a lot of things I know will have to happen. One step at a time, I guess.

He gets a private table in the corner, so we won't have to watch what we say. He orders his second gin and tonic and asks if I want anything, but I say water is fine. Once the waiter leaves, we sit in silence, both grappling with what we should say first. The usually refined Adrian Inoue now fumbles with a napkin, eyes darting anxiously from me to the floor and across the room. I stay still, hands in my lap, waiting patiently for my time to speak. It's only then that I realize that I have all the power in this situation. I'm not quite used to that.

"I should let you know," Adrian starts, cautiously. "I'm heading back to Chicago tomorrow. I was going to leave town as soon as possible, but…" He sets the napkin down and clenches and unclenches his fists before mirroring me and setting them in his lap. "I've been having a difficult time adjusting to being back. Needed a breather, I suppose."

I nod. I could tell him now, but I keep my mouth shut. I'd like to watch him squirm for a little bit.

And squirm he does. "If Chicago is too close, I completely understand," he rambles. "I can move back to LA. Or New York, or—I don't know, fucking Boise. Whatever you're more comfortable with. If I find out something about getting back to Velmyra, I'll contact you, but other than that, I'll leave you alone. We never have to speak to each other again, I promise."

I nod again. I still don't say anything, just to see if he keeps talking, but instead he looks at me, expectant. "Actually," I finally say. "I wanted to ask if you would move to Grand Rapids."

Adrian raises his eyebrows, obviously not expecting that response. "Oh."

"I figured it would be easier for you to come here since most of us are based here," I explain. "And you have more money."

"That's fine," he says with suspicion. "I'm fine with whatever you want."

"Good. That's what I want."

"I'm sorry," Adrian says, shaking his head. "I guess I just don't—"

"Don't get me wrong here," I say, firmly. "It's not because I forgive you. Or because I want to be friends or whatever. That's not happening."

He nods, but his face falls ever so slightly. "Right."

I sigh. "But I would be pretty stupid to not utilize you," I continue. "No one else seems to think so right now, but we are going to get back to Velmyra. Eventually. And when we do, we're going to be ready for her." I look him in the eye, paying no mind to how much he shifts in his seat as I glare at him. "You know what I did, right?"

He hesitates, but nods.

"You've been where I am. There are things you can teach me. Even if you don't have the power anymore, you remember what it was like." The intensity in my gaze wanes, and I'm the one to shift in my seat now. "You *are* my magic teacher, after all. You taught me how to use Residuum. Now, you can teach me this. And I have something you never had."

Adrian swallows. "And what's that?"

"An example of what not to do."

The nervous edge to his expression softens, mellowing out not into ease but into pity. That same pity Brennan gave me before he placed his hand on me. "Trust me, Violet. You're going to make mistakes of your own, with or without my involvement."

I reach out to the candle in the center of the table, running my fingertips through the flickering flame. It's comfortably warm, as if I'm running my hands through bath water. "We'll see about that."

When dinner is over, he asks me if I've released it yet. When I say I haven't, he throws a couple hundred-dollar bills on the table as he stands and tells me to follow him.

The sun has gone down, the fluorescent soul of the city igniting in its lampposts. We walk down a pathway that snakes around the hotel and down to the waterfront, running into couples taking an evening stroll. Eventually, the cement walkway ends and we go on foot across loose stone until we stop beneath one of the bridges spanning across the river. I protest—someone is bound to notice if I let it loose here, but Adrian shrugs it off. Chances are, people will assume it's kids setting off fireworks, he assures me. Even if someone calls the police, we'll be long gone by the time they get there. He steps aside, holding out a hand as if to say the floor is mine.

I step forward, rubbing my hands together, my feet just barely skimming the lapping water. My body shakes, though I can't tell if it's because there's a chill to the March air or if I'm terrified. Spreading my arms out as wide as I can get them, I arch my head up to the sky, not sure what I'm supposed to be doing. It's not using Residuum anymore, not channeling some power source. It's me, now. *I* am the power source.

I always have been, haven't I? That's what he's been telling me. Maybe I finally get it.

I breathe in.

Breathe out.

And I let it go.

I am part of the city's ignition, flourishing as torrents of fire blaze from my open palms, curling in tendrils of rushing heat and light, expanding beyond me, beyond my emotions, beyond my intentions and actions. The mirror image of the fire reflects back at me on the water's surface, the light almost too much to look at. But I keep shining, burning in incendiary splendor and asking the world to witness my light.

My energy wanes, and I eventually stop. I stay where I am, my face toward the sky, breathing in the sweet smell of smoke and heat.

And for the first time, the Infernal Mage doesn't hide her wild, untamable grin.

ACKNOWLEDGMENTS

In 2018, I was going through some shit. Dealing with loss after loss, figuring out who I was as a person, all that late 20-something fuckery. So, I did what I do when I hurt: I turned to stories. And along with writing, my love affair at that time was with a little game called Dungeons and Dragons.

What started as an exercise in self-therapy soon became a story about escapism, recovery, redemption, self-discovery, and refusing to deny yourself emotion. My love of storytelling, in the time that I've been writing this book, has only grown through my own games of Dungeons and Dragons and the connections I have made through that. This book is not only a love letter to that game and games like it, but to the thing that makes it what it is: community. And while I spent a lot of time to myself writing this, I could not have done it without the help of the strong support system that I've surrounded myself with. So, without further ado, here come the thanks.

The biggest thanks goes to the backbone of my entire life, my husband Cory. I knew you were the one twelve years ago when I chose making out with you over watching an episode of *Fullmetal Alchemist* (a very high honor). And I knew you were the one just a few months ago when you told me that the most important thing for me right now was to publish my book, and you would be there to offer whatever support you needed for me to get that done. You don't realize how rare that is, and I try not to take it for granted. You are steadfast and true, even when my own brain isn't. I cannot imagine writing this thing without you in the background encouraging me, and I hope I never have to write another book without you in my life.

To my family. Mom and Dad, you have always supported my artistic pursuits, and even if it wasn't the most lucrative choice, it was the thing that made me happy. I'm so thankful for your support in that. Hannah, I know you're probably not reading this because it's longer than five pages and it has nothing to do with BTS, but thank you for being there to distract me when I needed it and for being my ride or die, until the very end. Cole and Claire, you both have become awesome adults, and I can't thank you enough for never ceasing to make me laugh and believe that the world is a bit brighter with your generation in it.

The members of the High Noon Writers Club have held a variety of different roles in the production of this book, but first and foremost is the role of my long-suffering friends (I know, I know. I'll stop with the self-deprecating jokes, I promise.) Zachary Gale, "best man" is really the term to describe you, and not only because you were the best man in my wedding. You are such a fount of endless encouragement and advice, and you're the first person I go to in a crisis and always will be, writing or otherwise. Taiylor R. Wallace, my incredible editor, dungeon master, and creative comrade. You have elevated this book into something wonderful, and I can't tell you how grateful I am for your thoughtfulness and aggressive positivity, not only as a writing peer but as an outstanding friend. Blake R. Wolfe, since orientation week at school, you have been nothing but an uncompromising friend and confidant. Seeing you grow in your own writing and find success has been so inspiring for me, and I can't thank you enough for jumping at the chance to offer your own experience and thoughts when I'm panicking over the publishing process. Jayme Bean, the queen of hype, you have been so enthusiastic about this book since the first session of High Noon, and I am so absolutely appreciative for your willingness to talk it up to anyone who will listen and use your own experience in publishing to help me when I feel like I'm drowning. You all are invaluable parts of my life, whether it's as writers or as friends. I can't express how much you have done for the creation of this book.

I have worked with a few extremely talented people to help the book not just read well, but look and sound good too. Many thanks to Jay Pillerva, who illustrated the amazing cover for this book. Thanks also goes to Dewi Hargreaves who made the stunning map of Velmyra out of my incoherent scribbles. And thanks to Jennie VanderLugt, who has given a completely new voice to the story with the audiobook.

Also to all my incredibly patient alpha and beta readers. Avery Mills, you have been my go-to to send new pages to since high school, and that's not changing any time soon. Thanks also to my beta readers: A.R.K. Horton, Katherine Shaw, Ian Barr, Kester James Finley, Baylee Jean, and P.B. Breckinridge. You have offered amazing insights into the story, and it really would not have been the same without you all.

Excerpt from "The Good News Is You Won the Lottery, the Bad News is the Lottery is Post-Traumatic Stress Disorder" from SHAME IS AN OCEAN I SWIM ACROSS: POEMS BY MARY LAMBERT by Mary Lambert. Copyright © 2018 by Mary Lambert. Reprinted by permission of Feiwel and Friends, an imprint of Macmillan Publishing Group, LLC. All Rights Reserved.

Chapter images courtesy of Pixabay.

Other special thanks goes out to Shelley DeHosse, April Gray, Zack Koop, Tanner Maten, Breanne Stokes, and Tiffany Taylor.

And of course, to YOU, the reader! Thank you for taking the time to read this story. There was a lot of love and tears put into it, and I hope it brought you some needed joy, if only for a moment. And remember: don't deny yourself.

-Astrid Knight

A freshly born Mage.

A displaced King.

In the far reaches of the land of the fey, they will discover that some rules must be broken.

RULES AS WRITTEN

The Mages of Velmyra: Book Two

Coming soon!

ABOUT THE AUTHOR

Astrid Knight is an author and storyteller with a love of fantasy and all things strange. A graduate of Adrian College, Astrid has served as a contributing writer for anthologies such as Skullgate Media's *Tales From the Year Between* and *Welcome to Simmins, Detective Spencer*. They are also a co-founder and player for the actual play RPG Twitch channel, Atlaran Adventuring Company. *Perception Check* is her first novel. Keep up to date about all Mages of Velmyra news by following her on Twitter, Instagram, and Facebook @AstridKWrites.